A Sardonic Look at Life

A Collection of short stories, poems an

A Sardonic Look at Life's Vagaries

A Collection of short stories, poems and a play by Nigel Johnson

First published in 2021
Fiona Knowles-Holland

Copyright © Fiona Knowles-Holland 2021

The rights of the author has been asserted in accordance with Sections 77 and 78 of the Copyright Designs and Patents Act, 1988.

All rights reserved.
No part of this book may be reproduced (including photocopying or storing in any medium by electronic means and whether or not transiently or incidentally to some other use of this publication) without the written permission of the copyright holder except in accordance with the provisions of the Copyright, design and Patents Act 1988. Applications for the Copyright holder's written permission to reproduce any part of this publication should be addresses to the publishers.

ISBN: 9798500321725

This book is a work of fiction. Names, characters, businesses, organisations, places and events other than those clearly in the public domain, are either the product of the author's imagination or are used fictitiously. Any resemblance to actual persons, living or dead, events or locales is entirely coincidental.

Foreword

This book is a collection of stories and poems Nigel wrote for his writing group Wayward Writers in Mynydd Isa.

Once a fortnight, he would unfailingly delight members with his carefully honed observations on childhood, school days, life's disappointments and triumphs, faded gentility, theatre, the human frailty of unequal ambition, the savagery of war and the power of education – each populated by finely-drawn and superbly named characters. Also included here is a rare play script. Think Alan Bennett meets Barbara Pym meets Graham Greene's Henry Pulling in *Travels with My Aunt*.

The title of this collection, *A Sardonic Look at Life's Vagaries*, is taken from *A Laudation to Betty, Gilly and Inge* – fellow writers of the group - and pretty well sums up Nigel's style, drawn perhaps from 'Endless reading and the quirks of life itself' (from *Why Do I?*). Look to *Grandfather* for an exquisite portrayal of family life. And, once or twice in this collection, Nigel shows us his deep compassion for the horrors of the world at large, none better than *The Other Side*.

All these pieces embody Nigel's trademark wit and compassion, humour and humanity.

This book is published by his friends in honour and remembrance of a wonderful man who delighted, charmed and influenced all he met.

Fiona Holland
https://fionaholland.co.uk

Contents

21st CENTURY BLUES 11

A REAL FEAST 13

ADMIRATION.. 20

ALBERT 21

ALL AT SEA.. 24

ANGEL GABRIEL 30

ASPIRATION 35

BEING AN ARTIST.. 36

BETRAYALS 39

BIRTH OR DEATH 54

BLACK TUESDAY 57

"BLOODY ROYAL WEDDING" 62

BRADLEY WINSTON BOULDERSTONE 67

COLOURS.. 72

CONCENTRATION 79

CUSTARD.. 83

CYRIL BLAND 89

DETECTIVE SERGEANT COPPICE...............................92

DESERT ISLAND DISCS 99

DIARY...102

DOING IT AGAIN...106

DON'T PANIC...108

EIGHTIETH BIRTHDAYS 111

ELEVEN O'CLOCK 113

EYE WITNESS...117

FOOTSTEPS 122

GRAMMAR SCHOOL...129

GRANDFATHER..135

GREAT AUNT MAY..142

HARVEY..147

HE WHO IS MOST TIMID.......................................152

MISS HENRIETTA MAPLEY 156

HOME 163

CHILDHOOD or A MOTHER'S DILEMMA.................168

I OWN A DOG 170

I WRITE 173

WORDS 174

INAPPROPRIATE GIFTS 176

IT TURNED OUT WELL 180

IT'S A BOY 182

JOYCE MARSH'S BROTHER 185

JULIAN 190

JUST NOT FAIR 197

LAST REQUEST 199

A LAUDATION TO BETTY, GILLY AND INGE 204

LEFT SHOE 206

LESSONS 209

LINDA 216

LUCK 218

MADGE BRIMBLE 222

MAKING SENSE OF MRS HEDGE 226

MEMORY LANE 229

MICHAEL 233

MIRABELLA 239

MY SISTER 247

I MET MY WIFE AT THE AIRPORT AND THE SMILE WAS WIPED OFF MY FACE BY
SOMETHING SHE SAID! 250

NEVER AGAIN..253

NICKNAMES 255

NIGHT DREAMS..259

NOT GUILTY! 261

OUT OF SIGHT 265

PAIN..266

PARENTS 267

PARTNERS 273

PIPPI 277

POST-IT NOTES..280

PROBLEMS, EH? 283

RAIN or SETTING THE SCENE 288

RAINDROPS AND ROSES...290

RED 293

SESTINA 295

SEVEN DEADLY SINS 296

SHORTS 302

SMILE 304

SPRING 306

ST SWITHIN AT THE OLYMPICS 308

STANDING STILL 310

TABLOID NEWSPAPER : THE EDITOR'S DILEMMA 314

TAKING STOCK 316

TEACHERS 320

APOLOGIES TO TEDDY BEARS EVERYWHERE 324

TEMPTATION 326

THANK GOD FOR HARRY 328

THE BISHOP 331

THE BOAT 336

THE CATCH 339

THE DRIVING INSTRUCTOR 342

THE FALL 348

THE FLATS 350

THE GHOST WHO ATE UP COLOURS 353

THE GREAT IDEA..354

THE KING...363

THE LIGHTS IN THE WINDOW 367

THE LITTLE TERROR 371

THE ONE HUNDRED CLUB..374

THE OTHER SIDE 378

THE OTHER SIDE (2)..380

THE SCROLL..384

THEATRE SUPERSTITIONS..390

THREE BALLOONS..392

TIM HOLT 394

TO CREATE AN ANIMAL..400

TROUBLE 402

TRUST 405

TRUST II...409

TWO POEMS 415

UNCLE ABERNATHY'S ARTEFACT.. 417

WAYWARD WRITERS.. 422

WHEN THE TWINS WERE BORN … 425

WHERE ARE YOU NOW? 428

WHITE HOT... 431

WHY DO I?.. 433

21ˢᵗ CENTURY BLUES

2005

I woke up this morning to the wind and the rain
The water's cold, Cornflakes soggy, the milk is off again
The Postman forces the mail through, it falls with an ominous clunk
A pile of gaudy leaflets, it's just a load of junk
There is one envelope addressed to me, for me a personal word,
To inform me that my Council Tax has gone up by a third
The paper's full of bombs and Blair and lies and Blair and Cherie
Which leaves me 100,000 miles from feeling remotely merry
The daytime telly's a psychedelic dirge of fatuous chatter
With revelatory conclusions such as "if you eat more, you'll get fatter".
There's yet another make-over spot where the worldly and fashionably
wise
Drag a woman in off the street to insult and patronise
They pile the slap on the wrinkled old crone and tell her oh-so-brightly
That, if she follows this regime, she'll look like Keira Knightley
It's all too much, slink back to bed, there's nothing left to lose
I've got another debilitating dose of 21ˢᵗ Century Blues.

From under the weight of a heavy duvet
What could be seen as pessimistic
As the thoughts unwind and grind in your mind
You know you're just being realistic
Society's a rabble who babble and scrabble
To have more and more, and they fret
That they can't get enough of material stuff
As they sink up to their necks in debt
What's the point of learning with celebrities are earning
A fortune from 4ᵗʰ place in *Big Brother*?
Or they choose to undress on Page 3 of the press
Coz they slept with some Beckham or other
The young do as they please and they wallow in sleaze
They can all get degrees in binge drinking
And nobody's caring, for the future preparing,
Oh, for God's sake, nobody's thinking!

As things get more manic, there's no sign of panic
On the Titanic we've chosen to cruise
Ice on metal jars, on the deck 'neath pole stars
The band plays the 21st Century Blues.

It's mid-afternoon in October's grey gloom
The front doorbell chimes in the hall
It shatters the peace and there stands my niece
She was passing so thought she would call
She's welcomed inside and close to her side
Snugs a bundle that's worth more than gold
Her smile warm and wide, she's glowing with pride
It's her little girl, now five weeks old
She loosens her fleece, the babe sense release
Her arms stretch out, fingers unfurled
Her head turns side to side, her eyes open wide
Feeling – sensing her place in the world
A cute little grin – all right, then, it's wind
She gurgles and bubbles and coos
And, suddenly, where?
They're no longer there
My faith-breaking
Scrooge-making
21st Century Blues.

A REAL FEAST

We're having a feast today – "a feast of celebration" is how Matron describes it. We have been reprised. We have survived. They have not closed us down. 'They' is the Mulberry Homes Consortium. 'We' are Harold Downe House in Peckham, South London. The Consortium made a mess of its finances – over development, mis-investing, too optimistic forward planning – the gravy train hit the buffers. Things had to be salvaged from the wreckage – luckily we was one of these. Any fool could see matters was serious. It was all them hushed little clusters of earnest whisperers round the place – Matron with booted and suited officials, all grim determination and clip boards. Matron with off-duty staff and union reps. Matron with the worried families of residents, all these gradually withdrawing into the privacy and seclusion of her office. Of course, no-one talked to us inmates officially. Our families called by more frequently and attempted a display of optimism. "It'll be all right. Don't fret." And we talked amongst ourselves, but that didn't help because we really didn't know what the hell was going on! Even those of us who are still able to hold three or more thoughts together in our heads without at least one of them escaping. And there's precious few of us can do that. Now ... where was I?

Ah yes, the feast!

We have got the go-ahead. But I've told you that already.

So Matron decided on a community feast of celebration, and we all knew what that would mean – same as Christmas, Easter, Guy Fawkes – well, more likely Halloween these days. Billy Grainger liked to be dressed up as a Guy and pushed around in his wheelchair waving sparklers. Now the old girls do themselves up as witches and ghouls – not much of a change in some of them - and down two much Martini and Lemonade and dance the Conga.

So there's Xmas, Easter ... er ... and another. Ah yes, Founder's Day, all praise and thanks to Alderman Harold Downe, May God bless all who sail etc etc. He set up this place and we love it here – but don't tell Matron!

So now we have another feast exactly like all the other feasts – paper plates full of defrosted and reheated frozen food. Not that I wish to sound ungrateful nor nothing. But there's only so much enthusiasm you can muster for a pile of small ex-frozen sausage rolls. Small squares of tasteless cardboard mechanically folded over unidentifiable slabs of meat-like pulp. I douse mine in globs of acid-orange tomato sauce. Matron disapproves. "Mr Pilbeam", she complains. That is my name, Mr Pilbeam, Eric to my friends and normally to Matron, but she operates this teacher in the classroom thing. I'm 'Eric' as a rule, but 'Mr Pilbeam' when she's on the warpath or I've erred and strayed from my way like a lost sheep or she's talking money! "Mr Pilbeam", she says, looming over my plate of blood-stained dead pig and pastry bits. "You won't be able to taste what you have on your plate." Which is the whole point of the exercise, silly old mare.

Along with the inevitable so-called sausage rolls come mini vol-au-vents – small crumbling cups of flaking pastry over-spilling with what looks like cat sick but what luckily tastes of nothing (more ketchup!) and mini cheese cakes (just metallic sugar) and mini-trifles in paper cups with green and red jelly, bits of pale fruit and shaving foam cream. (Even I don't put sauce on them.) And cheese straws, no cheese, only straw (dipped in you-know-what!). White bread sandwiches, egg and cress or tuna and cucumber, made by the kitchen staff, not half bad and finally Matron's cake. Always the last to appear, triumphant in rock hard, clumsily applied, garishly coloured icing, hiding within a sponge cake that challenged the Trades Description Act as to what a sponge cake is, mostly because Matron's sponge is never the same twice and truly defies description. It could be as dry as desert sand and just crumble across the plate. Or suet pudding stodgy that clags up your dentures for days. Or firm like a three-day old loaf of bread. What it is is never sponge. But the icing can be chipped into shards and sucked on like boiled sweets.

In spite of all the well-meaning, these events are not feasts. I can remember feasts. I can remember real cakes. One in particular. Too soon after the war – in a hurry after the war – me and my Elsie got spliced. Life was still hard. Luxury a forgotten word. But we was determined not to wait. I wore my brother's hand-me-down demob suit which felted where it touched and his borrowed shirt and shoes. The tie and socks and underpants was my own. Luckily I had an interfering and domineering mother-in-law who handled everything. Elsie looked beautiful in a pastel blue day dress and a pill box hat with a veil.

And against all odds we had a cake. My eyes was out on stalks. Three tiers with small white pillars – white and glassy, acres of sugar icing – how the hell? The mother-in-law leaned into me, her scarlet red lips working hard, her eyes glinting, the ginger fringe of her hair bobbing vigorously. She fumbled the cake knife into my unsteady hands. "Only cut the top bit", she hissed. I must of looked as blank as I felt. "Only cut the top bit", she sighed with exasperation. A strong whiff of Californian Poppy. "Lord love us. Tell him, Elsie." She pushed us together and was gone "Only the top bit", whispered Elsie. She was already turning into her mother. But then she smiled the same smile that she was still smiling fifty years later. "Only the top bit. That's the cake. The bits underneath are not real. All wood and card and distemper."

So we only did cut the top bit, and it was a feast. Rich dark cake and dried fruit, oozing onto the plates the exotic smell of heavy rum. Still, to this day …" Anyway, soon it had all gone to the plate bearing guests and we didn't get any. "Family hold back", ordered the scarlet lips. Only the succulent smell and a couple of sultanas trying to escape off of the knife – and, of course, the indelible memory … Whenever I smell Xmas pudding and rum. That was a feast! And there was Derek's banana These fruits had vanished during the war. Achieved 'mythical status' as the modern saying goes. They was in story books and comics and unpeeled by apes in Tarzan films. But this was mystical treasure to wartime kids. But after the war they suddenly appeared at Bermondsey Market. They had been seen, like contraband, on London Docks and rumours had spread. But on this Saturday afternoon they'd appeared at Bermondsey Market and my brother Wilfred who helped run a fish stall then had got to the fruits in question. He came home with this brown paper bundle. He laid in ceremoniously on the green chenille cloth of the kitchen table and pulled back the rustling crinkled brown layers to reveal the cluster of golden curved fruit. "These, kids, is bananas." He eased back to allow Mum the privilege of distributing the treasures. She tore banana after banana from the clump and handed them around. "Now", she said, holding hers aloft, "this is what you …"

But Derek, ten years old, rash and impetuous as he always would be until fatally hurled off his motorbike four days before his 34th birthday, couldn't wait. He sank his teeth into the banana's yellow skin. A pause. A wrinkle of his nose. A gasp as he dropped his on the table. "Yeuch! It's bleeding horrible. Yuck!" And he scrabbled at his offended lips with his small dirty finger nails. Mum paused, her banana held aloft in anticipation of a good demonstration. "You daft little bugger", she erupted, her left hand giving him an accomplished slap on the back of his head. "Why can't you wait like anyone else?" Derek fell forward, his head to the table, bright red in paroxysms of tears of pain and humiliation. Mum continued, riding the storm, giving a superb demonstration of the unpacking and first bite of the white fruit of the banana. We all followed suit – a nihilistic act culminating in rich, fruity, sweet mouthfuls of creamy flesh. Hisses and sobs came from table level. Cissy, my oldest sister, hauled Derek, a heaving, sorrowful bundle, to his feet and wiped his eyes firmly with her hand. "Stop being a whingeing little bugger", she quietly intoned, "and watch this." Before his startled tearful eyes, she expertly peeled his deformed fruit and proffered him the white curved cone of flesh. Derek looked doubtful and suspicious. "Go on. Try it." He held it horrifyingly – looked forlornly at us all – and bit. Momentarily he froze and then sucked in the fruit. Bananas would never taste so good again. A real feast.

Matron has appeared with her celebration cake. The usual great slab but on this occasion trowelled with pristine white icing with some silver baubles and gold sprayed plastic flowers and leaves. Grand and almost marital. But what cake lurks within to cap this uninspired and uninspiring feast?

Derek was my only younger brother but I had three older ones. Wilfred, I've already mentioned, Earnest and Joseph. We was a lucky family. All three had been called up to war service and all three had come home afterwards, apparently unscathed. Of those, Joe was the least untroubled. Even before the war he'd been the odd one, something of a loner, a thinker I suppose you'd say. I found out later, as I did much about Joe, that he dabbled with pacifism before the war and could not easily contemplate the role of an active soldier. He came as near as it's possible, I believe, to be a Conchie – a conscientious objector – but he'd had good advice and went into the Medical Corp, but he was still trained to bear arms and fight. He could, though, live with active service amongst the medix, though he was never known to speak much about it after.

Except to Cissy, our oldest, who, with so many children in the family, had become something of a mother figure especially to the little ones. She went on to marry, long and happily, to a carpet retail manager but, ironically, never could have kids of her own.

Even I could see Joe was a troubled soul after the war. Dark eyed, slender and mournful he buried himself in his books and gramophone records. He worked as a landsman and gardener for the local council, quiet and solitary.

But what he confided in Cissy came out to me later.

It was to all intents and purposes the end of the war. Most of his duties there were of the clearing up kind. I suppose not unlike the tying up of surgical operations on the human body. Clearing out and clearing up the mess, what little that can be cleared up at such a time. They found themselves in Eastern Europe and knew they faced a big job ahead. Some prison camps the Americans had liberated - mostly and exclusively civilian prisoners that would need considerable care and treatment. The usual stuff – cleaning up, charting, feeding, lice, disease, perhaps some psychological damage, work for the mortuary boys.

But nothing prepared them.

It was in the middle of nowhere, he said. Tall dark trees, bleak skies, railway tracks, so much barbed wire. His descriptions were never precise, his voice distant, expressionless, his eyes unfocused.

It was all grey, he said. No colour. They got there at dawn in half light, the engines roaring unnaturally loud in the extraordinary silence. Half light and misty. Through a spidery, wooden archway. Words in German, he supposed, shaped into the arch. They crept forward, swaying with the movement of the trucks on the uneven surface. They could make out dark wooden huts on either side but not a light at any window. And banks to either side, against the huts, of what looked like dirty drifts of snow, or piles of old sacking and folded sheeting. There was a hint of a faint sun rise, a yellowing in the air. The vision cleared. Rows of huts, extending as far as the eye could see on either side – on into the amber gloom. The soiled snow banks were not that – nor was they piles of sodden sheeting – but they moved and unfolded themselves. They was people, cowering and huddled, in baggy, creased, filthy, striped uniforms who, responding to a curiosity they could not resist, was moving uncertainly forward, drawn to the unfamiliar sight of the steadily advancing columns of jeeps and trucks, hardly believing the emblems on their sides the white circles with the short red crosses.

These were the creatures – the victims – the shadows – the ghosts – the vestiges of humanity – the people they had been sent to tend.

Their lorry whisked them away to a clear space where they were to set up a field kitchen to prepare food for those unfortunate souls. "So many of them", he repeated over and over. "Their NCOs and Sergeants were practised in cheeriness for all occasions. "Focus on what you're doing, lads. A good hot meal. That's what we're here for. To them it will be a feast."

Eventually, as daylight firmly established itself, so did great steaming dustbins of watery gruel. "Not too thick for digestion purposes", advised someone. Trestle tables, piles of clean metal bowls, rough spoons stamped out of sharp tin. "Right, lads." A pile of rough black chunks of bread. "Ready, lads. Ready for the rush."

And then they came. A slow huddled mass. Grey. All grey. Slow and cautious. God knows the agony to them of the stench of warm, oaty, boiling food on the dry, col air. And all grey. The stretched skin, the scaly, scraped scalps, the wide, rheumy eyes. "Their eyes was too big", he whispered. Grey, purple parched lips. Rotten teeth. And enormous skeletal hands, knotted and grimed, unsteady and desperate, shakily holding a bowl. "We learned not to fill them too full", he said. "They couldn't bear the weight." And still they came. Some lucky servers were called back from serving at the tables. They were needed to replenish the empty dustbins over the glowing ranges. Joe readily withdrew and hid where the stirring and mixing needed to be done. For hour after hour after hour.

It was only days later when the medix who had not been involved in the feasting but in direct medical care reported back on the awful irony of those events.

The inmates had hurled away their spoons unused and used their scabbed hands to gulp down the steaming gruel. They had drunk the dregs directly from their bowls, what they had not supped up with the chunks of coarse bread. And, stunned and replete, they had retreated to wherever they had felt comfortable. And then had come the after effects. Extraordinary bloating. Excruciating pain that started in the bowels, up into the chest, and subsumed every limb. And so many of them died in agony, the weakest, the oldest, the youngest. "So many of them", he wept, over and over again. "So many. What should have been a feast ..."

Today we would have known to seek help. For post-something or other. But then ... there were too many who came back with awful memories. And you got on with it, if you could. Joe did. Tall, stooping and gaunt, he had his plants and gardens. He even wrote books about them.

Someone has persevered and pierced Matron's icing. Slabs of cake are being passed around. It's dark on the plate – dry, chocolate or even burned sponge?

My cake is put before me. "Wrap yourself around that, Eric, son. I dare you", said with a friendly grin.

I peer down. Wonder of wonders. It's fruit cake. And then the smell. Dark, rich rum. I hear a voice, long gone, and see the smile. "Only cut the top bit."

Sorry, Matron. This is a feast. A real feast.

ADMIRATION

'Twas with no little trepidation
That I set out to write about 'Admiration'
For at our previous convocation
I had expressed a reservation
That restricted the range of nomination
As to who should be subject to 'Admiration'.
But now I renege on what I said
For I have to admit to admiring Fred
Though, for my purposes, not Fred alone
He's intrinsically linked to Deputy Chairperson Joan.

For together these two are a representation
Of that stalwart wartime generation
Who suffered distress and deprivation
Found bombs and awful conflagration
For an extended period of duration
That taxes man's wit and imagination
With steely and grim determination
Balking not at evil's confrontation
And worse and worse abomination
Sacrificing so much for the good of this Nation.

So to you, Fred, though not alone,
I must include the doughty Joan,
With due respect, it must be said
I ask you both, dear Joan and Fred,
To accept this most sincere ovation
Of unreserved commendation.

ALBERT

Our Albert was off to Secondary school
And we knew there would be trouble
He's the untidiest beggar in the world
His bedroom is a bomb site with rubble.

In Primary school he could be contained
They only had one little shelf
And on this went all their daily needs
He could manage that just himself.

Senior school is a different kettle of fish
You need not one bag but three
A brief case for books, a hold-all for lunch
And a duffle for games and P.E.

On the first day of term Albert swaggered away
He'd insisted he'd go on his own
"I'll be alright – you see if I'm not"
Mum said, "We'll see when he gets home."

Mum had made Albert's favourite tea
And exactly at half past four
She heard a noise on the garden path
And Albert burst through the door.

His Mum looked down at Albert's feet
It was just as she had feared
"I know it looks odd", Albert said
"But me left shoe disappeared.

To catch the school bus dead on time
This trainer I had to borrow
But the P.E. teacher Mr Pugh
'll help me look for my shoe tomorrow."

His mother took his duffle bag
And said, "I'll wash your kit"
She loosened the cords and looked inside
And said, "There's not much of it.

There should be shorts and tracksuit top
Rugby shirt and gym vest too
And now you've only got one sock
When this morning there was two."

And so it went on day after day
And no left shoe appears
And what came home in his duffle bag
Could keep Oxfam supplied for years.

Mum cried, "What has happened now?"
Albert limped badly up the path
She ran out full of doubt and fear
But then began to laugh.

"A teacher lent me a left shoe
It's such a prat I feel
It was Mrs Brough who teaches French
It's bright red with a 3-inch heel."

Dad said, "I can feel a draught
Albert, come in and shut the door."
But his left foot clad in running spikes
Had nailed him to the floor.

The fourth day's shoe was bright yellow and red
With bells as a tinkling feature
The toe coiled up where a note was pinned
"On loan from the drama teacher."

The duffle bag was like a lucky dip
Jumbled contents without warning
Mum washed and pressed all manfully
To return them clean in the morning.

Mud caked rugby shorts for the 1ˢᵗ XV
Various shorts and sweaty sox
Speedo trunks and a blood stained vest
And a well-used cricket box.

And one night emptying the duffle bag
Mum pulled out her hand and cried "Ah!"
Amidst the shock of vests and stinking sox
She discovered a white sports bra.

Mum worried. She was up all night.
She said, "I feel a fool
But how did he get a white sports bra
When he goes to an all-boys school?"

Albert was ready for school next day
The sports bra washed and pressed
Dad said, "Now remember lad
That real boys wear a vest."

Came the great day, Albert burst through the door
His face was beaming bright
"I've found me left shoe, Mum", he cried
"Trouble is, now I've lost me right!"

ALL AT SEA

It all began late one autumn afternoon with the numbers flashing on my answerphone.

"You have one message. Message One."

It was a timid, light female voice that followed.

"Hello. Hello … Oh, I don't like these machines." There was a deep growling voice in the background, then – "Oh dear. Hello? I'd like to leave a message for Mr Nigel Johnson. Could you please phone me on 01244 755863. Er …" More background growling. "Do you think so? Oh dear … It's about a drama production in Guston." Long pause. "Yes … thank you very much. Sorry." And the message ended.

Guston was a small village about five miles away. The reference to a drama production whetted my appetite.

Later in the evening I rang the proffered number. My call was answered instantly. A deep gruff voice. "What?"

"Good evening. This is Nigel Johnson here, responding to a message I received on my answerphone earlier to phone this number."

"Who?"

"Nigel Johnson. I had a message earlier." There was a long pause,.

"Right." The voice called gruffly away from the receiver. "It must be for you. Who is it? Oh … Neville Jones. Are you going to take it?" Pause. Then the same soft diffident voice that had left the original message. "Hello, Mr Jones. What can I do for you?"

"No. This is Nigel Johnson. You asked me to call you."

Sudden realisation. "Oh, Mr Johnson. Thank you so much for ringing back. It's all right, dear. It's about the play. My name is Sylvia Penge and I'm hoping you may be able to help out with a problem we're having …"

It turned out that the Guston Village Players had undertaken a production of a play called *Bequest to the Nation* by Terrence Rattigan. The person who had adapted and was directing the play had had to withdraw 'for personal reasons' and they were looking for a replacement. Would I be interested and available?

Of course I was interested. The Rattigan play is one rarely performed. It concerns the late stages of the romance between Lord Nelson and Emma Hamilton and was filmed with, I seem to remember, Lawrence Olivier and Vivien Leigh. So I was definitely interested and, I will admit, not a little flattered, my reputation seemingly having gone before me and rendered me worthy of consideration as saviour of the situation. But in my onrush of intellectual curiosity and sheer vanity, I had overlooked one world – 'adapted'. It would not be pure Rattigan but a 'version' – the pit was there to fall into!

By agreement I drove out to Guston, a few days later, to meet up with Sylvia Penge. She suggested I park near the lych-gate of the Church of St Michael and All Angels where she would be waiting. From there we could walk to the close-by Old Vicarage to meet the lady who was the prime mover of this ambitious theatrical enterprise.

Sylvia Penge turned out to be everything her voice promised – a rather fussy, unassuming diminutive woman, of a certain age, with tightly permed fair hair, a rather pinched face, pale blue eyes, narrow lips. She was nervous to the point of breathlessness in that she could not stop talking. Her softness of voice with its rapid delivery allied to the smalless of stature compared with my not inconsiderable height led to my being able only to grasp about 60% of what she said. I remember the word "Sorry" occurred again and again. She was 'sorry' about the phone call – she hated answering machines and was 'sorry' if her brother seemed rude as he loathed answering the phone at all as he was rather deaf and wouldn't admit it so couldn't really hear what was being said and then got it all wrong and she was 'sorry' if she had been presumptuous in bothering me at all and 'sorry' to have dragged me out on such an unpromising day, grey and drizzling and cold, and 'sorry' and 'sorry' and 'sorry'.

It was a relief to arrive at the magnificently imposing red front door of the large Georgian vicarage. She stopped wittering in order to stand on tiptoe and reach for the brass bell pull. "Mrs Gossage is expecting us", she said. "She will explain everything I am sure." She paused for breath and smiled weakly and apologetically up at me.

The door swung open and a tall youth stood there – an extremely thin, gangling figure in a tight black knitted V-neck sweater, clinging black jeans, marble white, large, bony, bare feet, a long thin neck, a shock of tight dark curls above severe black framed tinted glasses that, in a sinister way, obscured his eyes and a thick, pursed mouth which made him look totally disdainful.

"Oh, Mrs Penge." There was no welcome in his tone of voice. "Mother is expecting you.

"Thank you, Tristan. This is Mr Johnson."

For an instant he remained unmoving. Then, "Good" and he turned away. "I am in the middle of something. You know the way", over his shoulder as he disappeared down the long hallway.

"He is so busy composing", confided Mrs Penge apologetically. "That's what he does. He is writing the songs for the play."

For me the first alarm bell. The word 'adapted' sprang to the forefront of my mind. "Adapted', with the addition of songs specially composed by a supercilious, lanky, callow youth. Oh dear.

After a hesitatingly apologetic knock by Miss Penge on a door to our left and a brief wait for the distant summons of "Do come in", we entered a grand sitting room decorated in Wedgewood blue, ivory and gold and I had my first, and I now reveal, my *only* encounter, with Guston Village Players' leading lady.

She lounged, decorously arranged, on a large pale blue settee. One arm trailed elegantly along the generously plump bank of cushions, the other supported her on the arm rest, her plump left-hand dangling languidly from a flashing, heavily braceleted wrist. She swung herself into a sitting position and proffered her right hand to me, the back of which was uppermost, as if inviting a deferential kiss on the scented and perfumed knuckles rather than a polite shake. "Welcome. Welcome both", she pronounced.

I took her hand between my thumb and forefinger and awkwardly worked it up and down.

"Dorinda, dear." Miss Penge was taking the initiative. "May I introduce Mr Nigel Johnson."

As I let go of her, our grand hostess swiftly placed both hands on the cushions close to the side of her ample thighs and, with apparently less effort than I thought would be required, heaved her generous self into a standing position.

"How good to meet you", she intoned. I recognised, in spite of her smile, the same disdainful mouth that her son had sported together with the revelation of slightly too prominent firm white teeth. She would have been 'Goofy' at school, I surmised.

She was an imposing figure. Tall and well fleshed . Her large bosom was in no way diminished by the white silk blouse that was generously frilled from the neckline plunging down the waist. This exposed an extensive amount of luminous, pink wobbling cleavage and a hint of shimmering red brassiere. An attempt had been made to discipline the hanging folds of her torso with a wide golden belt, below which she wore tight black trousers that flared below the knee. I noted that, in spite of her imperious height, she wore flat golden slippers. She needed no heels.

"I am pleased to meet you. Dorinda Gossage."

"Miss Penge fluttered. "I'm sorry. I should have said."

"Nonsense, my dear Sylvia" (though there was disapproval in her voice). "Mr Johnson, you sit there." She indicated a large, off-white wing-backed armchair. "Sylvia, ring for tea." And she sank back on to the settee.

Her lips were now composed into a plump pout. Her face was too round, too much weight compressing her eyes into narrow slips that no amount of carefully applied make-up could widen into anything expressive. Large dark false eyelashes merely compounded the problem. Her fair hair, fine and genuine as it was, would have flattered her far more had it not been scraped so severely back to reveal fleshy earlobes and a strong neck marred with unflattering horizontal creases of stretched skin. Large pendant diamante earrings reflected their sparkles onto her flushed, over-powdered jowls.

My attention was drawn away from Miss Penge's fluttering round in the background as Dorinda Gossage held sway.

"We have a dilemma, Mr Johnson, as I hope Miss Penge has told you." The narrow eyes slewed warningly in that poor little woman's direction. "Our problem being that our Director has become unavailable, for personal medical reasons."

A dramatic pause to emphasise the extreme delicacy of the poor man's condition was followed by Miss Penge's whisper, "He ..."

A furious scowl from our hostess and a rush to move on.

"We've been left, Mr Johnson, left all at sea, for that is indeed where we actually want to be." She paused, pleased with her knowing reference to the situation in hand, which left me somewhat perplexed.

"You see, Mr Johnson", she proceeded to explain. "We are proposing a piece based on Mr Rattigan's play, *Bequest to a Nation*. Our director, the Reverend Roundle, has redrafted it to accommodate songs composed by my son, Tristan. You met him in the hall. Musically he is extremely accomplished and has been thus ever since a boy. He gained a scholarship to Goldsmith's College in London but it was not to be. His tenure there had to be foreshortened for personal reasons."

Again the word hung in the air. Again a blast from Miss Penge. "He's very sensitive."

"Quite so. Have you rung for the tea, my dear? Perhaps a quick reconnoitre?"

Miss Penge departed from the room. The leading lady now uncontestably had centre stage.

"It is a marvellous and exciting concept. The work is now a comic light opera. We have rechristened it *All At Sea* and have introduced a middle act in which Lady Hamilton (a role that I have been persuaded to take on in view of the demands it makes and my extensive exposure in the theatre) in which Lady Hamilton, in order to be near her lover on the eve of the Battle of Trafalgar, disguises herself as a cabin boy and is smuggled on to the Admiral's flagship where much hilarious jollity ensues with mistaken identities and sexual ambiguity – think Viola in breeches in *Twelfth Night* (I could only think of Dorinda in breeches in Guston Village Hall).

Horatio fails to recognise his lover in disguise yet feels strongly attracted to the cabin boy. He reveals this in a ballad and in a comic duet with his friend and compatriot, Hardy, who in turn reveals in a dramatic aria his concerns for what he sees to be mental instability in the Commander of the Fleet. During a rousing drinking song with the crew – this is what Tristan is working on as we speak, but he's having trouble with words that rhyme with 'rum' – during that song (think Nanny and Oomp-pah-pah in *Oliver*) a seam in her disguisory garment fails and Emma Hamilton's true identity – all is revealed! (By now alarm bells are ringing wildly for me).

"Our other problem is that our Director, the Revd Roundle, was to play Nelson himself, but that cannot be … So …

She pauses. No way. No way would I play Horatio Nelson in this farrago.

So – a dramatic pause – joy of joys – Tristan has taken on the role. "Oh, Mr Johnson, can you imagine it?"

Oh yes. Oh yes. I could imagine it all.

"So, you see", a small voice at my elbow. Miss Penge with a tray of tea, "You see how much we are in need of your experience and expertise."

Two pairs of eyes, one squinting and one pale blue and waiting, gazed at me with hopeful expectation.

Think, I said to myself, think fast.

"And only four weeks away." It was Miss Penge – and thanks to Miss Penge, I saw a way out.

"Four weeks", I echoed. "That would bring us to where?"

"November 12th to Saturday 15th", informed the ruffled white blouse and pursed red lips in front of me.

"Oh no", I ejaculated. "Oh no. Confound it. What a shame." Two faces look askance at me. "Would you believe it? Oh dear. A wedding My niece's wedding. In West Bromwich. On that Saturday, the 15th. At midday. My niece, Helen and Bradley, her husband to be, I said I'll be there. On the Thursday. To help out. Isn't that typical. Of all the weekends in November – it had to be that one. In West Bromwich."

There was a long, very awkward silence. The Gossage slit eyes glinted at me with a mixture of total disbelief and sheer malevolence. She bared her teeth and hissed.

Miss Penge – bless her – saved the moment. She put down the tea tray. Again she was sorry – to have bothered me – a fool's errand – she was sorry – the first thing she should have mentioned should have been the date; it was all her fault. She was so sorry.

As the imposing red front door closed behind me I heard a cry that was anything but refined or decorous.

"Tristan. Did you hear that! Call the whole bloody thing off!"

ANGEL GABRIEL

The Angel Gabriel took a much needed gulp of cool, clear, freshly-scented heavenly air. He paused then became immediately aware of its calming effect. He was through necessity to conduct an interview of the kind he enjoyed least – with one of the lower caste of the heavenly throng. There had been a mistake. The encounter could be plagued by so many misunderstandings, the Great Angel's comprehension of the situation being so far above that of a lesser spiritual being. If he were not careful, he could be drawn into so much explanation and instruction that the whole point and purpose of the meeting could be blurred by philosophical observations that, at that juncture, may prove entirely inappropriate for his subordinate. Suddenly he was aware of a faint tinkling thrill on the passing celestial zephyrs – it was how an approach was announced, there being no door to knock or bell pulls to tug at in Heaven.

"Approach." He used the traditional accepted bidding word. He hoped his tone would not sound too stern. He was aware of how awe-inspiring he could seem.

The white vapours surrounding him swirled with a sudden vigour and dimly a figure appeared.

In all sense, the new arrival was lower than the Archangel. He was shorter and altogether less splendid. His raiment was dull in hue, his wings yet to achieve full height and maturity, their plumes still meagre in spread, too feathery, rather grey. He had yet to develop a halo so in contrast his hair, though fair, lacked life and lustre. It straddled across his head like wheat flattened in a storm – the top of his head was indeed positively table-top flat. His face was chubby, ruddy rounded cheeks, a rather protruding lower lip, a squarely cleft chin. His eyes were deep set, glinted a startling blue when they could be seen beneath generously thick eyebrows that gave a perpetual frown to his unprepossessing countenance. His shoulders stooped. His whole demeanour proclaimed uncertainty and unhappiness. He stood before his superior and added effectively to the whole impression by bowing his head. His arms hung loosely at his sides.

The Angel Gabriel felt an urge to put a comforting arm around his shoulders, such a sorry sight he presented. But such an action was not possible on the celestial plain – wings got in the way!

"What do they call you?" He tried to sound kindly but heard the unintended imperiousness in his voice.

The creature raised his face but could not dare attempt eye contact with his master. "Alf", he replied.

"Alf!" The Archangel could not help echoing the reply. "Alph", he said. "After the river …'Wagre Alph, the sacred river ran through caverns measureless to man, down to the something sea'. Poetry recital was not his thing. He had had trouble of late reciting from memory every verse of the Bible, a requirement of the job.

"No, your graciousness. Alf – A.l.f. – Angel of the Lower Flight. They call me Alf."

In spite of himself, the Archangel smiled. "Oh, I see", he said. He extended his right hand, tucked his crooked index finger beneath the boy's cleft chin and raised his face so their eyes met. He let his hand fall away. "You are in Archangel Michael's division."

"Yes, sir."

"Which is how you came to be responsible for the carving of the tablet."

"Yes, sir. Sorry, sir."

"Perhaps you had better tell me what happened."

"It was a mistake, Sir. The Mighty Angel …"

"Michael", put in the other.

"Yes, sir. He. He gave me the tablet to inscribe, choose the front and the wording …"

"On papyrus."

"Yes, sir, on papyrus And he withdrew. Leaving the rest to me."

Archangel Gabriel could see the picture. Alf was of artisan level – a kind of apprentice – who, with practice, would be expected to aspire to greater things. "So, Archangel Michael did not stay to observe your efforts."

"No, your graciousness. Currently he is occupied with a project of enormous significance. He is intent on providing divine inspiration for great earthly creativeness – the decoration of a ceiling and a beautiful carving of a human youth called D … D …" The boy stooped uncertainly.

"David", prompted the Archangel. He had heard of Archangel Michael's fabulous undertaking. To convey through divine intervention the greatest of God's creations to earth.

"That's it, sir. David. The Boy David. It is such a mighty undertaking, he can think of little else." The boy smiled at the Archangel. A gentle smile with just a hint of wickedness. "We tease him. Behind his back. Archangel Michael. We call it the Michelangelo Project. He heard us once, but he doesn't mind."

"But we are wondering off the point." The correction was more abrupt than he intended. "The tablets. What of the tablets?"

The boy's smile vanished. His head dropped. His voice sunk almost to a whisper. "There were eleven Commandments", he said. "I had the tablets, knew their dimensions and the font to employ. But I made an error in my measurements. The letters were fractionally too big – only fractionally." He stopped speaking. The Archangel could see a tear trickling over the pink bulge of one cheek.

"Go on", he encouraged quietly.

The boy took a deep breath. "I got to the end of the fifth Commandment and had filled one tablet. I realised that I had room on the second tablet for only five more Commandments."

"And there were eleven."

"Yes, your graciousness."

"So?"

"I had to get rid of one."

The realisation of the enormity of this menial's editorial decision struck at the very core of the Archangel's being – like a physical blow. Way above he sensed an Almighty rumbling of frustration and displeasure. The boy's as yet unschooled senses would not be attuned to this.

The Archangel straightened his back, flexed his wings and reacquired his sense of dignity. "You had to get rid of one of them!"

"Yes."

"Which one? May I ask?"

"It was the longest one. Number Seven on the list."

"Which was?"

"It was about men and women. Humans, you know, sir?"

"I know all about humans", came the knowing response.

"It was about how men and women they should always be equal, treat each other equally and with respect, honour one another. Something like that", the boy said. "Kind of equality."

There was a long pause. The air itself was still. The clouds froze.

"And?" Eventually the Archangel found his voice.

"I finished carving the other five. And handed them all in." Another pause. "I didn't tell anybody. I threw away the papyrus."

Archangel Gabriel looked down pityingly on the insignificant creature – Angel of the Lower Flight – who had changed the course of history single handedly. The boy burst into tears. He fell to his knees.

"What will happen now, sir? To me? Will He have to be told?" His podgy fingers knotted and unknotted themselves in his lap.

Now comes the awkward bit, thought the Archangel. "He – the Almighty – already knows." The boy's sobs suddenly ceased with one enormous gulp.

"How? He does?" he croaked.

"Oh yes. He knows everything. From the beginning to the end of time."

"Then how … why … did he let this happen? Let me do it?" The boy turned his face up towards the Archangel. His bulbous bottom lip quivered. He threatened to break into tears again. But Archangel Gabriel would have none of that.

"Rise to your feet", he commanded. "Wipe your eyes Your nose. Compose yourself." (Could I sound more pompous, he wondered?)

"Yes, sir." The boy did as bidden.

"God knows. He knew what would happen. What you would do. That Michael would be too preoccupied. That the omission of this 11th Commandment – Number 7 – would, will, throughout history, cause great disturbance and consternation between his separate creations, of men and women. Yet, not so separate", he mused. He pitied the boy. "You must see yourself as an instrument of the Lord. He knows the future. And was aware of the part you will play – have played – in it. He gives all his creatures – above and below – the freedom to act within the powers he has ordained. Freedoms that produce strengths and weaknesses. And he incorporates those freedoms – and their consequences – into his great and almighty plan."

The boy looked impressed – indeed, was impressed. For an instant his face cleared but, like a cloud passing before the sun, his brow furrowed, deeply bringing an expression of total bewilderment to his features.

"But", his brain was now working overtime. "But …" His eyes flickered from side to side. His lips tightened. "But …", he said. "Wouldn't it be easier if we was all told what to do and just did it?"

Matters had gone too far. Archangel Gabriel stirred himself mightily, raised one hand gracefully in admonition and pronounced, "That is a debate for another time. Go now." (He almost added, "And sin no more"). But, instead said, "Think over what you have done. Learn from it."

The boy's face was still dark with doubt. "But ...", he stuttered.

Archangel Gabriel interjected. "Remember, above all, God forgives you."

And a shaft of sunlight pierced the scene – temporarily blinding them both.

ASPIRATION

Everyone dreams a spot in the limelight
Everyone dreams a special moment in the sun
Everyone dreams a little taste of fame
Occasionally to feel they're winning in the game

Not enough the earnest slog of working
The daily grind of doing what's required
The box to tick, the uphill task, no shirking
No wit engaged, no inspiration fired

No moment when the world around seems glorious
When aspiration can uplift above the norm
When surmounting the raised bar can be victorious
And suddenly it's so worthwhile being born

Too often it is just enough to be there
To keep the nose clean, do not create a wave
To met the target, do as much as needs be
To hum the lowest note along the stave

Far too seldom chances will be given
For the spirit to engage, the soul to soar
For the inner eye to gain a glimpse of heaven
Or the inner being roar for more and more

They must stay in serious ranks assembled
Scratching black marks on a surface dull and grey
Close the blinds and let reality be dissembled
Hide then from the icy blizzard of winter's day

God forbid they'd want to paint, it, write a poem
Create a dance to match the swirling of the flames
Let alone burst out to meet the wildness of the storm
And plough through snow, raw flesh aglow
Relishing the freezing pain and aches.

BEING AN ARTIST

"I want to be an artist, Dad
I really want to draw.
I've scrawled and scribbled with crayons and chalks
Since I was only four."

At primary school Miss Gittings said
"That's quite a gift you've got
That Xmas card that you've designed
I really like a lot."

She looked at the things I drew
With favourable eyes
At the end of the year, in late July,
I got the School Art Prize.

In secondary school, more kids around
I found it harder there
Mr Babberstock, in his paint-stained smock
Was seeking artistic flair

His Art department vast and wide
I found it overawing
Pottery, wood carving and silk screen
It ceased to be just drawing

But determinedly I struggled on
With every best endeavour
I watched my school mate hit his mark
But could I? Hardly ever.

He'd smile and say "You do your best"
A rewarding tap on the shoulder
But time after time I failed to shine
It got worse as I got older

My A-level pass would be hit and miss
But for one element close to my heart
A three-hour written paper
Appreciation of History of Art

For Art I have loved in all its forms
From its primitive daubing on caves
Michael Angelo, Van Gogh, even Tracey's bed
To the very latest raves

My written paper pulled me through
And to Art School I was bound
My heart and spirit leaped ahead
My feet dragged on the ground

The work done round me in my classes
Was wacky, wild and rare
Mine was rated 'OK' or 'Adequate'
What I really lacked was flair

It couldn't last, my hopes they died
And shrivelled to a pin
In the ice-cold blast of reality
I threw the whole lot in

Shameful home to Mum and Dad
Who were supportive in their way
No criticism, no 'told you so'
Didn't really know what to say

Except "You'll have to find some work"
Not difficult to do
I drifted then from job to job
But to something I was true!

When I wasn't at work I pursued my Art
In active and passive ways
I did evening classes at the local Art School
These dragged me through dark days

I kept this up for nearly a year
Something of a fixture I became
Life classes, landscape, chalk, water paint, oils
Most people there knew my name

I helped a bit behind the scenes
Experienced in every medium
I longed for the evenings; it was when my sun shone
After day after day of tedium

Then a lecturer friend made a useful suggestion
He said I might rouse my ambition
A qualification at the local tech
To be a full time at technician

All this occurred many years ago
Though sometimes it seems like last week
Now the students and staff know to whom they can turn
If it's help or advice they seek

On the walls of my workshop hang some of my works
Students say, "Wow. They're wicked. Who did these?"
I half-lie to them, "Just some guys from the past"
And I glow from my head to my toes.

A conclusion I've reached as the years pass me by
And I know it may sound a bit daft
In the great world of Art I know I'll never shine
But in that world I have found my craft.

BETRAYALS

A ONE ACT PLAY FOR A FEMALE CAST

Cast
Mother:
Margery Ayling –A woman in crisis. Independent, aloof, formidable – but crumbling. Aged 78

Daughters:
Brenda - The oldest. Rother dull and dowdy, dutiful
Catherine - beautician, very smart, rather too much make-up, appears superficial and fussy
Alice - English teacher, bookish, very straight, determined, sensible
Sheila - the youngest. Ex-hippy, eccentric, unconventional, chip-on-the-shoulder

Journalist:
Barbara Avelon - very smart and professional, confident, cool, just too "nice"

The play hinges on mother's performance. She relives her own life in her speeches, fighting to keep her emotions under control. She has at last found "confessional" – but her wordiness must not come over as unnatural and forced. Her manner can be imperious but she is an ordinary woman; you wouldn't notice her in a supermarket queue.
Scene: Comfortable, traditional, furnished (old-fashioned but affluent) living room of Mrs Ayling's home (See final speech of play for details)
Two exits – one to hall and one to kitchen.
Time – the present. Early morning.
Alice and Brenda enter from hall. Brenda has just admitted Alice through front door.
Alice: (concerned) Where is mother?
Brenda: Upstairs
Alice: How is she?
Brenda: Very quiet
Pause

Alice: I can't believe it

Brenda: No

(Alice reaches in large shopping bag where she has all the day's newspapers)

Brenda: I don't want to. We were besieged by reporters all day yesterday. I don't want to read their filth.

Alice: There are none there now

Brenda: No. It's too early. Even they have to sleep and feed. They won't be long. Did you lock the door?

Alice: I pulled it to. There's the Yale….

Brenda: I'll go and bolt it. You check the back door is firmly locked. And put the kettle on.

(They exit – Brenda to hall, Alice to kitchen) Pause

(Re-enter Brenda, goes to Alice's bag, half pulls out a newspaper and puts it back with a shudder. Enter A.)

Alice: Tea…….or coffee? Have you had any breakfast?

Brenda: No. I'd love a cup of tea.

Alice: Black, no sugar. What about mother? Has she eaten?

Brenda: *(sardonic)* She's taken a tray to her room. Don't worry about her. Cereal, milk, coffee, toast – the lot.

Alice: The condemned eats a hearty breakfast.

Brenda: Not funny.

Alice: No. Tea – black, no sugar *(Exit to kitchen)*

(Brenda sits. Pause. Then Alice re-enters)

Alice: It's brewing. *(Pause – she sighs)* Gerry's gone to work. I don't think anyone there knows who his mother-in-law is. I've kept the kids from school. They saw the report last night on TV. Sophie is very upset. James is more bemused – a bit of him's rather enjoying it.

Brenda: I can't believe it. I can't believe it! *(distressed)*

Alice: Come on. I know it's hard.

Brenda: What the hell is happening? Let me see the papers. *(Grabs bag and hauls out newspapers)* Dear God! – Licensed to spy; "78-Year-Old Granny was a Spy".

Alice: Read them. Find out. Has she said much?

Brenda: No….she won't until we're all here. She looks very tired but calm, in control. *(Reads paper)*

Alice: I'll get your tea. You sure you won't have some toast…or an egg? *(no reply – she goes out)* Pause

(Knocking heard off in kitchen. Voices of Alice and Catherine)

Catherine: *(entering – over shoulder to Alice)* Milk, no sugar in mine. Brenda, I came as soon as I could. *(kisses her)* – I've taken the day off.

Brenda: Have you read these?

Catherine: I bought them all. *(shows bag full of newspapers)* I've only heard what was on telly last night.

Brenda: What are we going to do. (Alice enters with tea – china cups and saucers)

Alice: Take it bit by bit. Day by Day, hour by hour. Here *(to Brenda)* Drink this. It is what we British do in a crisis. A cup of hot strong tea. (They all sit drinking)

Brenda: It's like some dreadful dream. She won't say a thing. It's as if she's shut up shop. She does the usual, everyday things – calm, sedate even – meticulous – not a glimmer on the surface of what's going on underneath.

Catherine: That's typical of her. She's always been aloof, reserved. Always the correct thing.

Brenda: I've not dared leave her alone since the whole thing began.

Alice: You don't mean……

Brenda: No – she's no danger to herself…. I think. But she's so distant – she's pushed herself way out to sea.

Alice: Not waving but drowning.

Brenda: Not even waving.

(Pause)

Catherine: So?

Brenda: We'll wait for Sheila. Then I'll go and tell mother we're all here.

(Pause)

Brenda: It makes no sense at all.

Catherine: I can't believe any sane person could do such a thing. Sell out your own country – your own people – your own kind. But mother….she's not….

Alice: The type? Is there a type? I've thought about it. Nothing else all night. This is not the mother we know – certainly not that I know.

Catherine: This is her before we came along. When she worked at that experimental station place in London, after the war

Brenda: How do you know that?

Catherine: She told me about it once.

Brenda: Oh?

Catherine: She came to stay with us once. Emily was ill – glandular fever it was – and mum came to look after her while I was at work. I

41

had just got the business going. You remember…. Summer of '89. Well, in the evenings, after Emily was tucked up in bed, I'd sit and talk with mother. I used to do her nails. She often commented on how we'd all had full and independent lives before the children came along. She'd gone to London after her mother died and worked in a firm in London – she did tell me the name – dealing in long distance radar and remote-control things. She worked in admin. It sounded a pretty gloomy life. Post-war London. Dull office routine. Worked with some very odd people. She mostly filled her time with evening classes. And she was in a choir.

Alice: When she wasn't doing other things.

Brenda: That's how it must have been, routine, mundane.

Alice: Monday evening – Flower arranging; Wednesdays – Handel's Messiah; Fridays – back door of the Russian Embassy with a basket full of secret files.

Catherine: I really could do without this. I've cancelled all my clients today. At short notice too. I could lose some of them for good.

Alice: Oh, they'll survive for once without facials and exfoliation.

Catherine: Well they're cancelled. No going back.

Alice: This will increase your business. The tongues will be wagging. They'll all want to cross-examine you over the cuticle cream.

Brenda: I think we are straying from the point. Mother seems perfectly in control.

(Front door bell rings)

Brenda: That will be Sheila. *(Exits to answer front door)*

Alice: Now the fun will start!

(Pause……Sheila bursts in, Brenda behind her)

Sheila: Where is she?

Alice: Now calm down, Sheila.

Sheila: Don't tell me to calm down! I'm furious! That woman has…….

Brenda: "That woman", as you put it, is our mother.

Sheila: And I'm meant to respect that? That woman has hounded, criticized, condemned me for as long as I can remember – and all this time she was concealing the greatest act of hypocrisy that it's possible to imagine.

Catherine: Sheila, calm down. This helps no-one.

Sheila: It helps me. You know what I went through with her. Nothing I could do was right. My career. John. That damned business on

Greenham Common. How she sneered at me for that. Wasting my time with a coven of drop-out lesbian lunatics, she said.

Brenda: She seriously wondered if you were one yourself.

Sheila: Me? Rather that than what she is.

Brenda: She really worried about you – more than any of us.

Sheila: She worried about herself for the sake of appearances. I wasn't "respectable" enough for her high standards. By God, when I think back!

Alice: Ironical, really, when you think of it. Both of you on the side of the Ruskies. You might have woken up to find her in the tent next door.

Sheila: God forbid. Anyway, that wasn't it. We were trying to save the planet….

Brenda: We're not here to discuss you, Sheila. Any conversation we have ends up revolving around you. Sheila and her ideals – her latest "save the Universe project" – her most recent emotional crisis.

Catherine: Will you two stop bickering!

Brenda: I'm sorry. But this is all getting too much.

Alice: And you, Sheila, calm down.

(Sheila sulks. Front door bell rings. Alice goes to answer)

Brenda: Find out who it is first. Don't let anyone in. *(Alice goes out)*

Sheila: Where is she?

Brenda: Upstairs – having breakfast. Which reminds me *(grudgingly)* would you like something?

Sheila: Coffee would be nice.

Catherine: I'll get it.

Sheila: A little milk – no sugar.

Catherine: Right. *(Exits)*

Brenda: I do understand how you feel. Chalk and cheese, you and mother. Always were.

Sheila: *(sullen)* OK.

Brenda: It was hell here yesterday. Crowds of press in the garden, front and back. I called the police but they'd only take responsibility for keeping the front roadway clear. *(Enter Alice)*

Alice: That was reporters at the door. I told them "no comment" and to go away. And a letter for you Brenda. I've not unbolted the door

Brenda: Let me see (she opens the letter) Ah! I was expecting this. Excuse me (she goes into the kitchen as Catherine comes in with coffee for Sheila)

Catherine: *(to Brenda as they pass)* There's someone at the back door. Just standing there. *(Then to Sheila)* Here, Sheila. It's even de-caff.
Sheila: Thanks.
(Re-enter Brenda with Barbara Avalon, reporter)
Brenda: Come in, Barbara. These are my sisters. Sheila, Catherine, Alice. This is Barbara Avalon from......
Sheila: Not from "The Express"
Barbara: That's right.
Sheila: I thought you said, "no press".
Brenda: I did but.........
Barbara: Let me explain, shall I? You can't avoid the press – not in a situation like this. Your mother's story is public property whether you like it or not. I have advised your sister to do what is best, go with one paper. For exclusive rights, we'll make sure you're bothered as little as possible. The others will back off. And you'll get a better chance of having your side of events truly represented.
Sheila: *(Sarcastic)* By "The Express"!
Barbara: Yes. That's right.
Sheila: And what is a right-wing, fascist response to the problem of a spy exposed? Firing squad at dawn? Provision of a cyanide pill so that the decent and honourable course of action can be taken?
Brenda: I'd have thought that would meet with your approval, my dear.
(Sheila reacts with a withering smile)
Barbara: You disapprove of your mother's actions, then?
Sheila: Doesn't everyone – everyone who is honest.
Barbara: I'm not looking to prosecute – not even judge. I see it as my job to get the story – present the facts.
Sheila: As you see them.
Barbara: As close to actuality as I can get.
Brenda: We need some help here. You weren't here yesterday with them all clamouring around the house – even at the back windows. I can't deal with that. Giving Barbara sole rights makes sense to me.
Sheila: Giving?
Barbara: There will be a financial consideration, of course.
Brenda: Still under negotiation.
Sheila: God! She'll make money out of it!
Barbara: Money she may well need. She might have to get away for a while, until the fracas dies down. She may have legal costs.
Brenda: If they prosecute.

44

Alice: What?

Catherine: They wouldn't. Not an old lady – almost eighty.

Barbara: They well might.

Sheila: Morally they should. I wouldn't want them to, mind you, but they should.

Alice: Oh my God!

Catherine: She couldn't face that. At her age.

Sheila: She's like nails. Hard. She'd cope.

Barbara: So that's why I'm here. To help. OK? *(General acceptance)* Right. Let's get on. *(They gather round her, backs to entrance hall. She, business-like, consults her note book).* Brenda filled me in with a lot of background over the phone. Your mum's education – left school at fourteen – various clerical jobs – moved to London when her mother died. That's when she was employed at P&F Systems Ltd.

Catherine: That's it. P&F Systems. That's when it happened.

Barbara: This is where I need your mother's input. Then she married – Cyril Arthur Ayling. 1946. Register Office, Clapham. Then five children – the four of you and a boy, Dennis.

Alice: I think we ought to keep him out of all this. He was only ten when he died. I can't see the need even to mention him.

Barbara: It's all part of the picture. I want to provide my readers with a comprehensive picture of this woman.......*(Mother appears unnoticed at the hall door)*.......not just the one dimensional, tabloid 'grandmother spy' image.

Brenda: And Dad. How much of this did he know?

Sheila: Nothing. He could have known nothing. He wouldn't have tolerated this. He was as straight as a die, was Dad.

Barbara: Ran his own ironmongery business, didn't he?

Sheila: Worked hard all his life. Town Councillor. Parish Councillor. Almost Mayor at one point.

Barbara: And he passed on twelve years ago.

Sheila: Very sudden. Collapsed in the street and was gone. Within weeks of retiring.

Barbara: Very sad.

Sheila: But all taken very much in her stride. Surface hardly even ruffled.

Alice: That's not fair, Sheila. She's never been one to show her emotions. We all have to deal with those things in our own way.

Catherine: I thought I got pretty close to her at times, but Dad was a no-go area. She didn't even seem to miss him.

Barbara: So, what else did your mother do, apart from running the home and bringing up a family – I mean – as you all got old enough to begin leading your own lives?

Catherine: Mum? Well, she was just there. No particular outside interests.

Brenda: She did much of the bookkeeping for Dad's business.

Catherine: She even took over once – Dad had prostate trouble.

Alice: "Men's problems" as she put it. She didn't like to go into too much detail.

Brenda: Yes, she ran the business. Single handed for a while.

Catherine: With Geoff.

Barbara: Geoff?

Catherine: Dad's storeman and assistant. Worked for him for decades.

Barbara: So very much the mother and housewife.

Alice: And an avid reader. That's where I got it from. Regular piles of books from the library. Every evening she would disappear with her book. We were left very much to our own devices, with dad, downstairs.

Sheila: He was a wonderful man – Dad. I don't want him – his memory – dragged down by this. She didn't give him much in his lifetime. I don't want her to pull him down now.

Barbara: To be fair, she emerges from what you tell me as being very supportive. A traditional role, very much of its day. Looking after the house. One foot in the family business.

Sheila: But there was never any welcome – any warmth. She's never ever been a woman who relaxes much. Never known how to enjoy herself.

Brenda: Having fun is an embarrassment to her.

Alice: Christmas and birthdays. Everything in keeping – parties, candles, presents, a tree – but it was all just going through the motions with her.

Catherine: Nothing spontaneous.

Alice: Highly organized – precise.

Brenda: But dead in the middle.

Barbara: Housewife. Mother. Quiet life. Reserved. Er…devoted? Is that fair?

Brenda: Devoted. I think so.

Alice: Yes.

Sheila: Certainly determined. Something of a control freak.

Brenda: Not again Sheila.

Barbara: I don't feel I'm getting far. Circling around the subject. Not getting to the heart of things. *(Mother steps forward)*
Mother: Maybe I can help *(Consternation)*
Barbara: Mrs. Ayling!
Brenda: Mother
Catherine: Mum *(Pause)*
Mother: Well?
Brenda: Mother….er….this is Barbara Avelon.
Mother: *(Curt, aloof)* From "The Daily Express". I've read your column. Quite readable. Human interest.
Barbara: I was hoping for an interview….
Mother: Well, I am human – if cold and aloof – and suddenly of undoubted interest.
Brenda: Mother, I can explain….
Mother: No Need, Brenda. I've left my tray at the top of the stairs if you would be so kind. *(Brenda goes out to the hall)*. Miss….er…Mrs Avalon?
Barbara: Barbara, please.
Mother: Has anyone offered you a drink? Tea? Coffee?
Barbara: I'm O.K, really. Not long had breakfast.
Mother: Right. How can I help you?
Barbara: You realize that my paper is being offered sole rights for your story. Such an arrangement will benefit you in several ways; firstly….
Mother: I am offering you my co-operation. I'm sure Brenda has talked matters through with you.
Barbara: I…I….yes. Well…
Mother: You were itemizing aspects of my life. Archetypal housewife and mother…. Rather dull it all sounded.
Barbara: It was the bare bones. A starting point.
Mother: I have little to add. Nothing to remark upon….
Barbara: Except?
Mother: Except? (Brenda re-enters with tray)
Sheila: Except what we really want to know – **need** to know, mother. Why?
Mother: Always straight for the jugular, Sheila.
Sheila: It's bite or be bitten, mother.
Barbara: Mrs Ayling – can you tell us why?
Mother: Before I tell you how, where and what?
Alice: No games, mother. No games.

47

Brenda: I can't stand this. (Brenda exits to the kitchen)

Barbara: All this is in the files that we have. "How", we know. Gestetner copies and accommodation addresses. "What"? Details of long-range aerial reconnaissance system – too scientific for the majority of our readers. "Where"? Clapham, London. "When"? we know that. But "WHY"?

Alice: That is the question. *(Brenda quietly re-enters)*

Mother: Do you know what it is like to stand and hear yourself dissected? – "Deconstructed" is the modern term, I believe – by those who are closest to you? To hear your faults – your dullness, coldness, unfeelingness – stretched out across the operating table, tightly, remorselessly pulled apart and heartlessly exposed as scalpels are raised....

Brenda: Don't, mother, don't.

Sheila: We're going for the sympathy vote.

Alice: Sheila!

Mother: So you all want to know "why".

Alice: Not now, mum. It doesn't matter.

Mother: Oh, but it does. Sheila – doesn't it?

Sheila: Yes, it does. More than anything.

Mother: The "why" is easy. I was young. I tried to make sense of a world that defied any attempt to do just that. The War left things as unfair and as out of balance as they had been before it started. Maybe even more so. The Allies positively crowed with victory. And rightly so. There were attempts to make sure that Germany and her allies were not left in the desperate plight they had experienced at the end of the First War – they didn't want the same disillusionment and dissatisfaction to breed again another Hitler and a fight for German dignity and superiority. But nobody looked towards the poor end of the allies, Russia. I felt for Russia. A fine people, a splendid history, a great culture – torn apart by revolution and war, threatening to plunge further and further into degradation and chaos. They needed help, stability. The balance had to be maintained – the power balance. Technically and strategically they should not get left too far behind. *(Pause)* This all suddenly sounds very hollow, doesn't it? It's my prepared speech – now that I have to face the world – now it's all coming out.

Sheila: It doesn't tell us "why" – just gives us reasons, cold, empty, logical reasoning.

Brenda: Sheila!

Mother: No, she is right. At the jugular again.

Alice: Why could you betray all you should believe in – all you must, at some time, have believed in?

Catherine: And us…. Your family, father, everyone you had known and lived alongside – neighbours….

Alice: Those who fought for you, died for you….

Sheila: Gave you the opportunity to do what you did.

Mother: That didn't seem to matter. We were all lucky to be alive. Life or death were just a matter of chance. The only way out of the mess was to give both sides every opportunity to prosper – the Russians as much as anyone else.

Sheila: You're not answering the question. What about us?

Mother: You weren't there when all this started. None of you – not even your father.

Catherine: And did things change – when he came along?

Mother: At first, no. we never talked about things like that. Your father was a simple man – no, that sounds terrible. He was an uncomplicated man. Never a politician. He had "done his bit in the War", as we used to say, and now wanted the settled, peaceful life he had fought for. So he worked – in the shop and on the Council – he was a school governor – he worked and worked and worked. That is how he justified to himself his own luck in surviving the War. So many didn't.

Sheila: And he never knew?

Mother: Oh he knew. He knew.

Sheila: I can't believe that!

Alice: Never!

Mother: He knew. He knew there was something – something between us. He could tell there was a shadow – a blight – something unmentioned and unmentionable. He was a sensitive man – he carefully chose not to tread on that particular spot. In a million careful ways, he skirted around that emptiness in our lives. And no matter how horrible it became, I could never tell him. When he died, I felt his strength go from me – his decency – his reassurance. I suddenly realized how much I had come to depend on him, and his discretion, his reluctance to intrude. And yet he gave so much – so much trust. I felt then, I could have – should have – entrusted everything to him. He would have coped – he would have shared the hurt.

Brenda: The hurt?

Mother: I was betrayed. Russia changed – or the truth within Russia emerged. Stalin and his hideously vile regime. I had sold my life, myself, my peace of mind for a system that was so awful in its cruelty and inhumanity, so corrupt in its very essence – I was just one of millions of sacrifices made in its name. But I had stopped. I had married and then when I found I was pregnant – with you, Brenda – I gave up work. We did in those days.

Sheila: But why? I still can't see. It was such a wild radical thing to do.

Mother: Not then. It was a different world then. The ghastly, the outrageous, the inhuman, the bizarre was what surrounded us. A few leaked documents seemed at once both pointlessly harmless and also greatly and personally significant. There was no perspective, no rules.

Sheila: But there are rules that apply – whatever the circumstances. Basic rules of human decency, of honesty, of humanity. Rules of faith, loyalty, love that outweigh anything awful that life has to throw at you.

Mother: I know that now – and have for a long time. But what's done cannot be undone. You have to live with it, or in spite of it.

Sheila: I refuse to believe anybody could be so naïve as not to foresee all that you've said. You're a logical person. Reasoning, Controlled. You must have known.

Mother: But I was also so young. I was naïve. I did believe, even in the muddle of the chaos after the War, that order was re-attainable. Good had just conquered evil, after all. There could be justice.

Sheila: Rubbish!

Mother: I had passion – that's it – passion. A belief that there would be a better future and I could help make it. Suddenly I was alone in the world – in London – and I could make my mark.

Sheila: But you are not a passionate person.

Mother: Not now – not for a long time. But I was. By God, I was! I was like you, Sheila. Ideas inflamed me. Only half understood, I know that now. But ferocious in the effect they had upon me. They swept me on, and the more successful I was, the more passionate I became. So much so that you enter your own state of reality. You know this, Sheila. All your enthusiasm. Any way you could, you would channel your natural restlessness into something that resembled purpose. Lost causes, you built up a collection. John - that awful man – cynical, dispiriting, self-absorbed, one of life's exploiters – you adored him, hung on to every bogus word. The number of sick and injured animals and birds you brought into the house when you were little – and not so little – all needing help. You befriended the grubbiest of children at school and brought them home for tea – shoeless, knickerless, huge appetites. You were proud of them. Not patronizing in the least. Just thrilled to be of use. And Greenham Common. I had to douse the flame in your eyes. I couldn't let you sell out to an ideal that would eventually prove disillusionment, as they always must. But the harder I fought you, the further you went.

Sheila: And I have that from you? No, mother. There are levels to which I would never descend. Don't use me to justify yourself. "Chalk and cheese" Brenda said. She's right.

Mother: And Brenda. Always right. Saddled now with the solemn duty of "looking after mother". You're so like your father, Brenda. He'd have taken me on in old age. Irrespective of everything.

Brenda: Yes, mother.

Mother: Catherine, you were the easiest, hardly ever a serious thought in your head. You'd always be the happy one.

Catherine: *(bridling)* I've done very well. A thriving business, Michael, the kids.

Mother: You've done extraordinarily well, with your father's uncomplicatedness. Your fine. Michael's a lovely man and ......I was going to say I'd do anything for Emily, but perhaps I've forfeited the right to make promises like that.

Catherine: You'll have to give me time, mother. Mike's O.K but Emily makes up her own mind.

Mother: And you, Alice?

Alice: I shall write a novel out of this.

Sheila: And make more money out of it.

Alice: Not really a novel. But I must learn to look at it that way. To take into account the whole of the saga. Whatever, it's not about you, mum. I don't recognize you in any of this.

Mother: That is your strength, Alice. To see objectively with the eye of an artist. It's also your weakness. Don't stand too far adrift. It's not a good long-term strategy. You need something else.

Barbara: Spoken from the heart, eh, Mrs Ayling?

Mother: Good God, I'd forgotten about you. What will you make of all this?

Barbara: There is enough here for a novel – but I'm only after an article.

Mother: I feel utterly exposed and utterly alone.

Brenda: Mother....

Mother: And utterly betrayed. I am the only stranger in this room. I feel we must start again – but I don't think there will ever be enough time. *(Pause)* Miss Avalon, come with me. We must agree what goes into print. You see how naïve I still am in saying that to a Grub Street professional! At least when Cleopatra clasped the asp to her bosom, she knew it would bite. We'll go to the dining room, then I shall go to my room for a rest. This way, <u>Barbara</u>. *(Exits)*

Alice: We have just spent ten minutes in the company of a total stranger.

Catherine: You must keep an eye on her.

Brenda: I will.

Sheila: To live with such loneliness all these years and we didn't know. And poor Dad.

Catherine: I'm going now. I've got the kids. I'll keep in touch, Brenda. Let me know if there's anything I can do. I'll call by tomorrow.

Brenda: Thanks. Take all your papers.

Alice: I don't think they can add much we need to know.

Catherine: Goodbye all. Will be in touch.

Brenda: 'bye Cath.

Alice: 'bye……Are you alright, Bren?

Brenda: I'm O.K.

Alice: Look, Mother's going up to her room. Why not come for brunch with me? Take a break.

Sheila: She can't be left alone in the house.

Brenda: And I must see Barbara off.

Sheila: You've got to discuss the fee!

Alice: Sheila!

Sheila: I'm sorry, I'm sorry. I shouldn't have said that.

Brenda: Old habits. *(Sheila smiles)*

Alice: What about you Sheila?

Sheila: Can I cadge a lift into town? I'll be back tomorrow, Bren. Tell mother I don't want a fight.

Brenda: O.K. Let's go out the back way. Could you bring the cups? *(They all take the cups and go)*

Alice: *(as they go)* I'll tell Gerry everything tonight when he gets home. Though what I'll say to Sophie I've no idea….

(Pause)….(Enter Barbara)

Barbara:

(Over her shoulder) Thank you, Mrs Ayling. I'll tell Brenda you have gone up. Goodbye. *(She sees the room is empty)* Right. *(takes out mobile phone)*

Express? Copy. Yes. 450/97/872. Right. Headline. SPY GRAND-MOTHER UNREPENTANT. Copy. It was like being in Olde – that's O-L-D-E England, the country of Noel Coward, rationing and "Brief Encounter". I sat this morning in a comfortable suburban villa, on the outskirts of conservative small 'c'....traditional, half-timbered Chester, and took morning coffee with Margery Ayling, elderly widow, mother and grandmother. She was surrounded by her four daughters, all supportive of her yet in varying degrees of incomprehension. Yes, amongst the chintzy curtains, embroidered cushion covers, fringed parchment lightshades, the Axminster carpet, antimacassars and bone china, I accepted the hospitality of a spy. The dignified, vaguely distinguished articulate woman sitting opposite me had sold her country to its most feared enemy – and felt no regret – only maudlin self-pity that somehow her life had been blighted, so she claimed, by the fact that her actions of betrayal had been successful neither as a personal statement nor as a political act. As she whined on, I thought of the lives of innocent people she had put at risk or even caused to be lost. I thought of other mothers and daughters who had lost their loved ones or who themselves had suffered.

(During this speech, the curtain descends or the lights dim, whichever is more appropriate to the production or felt more dramatic)

BIRTH OR DEATH

The girl looked up at us from across the impossibly large desk. Her attitude was neither welcoming nor forbidding. She was stockily built in a mid-blue baggy jacket with a cream open necked blouse. Her face was plump and pasty, untidily framed in a mass of dark hair. Her eyes were blank. Her lips, outlined in bright red, shaped the words emphatically and precisely.

"Birth or Death?" She was cool and insistent.

My mother, at my side, shifted her handbag nervously from one hand to the other.

"Yes" she responded.

The girl's eyebrows circled enquiringly – a small sigh of exasperation escaped her now relaxed lips.

"Yes," went on Mother. "A death."

"Take a seat."

The girl reached into a drawer on her right and fumbled about. She pulled out a broad, flat, leather bound book.

"It's the wrong ledger," she announced almost to herself. She rose from the desk and walked behind us to the office door. She held it open and looked purposefully at us.

We rose and made our way out into the waiting room. I noticed the girl was much shorter than I anticipated. Her unkempt blue jacket was matched by trousers that were full in the leg. They served to emphasise her shortage of stature and the broadness of her shoulders and hips. She looked out of proportion, almost stunted in growth.

She closed the door brusquely behind us and efficiently turned the key in the lock.

"Take a seat." The same phrase, the same dull tone.

She walked across the room to the outer door and exited, closing the door behind her.

We sat side by side on the black upholstered bench, the only item of furniture in this featureless space. The walls were grey, the floor linoleum tiles of a mottled darker shade. The two windows opposite us were unadorned with curtains or blinds, the opaque glass was dirty enough to further dissuade the cold grey light of the afternoon to penetrate. We sat in silence breathing in the stagnant fustiness of the confined space. There was an unnatural silence, not an echo from the busy street that was several storeys below outside.

Suddenly the outer door burst open and a tall, stern looking man, horn rimmed glasses, a prominent nose and thin dark lips entered. He didn't close the door but proceeded to the office door which he knocked on peremptorily immediately trying the handle. A pause. He knocked again.

"There's no one there," I offered. "The girl in the blue suit, she's just gone out."

He glanced at me almost disgustedly peering down his long nose. He sighed in exasperation and crossed the room, stepping out into the corridor, closing the door behind him.

Again, we waited. There was nothing to say. I felt my mother's right hand slip around my arm. With her other she balanced her bag on her knees. The silence resettled itself, colourless and stale.

The outer door reopened. It was the girl returning, a large dark grey ledger under her right arm. She left the door ajar this time, crossed the room before us without acknowledgement – her dark blue suit was almost a flash of colour in the bald featurelessness of the ante room – and swiftly unlocking her office door, disappeared within closing it firmly behind her.

I want to stand up but my mother's firm grip on my arm restrained me. I sat back.

The tall man's upright figure suddenly filled the frame of the open outer door. In what seemed a single swift movement he crossed the room, knocked on the door opposite, turned the handle and was inside, the door firmly closed behind him.

I glanced down at my mother. She smiled weakly back, her eyes sad and watery.

From inside the office came the low rumble of the man's voice, then a replying higher timbre of the woman. The man's response increased in volume and, in spite of not being able to identify the words being spoken, it was easy to recognize the increasing agitation and anger. The woman's response became equally more shrill and protesting. A crescendo of gruffness from the man then sudden silence.

A pause.

The door opened. The man appeared, eyes glinting, red patches of anger on his gaunt cheeks, his lips tight. Unceremoniously, he pulled the door shut behind him and left the room.

From behind the closed door came the unmistakable sound of a woman's violent sobbing.

I rose to move towards the door but my movement was curtailed by my mother's stern tone.

"No", she said. "This is none of our business." She rose and hooked her bag over the crook of her right arm. "Come on." And she led the way out into the corridor. Instead of heading for the stairwell to the left, she turned to the nearest door on the right, knocked briefly and went in. I followed as far as the door.

Three women sat in the room, each at a desk with their backs to the centre of the room. The one to our right I noticed looked up at us – a profusion of blond hair and a pleasant toothsome smile.

"We've come for an appointment with the Registrar …" my mother began.

The blond girl rose.

"I'm afraid you've got the wrong room", she said pleasantly.

My mother pressed on. "No … we were waiting outside the Registrar's office. There was some kind of altercation with a man. The poor girl's in floods of tears."

To our left the second woman rose. "Oh my gosh," she exclaimed. "He must have told her."

The woman directly opposite us turned in her swivel chair to face us. Much younger than the other two, she looked anxious and concerned.

The blonde spoke again.

"Leave it to us", she said reassuringly. "I'm sorry……"

But Mother had turned abruptly to leave the room. I had to execute a nimble sidestep to avoid being mowed down.

"Come on", she hissed as she passed me. She paused at the head of the stairs, her gloved hand on the metal hand rail. "We'll make another appointment. I don't think Dad will mind, do you?" A wave of sadness crossed her face but seemed to evaporate as soon as it had appeared. "I think a cup of tea is called for." She caught my eye and smiled clearly.

She moved down three or four steps and paused to allow me to draw abreast of her.

"And …" she asserted firmly, more like her usual self "and a nice thickly buttered toasted teacake. Yes, just the job."

And the hustle and bustle of the offices around us, the distant clamour of the busy street, the comings and goings of the world outside seemed to welcome us as we made our way downwards.

BLACK TUESDAY

At last they've given it a name – Black Tuesday – when the nation groggily raises its head from the torpor of prolonged Christmas and New Year festivity, frivolity and indulgence, groans, clears its eyes and its throat and reluctantly acknowledges, in the bleak winds and squally showers of yet another grey unforgiving January, that life must, in spite of all, go on.

And so it is with the Wayward Scribes. Through the warm heady fuzz of scented woodsmoke from the failing Yule log fire, through the warming fumes of too frequently reheated mulled wine, the week-old fermenting sherry trifle, the oozing hot sugar scent of yet more warmed up mince pies and Christmas pudding slabs sizzling in frothy brandy butter, through this mind-numbing, eye reddening, mouth drying fug – and we berate today's youth for indulging in a drug culture! – through this murky miasma, indistinctly at first, appears the disapproving countenance of the formidable Madam Chairperson herself, like the Cheshire Cat reconstituting itself but without a smile, like the ghost of Christmas future, she wavers in the sticky mists, most prominent her reproachful frown and firmly downturned lips. Her voice is heard, terse and reproachful. She exhorts her cohorts to up-pen and follow her; she has laid aside her tawdry decorations, quickly crusting sweetmeats, discarded her turkey carcass and curling chipolata sausages, returned to the attic her carol sheets and her trumpet, dispatched Ted to conquer the piles of washing up – take a chisel to the roasting tins – with firm instructions not to relax until the home is shining from cellar to eaves, and she is ready to go. Such a fine example can only spur on her followers, who unsteadily fumble their way through piles of torn Christmas card envelopes, discarded wrapping paper, exploded crackers, searching for writing pad and biro. The screwed-up bale of Madam Secretary's last Minutes is uncertainly straightened out and the topic for January 4th 2011 is blearily deciphered :

Sisters.

It takes a while for the penny to drop, the rusted cogs of the mind to turn gratingly.

Sisters – the Nolans, March, Bennet, Andrews, Beverly, Scissor (ah! One for the youngsters!) and then the most seasonal sisters of all, the ones we're all too familiar with but to whom we can never give a name, for they have as many nomenclatures as they have manifestations. Yes, we recognise them in an instant and the role they play in the rich drama of life.

Their lives have not been without incident.

They were born into apparent wealth. Their mother – a hard and determined woman – determined to improve her fortunes after a lowly start in life, convinced that she deserved better than fate had so far allotted her, ruthlessly pursued and won their father. He was an older, frail man – a member of the landed gentry. She, a considerably younger woman, not pretty but striking in a wild and hawkish way. She was his fifth wife. This may have encouraged her to pause and consider the effect that four divorces might have had on her new husband's pecuniary arrangements, but it didn't. She became the lady of a somewhat shabby manor but she determined to sort that out.

Within two years she had presented him with two daughters. That done, she withdrew with the babies to her own apartment in the west wing of the house leaving her husband dissatisfied that she had failed to produce a male heir, gradually closing in upon himself in the grip of profound disappointment and disillusionment. His ever-weakening body was joined in concert by an enfeebling mind and, as he retreated, so his wife, always one for grasping the main chance, looked outwards to establish herself in society.,

Her daughters, once of age, made their first steps into the wide world. They needed, above all, contacts and so were sent to attend Countess Herzog's Distinguished Academy for the Cultivation and Refinement of Young Ladies. As important to the girls as passing any entrance examination was the generous donation their mother made to the Countess Herzog for the betterment of the old dowager's circumstances and the discreet settlement of her extravagant gambling debts. The old lady was a frequent attender and a *force celebre* at the gaming tables. The spinning wheel obsessed her and she had once had one installed at the academy – for to better the young ladies in their facility with use of mathematical numerations – but parental common sense and disapproval had intervened, mainly that of the Roman Catholic Cardinal de Vere Monsooth who had several of his own daughters as pupils at the establishment.

The girls appeared mid-term at the Academy. And a curious paring they presented. The older girl was far more fleshy and rotund than could ever be fashionable. Her round sweaty face had, appropriately perhaps, mean little currants for eyes and a tiny pursed mouth that suggested that she was constantly sucking in tuttings of disapproval. Her hair was remarkable – rich, copious, auburn ringlets – the envy of any girl – but it did little to counteract the overall unhealthily pallid puddingness of her countenance and stature. Indeed, her white moon face suggested a doughy, dull and uninventive brain but as such was misleading. Hers was the most devious, fertile and waspish of minds; her demeanour was one of spite and resentfulness. An unappealing combination.

Her sister was narrow, angular and unnervingly over-tall. She had an unruly shock of carroty hair, bright green eyes with an off-putting squint in the right, enormous bony, manly hands and feet of the size rarely catered for by any fashionable and respected creator of fine ladies' footwear. The turn in her right eye, the thick drooping lips and a preternaturally furrowed brow gave her the appearance of lack of intelligence. And rightly so – the proverbial two short planks had greater discernment than she. But together, they were a formidable duo - the squat one's cunning and heartless intelligence allied to the looming size and unladylike physical prowess of her sister.

For many reasons they were social outcasts at the academy, but primarily because all the young ladies knew that their mother was not really 'of the right sort'. She had no 'family'. Rumours abounded – she had been a stock herder's daughter, child of a tinker and a laundress, a gypsy, bastard offspring of a disgraced holy sister or – horror of horrors – herself an actress and showgirl. The sisters fought back; one with unsubtle, physical bullying – twisting arms, kicking shins, pulling ears and hair, violently tweaking noses and, most effectively, hefty punches in the solar plexus which could result, amongst the more delicate girls, in wide eyed gasping for breath followed by subsidence into unconsciousness. Countess Herzog, on one of her rare appearances, would huff, puff and whine with high disapproval and displeasure but reflection on the parlous state of her personal finances and unavoidable recourses to the spinning wheel lent tolerance to her dealing with the sisters.

The rounded little sister fought her corner with greater subtlety but with as devastating effectiveness. The well-chosen word – even an inspired selectivity, one might say – was her weapon. Her sister's retribution was instant, brutal, masculine; hers was insinuating, spiteful, undermining, feminine – each attack an attrition, a thousand piercings of the tender, semi-formed, delicate being that is the refined young ladies' psyche.

After careful mental unsettling of her victim, she would make the powerful final lunge of attributing a nickname to the unfortunate girl which not only caused an initial piercing wound but, in its being taken up by her best friends and acquaintances, succeeded in protracting itself into a long term – even life time – effectiveness. A stout, ruddy faced girl who refused to surrender her birthday lavender truffles was given an epithet that, being translated, could be rendered as 'cheeks of a sow'. Not terribly injurious, one would surmise, but the cheeks were not those of the face and vocabulary of that language benefitted from some fifteen different words for sow – her selection being a female hog who is raddled, diseased, rolling in its own ordure and on the point of painful death. A small, inoffensive girl whose recourse to dramatic weeping was deemed too frequent was designated 'slug breath', there being eighteen words for 'slug', this one a peculiarly revolting clammy grey sausage-shaped beast which fed solely on decomposing flesh usually in the drains of abattoirs, its breath being the word for the final exhalation of a cow dying from gut cancer and udder rot (there are 47 words for breath).

The sisters grew daily to be more hated and feared than they were the day before. Cruelty and unhappiness emanated from them, and lingered perniciously in the lives of their victims. Poor 'slug breath' had the final ignominy, as an old woman on her deathbed, hearing her grandchildren, who were pouring over their grandmother's yellowed and dogeared school books, innocently asking what was slug breath and why was it inscribed all over grandmama's Latin primer. Their mother closed the book and said, "Oh, look, dears, it's starting to rain."

Just after the girls graduated from the Countess Herzog's academy – they passed out with Distinction (the Countess was still a devotee at the altar of roulette), the tree of their fortunes was severely shaken and the fruit thereof plunged into the mire. Their father, now a total recluse, died and his creditors moved in. Everything was seized to be sold. His widow and her girls would have been destitute but for yet another display of the mother's opportunism. Another widower, rendered vulnerable by the sudden death of his gentle, much loved wife, unprotected from the guile and machinations of the hawk-like woman. In the confusion of his grief, she appeared as a much-needed support, a mother for his newly-orphaned only daughter and also the provider of two caring stepsisters.

Soon marriage was proposed, announced and expected and the invasion was complete, total take over accomplished entirely on the new wife's terms. Past experience had her seek out a more realistic appraisal of this husband's financial status and she saw that, with careful husbandry, she and her daughters could lead a comfortable life to be enjoyed on the peripheries of society. Her new step daughter must learn her place, coming very much fifth in the scheme of things, making herself useful even in the lowliest of domestic chores. She endured much humiliation at the powerful hands and viperish tongues of her stepsisters. She was punched, bruised and winded – and duly given her nickname. A cleverly devised portmanteau word – Er-ay-la – a female slave of peasant stock, much akin to an untouchable on the Indian Continent and a sint – a swine herder – the lowest of farm labourers whose house was the sty, where food was the swill of the pigs.

Sint er-ay-la.

The sisters clung to each other in cruel satisfaction.

Their mother smiled, grimly proud of what she had created in her daughters.

It was at this moment that a large cream envelope was delivered to the great oak front door. The mother received the letter and noted with some pride and considerable interest that it was embossed with the royal crest.

"BLOODY ROYAL WEDDING"

Now it would be unfair and indelicate to suggest for a minute that this is the kind of language that Patricia Porter would habitually resort to. Heaven forfend! At times of stress she might, on a bad day, resort to contemplation of such a profanity : on a worse day to a hissing whisper of such a word – but you would have to be physically very close to catch it – closer than anyone ever got to Miss Porter! So imagine how bad the day that occasioned an easily audible utterance of such a dubiously phrased outburst.

Except it wasn't quite daytime.

She had had a particularly restless night, turning and turning again, twisted bedding, an unrelentingly hard and lumpy pillow, an aching back and neck, a cramped hand – the full works. And now, in the cold light of dawn, she struggled to a sitting position, flung her legs over the side of the bed, the better for her clenched toes to search for her quilted pink mules amidst the shaggy pile of her arctic white deep-piled carpet as her ever-reliable alarm clock sprang into its harshly unwelcome vibrating braying sound accompanied by its undeniable flashing yellow light.

Hence the curse. The alarm acted as if in mockery, roundly waking up one who had been awake for hours – rudely trumpeting its own pointlessness on this particular morning.

Patricia Porter blushed as the ill-chosen words shattered the grey morning stillness. She had succeeded in embarrassing only herself, alone in her ordered bedroom.

It was all the fault of that damned Jacky Pulse-Strebling.

I must explain. "Damned" is allowed. It is not a word of outright vituperation. It creeps in within the bounds of acceptability – just! And has been heard on Miss Porter's prim pouting lips quite frequently, to her own annoyance and the casual listener's total indifference.

Jacky Pulse-Strebling.

Let's fill in the background here. Patricia Porter is the Head of the local Junior school – or, as she has had her position re-designated, the Principal – she's after Academic status. Prim, precise, particular.

Miss Patricia Porter the Principal of St Peter and St Paul's Primary in Pardoner's Lane, Upper Pimlott.

Jacky Pulse-Strebling is the teacher of St Peter and Paul's Year Six. She is a long-standing member of the school staff, far outweighing Miss Porter's two- and three-quarter terms – almost a whole year. And Mrs Pulse-Strebling represents everything that Miss Porter does not, and of which she disapproves.

Jacky Pulse-Strebling (or 'PS' as she likes to be known to her colleagues (but NOT to Miss Porter) is perceived as a force for chaos in Miss Porter's ambition for a highly organised and well-ordered life at St Peter and Paul's. Principal Porter's maxims are that "A tidy life leads to tidy minds", that "a successful society stands on sound supervised structure", that "everything finds a place when everything is in its place" (had she the wit, she would see that this last bears very little scrutiny – but let's move on).

PS is as tall, broad and imposing as Principal Porter is diminutive, slender and overlookable. PS wafts through the school like a galleon in full sail. She chooses clothing that is full, loose and flowing. Her progress down the narrow central corridor leaves not an atom of the normally still stale air undisturbed and the draft of her passing inspires the dangling notices on the walls into a kind of paper Mexican wave, the flapping of such in turn responding to the breeze of her displacement. Her crown of reddish full curls always seems restlessly bobbing, her red framed glasses glint and wink, her chins wobble winsomely and her two prominent teeth give her full red lips a certain appealing ridiculousness, indicating that a full beaming smile is ever looking to be freely released. PS is an unintentioned and innocent Lord of misrule to Principal Porter's developing regime of stern and sterile obsequiousness – not her fault, she has a school to promote from near failing standard to that of excellence, and in as short a time as possible so that she can use acclaim at her own success to move on to brighter and better things.

So she could have done without the Royal Wedding and PS's instinctive theatrical response to such an event. Miss Porter, as newcomer, had been unable to avoid in her first year PS's Halloween and Guy Fawkes School Party, the Pantomime, the Xmas Carol Service and Party, the school Play at Easter – 'Wind in the Willows' with 30 riotous Year 4 rampaging weasels – all this she faced with forbearance. Next year would be different. She already had in hand an annual report critical of PS's professional acumen and demeanour which should see her wings trimmed for the foreseeable future and would serve – together with the excuses of financial cutbacks – to curtail her extracurricular activities. She had thought Wind in the Willows would be the end of it – School Sports Day she had already knocked on the head. But she had not reckoned with the Royal Wedding and PS's enthusiastic determination for St Peter and Paul's to do their own version of it.

She could do nothing. The local Bishop (Chair of the Governors) saw it as an ideal opportunity for a celebration of the importance and validity of marriage within the community and PS was off into her usual extravagances of scenery and costumes and props and lighting and sound effects and wholesale involvement from the infants to the dinner ladies and parents and, in this case, the local police (the whole school had to cross the road to St Peter and Paul's Parish Church for the actual ceremony) and the local livery stables for use of a coach and horses. In all this, Principal Porter's role would be one of imperious detachment and grudging smiles of patronising approval. She was horrified when word reached her through her loyal, if dull and unimaginative secretary, that the Royal Wedding Organisation Committee, chaired of course by PS, might prevail upon her as Principal to take on the role of Her Majesty the Queen – thankfully this had come to nothing. But everything else had come to something, a very big and complicated something.

The reason for her restless night and the unwelcomeness at the start of this new day was that she had endured with a tight bleak smile the exigencies of the Royal Wedding's Trial Run – a whole day of mad carnival chaos – and now finally the real thing. So much in her eyes had gone wrong – her memory of the day was a jumbled nightmare, with dozens of eventualities vying like contestants in a hellish X-Factor for title of 'Worst Moment'. The winner inevitably the horses evacuating their bowels noisily, steamingly, smellily, great coils of ginger turd smashing on to the crisply white lines of a number of the hop-scotch markings on the pristine black tarmac – to delighted groans and jeers of the children. But in her mind Health and Safety and Environmental Health – the possibility of excited members of reception and infants lunging forward for a close and tactile examination of this rural phenomenon. But the practical horse owners were there immediately with shovels and buckets engendering joyful bidding cries from parent-helpers offering increasing prices for manure for their rose beds. Each cry and shout, no matter how good natured and jovial, a stab in the back for Principal Porter.

Then Kylie Smith, the elected Princess Kent for the Day, had been sick through over excitement, had vomited all over herself and Prince William (luckily neither in costume). Both had to retire for a cleaning-up and re-emerged in items of clothing from the emergencies cupboard – mostly old P.E. shorts and ill-fitting gym vests. Kylie (a pretty girl too aware of what was and was not fashionable) had fled in a fit of shame and locked herself in a lavatory cubicle. Prince William, a boy of extraordinary blond good looks but of little brain or awareness, had proceeded stoically with the rehearsal but with a new partner, Stacy Hulme, who had no part to play in the actual proceedings as her father, a local publican and republican, had objected vehemently to the whole enterprise and had withdrawn his daughter's involvement and even planned to remove her from school for the day. Leaving Stacy free to step in for the trial run. An unprepossessing sight, a bespectacled lanky and gloomy child in ill-fitting blue and grey school uniform. she clung grimly and self-consciously to an unyielding Prince and performed immaculately, though in the demeanour of one attending a funeral rather than a replication of profoundly the most joyous and celebrated weddings of the century (and it is only 2011).

The fanfare mis-sounded like an over-amplified passing of wind on the borrowed public address system and the vicar had forgotten to unlock the church door and the police were late and there were tears when the banquet cum tea party also turned out to be a rehearsal – the real food would not be available for 24 hours as was indicated when the caterer's van turned up but couldn't get through the school gates because of the turmoil, so disgruntled delivery men had to lug large boxes and crates of consumables through the thronging procession and managing to knock over and tread on David Cameron, the Prime Minister, who wasn't looking where he or anyone else was going and ended up with a cut hand, torn trousers and a badly gouged leg. Luckily his mother was one of the parent helpers present, a Treasury woman of great common sense who swept him up with a "You stupid boy – look where you're going. He'll be all right. I'll sort him" and disappeared inside to the school office which doubled as casualty room. Momentarily Principal Porter had panicked. Dear God, that could have been a case for damages!

Shattered, at the end of a very long day out of her comfort zone, Principal Porter had confronted PS, as the last of the clearing up was done, with her apprehensions.

"Never fear, Pat", PS wobbled, energetic still after so long. "As we in PODS always say (PODS – Pimlott Opera and Dramatic Society – of which she was a figurehead), 'a bad dress rehearsal means a great performance'". Patricia Porter was unconvinced and aggravated by the woman's lack of concern and apprehension. Her lip clenched. Masses of red copper curled hair, wan cheeks. Her brow furrowed. PS was oblivious. "I can't wait. Oh, while I have your attention. What about the Queen's Jubilee next year? If we book the coach now …"

"Is that my phone?" Miss Porter mouthed in true preoccupied Principal mode. "Excuse me." And she went.

So it was in a far from fair temper and with uncharacteristic irritation that Patricia Porter slammed out of her front door to face the day itself. Her car stood in the driveway. She reached it, paused, swung her brief case aloft to crash it heavily on the car's roof and stood, shoulders slumped looking despondently at the door handle. She raised both hands and slapped her palms noisily on the car.

"Bloody Royal Wedding" she spat out fiercely. She had left the keys on the hall table.

There was a footfall below her. It was the postman, always jolly.

"A big day today, Miss Porter. My little Sinead is really looking forward to it. These are for you." He handed a couple of letters to her and winked confidentially. "Don't worry. It may never happen." He walked away chuckling.

Patricia Porter took a deep breath. "Bloody postmen" she hissed almost inaudibly. Then her back straightened. Principal Porter was in charge again. Principal Porter perpetually prepared. Precise. Possessed. Purposeful.

She took her handbag off the crook of her arm. She smiled grimly. She always carried in her purse a spare house and car key. She began to compile 101 reasons not to celebrate Her Majesty the Queen's Jubilee – starting with the unavoidable absence of Mrs Pulse-Strebling. Such a shame!

BRADLEY WINSTON BOULDERSTONE

In every litter there is the pride of the litter – and the runt. And there is nothing quite so much like a squirming, sauntering litter of puppies then a gaggle of eight- and nine-year-old boys in the same class of their local primary school.

We were such a litter.

Our pride was Bradley Winston Boulderstone, broad faced, broad chested, a good 6" taller than any other in the class, well-fleshed, healthy rosy cheeks, close cropped ginger hair, and a permanent expression of total earnestness as if the awareness of his prominence in our tiny society was weighing on him, depressing his blonde eyebrows into a frown and something of a scowl and the downward edges of his thick lips into a permanent loss of temper. But this was to do him an injustice. He was taciturn and not given to easy demonstrations of temperament, but always fair and pleasant enough.

But rule the roost he did, with an easy authority that sprang a great deal from his privileged background. His father was reputedly the wealthiest man in our small town, owning the General Store which, in those early post-war days, was developing rapidly as people's expectations and spending power expanded. Indeed, he had purchased the shop next door and was expecting soon delivery of his first electrical goods – cookers, fan heaters, fires that glowed like real coals and – wonder of wonder – fridges.

It was Bradley's birthday and his father had prevailed upon the Headmaster to allow Bradley to bring his birthday present to school to show off to all at playtime. We all stood around in awe.

A sturdy metal frame – shining bottle green – *Raleigh* in gold and black gothic script. White walled tyres, gun-metal Sturmey-Archer gears, black leather seat and tool bag, shining silver handlebars with a bright chrome and blue enamel bell and a slick hooded front light. Bradley swung one pink, podgy leg over the crossbar and posed effectively. He rang the bell. "This is the latest model", he announced. "The Raleigh Tower. My Dad says I can have a gold flash painted down the front forks. I'm gonna call it *Lightning Bolt*." Then, just as assuredly, he dismounted. (The privilege from the Headmaster did not include riding the bicycle on school premises.)

So we stared and shuffled awkwardly around the machine. One of us hesitantly stepped forward and placed his grimy hand on the shining saddle. Bradley glanced down, his green eyes flashed briefly and he growled, "No touching – not *you*, Micah Bingham!"

The slight, shabby figure winced as if threatened with a blow, quickly withdrew and shrank into himself, staring intently down at his feet.

Bradley, clutching his paper bag of Pontefract cakes, wheeled his bicycle away towards the school front door. We all followed, but not a subdued Micah Bingham.

He was the runt of the litter.

One of a family of twelve children who lived in a two-up, two-down farm labourer's cottage on the local squire's estate, Micha Bingham was the true embodiment of deprivation. Small, skinny, dirty, his bony limbs swamped in a stained and tattered jumper far too big for him, copious worn corduroy shorts, a voluminous swathe of wrinkled stockings around his narrow ankles and hefty faded greying black boots connecting him too firmly to the ground. Sad eyes gloomed from beneath an unruly shock of black hair. He stooped and sidled around his world – his whole demeanour suggesting apology for even being there.

Most noticeable was his smell and it was for this that he was most shunned. A sickly sweet, acrid aroma – burnt sugar and vomit that pervaded the air around him. We stayed away. There was even a childlike theory that the smell was artificially induced (by whom? we didn't ask), a deliberate attempt to repel the more unkind and boisterous of us from abusing his fragile, skeletal body. Our teacher, Miss Hampton, paid close regard to Micha. We noticed but didn't mind. On cold days she sat him at the desk nearest the convected warmth of the classroom's large black metal coke-fuelled stove. Perhaps the only other warmth he experienced, she reasoned, was that of sleeping fully dressed five or six to a bed. At this time Micha Bingham sat and gently steamed – and his distinctive and repugnant stench invisibly felt its way around the room.

It was time for our 'story telling' lesson. We had all had a double lesson to write a story and now had an opportunity to air our efforts. Stories would be read out aloud by Mis Hampton or, in the case of the more confident and competent, by the authors themselves. Micah

Bingham never took part in this exercise. He appeared to write his story like everyone else – head down, eyes screwed up with effort, pink tongue forced between tight lips, his pencil moving vigorously over the paper. But this was all arid imitation. He could neither read nor write : the end product was a page of scribble.

But on this occasion, Miss Hampton asking for volunteers but really knowing whose turn it was, up shot Micah's hand.

"Please, Miss, me Miss. Please, Miss!"

Miss Hampton glanced in his direction and paused. His hand dropped and he looked directly at her. Mis Hampton looked away from him.

"Miss. Miss. Please. Me, Miss."

Miss Hampton blushed – embarrassment, not anger.

"Ah, right, Micah Bingham. Do you have a story for us?"

"Yes, Miss. Yes." He waved his paper sheet of scribbles at her. Another pause.

"Well, Micah. If you're sure, perhaps you'd better read it yourself."

Micah scrambled on to the platform next to Miss Hampton's desk, looked down at his story and cleared his throat. The class was tensely silent.

"Let's have the title first, Micah. Do you remember the title?"

"What Makes Me Happy, Miss."

"Very good, Michal. You may begin." I can imagine Miss Hampton at this moment crossing both sets of fingers and offering up a brief but very heartfelt prayer.

Micah took a deep breath and began, earnestly reading from his creased sheet of paper.

"What Makes Me Happy. What makes me happy is I have my birthday next week. And I will be very happy. And I will have presents and a cake. And I will have a good present from my Da. And I will be happy. And it will be my own bike. And it will be bright red with wheels and white stripes. And my Da will paint it with gold flash. And I will call it …" A pause. He looked up, flush-faced, bright eyed, defiant. "Call it … Call it … *Thunder … Bolt*. And my Da will let me bring it into school for playtime. And that's what makes me happy."

A long, awkward pause. Total silence. Micah realised the responsibility was his. "That's what makes me happy. The End."

Miss Hampton stood.

"Thank you, Micah Bingham. That was a very good effort."

Micah looked up, his attempt at a beaming smile marred by uneven, broken and missing teeth.

Miss Hampton diplomatically whisked his story from his hand. "Now you may return to your seat."

Next Wednesday really was Micah's birthday. As we filed into class we saw the small white paper bag on Miss Hampton's desk, half a dozen Pontefract cakes she supplied as a small gift for any child whose birthday it was. Micah glowed with joy as she handed the bag to him after she had called the register.

"And today's birthday boy is Micah Bingham." He clutched the bag to his chest. "Happy Birthday, Micah." And she led the class in a brief round of polite clapping. That was Class Four's birthday ritual.

The morning moved slowly until playtime. Micah was last out into the playground. He always was. Miss Hampton saw that he always had a spare bottle of milk and, for that, he cleared all the foil bottle tops and spent straws into the wastepaper bin.

He stood isolated and forlorn on the dark tarmac. He had two problems and we all knew what they were. Fifteen minutes to produce a bright red and white bike called *Thunderbolt*, and find five friends to share his Pontefract cakes with. That was part of the ritual – the birthday boy or girl's five best friends spent the rest of the day, with him or her sporting blackened teeth, tongue and lips.

Micah edged forward. The bag of sweets was now grey, damp and compressed in his bony fist. All was still.

Then Patrick O'Hannahan moved towards Micah. He was the nearest we had to a class bully. Apart from being an expert in the sudden and unexpected delivery of dead legs, tweaked ears, Chinese burns, slapped cheeks, hair pulls and stamped feet, he was the most accurate spitter in the face or hair and had a mean and spiteful tongue. His thin lips contorted into a cruel smile.

"So, Micah Bingham. I thought today was the great day when you …"

A huge, fat, pink fist shot out of nowhere and floored him into silence. He lay huddled on the dusty ground looking up at his assailant. It was Bradley Boulderstone. He didn't need to speak. His fierce, flashing green stare told Patrick O'Hannahan that he had better stay where he was and there would be no further talk of bright red bikes and Thunderbolts.

Micah gaped up at Bradley. He began to sink into his apologetic stoop.

Bradley directed his gaze to him and what might have been a smile shadowed across his staid, firmly set lips.

"Ay, Micah", he said and he extended a large fleshy hand, palm upwards.

Micah needed no other cue. He hastily unscrewed his dank paper bag and placed a sweaty, misshapen, strongly scented Pontefract cake on the plump cushioned palm.

"Ee – tah!" said Bradley and his gaze left Micah and fixed turn by turn on each of the four boys nearest to him. They, as if mesmerised, stepped forward and took a Pontefract cake from the tiny boy. As Bradley did, so did they all commit the sickly-flavoured liquorice disks to their own mouths.

And that was Micah Bingham's birthday – standing in the playground surrounded for at least one day, or at least one morning, or for at least one playtime, with his five friends, all grinning their blackened grins.

COLOURS

16th June 2005

Douglas Haig – 'Dougie' to the lads – had always considered himself to be a down-to-earth, practical man. Throughout his six decades, he had evolved a philosophy – if that was not too grand a way to put it – that there was little in life that could not be tackled with a modicum of practical application and a large amount of common sense. His older daughter, Sally – the bookish one of the family who had gone on to university and become a primary school teacher – had bestowed on him the term 'pragmatical'. He enjoyed this. A word he himself would never have come up with. A man of few words – another asset he felt in life – he had never taken to books and writing. He had found school studies something of a struggle, made the most of the hands-on subjects at his Secondary Modern School – Woodwork, Metalwork, Car Maintenance – and moved on as soon as he could to enlistment with the Army's Junior Leaders Regiment, secondment to the Army Apprentices Scheme and thence into the Royal Artillery where, in a successful and satisfying career over several decades, he rose through the ranks to that of Company Sergeant Major, shunning proposed promotion to the ultimate Regimental Sergeant Major, this being the highest rank of non-commissioned officers and offering a degree of prestige that attracted an elitism and isolation that he did not relish – and much more paperwork. Heaven knows, as the army establishment self-modernised, even the lesser CSMs had recourse to greater and greater piles of forms to complete and reports to make.

He had met and married Margaret early in his army career. She was from an army family (her father being in the Signals) and eventually along had come two daughters, first Sarah (always known as Sally) and three years later, Elizabeth (or Lizzie). Family life had progressed on a contented if predictable course, he earning respect in work with his calm, natural authority and total reliability. Got a problem? Go and see Dougie Haig. Need a rife sight repaired or adjusted? Ask Dougie. The wooden frame of a target or its metal lifting mechanism re-built? Consult Dougie. How best to maintain equipment? Prepare and polish up kit for a trooping parade? Get the lights flashing in sequence of the Sergeants' Mess Disco? Prepare the equipment for the start of season cricket match against the officers? Ensure that the gallons of home brew was 'vintage', for this year's Regimental Founders Day? Ask Dougie. Always get Dougie. She – Margaret – was much preoccupied with bringing up the girls, yet finding time to organise events to raise funds for the Army Benevolent Fund and get involved in the social events of the various army camps they moved to, mostly following the pattern of the girls' lives – Mother and Baby Groups, Toddlers Clubs, Nursery Classes, Parent / Teacher Groups etc. etc.

A major decision had to be made on or about Sally's twelfth birthday. Her school reports over the years had always been favourable and it was felt she would really benefit from a grammar school education. Dougie was impressed that university was mentioned as an achievable if distant goal. The peripatetic nature of army life would not help. The girls would benefit from a far more stable, less changeable period of secondary education. Dougie was being posted to Aldershot for at least three years. The scheme was for them to buy their own house in that area and, whatever Dougie's future postings, for Margaret and the girls to stay behind in Aldershot for as long as necessary. The plan went into operation but 'the Gods are smiling on us' as Margaret put it. After three years, Dougie was offered the post of Armourer at Aldershot which meant a far more permanent posting in view of the security concerns that came with the housing of arms and ammunition. He was stationed in Aldershot for more than ten years, apart from a couple of brief turns of duty in Northern Ireland, which saw them through to Sally finishing her teaching qualification and moving up to Chester where her fiancé, Gavin, lived (she had met him at university) and Lizzie working as an IT Consultant in Manchester. The path for Dougie and Margaret was clear as his army career drew to a close. They could sell their now over-large home in Aldershot and move to be nearer the girls. Downsize, they thought, to a bungalow somewhere near Chester, perhaps on the North Wales side. They had holidayed in that area – Llandudno, Anglesey, Snowdonia – and it held great appeal.

All went as planned and it was good it did, as a cloud was gathering over the hitherto tranquil domestic life of the Haig family, a real darkness was to affect all their lives.

After too long a wait, Sally found she was at last pregnant. She and Gavin were delighted but Margaret was ecstatic. Sally joked that her mum had wanted to be a grandmother far, far longer than Sally had wanted to be a mother, which was quite possibly true. Dougie warmed to the obvious excitement and happiness of the others, but he had a somewhat ambivalent attitude towards babies. With the advent of Sally, he had been thrilled, nervous, happy but rather more dismayed than he had hoped when the writhing, weeping bundle finally appeared. She made him feel so awkward, so big, so unprepared. He wanted to hold her, needed to be shown how to hold her, but in doing so felt as if he was in the centre of an important gathering and was handed a crystal goblet of enormous value and indescribable delicacy – it would only be a matter of time, feeling the clumsiness of his large hands and blunt, stocky fingers and under the unwaveringly intense scrutiny of the surrounding throng, before the too precious object slipped from his grasp and fell disastrously to the floor. Handling a new baby, he tended to freeze until someone, usually Margaret, had confidently lifted the child away from him. He had been astounded by Margaret's handling of the children. He had watched, bemused and in awe, for long periods of time at the way she cuddled, cradled, positioned the child, deft, experience gained from instinct, he supposed; how she took every opportunity to gain the child's attention, maintaining eye contact, delivering a continuous stream of burbling, cooing, giggling, laughing, singing, chanting, a language of baby-talk nonsense sprinkled with suddenly recognisable real words, and the magic of how each baby responded, gazing intently upwards, echoing the gurgles, giggles, smiles, laughs and eventually the sounds that her mother so unselfconsciously produced. It's all in the eyes, he thought.

He sat stolidly, cradling the little creature and was glad within the time for brightly coloured story books came when he could concentrate on reading, however haltingly at first, the repetitive text and enjoy the concentration of the baby on the rainbow pages rather than on him. Besides which, babies served to undermine the great credo of his life, that common sense could counter all. Babies, he discovered, had no truck with 'common sense'. Doing the sensible thing, the reasonable thing, the practical thing was no part of a baby's existence, and he was only too glad when Margaret intervened at times when his very raison d'être was being most seriously challenged by a determined offspring.

Eventually, he knew, children would grow up and gradually become more responsive to rhyme and reason – they would enter his world more than he had to enter theirs. Then his feet would feel solid ground beneath them again. Then he could breathe easily, relax and enjoy them fully. Then the giant fingers that had flinched from delicate nappy folding and safety pin juggling, with precision of affixing teats to bottles, the tying of Lilliputian tapes, ribbons and the doing up of sequin-sized buttons, could relish the role of building Wendy houses, dolls houses, nursery furniture, repairing prams, pushchairs, tricycles, bikes, teddies, dolls and finally motor scooters, hairdryers and typewriters.

Now – he breathed deeply – the whole process would start again.

So Sally, with the help of a midwife, several nurses, Margaret and a stunned Gavin, brought Olivia into the world. Dougie, called in from the corridor, marvelled at the shock of thick black hair on the new baby. Margaret said she looked like Sally, Gavin that she looked like Margaret and Sally that she looked like Gavin's sister, Hazel. Dougie thought she just looked like a very pretty little baby. But soon the baby was recognised for something else.

As time passed, a certain limitation was noted in her responses to the world around her. She would turn her head to odd angles and flail about with her arms. At an age when she should have been able to, she showed an inability to focus her eyes on anything at all or respond to movement of colours and lights. The conclusion was reached that she had little or no sight. It pained Dougie to observe the reactions of the family. Sally and Gavin were pale and drawn, intently focussing on the advice and opinions of the doctors and consultants, drawing hope where they could. Dougie would catch Margaret in a quiet moment with full tears rolling heavily down her cheeks and she would catch his eye and a weak if determined smile would force her lips apart.

Dougie felt anger, deep and swelling. Something must be done – had to be done. But time was needed. Investigations into the causes of her condition would not be appropriate until she was considerably older – there were several possibilities, most having some kind of remedy that would produce partial or even total sight. And there would always be advances in medical techniques. This was the forward projection that offered Dougie the least comfort.

Time passed.

Dougie felt more 'at risk' with her than with either of the other two. He and Margaret spent a great deal of time with Sally who, since Olivia's diagnosis, had not even entertained. He thought of returning to work. Dougie watched closely the behaviour of the tiny girl. She was so restless, her head ever swivelling to catch the slightest sound, her hands roaming, groping, feeling, reaching, her nose twitching, nostrils distending and retracting, her whole being alive with compensating for the sense that she didn't have. And always a huge toothless smile when her senses met and recorded a new, stimulating experience.

And she didn't wait for Dougie to enter her world; she invaded his. With Sally and Lizzie he had been able to sit quietly with one or the other relatively inert in the crook of his arm. But, no, this was not good enough for Olivia. She turned, twisted, reached out further and further. She explored, leading with her hands. She clambered over his chest upwards, pushing herself down into the rise and fall of his chest, pressing down an ear, he could swear, to hear his very heartbeat. And his voice, or a cough, or a quiet whistle (as he was wont) would attract her even higher where her tiny hands explored the adventure playground that was his face, the mound of his rough chin, the wide elasticity of his lips, the hard evenness of his teeth. He enjoyed her startled reaction to the sudden emergence and withdrawal of his tongue, and her search for it again. Her fingers poked unceremoniously up his nose and painfully pulled on his moustache. She swung on his ears, prodded his firmly closed eyes, gently ran along his eyebrows and hauled cruelly on his steel grey hair. His gasps of pain had her lunge down to explore his mouth again. There was no delicacy in observing any roles of intimacy with this child. She plunged at life with a sense of physical urgency that was as welcome as it was violent.

But gradually, most probably out of satisfaction that what was above her held little novelty, she learned to sit in the crook of his arm, comforted by the steady, bass notes of his voice as he read to her from the colourful pages of a book she had yet to see. Sally had carefully chosen books that offered plenty of opportunity to the reader for onomatopoeic sound and Dougie dutifully obliged. He had moved on to 'The Little Red Bus' that roared and purred and clattered and spluttered and screeched and pinged and honked – he did them all, but was far from convinced that any true meaning to the story was getting through to Olivia. He bought her a toy bus – large, red, plastic and she delighted in being sat astride this and guided around the room. That, to her, was a 'red bus'. But Dougie knew there was more.

Olivia happily went in the family car. She walked the street with her 'Gander', as she called him, straining on to the reins of her harness. Dougie was impressed with her almost total lack of physical fear. The next move had to be a ride in a real 'red bus' and this was achieved with little complication. The first ride was a nervous one. Only a short ride; she clung to him, wide eyed, alert to the strange noises, the precarious swaying of this new world, the harsh urban smells, the strange voices. But as ride succeeded ride, so her confidence increased and she would stand on a seat, her Gander's hands round her waist, her cheek pressed against the smooth coldness of the grubby window or her hands clasping the chrome rail along the top of the seat. She swayed with the vehicle and smiled broadly,. She could tell Mummy and Nana that they had been on the 'red bus'. But it wasn't – it was a green bus, and that worried Dougie. It was an innocent deception, but it niggled him.

He worked out a plan to introduce Olivia to colour. 'Red' had to have its own meaning and not just be an undistinguished part of the bus. Olivia must see colours. Or, rather, experience colours through touch, taste, smell and sound.

Red would be hot – the radiant heat of an electric fire, the burst of taste of a strawberry or a tomato, the warm blast of a hairdryer, the loud blast of a car horn and, of course, a bus, for the time being, would always be red.

Blue was cool – air fanned near her face, water in a bowl, a glacier mint (though her little lips pursed at that).

Ice cream was too cold – that moved on to white, with snow and the smell of fresh laundry, the tingle of toothpaste, feeling her teeth with her fingers.

Green – the scent of lettuce, newly mown grass, parsley, vegetable odours, spearmint, apples, grapes, cabbage (she resisted), spinach (she rejected).

And so his list grew. Silver – tiny bells and granite-shiny cutlery. Gold – Nana's jewellery, the sun's warmth, the clash of cymbals, honey and honeycomb.

The game began. "What colour is the bus, Livvy?" ("It's *Olivia*, Dad" – from Sally.)

"The bus is red."

"What colour is this, Olivia?" Handed the fruit she said, "Orange."

"What colour is this?"

A sprig of foliage from Nana's flower arranging a quick sniff and a rustle of figurers through the leaves. "This is green."

Then a role reversal. "What colour is this, Grander?" Her cheeks pressed to the carpet.

"That's brown, Livvy." (Sally was out shopping.) Brown, the colour that was chocolate, and cosiness and Gander's humming, deep and tuneless, and the smell of polish on his smooth shoes, earth scrunched into her exploring hands.

The ruse had worked. Olivia had experience of colours, and had garnered the idea (the 'concept', corrected Sally) that colour was a sensation which was transferable. A bus was still always red – but also Nana's scarf could be red, and Olivia's new dress, and a balloon. Until ....

Gander took her off in the red bus that was green to the park – a place familiar to Olivia, that she delighted in. The wind was strong that day and, as they played the colours game, it whisked their voices away, so they shouted and laughed. Olivia plunged at the ground – yes, the grass is green. She held onto the cold steel of the park bench – yes, it's silver, but the horizontal wooden slats of the seat were brown. Olivia waved a mitten at her grandfather. "What colour, Olivia?"

"It's yellow, Gander."

A gust of wind made her stagger. "It's only the wind, Livvy." He reached down, steadied her and lifted her to stand on the bench. He sat beside her. He turned her and she stood to face the wind. Her face was hot – red – with exertion and excitement. "Feel the wind", he coaxed. She stretched her neck to fully expose her face. She stretched her arms forwards and upwards, her hands clenching and unclenching to expose every square millimetre of flesh to the wind's buffeting chill – her hair strained backwards from her forehead, her scarf and coat flapped vigorously, her sightless eyes smarted and streamed with joyful tears.

"Gander", she cried. It was the game. "Gander. What colour is the wind?"

She did not have eyes to see the slump on the shoulders of the large figure behind her, the dropping forward of the head, the face crumpling into severe expression of sadness and futility, the large tears plunging down the cheeks.

She did not need eyes to feel the slackening of the grip of the large hands around her waist, to sense the need to turn towards him, to know that suddenly everything had changed. She moved into him and reached up to the now unfamiliar contours of his face, and felt the dampness on his cheeks.

And she wondered why Gander's face was covered with blue.

CONCENTRATION

"Oh, Dad", asked the boy,
"Why do they call them 'CONCENTRATION?'"
"Read this", came the reply.
The boy looked down, his brow furrowed in CONCENTRATION
And he read –

"Will you please silence those children?
I'm trying to concentrate!"

"But darling, you don't usually
Bring home work at weekends."

"This is very important, my dear
A big job. One of the biggest.
Could do me a lot of good,
If I get this right.
So keep the children quiet.
CONCENTATION is the keyword.
You wouldn't understand, my dear.
It's all logistics, timetables,
Co-ordination of rolling-stock,
That sort of thing,
All to be planned urgently.
Needs CONCENTRATION.
Tell them Daddy will have time to play tomorrow.
Daddy loves them.
But he has work to do.
Plans to prepare.
So many cannot be expected to move themselves
Tomorrow play
Today CONCENTRATION
CONCENTRATION, CONCENTRATION
Don't disturb my CONCENTRATION."

------- X ------- X -------X

"Why are you so funny about the CONCENTRATION?"

We must get an efficient and effective
Chemical reaction.
So the CONCENTRATION must be right
It's a big order,
Especially in these hard times.
We get this right and there will be more
Profits will soar.
So when the tablets hit the acid
The effect is immediate – powerful –
A thick and concentrated gas
Speedy and efficient.
The right CONCENTRATION
So double check all the valves and dials
Carefully
And achieve the appropriate CONCENTRATION
CONCENTRATION, CONCENTRATION
Don't misjudge the CONCENTRATION."

------- x ------- x -------x

On the slate-grey, black and desolate landscape
A sudden CONCENTRATION
Of huddled human forms
Black on grey
And encircling them
A CONCENTRATION of grey uniforms
Grey on grey.
"Move them on! Quickly!
Women, children and feeble to the left.
Men and workers to the right."
A CONCENTRATION of victims.
A CONCENTRATION of persecutors.
A CONCENTRATION of fear.
A CONCENTRATION of hate.
CONCENTRATION, CONCENTRATION
God forgive this CONCENTRATION."

------- x ------- x -------x

I shall sit here
And pull my legs tight against my chest.
My knees to my chin.
Bone on bone.
My arms wrapping rightly around.
I will feel the roughness of the boards
Chafing against my bent spine.
But not so much the gnawing cold
If I curl myself into a ball
And concentrate. Concentrate
And pretend I forget
The awful journey to this place.
The endless swaying, the human stench
The queuing when we arrived.
Mother and my sisters pushed one way.
~Father firmly gripping my arm
As we stumbled the other.
And I'll forget that was the last time I saw them.
If I concentrate. CONCENTRATION.
I see them now at home.
In the garden, under the flowering cherry
Mother and the girls sewing, giggling and sewing.
Father arriving home from his surgery
They are waiting for me now –
As I concentrate.
So I will concentrate.
CONCENTRATION – blocks out the groans
The sobbing, the sound of distant shots
The screams
That even the roar of the engines of
Stationary motorcycles
Cannot stifle.
CONCENTRATION
The sickly cloud of yellowing smoke
Spreading into the leaden sky.
The nauseating sweet smell
That always comes with the smoke.
So I will concentrate.

CONCENTRATION, CONCENTRATION
Don't disturb my CONCENTRATION.
All I have left is my
CONCENTRATION

------- X ------- X -------X

The boy looks up from his reading,
His brow furrowed in CONCENTRATION and deep sadness.
"I see now", he said simply,
"Why they call the camps CONCENTRATION."

CUSTARD

As soon as Sheila let herself in through the front door and firmly closed it behind her, locking out the cold winter's evening air, she knew all was not right within. As she stood inside the dimly lit hallway, taking off her mac and scarf and hanging them on a hook on the dark wooden coat stand, she could hear the stumbling about and mutterings from the floor above. It was her father. What had riled him this time? Swinging her handbag loosely at her side, she made her way to the brighter lit, warm glow of the small back kitchen. There she found her mother stooped over the stove earnestly stirring the contents of a large saucepan. There was a welcome smell of food preparation – the sweetness of pastry baking, the comforting familiarity of boiling veg. Without pausing or turning towards her, her mother welcomed her. "Hello. Is that you, dear?"

Sheila paused in the doorway. "Hi, Mum. What's up?" She cocked her eyes towards the ceiling but her mother continued concentrating on the steaming pan.

"Hang on", she said. "Just let me … Ah, that is it, I think." And she lifted the pan off the flame. Sheila could see it was custard. Needing constant stirring to avoid the cushioning, clinging yellow mass sticking to the pan, even when it was off the direct heat. Mother peered in. "Perfect", she said, and raised the coated wooden spoon gently dropping its tentacles of creamy gold. She extinguished the gas flame and placed the pan back on the hob. She turned towards her daughter, her round face flushed with the heat, her glasses steamed up.

"Now, what were you saying?" She smiled brightly.

"I said – What's up? With him upstairs? He's banging around and cursing."

"Oh, don't ask. It's that pothole."

"Not still that ruddy pothole!" exclaimed Sheila (only she didn't say 'ruddy').

"There's no need for that language" corrected Mum. She took her glasses off to wipe them on her apron. "We've got enough of that from him."

"Well!" Sheila's gall was rising. She was still young enough to feel resentful at being treated like a schoolgirl. "If it's good enough for him …"

Her mother cut in. "Never mind about your father. It's when you hear me use that language that you can start." She looked directly at her daughter, her smile not faltering. Her daughter smiled back. "Now", continued the older woman. "Wash your hands, there's a love, and lay the table. Tea's almost ready. I've already laid the cloth."

Sheila had barely taken her seat at the dining table in the living room before her father appeared. He had changed out of his work clothes and put on his customary, well-worn Fair Isle jumper. "Hello, Father. Lovely day, isn't it?" She admired how precisely she had captured a tone of bright sarcasm.

The retort was gruff and mumbled. Could have been a reluctant greeting, she mused. More likely just inarticulate bad temper.

The meal proceeded in virtual silence, but with food that good there was not much to be said. Finally the subject had to be broached. "I've thought what to do", said Dad.

"Oh, yes", responded Mum.

"I had a word with Mike Briggs."

There was a sharp intake of breath from Mum. A mixture of disappointment and exasperation. She had little time for Mr Mike Briggs. She had met him a few times at the Work's Club social events. A tall, thin man with a long, pale gaunt face. Protruding eyes and teeth, prominent ears. His hair, slicked down onto a severe side parting with a copious layering of Brylcreem, looked unnaturally gloss black, as did his full military style moustache. It had taken her a while to realise what made his face look really odd. It was, just above his glassy grey eyes, an almost total absence of any kind of eyebrow. This, with his dark hair and moustache, gave his face an imbalance. He reminded her of the figures you get in the old silent movies, with their abnormally dark hair and their almost white faces. But his worst feature was his thin, narrow lips and his aggressive manner of speech, his reedy voice emerging almost with venom, a fine spray of spital hissing forth. He displayed utter confidence; there was not a subject about which he did not have an opinion, on which he was not an expert.

"You've asked me so I'll tell you …" he would spray and then hold forth at considerable length.

"Mike Briggs", went on Father. "He said …"

"You asked me so I'll tell you", whispered Mum. Sheila giggled. Dad paused, lengthily, waiting until he judged the ensuing silence appropriately respectful.

"Mike Briggs says we should write a letter of complaint to the Council." Dad dug his spoon into his rhubarb crumble and rich yellow custard. Mum's spoon froze half way to her mouth. Sheila shuddered inwardly at the ominous use of the word 'we' and all that that suggested.

She knew that the last thing her father ever would attempt would be an exercise involving the written word. He had enough troubles understanding the written word let alone creating it. As a child he had suffered a serious accident. He had been with other boys playing in a ruined building near the Rec when he had slipped, fallen some distance and impaled himself on some rusting, dislodged railings. His long stay in hospital and subsequent period of enforced inactivity had resulted in an attack of rheumatic fever. He had almost died. But he struggled on. By the time he was considered fit enough to resume some form of normal life, his school age had passed, as had any chance of him becoming meaningfully acquainted with the written word. The last letter they had written as a family was one of condolence when a distant relation had died in a car accident, and that was a traumatic undertaking, mostly because of her father's frustration at having to have all his sentiments transposed by her and her mother into a written formality totally alien to the man himself. And that starting from a base of respectful sadness. Now, with the underlying mood being one of anger, Sheila just could not contemplate the consequences.

Nervously she spoke up. "I've promised Sally I'll be out at hers tonight. Her Mum and Dad are out. She'll be glad of the company." She was not lying. The girls had promised themselves an evening of 45's on Sally's Dancette record player, a pile of girls' magazines and, most secretly, a few surreptitious lemonade shandies.

Dad sucked his lips in. "I want to get on with this bleeding letter" he muttered (but he didn't say 'bleeding').

"Ronald, there's no need for that", said Mum quite sparkily. "Look. I'll give you a hand. You can't expect Sheila to spoil her plans."

Sheila stood up. "Talking of which, I'd better get going. Sally'll wonder where I've got to. Tell you what, Dad. You and Mum compose the letter and I'll copy it out in my best handwriting tomorrow night and post it the next morning."

"And that's more delay", retorted Dad. "It's already been weeks. I want it written tonight and in the post."

Sheila paused but Mum cut in. "We can manage that. Off you go, Sheila. Have a good time."

Dad's spoon rose to his mouth and his teeth clamped down on a generous mouthful of glistening rhubarb crumble running with lemon bright glossy custard.

"Right", said Mum, coming back into the living room, the dishes washed and draining at the sink. "About this letter."

Dad promptly moved from the comfort of his brown leather club style armchair. "Right", he returned. "We need pen and paper."

Mum waved an old exercise book of Sheila's under his nose. "Come on. Sit at the table. Let's make a start."

She sat, her pencil poised. He positioned himself opposite her.

"Right", he said. "Dear … er… Mr …" He didn't know his name. "Head of Highways Department."

"We'll put 'Sir'. Dear Sir", and she wrote it down.

"Right." His forehead was drenched in total concentration. "Right. Dear Sir. There is a pothole outside our gate."

Mum copied him down obediently. Her plan was to doctor the letter when she did the proper copy later, "… outside our gate", she confirmed.

"Right", said Dad. "Our gate is at Number 2 Aubright Road."

"You don't need to put that", Mum corrected. She couldn't stop herself. "We put our address at the top of the letter so they'll know where it's from."

"Right", acknowledged Dad. "Our gate". He paused, "is at the address at the top of this letter."

Mum wrote obediently on.

"The pothole is dangerous and is getting worse" (pause) "and I am blinking fed up of it" (except he did say 'blinking'.)

Mum was abrupt. "You can't say that – 'Dangerous and I am not happy about it.'"

"I am really not happy about it!"

"'I am far from happy about it'. That will do."

"If you say so. But that's not how I really blooming feel" (though he did not say 'blooming').

"My lady wife, Mrs Vera Duffield, has already telephoned you twice about this and my daughter, Miss Sheila Duffield, called in during her lunch hour at your office ..."

"To report the matter", contributed Mum.

"To report the matter. We have been waiting now for six weeks."

"Is it that long?" queried Mum.

"It is that long." Dad was indignant. "It is that blinking long" (but he didn't say 'blinking'). "Right. Now. I want something done about this immediately before there is an accident or some such. I pay my rent like everyone else."

"Like everyone else", echoed Mum.

Dad paused. "Well, is that enough?"

Mum glanced down at her script. "I reckon so", she said. "It makes the point."

Dad continued. "So. Finish it. Yours ... er ... what?"

"Faithfully", offered Mum.

"Doesn't sound right", said Dad. "Yours ... er ... sincerely... Yes, that's better."

Mum scribbled dutifully. "Yours ..." Her pencil scratched ... hesitated ... scribbled out ... then wrote confidently 'Yours faithfully'.

Dad bridled. "Why 'faithfully'?" he asked.

"Because I can't blooming spell 'sincerely'" she said (only she didn't say 'blooming').

Dad's eyebrows shot up. He accepted 'faithfully'. He knew when not to push his luck.

But the mother did not finish there.

Next day, Sheila was instructed to buy, in her lunch hour, some matching writing paper and envelopes – Blue Basildon Bond it had to be. She brought that home and neatly copied out the letter. Her father signed it.

But they had no stamps. Sheila offered to take the letter and see it posted. Dad would hear none of it.

"I want to see that letter posted myself good and proper. There's a post box outside the works. I'll do it tomorrow. You bring the stamps. If it's the last blinking thing I do" (only he didn't say 'blinking').

The following day the letter was addressed and stamped. Dad stood in the living room looking at it proudly. He put his cap on his head, flung his snapping bag on to his shoulder. He heard Sheila at the front door.

"Dad", she called. "There's a man out here. From the Council. They've come to do the pothole. Will that be convenient?"

Dad seized the letter and hurled it across the room. "I'll give him 'convenient'." He looked at the crumpled envelope skulking on the carpet and had to grin to himself. "A waste of a flaming stamp", he said (only he didn't say 'flaming').

CYRIL BLAND

Please spare a thought for little Cyril Bland
Who decided to take his life in hand
Shake his being to its very core
Go where he'd never been before
Straighten his tie, polish his specs
He was going out to tackle the opposite sex.
Out into the world like a rampant Viking
Find a woman to his liking
Seize her, woo her, be her lover.....
But first he'd better ask his mother.
The s-e-x word surely would offend her
So he broached the subject of the 'opposite gender'.
Mum bridled, frowned and pursed her lips
"I knew one day you'd ask me this.
But not so soon, that was my fear
You've only just entered your 40th year.
But it had to come, I always knew it.
Listen to my advice, or else you'll rue it.
Ask her out, not too much fuss
Tell her you'll meet her off the bus.
Go for a burger, pizza or such
Let her insist on going Dutch.
Then just a walk, that's all, I think.
You don't want a woman who likes at drink
Certain things will have to wait
No holding hands till your 17th date
Things like that come far too soon
No kissing till your honeymoon.
Make sure she's respectable, decent and clean
Some women, you don't know where they've been
And should you be in any doubt,
You bring her home - I'll sort her out!"
Mum's smile was grim as he left the house
With all the confidence of a sugar mouse.
He sat in the back of dingy pubs,

Lurked in the dark of dodgy clubs.
But his Brylcreemed hair and watery smile
Made all the totty run a mile
While his dew dropping nose and sweaty palms
All too easy for them to resist his charms.
Once the 31st girl had firmly said "No."
He began to lose his get up and go
The 64th 'No' was the event
When his get up and go finally got up and went
Over lukewarm flat bitter he shed a tear
When there suddenly was a voice in his ear.
"Are you alone, mister?" a voice husky and deep
His eyes slid to the side to take a peep.
Almond eyes, moist and dark, raven hair, dusky skin
Cyril couldn't believe that his boat had come in.
Parting full carmine lips, even teeth, pearly white
Cyril trembled within - could this be the night?
She moved closer to him and before he could think
He found himself offering to get her a drink
Long lashes fluttered demurely, the more to entice
"No alcohol, thank you, just soda with ice."
Cyril's heart leapt within him. He heard his mum's voice.
"Take one who doesn't drink to be your first choice."
"Shall we have a dance?" Sweet breath his hot face fanned
and he felt his fist swallowed in her enormous hand
She slunk on to the dance floor, swaying bosom and hips
The red silk of her dress, the dark red of her lips
One long arm snaked around him, smooth, glossy and tanned
Any more, thought poor Cyril, and I'll be unmanned.
Her soft lips brushed his cheeks, her scent musky sweet spice
Cyril thought to himself, "This is really quite nice."
"Now, I won't be a minute." Her warm breath in his ear
"When a girl's got to go … No, you wait right here."
Cyril thought, as he watched her slink into the throng.
"I think I can wait, but I don't know how long" For all that flat beer
he'd drunk when he was sadder
Was having its full effect on his poor bladder
And, as the D.J paused to turn over the vinyl,
Cyril decided to make a rush for the urinal
And there she was, doing what a girl had to do

But like man does it, and in a gent's loo.
She turned, sneered at him, a rough deep bass croak
"All right. What the hell? So I'm really a bloke!"
Cyril gulped, sobbed and fled to the cold of the street
The wet pavement echoed to the stomp of his feet
He rushed home to his bedroom, in the door turned the key.
He sat down on his bed and he grabbed his diary.
As he wrote that days entry, he felt his face burn
"I have just been where I'll never return.
And I swear to the gods", he so shakily penned
"That was my first slash and last girl slash boyfriend."

DETECTIVE SERGEANT COPPICE

It might be helpful at the outset, when considering the mystery of the Great Lover, to focus on the protagonist to whom fell the task of investigating the phenomenon. I refer to Detective Sergeant Coppice – Detective Sergeant Marilyn Coppice.

Picture her, as was her wont, hunched over her investigation note pad, her black biro hastily scribing her observations in a neat, easily legible hand.

D S Coppice was – er, sorry, is – a big woman. That is not a euphemistic way of indicating that she is fat. But she is big. 6'2" in her large stockinged feet. Broad-shouldered and hipped but with a convincing waistline. A wide plain face, with well-shaped lips, deep solemn brown eyes and impressive eyelashes that add a definite femininity to her features. In spite of her choice never to wear any make-up, there is no doubt that she is a woman – her auburn hair expertly cut well above shoulder length was – sorry, is – gently curled and flattering to her expansive forehead and longish neck.

Return to her stooped and concentrated over her note pad, her dark business-suited frame and large hands dwarfing the pad, her long thick fingers looking painfully contorted in operating a pen that appears of Lilliputian dimensions. Towering over most of her suspects and witnesses, she easily conveys an impression of authority, earnestness and solemnity. And thus stands her reputation within the station. She is isolated by her size and the determination with which she approaches her job. She has passed the latest tier of her promotion exams and is looking for the occasion when she can demonstrate her prowess.

And now it presents itself, she is well in position to take advantage of the opportunity. In the village of Upper Grassington, at the local Post Office, has occurred what appears to be a grisly suicide. The Post Mistress, Margaret Brackley, a spinster of a certain age, living with her somewhat frail and delicate twin sister, Maisie, also single, had consumed a gruesome cocktail of prescription drugs by imbibing a copious supply of not-the-best brand of whisky. ("But she never ever drank alcohol" protests the distraught Maisie, living now with the guilt that it is to her supply of medicines that Margaret had recourse to to end her life.)

D S Coppice was the ideal investigating agent. She was a local girl, having grown up in the five parishes that encompass Upper Grassington and come together under the aegis of The Church of St Edmunds on the Hill in Lower Grassington. She is known in the area.

Maisie, between sobs, and in a series of interviews, each cut short by her inability to go on ("I'm sorry, my dear, it's just too much at present") has confided to the towering policewoman details essential to the case. The Post Office had been failing. The new retail park and supermarket in the nearby market town of Winsborough, the increasing dormitory nature of the villages themselves and finally the ever increasing likelihood indeed that the Post Office facility would be closed. Margaret had taken unofficial business advice and been persuaded into fiscal adjustments which were at best very ill advised. ("He had told Meggy they would be all right as a temporary measure – if it could all be put right quickly – like a short-term loan" blurted Maisie.) There had been the transfer of monies between separate accounts – the shop, the Post office, the off-licence – governments funds had been inappropriately drawn upon to subsidise elsewhere. But now the closure of the Post Office counter was imminent, matters would be brought to account. Literally. The unjustifiable imbalance would become a public matter – criminal charges would likely ensure ("She couldn't face the shame" wept Maisie. "And then *he* just disappeared").

D S Coppice could not overlook the importance of the 'he' in the matter.

Maisie could provide certain details. 'He' was – or, perhaps is – a Mr Guy Lazenby-Brooks.

"He was a lovely man", breathed Maisie. "A real gentleman – a something of a charmer." She blushed. "He popped in for the odd stamp, at first, or a packet of mints (strong and sugar free), maybe a bottle of whisky or some cheese and an apple if he was off walking. Then he'd pause for a chat, and a cup of tea and a biscuit. I'd watch the shop whilst he and Margaret would talk business. On half days, they'd both go walking with sandwiches and a flask of tea and it was all right to start with but Meggy grew less happy with the business arrangements – and some money that he'd borrowed from two of the accounts. She'd changed – really down, she was. I couldn't do anything", and she subsided into sobs.

D S Coppice noted in capital letters, VICTIM TOOK OWN LIFE – QUESTION MARK. A TEETOTAL DRINKING WHISKY? TOTALLY OUT OF CHARACER. WHO IS THE CHARMING GUY LAZENBY-BROOKS?

Maisie was unable to be helpful other than a physical description and a full endorsement of his ability to charm. "A real gentleman", she opined. She did know that he had been staying for some time at the Royal Oak in nearby Middle Grassington. Perhaps Mrs Patterson, the landlady, could help.

The policewoman was not a drinker or frequenter of rural pubs. She knew of the Royal Oak but had never been there.

It was a Wednesday, late afternoon, a known lax time in the trade, when she chose to call on Mrs Patterson.

"Guy Lazenby-Brooks? Do I know Guy Lazenby-Brooks? Do I *not* know Guy Lazenby-Brooks! I wish I had never heard of Mr Guy Lazenby-Brooks."

And the whole saga tumbled out. Marilyn Coppice was ushered through to the private quarters to the rear of the Saloon Bar. "Herbert, watch the front, will you, love? I could be some time", as Dora Patterson closed the door behind them. "Something to drink, luv?" she offered, swinging a gin bottle aloft in her well-manicured scarlet talons. Marilyn shook her head. "You're on duty, I suppose. Fair enough", and she poured herself a generous quaff.

Guy Lazenby-Brooks had taken, for an indefinite amount of time, use of the two rooms for let at the Royal Oak. He was quiet, kept himself to himself, polite, respectful, paid in advance, at least for a while. "A man of clean habits, tidy, took real care of himself and his person, neat." Dora Patterson was sure of this. Her informant, her eyes, were old Mrs Briggs who did for her around the place. She had access to the guest accommodation for cleaning and bed making purposes and emerged with a full report. "No mess, my dear", she confirmed. "Even 'is drawers is tidy. Keeps one for his soiled smalls. All folded. Good quality aftershave. Wet razor. Sink wiped down. Magazines on antiques and the like. And a book on politics and parliament. Don't keep up his diary but his address book is full. Mostly London. And there's even a Lord in there and a right Honourable. Oh, and an invite to a do at Tony Handgarten's in his suitcase – very expensive leather and smells nice."

Guy Lazenby-Brooks had passed the test with flying colours and Dora Patterson warmed to him.

"I was lonely", she confided. "My Derek and me had come here from Chingford, Greater London. Derek had always wanted a country pub. We sold up our large news agency – they were hard times – the competition was all foreign – Pakistani (their families work for them for nothing) that and the supermarkets – so we sold up and came here. At first it was all good but the new regulations moved in – no drink and driving did us seriously down, look at the size of our car parking – and the smoking ban and music restriction really did for us. Derek had his problems" – *prostate*, she mouthed, her scarlet lips emphasising what her whisper could not convey – "and suddenly I was on me own". She didn't pause for breath, not even a hint of a misty eye. "But I've carried on. Then up turned bloody Guy Lazenby-Brooks. God, he took me in with his business acu – acu – acumen and so-called bloody experience. He could turn the place around. Cash in on the food, he said, give the punters a dining experience. I would do front of house, bring in a restaurant manager and a chef – a bit of refurbishment – it'd be a gold mine. He was what I needed – a shoulder to cry on, to lean on, a way forward – we drew up plans, budgets, he had contacts, he said, in the catering world for refurbishment and supplies. I took out a second mortgage – a loan on the business plan. He handled the investment – you can see where this is going. Well, it's then he went. Out of the door and off. I am clinging on by my finger nails, dear. Hand to mouth. Hand to mouth. My Derek will be turning in his grave."

The pattern was clearly emerging. In capital letters CON MAN. WELL EDUCATED. LONDON BASED – QUESTION MARK. WHO IS GUY LAZENBY-BROOK? WHRE IS G.L-B. – QUESTION MARK

"I've no idea who the bleeder is. But there's someone who might know. That Lady Snotty Nose up at the Manor. Word came to me he was sniffing around up there. Mrs Briggs found his lordship's business card in his sock drawer – hidden inside a cigarette case."

Lady Snetton was very accommodating to the towering cumbersome figure at her front door. She talked in the conservatory away from her husband who was tying flies in his large, wall-panelled study.

"Have you met Guy?" she enquired, her eyebrows arching, her eyes narrowing.

"Not yet." Marilyn had her note pad and pencil poised, ready.

"Because, my dear, he is a great charmer. He totally took me in – and I've met some in my time, believe you me."

There was a groan from within. "Almost finished, Bobby. Time for tea."

Lady Snetton continued, not missing a beat.

"Tall, extremely good looking – think a younger Michael Caine – immaculately dressed – and that voice – positively chills-up-the-spine purring."

A bark from within. "D'you hear? Tea time."

"Preferable to feral roaring", she pointedly continued – the faint sign of a wince around her wrinkling nose. "Such a breath of fresh air around here." She glanced at the study door. "Considerate. Attentive. *Civilised*", she breathed. "We had – or appear to have – so many people in common. And he had taken this country retreat to work on his new venture. Actually started seeking my advice."

"Damn and blast. Cut me bloody finger on a Blue Ice Steamer. First Aid."

With a sign of annoyance, she rose to her feet and, all done with seamless almost balletic elegance, she took from a drawer a roll of Elastoplast, crossed to the sliding door, opened it and hurled with vigour over arm the pink coil into the room, hastily pulling the door shut. Without pause she crossed back to her chair.

"Missed. Bad luck", came from within.

"Pity", she spat and smiled serenely. "You see?", she asked.

"He had a venture, for charity, to do with a Young People's Welfare Trust for Prince Charles. He wanted me on board and our support, Lord and Lady Snetton. Any financial input on our behalf he assured me would be minimal if at all, but he would require our influence and events-opening skills. Easy peasy!" She paused meaningfully, deciding whether to go in and how far to go. After a while, "We became very close."

Marilyn's pen was poised over her pad. She did not write this down. Lady Snetton's confidence in her increased.

"I need say no more. Henry, my husband, Lord Snetton, is often away on shoots, attending at the House and such like. We've always had a healthy attitude to matters such as this. The rule is to keep it away from home. I broke that rule, but otherwise …"

From within, "Hasn't that bloody policewoman gone yet A man could die of thirst in here."

"I became truly committed – you might think perhaps I should have been." She smiled broadly. "But not all common sense deserted me, always one foot in reality."

"Damn it, woman. I could bleed to death in here."

"As I said, never far from reality. It came to a head over dinner. I invited Guy formally to meet Henry and some friends. He, very effortlessly, oozed charm – witty, urbane. But then … again reality struck. The first course. Who would use his fruit knife and fork for the game terrine? The scales fell from my eyes. Next morning, I phoned Basil Terrington. I had Guy down as a flim-flam man (that's American for con man : we were seconded to Washington DC back in the 80's). But, nevertheless, one of us. If the Honourable Basil Terrington had no heard of Guy, then …

"He hadn't, not the faintest. Just within the nick of time. I immediately closed my cheque book to him, and the door and drew up the drawbridge. He didn't protest. He knew the game was up."

"Bloody hell, woman. Tea. Tea. And a plate of Battenburg."

"Reality bites", she said.

Next morning, D S Coppice was busy in her office – not to be disturbed – transcribing her notes into a report. Her phone rang.

"A call for you, Serge. Says it's business. Won't give his name."

Marilyn signalled her impatience with a sigh of theatrical proportions.

"Put him through." A pause. "Hello, Sergeant Coppice here."

"Ah, at last. Detective Sergeant Coppice? Detective Sergeant MARILYN Coppice?"

She was alert. The voice. Plummy. She could feel it actually caress her right ear.

"Yes, sir."

"I understand you wish to speak with me. I am Lazenby-Brooks. Guy Lazenby-Brooks."

"Yes, sir. I would welcome that." She felt the muscles in her stomach tighten. All her Christmases come at once.

"Very good. You will know the Grassington Strand Hotel, just outside Winsborough, on the Tilbury Road. You can find me here. After lunch I take coffee and brandy in the orangery. Shall I see you early afternoon, about 2.30?"

Marilyn felt like a school girl summoned to the Headmaster's study.

"Yes", she agreed, feeling very uncertain. "Yes, that will be fine."

"Good. Very good. I shall look forward to it. I would invite you for lunch but I fancy that might well be inappropriate. What say you?"

She could feel his presence. "No. No. Thank you. Two thirty will be fine."

"Until then … Marilyn. Goodbye."

The line went dead.

Two hours later, Detective Sergeant Coppice left the station, leaving details of her expected whereabouts, saying she anticipated being gone for most of the afternoon.

And that is the last that was ever seen or heard of her. Her car was found parked at the Grassington Strand Hotel but there was no reported sighting of her. No trace either of Guy Lazenby-Brooks as a resident of the Hotel or a casual guest.

Oh, and the Grassington Strand Hotel does not have an Orangery.

DESERT ISLAND DISCS

Being invited to be the castaway on *Desert Island Discs* is one of those pleasurable fantasies that can be enjoyed on a cool winter's evening lying cosily on one's back in a warm bath – the bathroom candle lit, the flickering lights filtered gently through the rising scented steam, the tiles and mirrors gradually misting. A loofah balanced on the raised big toe, a plaster yellow duck on the other, the mind idles through the pleasures of being a celebrity for a day – a limousine and personal driver, escorted to the studio, the obsequiousness of various BBC Tristans and Arabellas, the one-to-one attentions of Kirsty Wark, every idle, carelessly-expressed, wandering verbalised thought of yours being treated and recorded with the utmost respect – to be severely edited later down to the required duration. And then the choice of your eight discs. In the comforting warmth of the bath, your imagination wanders, through previous memories and treasured experiences, through orchestras and bands, voices and choirs, flutes, guitars, organs, trombones, timpani and strings until you float off into a semi-conscious haze.

It is the next day that reality begins to bite. What would your eight discs be? You take out pen and paper, sit at a garishly reflecting polished table top, in clear unforgiving daylight and you begin your selection. It's impossible – for every choice you make there are tens of reluctant rejections : Walking with Aled Jones through the Air or with Nancy Sinatra's Boots that are made for : Water with Handel's Music or with Britten's Sea Shanties : Roses with Bizet's Carmen or Ireland's Blooming in Picardy : Imagine with John Lennon or Dream with the Everly Brothers. You are suddenly on the rack of indecision. Even if you are able to make the frankly impossible choice of only eight, you still face the final excruciating test – if all your eight discs were washed out to sea, which ONE - ONLY ONE you realise with mounting hysteria – would you try to save? Only one – to listen to over and over and over again for the rest of your days – is there any piece of music in any genre from any period of history, from any geographical source that can stand up to regular and frequent repetition in any place, let alone on a desert island?

Ah, that word 'desert'. Don't be misled. It doesn't necessarily mean the cliché gentle golden sands, lapping crystal and turquoise waves, clear blue skies and frothy clouds, gently swaying lush tropical vegetation, tall exotic palm trees, generously dropping to earth, almost as you will it, plump ripe coconuts full of rich, cooling, nutritious white creamy milk. Rainbow fish flying out of the waves into your eager hands, crabs scuttling readily from beneath rocks, small mammals exposing themselves from the undergrowth as offerings for your next meal. Oh no!

For 'desert' read 'deserted'. And really it could be a stony outcrop in the chilly Atlantic where you sit huddled against the winds, clasping to you your wind-up gramophone and your eight discs, their covers becoming soggier and soggier. You are an alternative wildlife – gulls, puffins and guillemots, pecking and swooping at you either in inquisitiveness or territorial aggression, covering you in vicious pecks, scratches and layers of bird lime – which, though stinking and noxious, does provide some protection against icy gales and stinging shards of freezing sea water, adding a further crust of dripping salt.

Reality now really strikes home – which, of course, is where you are desperate to be but now never will. This and the isolation and deadening loneliness.

There are reasons why I cannot deal with abandonment on a deserted island in a light-hearted and facetious manner.

This is why, with all due respect to our Lady Chairperson and Madam Secretary and to honourable members of our group (as well as the other ones) I am daring to refuse, on principle, to write anything on this topic. I can't even contemplate choosing a book (other than the Bible and Shakespeare) or a single luxury item let alone wasting time wondering what it is I cannot do without.

Actually, I do have a choice of book : Professor Harold T Shoulderstrap, The Department of Anthropology at the University of Minnesota – his treatise on '173 Ways to End it All". But, as most of these require either a tall building or a fast-moving vehicle or an assortment of drugs or at least an offensive weapon or unmitigated exposure to the infantile warblings of One Direction, and hardly any section features guillemots, puffins or airborne avian faeces, I suspect it will be of little use, so hope and optimism are finally extinguished.

With respect, ladies and gentlemen, I respond to this week's writing requirement with unabashed and unalloyed silence.

Although feeling obliged to add that, if there is one thing I cannot do without, it would be a sense of humour!

DIARY

It is bad enough to experience life-long shame about a particular failing – especially as one who has always had a vested interest in matters literary – without discovering that one shares that shortcoming with no less significant a figure than this country's First Minister, the Rt Honourable Anthony Blair, or 'Tone' to his friends and fellow conspirators. Neither of us has been able, over any significant time nor for any sufficient length, to maintain regular entries in a diary.

The problem is decidedly his, as he puts out his grubby, grasping, beautifully manicured hand to seize the four million advance cheque on his soon-to-be-written memoirs. My problem is the regret that I really should have been doing it – but I understand that one of the advantages of advancing age is that more distant memories become clearer. I shall have to wait and see.

But – not to do myself a disservice – there was one point in my life when I kept a diary for almost a year – well, seven months and three and a half days. Not only that, but I have an album of small grey and white photographs that chronicle the same period.

I was in my mid-teens and still in school. The brief period I always zoom in on is the weekend of the cricket tour and the plane crash. Let me explain.

A warm summer's weekend in July. A two-day visit of the 1st XI Cricket Squad from Dover College. They arrived on Saturday, just after lunch, and soon the match was underway on the pavilion pitch, part of the extensive playing fields high on the cliffs over the English Channel.

The squad had arrived with two members of staff – their true coach, a tall stooping elderly man (don't forget, all this was viewed from a teenage perspective – he must have been all of 50!), tortoiseshell glasses, greying hair brushed severely back from his corrugated forehead, a large box shaped nose and an old pipe, rarely lit, protruding from full, fleshy lips. His manner was easy, movements leisurely, eyes sharp and attentive.

The other was much younger, extremely dapper in blazer, white flannels, fastidiously blanco-ed tennis shoes and a striped cravat – indicating a regiment, a college, a sporting club, a sign of authority – which belied the otherwise youthful appearance of the man, a generous quiff of fair hair overhanging his forehead, fresh complexion, a pleasantly rounded face, not over tall but with a stocky build most noticeable in the way his bulky thighs strained at the white material of his cricket trousers – a sure sign of an athlete. His top lip was thin, peeling back to reveal even white teeth in a smile that did not radiate sincerity, his eyes very blue and restless and – the summer breeze momentarily lifted his light brown quiff – a forehead extraordinary crisscrossed with deep frown marks, horizontal and vertical, the most noticeable being a severe furrow plunging down towards the bridge of his nose.

As the game progressed it was noticeable that wherever the older man was, a small gaggle of his players would gather to observe with him and discuss the finer points of the teams' progress. The young man, not relaxed, peering all about him, remained a solitary figure. He could well have come to the match on his own.

The afternoon wore on. I was there as a spectator purely because several good friends of mine were caught up in the home team.

It was later that evening, after the match, when we were idly chatting over the day's events, when a figure burst in on us. A plane had crashed on the playing field.

I'm afraid this is an example of schoolboy hyperbole and diarists' licence. In fact, a small, private monoplane, having to thwart an attempt at crossing the Channel, had had to force land on the largest, flattest green expanse it could find. We had rushed out to see it – but returned later, when the fuss had died down, to get some photographs. It was my closest friend's year of the camera – box brownie – and the reason why my diary of those months was so well documented with monochromatic photographs. He took snaps of the machine from all angles, some I took with him posing, some he took with me posing – until we were interrupted by a small car pulling up on the road nearby.

Two young men got out, one with a large black camera. "Professional", muttered my friend cramming his puny box brownie into its unimpressive carrying case. They had come to see the plane, a photographer and reporter from the local paper. They asked the way to the Headmaster's house to get an interview. The reporter introduced himself. "I'm with the Dover Express", he said. "Julian Pettifer." And he turned his attention to what his photographer was doing.

After Sunday lunch we returned to the pavilion for resumption of the match. We noticed across the fields that the plane had gone.

A group of us settled on a couple of benches. Our College's innings was drawing to a close. Their young teacher appeared and sat down with us. He spoke. His voice was light, his delivery crisp, precise, a slight thickening of his esses (ss). And in the next half hour we learned a great deal of him and his view of the world and of the advice he obviously felt authorised to offer to a captive audience of slouching adolescents. We became aware of his public school education; how he had entirely justified his parents' financial outlay by achieving extraordinarily creditable A-levels and becoming Head Boy and Captain of all major sports; how Oxford had beckoned and awarded him a First Class degree; how he had become part of the English athletics team – a middle distance runner (hence the thighs); how he would have a spectacular career in journalism and politics; what a good thing university life was; how it should be aimed for; how Oxford Colleges were full of women begging for it – especially from him – and how nurses with glasses resident in nurses' homes were the most likely 'push over' (as he put it!); how he loved his alcohol and could drink anyone under the table; how he was working at Dover College for one term to fill a gap year; how they wanted him to stay on as a Senior English teacher with responsibility for heading the team that coached all school games with promise of a headmastership in the near future; how he was considering this but felt that the Westminster village and Fleet St beckoned and how – he paused and looked into the middle distance, "That's your HM approaching, isn't it? Right." And he was up and gone. Bigger fish to fry.

He left us undeniably in awe and breathless. Sitting at the feet of a true paragon we had been, our adolescent eyes deflating as his became more aggrandised and resplendent. There was only room for him in his world. No wonder he had presented such an isolated figure. It had been like staring into too bright a light. We didn't need to speak. We just looked at each other. A faint whiff of his brilliantine hung on the balmy air of a summer's Sunday afternoon. I can't remember which one of us started the quietly mocking laughter.

There is a coda to this incident.

Not long into the autumn term, my photographer friend – ex-photographer now the craze was over, partly due to the expense of developing at Boots the Chemist – produced a national newspaper.

"Look at this." A large photograph on page two. A cluster of young men. Four dark, extraordinarily copious mops of hair, one in the middle with a distinctive blonde quiff. "Do you see who that is?"

It was the young teacher from Dover College – lips pulled back – teeth on display. The headline? "The Beatles back Oxfam." The young fair-haired man, working temporarily for Oxfam, had garnered the support of the most prominent rock group in the world. This would do no harm to his career and aspirations.

I read down the article. "Yes, it is him", I said. "Mr Archer – Geoffrey Archer."

DOING IT AGAIN

Flo was a girl who just couldn't say 'No',
Of her vocab it wasn't a part.
Whilst a sensible girl would lead with her head
Dear Flo, she would lead with her heart.
Down life's sweet primrose path she'd prefer to be led
From its dalliances she could not refrain
And when other girls would say 'No', 'Nein' or 'Niet'
Flow would simply coo, "Do it again".

So to France she set out, to Paris in Spring
Her linguistic problem to stifle
When she met Frère Jacques on the rive gauche of the Seine
Near the tower known as Eiffel.
And as darkness fell she knew that she had
The same problem as before.
Flo found that in French she just couldn't say 'Non',
But, with a Gallic sigh, "Do it *encore*".

Then to Italy, determined to be
In Venice an earnest sightseer
When, not to her surprise, by the old Bridge of Sighs
Swept away by a suave gondolier
Not on the canal, nothing so banal
But in his S80 4.4 litre Volvo
In the throb of his arms Flo succumbed to his charms
For she couldn't say 'No', but "Do it *di nuovo*".

On the very same pretext, o Germany next
Cruise the Rhine in a smart German bateau
Where she met creepy Hans, putty in Hans' hands
Plied with schnapps and rich Black Forest gateau
Hans thought with tight lederhosen and small black moustache
He was his Fatherland's most famous leader
But confronted viz dis schwein, Flo just couldn't say 'Nein',
But "Achtung, mein Herr, now do it *wieder*".

So further Flo ran, to distant Japan
The pure life of a Geisha to adopt
What harm could there be, in dishing out tea?
One look in his almond eyes, her heart stopped
Known as Tokyo Joe, he was Bert Harahito
On his sake and hers she did feed. Oh,
Her kimono fell away, she couldn't say 'ee-e'
But cried "Ah so! Do it *mo-ichi-do*".

So when all else fails, Flo flies to Wales
Her linguistic fault to be forgotten
But on the banks of the Dee, he fell to one knee
It was Dai the Lover from Shotton.
She just couldn't say 'No' (or, in Welsh, *'eto'*).
Now the children she's had with him
The eleventh's on its way. But she can finally say
"Now, Dai, I don't think we'll do it *na ddim*."

DON'T PANIC

She is the mother of the bride
All is booked for imminent Eastertide
Invitations sent out far and wide
To bask in shared maternal pride
On this day
When she'll say
Standing at her husband's side
I love you
Yes, I do.

Then the phone rings in the hall
Leave the room to take the call
Bringing news that will appal
The bridegroom's slipped and had a fall
Both leg and arm
Have come to harm
But his progress this will not stall
He will be there
In wheelchair
Don't Panic

With shrieking bell the telephone rings
Desperate news again it brings
Amongst several other things
The best man has mislaid the rings
The bridesmaids' gifts
Also gone adrift
Lost in the stag night's carousings
The bridegroom's suit
Is lost to boot
Don't Panic

That phone again. What will it say?
The baker's van is on its way
He set out earlier in the day

But it appears he is gone astray
What a mistake!
With the cake!
Now he's a hundred miles away
The baker wailed
"My sat nav failed!"
Don't Panic

The hair dresser – such a gay, young fellow
Has turned the bridesmaids' hair bright yellow
The poor bride's mum – who'd dare to tell her?
"She'll wall herself up in the cellar)
No, do not laugh –
The reception staff
Have all gone down with salmonella
300 to seat
With nowt to eat
Don't Panic

Oh, truly now her goose is cooked
The photographer has doubled booked
The vicar's ill and up he's chucked
So much bad luck cannot be brooked
For painting his pipes
With candy stripes
The organist's sacked – will not conduct
He's had to fire
The entire choir
Don't Panic

The screaming bride disrupts the quiet
"What stupid impulse made me buy it
Before I'd started on that diet?
Oh, cruel fate
I've lost too much weight
It won't fit no matter how I try it
My wedding dress
Is just a mess."
Don't Panic

The bride's mum quells her daughter's wails
She'll cope, no matter what else ails
She knows a staunch heart never fails
She looks down : her complexion pales
In her dire stress
She's plucked her dress
And broken one of her finger nails
That loud crack
Is the camel's back
Now panic -
Oh yes, PANIC!!!

EIGHTIETH BIRTHDAYS

It was a happy accident
(Though some may say quite silly)
That 80th birthdays should coincide
For Inge, Betty and Gilly.

And birthday wishes did abound–
On that I will not linger –
Taroo-la-lay : oh frumptious day
For Betty, Gilly and Inge.

240 candles they were lit
Balloons, streamers and confetti
To celebrate the natal days
Of Gilly, Inge and Betty.

At which of these three wordsmithesses
Will excellence point the finger?
Which will be our poetess laureate?
Will it be Gilly, Betty or Inge?

For one has tales of swimming far
After plunging off the jetty
And waterlogged struggles, a fight for life
That was Gilly, not Inge nor Betty.

And one breathes poems Wordsworthian,
With the beauty of a lieder singer
Of flowers and trees, of birds and bees
Not Betty not Gilly – but Inge.

Then one has humour, wry and keen
With quips we'll ne'er forget
A sardonic look at life's vagaries
Not Gilly nor Inge – but Bet.

Which has the Wayward Factor X?
Is it Inge, Gilly or Betty?
It takes a braver man than me to decide
For I'm too much of a wetty.

'Tis insidious to choose 'a best'
Let joy reign unalloyed!
Let's celebrate we've got all three
Inge, Betty and Gilly Boyd.

ELEVEN O'CLOCK

As Lynne Masterson reached for the best china cups and saucers from the kitchen dresser, she glanced at the wall clock. It was almost eleven, and her self-invited visitor was due in two minutes. She did not know how prompt would be the arrival of this visitor as she was unaware of her exact identity. She knew it would be one of the Hesketh-Solomon sisters but would it be the efficient and particular one or the other, frivolous and lackadaisical?

It was her home help, Mrs Danby, who had taken the phone call that morning whilst she was out on the school run.

She had returned to ...

"Oh, Mrs M." It was Mrs Danby who was poking about in the cupboard under the stairs as she arrived. "There's been a phone message for you." Poke. Poke.

Lynne could see nothing written on the telephone pad, which was not Mrs Danby's way anyway.

"And the message, Mrs Danby?"

Mrs Danby emerged red-faced, her grey curls escaping restraint. "Oh yes. She'll be here at eleven. I told her OK." She plunged back into the dark opening. There came a muffled, "I lost the doofah off the hoover."

Lynne waited patiently.

Eventually. "Mrs D, who is coming?"

A pause. Mrs Danby emerged triumphantly waving a small metal nozzle about her head. "Found the varmint", she grinned. "Now ..." She looked at her employer expectantly.

"The phone message. Who will be coming at eleven?"

"Ah yes, dear." She pushed back her straying tresses with a plump, grubby fist. "It was one of the ladies from the big house, but they both speak so grand I never know which is one, which is the other. But one of them's coming."

'The ladies from the big house' were the Hesketh-Solomon sisters but that description of them was no longer accurate. They had once occupied Grayton Manor, but their independent family publishing business had hit hard times and they had had to sell up and decamp to the lodge house at the entrance to the estate. There they lived as grandly as one can in such restricted surroundings – on the surface quite contentedly, their dignitas intact.

There were two sisters, the older one Clytemnestra and the younger, by several years, Persephone. Their mother had been a rather austere and unworldly Professor of the Classics; their father had imported his publishing company to London's famous Pudding Lane just before the first war.

Clytemnestra would be meticulously on time. She was tall, long-faced, spectacularly nosed, angular, determined in gait : an almost masculine presence. Persephone was too conventionally the exact opposite. Much shorter, well rounded, a very mobile face, eyebrows ever on the go, full lips constantly working around slightly prominent teeth – ready smile and frequent pursings – her hair reddish and loosely permed, forever flopping, her cheeks and chins ruddily wobbling, her voice light, tremulous and swooping. She would be late – disorganised and self-obsessed.

Eleven o'clock. The door bell rang. "Clytemnestra" concluded Lynne.

"It'll be her", said Mrs Danby, scampering with her bit of hoover up the stairs.

Lynne opened the door.

"Good morning, Lynnette", came the brusque tones of the elder Miss Hesketh-Solomon's confident voice. "So good of you to see me." She walked past into the kitchen.

Lynne offered a quiet "Good morning" to the recently disturbed empty air. Inside she bridled. No-one had called her Lynnette since her christening, too many moons ago. She had persuaded the sisters to refrain from calling her Miss Masterson, but they could not adjust to the total informality of Lynne. Lynnette was acceptably less familiar.

She went to the kitchen. Clytemnestra was already seated at the table eying the plate of foil wrapped, plump, chocolate biscuits. She looked at Lynne with a semi-scowl. "My favourite", she said, almost disapprovingly. "You know you shouldn't. I can never resist."

Lynne moved to the kettle.

"And you will have …"

"Yes, please, Lynnette. Just a drop of milk. No sugar, as you know. I always enjoy your coffee. It's very palatable – for instant!"

Once they were both settled at the table, the older sister began to come to the point of her visit.

"I am concerned about Persephone. Indeed, perhaps even more significantly, Dr McNabb is concerned about Persephone. Frankly, it is her weight and sedentary lifestyle. She needs to get up, get out and do." She helped herself to a second biscuit and removed the shiny, crinkled wrapping with precise dexterity. She neatly folded the piece of foil. "But where can she get out and do? Dr McNabb's physiotherapist has provided details of some suitable exercises but these she can do from an armchair. Not, I feel, really what the doctor ordered. I have an idea."

Lynne's heart sank. Clytemnestra's ideas were not infrequent, but had little durability. They involved her gaggle of well-placed elderly female friends taking over the village hall for a few hours a week – usually ten o'clock till one on the first and third Thursday of every month, and indulging in self-improving, conducive but select decorous activities. Art Appreciation, Play Reading, Poetry Appreciation, Embroidery, Musical Appreciation had all come and gone with remarkable rapidity. What now?

"I intend to establish a Movement with Music Group. You will remember Eileen Fowler." Lynne's expression was blank. "No, you are too young. The ladies will gather twice a month as of yore. This is why I am here. To arrange prior booking of the village hall." The second biscuit had gone. Already she was stripping a third. "Of course, I accept that any function held within the demesne of the village hall must be promoted within the village for the availability of all-comers. That is democracy, after all. But I fear Persephone will never perform her stretches and bends before too many prying eyes. I must have exclusivity." (And that's not the only reason, thought Lynne, amazed at her own waspishness.)

"And that brings me to the nomenclature of event. We need a gramophone, records of an appropriate nature and I have managed to procure from W H Smith's in town what is called an 'exercise video' by Gloria Hunniford. Her antics have a grace and decorum of a type that I feel Persephone may achieve."

A pause.

"Another coffee?" proffered Lynne.

The cup was already pushed in her direction. "You know me too well, my dear Lynnette. Just a drop of milk. No sugar." The third biscuit had vanished. "I have puzzled long and hard over a title for this venture. Of course, there is 'Weight Watchers' but that, though alliterative, is clumsy and perhaps too familiar if we wish to maintain exclusivity. My nephew, who called by yesterday on his way to do some filming in Oxford – a small part in Midsummer Murders – suggested, but he is facetious and flippant, 'Fun for Fatties'."

There was not the slightest indication on her severe features that she found this the remotest bit amusing. "I thought of 'Grace and Beauty', 'The Dancing Hour', 'Step and Glide'. Rupert again offered 'Pound Stretchers'. He thought it most amusing, but I fail to see the relevance. But then I had it. In a blinding flash. I shall call it 'Enlightenment'." She paused, a naked fourth biscuit in her long, pointed fingers. She added impatiently, "It is in the nature of a pun, my dear Lynette. 'Enlightenment'. When we shall all not only see the light but become lighter. Well?"

"Very good", approved Lynne moving the refilled cup across the table. And added, "When there might be refined consideration of certain weighty matters."

Their eyes met. Did Lynne detect a rare glimmer of appreciation and acceptance in the usually icy pale blue ones opposite her? A slight relaxation in the firm set of the lips? The faintest hint of the beginnings of a smile? Perhaps not.

There came a typically curt reply. "Yes, dear. An acceptable cup of coffee ... for instant."

EYE WITNESS

Miss Moncrieff was Scottish, tall, gaunt, totally unyielding and – in our eyes at least – incredibly old. She ruled us with an iron fist – no hint of a velvet glove. Imagine our surprise when her strict regime showed signs of softening – a noticeable change of tone and direction. It was towards the end of our time with her – the 11+ had come and gone, as had the announcement of the result of that exam. And now we were on the home strait. There was to be a relief from the hitherto inevitable routine of learning by rote, the unison chanting of times-tables, rules of spelling and grammar, capitals of the world's countries, the dates of Kings and Queens of England in chronological order and, not least, the Ten Commandments.

We were to undertake a 'project'. We were to find a person in our neighbourhood who had been an 'eye witness' to an interesting event. We were to write an account of that witnessing and read our finished piece to the rest of the class. The best three would then be read before the whole school and the Headmaster himself would choose a Winner – details of the First Prize yet to be announced.

At this time, we lived on the ground floor of a double fronted Victorian house in Amblers Crescent. The house had seen better days but we had lived in worse – my father, mother, older brother and I. Father had come back after the War with 'nerve trouble' and found it hard to hold down a job, even though he was a trained mechanic. Hence our moonlight flits and sudden changes of residence – and our ending up in the gentrified dilapidation of No. 17 Amblers Crescent – peeling paint, cracked tiles, crumbling stonework and creaking floorboards.

I was determined to win first prize and hoped beyond hope that it would be a new book. But who would be my 'Eye Witness'? *Not* Father; he was reluctant to talk about his wartime experiences – indeed, even becoming distressingly upset at any references to them. My mother advised me that it would be best to look for a cooperative old person – such would have more experiences to draw upon, not that there would be a dearth of those so soon after a six-year period of universal warfare.

I thought and thought – and eventually thought of Mr Kamzoil, a frail and stooped old man who lived at No. 17 somewhere above our ground floor. The entrance hall and staircase were communal, so we met in passing the other residents. On the first floor were Mavis and Mandy, the comptometer operatives from the War Office and Mr Kamzoil. One large front room was used to store the landlord's furniture and personal effects, and so was kept firmly and ostentatiously locked – metal brackets and large padlocks.

I had had sight of Mr Kamzoil – black homburg hat and heavy coat, the collar upturned. Eyes cast down, he crossed the hall and made halting progress up the stairs. He looked incredibly old – even older than Miss Moncrieff – and I decided he had the qualities of a good 'Eye Witness'; also, geographically, he was very convenient. I didn't even need to go outside.

I found myself standing on the worn lino of the dark landing, my notebook and pencil clasped in my left hand, knocking with the other on the dark brown flaking paint of Mr Kamzoil's door.

At first, nothing. Then a noise from inside, a muffled voice. "Who is there?" A pause. "Come on. There is somebody there."

"It's me, Mr Kamzoil, sir. John Kelsall from downstairs."

"What is it you're wanting?" The tone was not friendly.

"I need to talk to you, Mr Kamzoil. It *is* important … please, sir."

The handle turned and the door slowly scraped open.

"Yes, my boy?"

I went on to explain what I wanted in such a nervous, fractured, unclear manner that I was amazed he grasped the gist.

"Then you had better come in."

The room was only a little less dark than the windowless landing – bare floorboards, a table, two upright chairs, a chest of drawers. A colourless room, dull and dun.

"Sit here." He indicated one of the chairs at the table. He sat opposite me.

"Oi veh. A proper interview, my boy. You are a real reporter."

I placed my notebook and pencil on the table's faded oilcloth.

"Yes, sir."

"An 'Eye Witness'! You want an Eye Witness?"

I nodded. His face was lean, his eyes bulged and his nose seemed enormous. His lips moved from a narrow smile to a grin turning down. I noticed he wore his homburg hat and, to my surprise, had long curling tresses of grey hair falling close to his ears.

He breathed deeply, as if reaching a serious decision.

"I am going to turn the tables on you, I think. I will make you *my* Eye Witness."

There was a pause. I lowered my eyes. Things were not going according to plan.

"Look at this." He extended one hand towards me and with the other pulled the cuff of his ragged cardigan up, exposing a fleshless, pale forearm. I looked at it.

"Look carefully", he ordered.

I strained my eyes in the grey half-light. I saw the proliferation of white hairs on the arm and – what was that? – someone had written in a grey, blue, purply ink a string of numbers running up his arm. My mind went blank.

"Well, my boy?"

Instinctively I reached for my notebook and pencil and, with rough black strokes of my best writing between the faint green lines on the white page I copied out the numbers precisely.

There was a long pause. I slowly raised my eyes and looked into his. His were deep and solemn. He seemed to recognise the blank incomprehension in mine.

"One day, my child, you will understand. It is not my task to shatter innocence – that is the task of history – and education. All I ask is that you remember what I have shown you. It is so important you remember."

He withdrew the naked arm and swiftly recovered it.

"You are my Eye Witness. You have just seen what I cannot look at without seeing again what I was made to witness. And I would have plucked out my eyes and howled like the mighty Sampson blinded in the deserts of Gaza rather than see what I was forced to witness."

His shaking claw-hand moved to grip savagely the woollen covering of the offending arm. I raised my eyes to his. They were even darker now and set in his quivering face were brimming with tears. I was amazed and growing frightened. He licked his dry lips. "Now – it is better you go." He breathed gently and hoarsely.

I needed no second bidding. I rose to my feet, my chair grating harshly on the bare, rough wooden floor.

"Wait!" he commanded.

He pushed himself to his feet, such a mighty effort to raise so slight and slender a frame.

I froze.

He crossed with shuffling steps to the chest of drawers, opened the hinged lid of an old silver and dull red biscuit tin, took something out and, returning to the table, threw it in front of me. I looked down. It was a bar of Fry's Chocolate Cream.

"Take it", he whispered. "A good reporter deserves his fee."

I picked up the bar together with my notebook and pencil. I moved to the door, twisted the rough Bakelite doorknob and suddenly remembered my manners. I turned back to him. "Goodbye, Mr Kamzoil. And thank you – thank you very much."

He stood – a black silhouette against the square of the window behind him – the light of a grey afternoon struggling unconvincingly to make some impression on the shabby interior.

"You are a good boy, my Eye Witness! Maazel tov."

And I left the room, closing the door firmly behind me.

Back downstairs, I sat on the edge of the doubled bed I shared with my brother. This room was lighter. The street lamps had come on outside and cast dramatic shadows across the stained walls.

I looked at my notebook. Total confusion. A set of meaningless numbers – Sampson and blind men crying out in the desert – a scrawny bare arm – an old man with long curls and – worse – an old man who cried. And I am an Eye Witness to all this?

I carefully unwrapped the chocolate bar he had given me. I felt the combination of dark bitterness and white sweetness on my tongue. I lay back on the bed, gazed at the familiar cracks on the ceiling. And the scraping, shuffling noise above of an old man moving about his spartan bedsitter. Now I knew. I smiled and took another bite. Not the noises of giant rats scuttling between the ceiling and the floorboards above, that could, if they wanted, force themselves through the fragile cracked ceiling and attack us in our sleep – as my brother had confidently assured me when we lay awake in the darkness waiting for sleep. I had pressed up against him and buried my head under the protection of my pillow. I was stupid then. Now I knew there was nothing to be upset by.

But there remained the mystery of the skinny old man's arm and the numbers.

The chocolate cream tasted good.

I thought the explanation would prove equally silly and childish.

More shuffling over my head. A louder sound as a chair rattled across the bare boards.

Another bite of chocolate. I carefully wrapped up what remained before my brother came home – keeping it for myself on another day.

After all, I concluded, gazing upwards, then are worse things in life than this.

FOOTSTEPS

I can't say when precisely the footsteps began their nightly patrol but I can remember that eventually they didn't just end but kind of faded away, grew less distinct, then silent. But life was chaotic at that time. There are so many confusing memories.

You see, we'd been bombed out. Our small terraced house in Finsbury Park, North London, had been 'blown to smithereens' – that was a term we schoolkids enthusiastically adopted – together with the two houses either side. Luckily (as Mum said – she was always determined to take an optimistic view), luckily, we had all been away from home at the time and even more luckily, it meant that, as a family of five with our dad being away at the war, we were given a priority billeting AND in an area that was not directly under Bombers' Alley, in Crouch End, just to the west of Finsbury Park. The German bombers droned across the Channel heading from the South for London Docks and peeled off to the East, unloading surplus bombs as they went. Crouch End was to the west – luckily for us, said Mum

Our 'billet' was two large rooms at the top (the second floor) of an old Victorian house. There was a large landing with a window overlooking the city (Crouch End is very hilly and we were at the top) and a single battered door that led into the first room. Equipped with a sink and a small gas stove (just two rings and a grill), Mum called this our living room, and the other became the bedroom, a large double bed, a camp bed and a mattress to accommodate us all. But, curiously, in this room there was a crudely constructed walk-in cupboard, wide enough to take a single bed mattress but somewhat longer. "Well, I …", said Mum. "How's that for lucky?" She looked at me. "Danny, this can be your room." Problem solved. Mum and the three girls in the big room and me, the only boy, in mine. I was thrilled. It was like a den or a camp or, more importantly, all mine. If I placed the mattress near the door then, at the far end, was my space for all *my* things. I stuck a hastily crayoned notice on the door. "No Girls Allowed", and Mum agreed.

It was Piggy Brewer who threw a cloud over proceedings. I went back to school after our 'move' – a much longer journey now but with the welcome novelty of different streets and neighbourhoods to explore on the way – and he said he knew the street we were in. That was one of the causes of Piggy's lack of popularity – he always knew everything about everything.

We called him Piggy because that's what he looked like. A fat, pink puffing boy, large round face, tiny glinting cramped eyes, and a broad upturned nose – you could see up his wide nostrils without even trying – and a tiny, clenched mouth. He shared my desk and I had a regular close-up view of his podgy pink fist clamped clumsily around his pencil as he struggled to write – like a troll, I thought – and I saw his intense concentration bring a flush to his ballooning cheeks, and his red tongue protrude squirmingly from the plushness of his lips and his breath erupted in gentle undeniably porcine grunts from his dark moustache.

"I know that road", he confided to me. "And that house." I doubted him, but he added, "My Aunty Dolly lives down there. That house you're in, they bombed next door." My heart stopped. We are next to a bomb site, huge timbers shoring up the wall to our new home. He knew what he was talking about. "All the people was killed", he continued. "And … (he paused for effect, looked secretively over his shoulder then back to me) … and it's now haunted. All that part of the street, my Aunty Dolly says – haunted by all them dead families." I made a weak attempt to show disbelief of him, but the point had been made.

It was about this time that the footsteps started, on the creaking landing, just outside my room.

And it was at this time also that Maisie, my four-year-old sister, came in off the landing (my mum had put a barrier of chairs across the top of the stairs and secured the landing as a place to play and announced she had just been talking to Mrs Elliott.

"Don't be silly, dear", said Mum, distracted as she dealt with a large saucepan of watery stew on the gas ring. "You know Mrs Elliott has gone away."

'Gone away', that phrase again. So many people and things had 'gone away'. Our house had 'gone away'. Our Dad had 'gone away' though Mum did have a printed letter from the War Office that he was only 'missing'. (Mum said he was in the Orient, a place called Singapore, and it was very jungly there so it was easy to be missing. She was sure that was all it was.) And Sally, our poor Welsh Corgi, had 'gone away'. She had put up with a lot of messing from a family of over-enthusiastically loving children but had started to snarl and snap. Mum said Corgis could do this and she was dangerous to children so a kind farmer had come from Wales to take her to live with him on his farm where she would have lots of fun and farmyard friends and no need to growl and grumble. But I had seen Sally being led away by Mrs Elliott one afternoon as I came home by an indirect way from school and I knew where the vets was and I knew about the encouragement by the Government for people to have their pets put away as part of the War Effort, for no cost at all.

And now Mrs Elliott had 'gone away'. She had lived in the next-door terraced house to us. She was a very old lady, stooping, white hair in a bun, glasses, always in long, loose dark coloured dresses with baggy cardigans (camphor, Mum said the smell was) and often as not an old green shawl. But she was not like all the other old women – bossy and nagging and bad tempered. She was calm and kind, often with a few sweets for us in a screwed-up paper bag – and she helped Mum when she could. She loved doing the ironing and there were lovely evenings in our home : Mum would screw the iron's plug into the overhead light fitting, the radio would be on – Workers' Playtime, Have a Go, Edmund Ross and his Orchestra – the gas fire would splutter in the grate, there'd be one standard lamp lit by the ironing board, and the smell of warm neatly laundered linen and the hiss of steam. That had all 'gone away'. And now Mrs Elliott with her home next door. I got angry with Mum and she said 'Don't be silly. Not in front of the little ones. Mrs Elliott, lucky for her, had, on a last-minute decision, gone to live with her niece in Northampton, where there is no bomb. I stormed out onto the landing, sat on the window sill at the sash window and seethed with indignation. Northampton – I knew she'd made that up. I knew there was a Southampton Docks and all the ships. But Northampton. How stupid did she think I was? Why not Easthampton or Westhampton? I pressed my forehead to the cold window pane and wanted to cry.

------- x -------

These temper tantrums. I do worry about our Danny. He's got such a temper on him. He's such an inquisitive boy, so determined and demanding – so unsettled. Just him and three little girls. And all this change. He needs his Dad, that's what. Can you blame him for not believing me about Mrs Elliott and Northampton?

And now there's Maisie. Coming in off of the landing saying she's spoken to Mrs Elliott. And she's told me stories that Mrs Elliott's meant to have told her. Three Little Pigs, Red Riding Hood's just two

124

of them. I let her tell me – better out than in. But I worry if she's taking after Danny – fanciful and restless.

Danny's got his little room – that's good. And he's got the landing window sill he can go to and read – he's always got his head stuck in a book. Well, he can do that uninterrupted out there. So that's lucky for us.

I decided to take Maisie's stories from Mrs Elliott on board and use them to get the girls to sleep. Maisie loved this, it made her feel important – but I still worried that the stories kept coming. And they weren't from Nursery school. I asked Miss Holdsworth, her teacher – without, of course, telling her the full reason for wanting to know.

And then, one evening, all was explained. I'd settled the girls, even Danny had gone to his room early for once, and I went out on to the landing to check the chairs. They were there – blocking the stairs. And a movement caught my eye, over by the window. A moving shadow and a sudden glint. I froze, looked through the evening gloom and saw – Mrs Elliott!

Sitting hunched in the window seat, white hair in a bun, steel rimmed glasses, her head turned to one side, her shoulders hunched under a dark shawl, a long skirt almost to the floor. My hand reached to steady myself on the door knob behind me.

The figure moved slowly and turned to face me. I breathed deeply and felt myself shaking. It was not Mrs Elliott. Everything else was like her but not the face. This one was long, a wide compressed mouth, a nose too big and a large forehead. She looked bad tempered but immediately relaxed into a beaming smile that seemed to warm the gloomy scene.

She rose awkwardly to her feet. "I'm sorry, dear. Did I startle you?"

"No, I just wasn't expecting …"

She moved towards me. Her voice was gentle, quite refined, I thought. Scottish, I guessed.

"I was just looking over the city. A lovely vantage point, I find. I hope you don't mind. I come up here from time to time." She waited for my response.

"No, that's quite all right. It's just that no-one normally comes up here but us."

"That's probably why I like it here. The quiet and seclusion. There's lots of noise and kerfuffle downstairs, comings and goings."

Another pause. I couldn't think what to say.

"I'm Moira Makillroy", she said. "I'm a friend of Maisie's." As if to emphasise this, her pale hand rose towards her throat. Her white fingers played with a richly bejewelled brooch with white and blue stones in the shape of an ornate letter M.

The mists cleared. "You're Mrs Elliott! She thinks … she calls you Mrs Elliott to me .. she says …"

Again the beaming smile. "Yes, mystifyingly, she calls me Mrs Elliott. So I let her!"

"And you tell her them stories."

"She does enjoy them so. They're all ones I knew as a child, and told my children and my grandchildren."

"Maisie loves them – over and over again."

"Well, Maisie's welcome anytime – anytime at all."

"If I'm honest, it's a great relief to me to meet you at last. I was a bit worried."

The clouds shifted outside, the landing darkened and Mrs Makillroy's silhouette grew even more indistinct.

I couldn't think what else to say.

Then, a cry from inside – it was Maisie disturbed in her sleep. "Mummy, where are you?"

"Scuse me. She'll be frightened if I'm not there. Oh …" I looked at the chair barricade. "Sorry. Shall I move them for you?"

"No, don't worry, my dear. What's a few chairs. Off you go to Maisie."

And that's what I did, whispering, "Well, goodnight then", pleased to have met the other Mrs Elliott.

------- x -------

And that's how, eventually, I came to meet the mother.

Maisie, of course, had seen me straight away and come across to the window seat and called me Mrs Elliott. And we had laughed and giggled and told stories. She had confided to me secrets and wishes and longings. And I had listened.

The boy, when he came out, just didn't notice me. His expression was scrunched into worry, frustration and unhappiness. He muttered to himself angrily about what was disturbing him – lies, unfairness, changes, his daddy. He would sit tightly on the sill, bony knees up close to his chin, feet crossed, shoulders hunched, scowling at yet another book he opened close to his face. But as what he was reading gradually penetrated his concentration and his imagination responded to this text on the page, his brow cleared, his knees lowered and his long legs relaxed and stretched along the sill and his lips gently moved with the words. And I knew then he was lost to me.

His mother I had seen many times before our only and final encounter. She tended to emerge late in the evening and fiddled with the chairs. On good evenings she crossed to the window, gazed out over the black and silent city and breathed deeply, her dark eyes full of wistfulness. On bad evenings she took a chair to the darkest corner of the landing, away from the window, and sank down on it, her body heaving with silent sobbing, her eyes screwed up against the bitterness of scalding tears and her mouth a gaping, hurting wound of desperation. Whitening knuckles would be forced between her teeth to prevent the outcry of anguish that was lurking there. After all, she was mere inches from her sleeping children – she would protect them from the animal howls that her whole body yearned to unleash. Then she would stop, like a fawcett being turned off. She would rise briskly to her feet, panting like a runner at the end of a long race. Her shoulders would strengthen and, with a huge sigh, she would adjust the scarf turban around her head, roughly towel her dampened fae on the raised skirt of her worn gown, drop this and smooth it down correctly, wipe her eyes with delicate sweeping movements of her fingers, and stride off back into her home – finally and firmly shutting the door – a soldier poised for the next battle.

At times like this she would not see me – but once in a relaxed mood, when she least expected me, there I was Nora Makillroy – to solve the mystery of Mrs Elliott and her stories.

Then again I was left to my lonely pacing up and down, up and down.

-------x-------

It was quite a while after my temper tantrum over Mrs Elliott going away that I picked up a letter addressed to Mum in the hallway as I came home from school. Mum read it, looked at me and smiled knowingly. She handed it to me. "There", she said, not a little triumphantly. I didn't recognise the handwriting. It certainly wasn't Mum's but the postmark was Northampton. It was from Mrs Elliott – Agnes, it was signed – who was nicely settled in with her nieces.

That night, I finished the last chapter of "Tom Brown's Schooldays" sitting as ever on the wide landing window sill. And as I stretched my legs and raised myself from the sill, I dislodged something with my foot that fell to the floor. I stooped and picked up a glittering, metallic and glass object. It was like a brooch, in the shape of an ornate letter M blue and white stones. M for Maisie, I thought. She'll love this. Goodness knows where it had come from!

GRAMMAR SCHOOL

We knew the letters were posted by the school on Monday 14th and would be dependably delivered by our regular postman on the early morning of the next day. That is how it worked. The scholarships were sat within the lofty panelled walls of the Old School Hall and two weeks later results were dispatched. It was an annual ritual. And the recipients didn't even have to open the large cream envelopes bearing the school's crest in green and gold to learn of success or failure. The envelopes of successful candidates were stuffed thickly with forms for completion, instructions for the start of the new school year, a booklet of school rules and details of uniform required and the necessary academic equipment. The envelopes for those not chosen were thin and flat – just a folded single sheet of unwelcome information.

I was up early that morning. Dad had gone to work at the crack of dawn, on early shift at the local steelworks. His first words to me were not exactly encouraging nor dismissive. "We'll see", he said, cramming his greaseproof paper wrapped sandwiches into his stained canvas bag. "We'll talk about it tonight, when I get home." He couldn't linger. The works bus left the corner of our street at exactly twenty past. "See you then, Mum", he said and went.

Mum paused as she placed his used breakfast dishes into the steaming bowl of water in the sink. She pushed back a lock of dank hair that had fallen across her forehead with the back of her soapy right hand. "Don't think he's not interested", she said. "He's worried. All that expense for grammar school. We've never had that in our family before. We've always gone straight into the works at fourteen. Dean's all right now, since he went into the army ..." Her words trailed away. She had now got used to one of her brood having left the nest and flown away so far.

"I most probably won't get in, anyway", I offered, in an unconvincing attempt to be conciliatory and not add any further to the anxieties of the morning – though both my mother and I could easily remember the evening when Miss Rumbold, the Headmistress of my Elementary School, had turned up on our doorstep unannounced some six months before. Mum had answered the door.

"Oh, Miss Rumbold."

"I am sorry to arrive without warning, Mrs Blackstock, but I'm just on my way home from an Extraordinary Governors' meeting at school."

Dad was in the back kitchen at the table, reading his newspaper. He looked up startled. "Who's that?" he hissed at me.

"It's Miss Rumbold. My Headmistress." My heart was thumping. I felt true alarm.

"Oh? What's she doing here?" And he leapt to his feet, grabbed the tea cloth as he passed the sink and went quickly and quietly out of the kitchen door into the dark back yard.

Mum was ushering Miss Rumbold into the kitchen. I stood up and backed away to stand against the wall.

"You'll have to take us as you find us, I'm afraid, Miss Rumbold." Mum smoothed her apron and patted her hair down nervously. "Do have a seat. Victoria, a chair for Miss Rumbold."

I darted forward and eased out one of our four unmatching wooden chairs from under the fading, chequered oilcloth that covered the kitchen table. Miss Rumbold moved across and sat down. She placed her large black handbag on the table and removed her leather gloves.

"Thank you, Victoria", she said brusquely.

Mum paused then uncertainly took a seat opposite her unexpected visitor. I gently retreated to my place by the wall.

"I expect you'd like to speak to Mr Blackstock ..." Mum began, looking uneasily at the abandoned newspaper and Father's chair untidily pushed back from the table. She glanced up at me.

"He's out back", I volunteered and felt myself blushing. It sounded so coarse in view of the presence of my school's senior teacher. 'Out back' was the euphemism we commonly employed when one of us was using the outside privy.

"He's gone out. He's in the yard, I think. I'll go and see", I muttered on, embarrassed, but I didn't move.

"No", decided Mum. "He won't be long."

Miss Rumbold sensed an obvious tension in the air and she determined to relieve it.

"Please don't worry, Mrs Blackstock. I am the bearer of good tidings. Victoria, as this concerns you above all, I think you'd better come and sit at the table. Here, by me."

I instantly obeyed, slipping nimbly into the chair indicated.

"As I said", she went on. "I've just come from an Extraordinary Meeting of my school Governors." She paused for effect, to allow the weight and sobriety of her statement to strike home. "It is a meeting we hold every year at this time to discuss the possibility of our presenting suitable candidates from our student body for scholarships at the local grammar schools." She paused again. "Victoria's name came under consideration and it was unanimously agreed ..."

The back door clattered open and Father burst in. Instantly I could tell where he'd been, to the cold-water tap set in the moss-covered bricks of the back yard where he had attempted to spruce up his appearance. His hair had been flattened down with water, a rather ludicrous attempt at a centre parting achieved, his face glowed, damp and pink, all traces of the grime of his working day obliterated, his collarless shirt was buttoned to the neck – but, above all, the give-away was saturation of the shoulders and upper chest of his shirt and knitted waistcoat and the soaking, screwed up tea towel in his right hand.

Stiff and awkward, he almost bowed in the direction of his visitor. "Ah ... good evening ... Miss ... Miss ...", he stuttered.

"Henry." Mum took the initiative. "This is Miss Rumbold – our Victoria's headmistress."

Miss Rumbold looked Dad directly in the eyes. "Good evening, Mr Blackstock. Won't you take a seat?"

Dad's eyes widened noticeably. Take a seat? In his own kitchen? By this woman? Take a seat?

But, take a seat he did, hurling the soggy tea towel neatly into the sink as he passed by.

"I've been explaining", continued Miss Rumbold, "about Victoria's progress and achievement in school. We – that is my entire body of School Governors and myself – are entering Victoria as a scholarship candidate for the Girls' Grammar School in Heverbury – for entrance in September this year."

Father gave an audible gasp.

"It is something we've never done before, enter a girl for such a scholarship. Boys aplenty, over the years, with some success. But never a girl. But Victoria's prowess in all areas of her academic pursuits is so impressive in its excellence that we feel it would be a serious disservice to her if we did not encourage her advancement in this way. I am particularly pleased to receive this unanimous endorsement from my Governors and, I admit, I am not a little excited."

She delivered this last with stony face, hands clasped tightly on her bag, her back ramrod stiff and upright, her eyes straight ahead.

There was a long pause. Mum glanced anxiously from person to person. Dad looked down at the table, slowly and deliberately rearranging the pages of his newspaper and then folding it tightly in ever decreasing oblongs.

"Well, Victoria?", Miss Rumbold broke the silence, glancing down in my direction. Mum and Dad both looked at me.

"Yes, Miss", I whispered hoarsely. What else could I say?

"Mr Blackstock? Mrs Blackstock?"

"Well …" Mum searched for words. "Well, Miss Rumbold. It's all very nice, I'm sure."

A rumbling clearing of Dad's throat. He pushed his tightly folded newspaper away from him and flattened his damp hands on the table surface.

"I'm not sure", he began, "that 'nice' really covers the matter, Mother. Indeed, it is nice to hear our Victoria is so highly regarded in her studies. Indeed, that is very nice. It is so, Miss Rumbold. But … Grammar School. That is something else, Miss Rumbold. That really is another matter. We shall have to think about that."

"Father!" Mother's interjection was something between a warning and a plea.

Miss Rumbold bridled. She had not anticipated anything less than joy and enthusiasm as a reaction to her glad tidings.

"I said it needs thinking about, Mother." I saw Dad's top lip grow narrow. He was unhappy and was displaying his stubborn streak.

"Mr Blackstock." Miss Rumbold persevered – a woman of authority, she could not easily abandon that demeanour. "This is a rare distinction we are bestowing on one of the girls from our community. No, more, a unique distinction. Now is not the time for thinking. All that has been done by my Governors and, in all modesty, by myself. The decision is made. I am here to inform you that our confidence is firmly placed in young Victoria and we look forward to offering her as our first Girls Grammar School scholarship candidate. It will mean lots of hard work for her and for her teachers and I can assure you…"

"What can you assure me, Mis Rumbold? Just what, may I ask?" Dad was rising to his feet, his chair scraping back harshly on the kitchen floor tiles. "It would seem to me that what you have said tonight raises more questions than it gives assurances." He paused and breathed deeply, not a little daunted by his own speechifying. "I've some questions. How's all this going to be achieved? Supposing our Victoria is clever enough. And I'm not saying she isn't. No, I'm not saying that. But what happens then? It's an expensive business, all this Grammar School lark. Uniforms and … books … and necessaries … and uniforms." Words were failing him. "And the fares. The bus to and from Heverbury – every day. And what afterwards – after Grammar School. What's there round here for a girl with Grammar school exams behind her? And years after she should have left school to find paid work, what then?" He stopped, breathing heavily, his forehead clamped in a deep frown, his eyes defiantly glinting, his cheeks and nose flaming red, his top lip now completely vanished. "Those are question I have", he growled.

Miss Rumbold exchanged the mantle of campaigning educationalist for the mask of calm diplomacy.

She rose to her feet, not a little dismay in her eyes.

"Thank you, Mr Blackstock, for hearing me out. Perhaps it was not my wisest move to arrive out of the blue, so to speak, without prior warning, but I was so … I felt so … Please think about it, Mr Blackstock … Mrs Blackstock. Victoria could achieve so much. I think I'd better be going. My family will wonder where I have got to."

She slowly put on her gloves and picked up her bag,

Mum rose and spoke. "Thank you for coming, Miss Rumbold. Victoria will see you out." She glanced at her husband's impassive form. "Father?"

Father shuddered to life. "Yes, thank you, Miss Rumbold. Thank you."

I led Miss Rumbold to the front door and held it open for her. She squeezed past me. Her lavender fragrance seemed out of place in our front entry. She paused. "There's a whole world out there for girls like you, Victoria. But we have to fight for it. Believe me in that!"

And she was gone.

I returned cautiously to the kitchen. Dad had gone – the back door left open. Mum stood by the stove, the letter in her hand.

"I didn't even offer her a cup of tea", she said bleakly.

And now the morning had arrived. Red letter day. Just the beginning of mine and Miss Rumbold's fight. If I gain the scholarship, lines will be drawn in the sand and battle will commence.

"I most probably won't get in anyway."

My words echoed in my mind. I knew they were a lie. I knew I'd found the scholarship papers well within my grasp.

"Don't talk nonsense", scoffed Mum. She dried her sudsy hands on the kitchen towel. "And don't you ever …"

There was a clatter as something was pushed through the metal flap in the front door.

"You'd better go and see", she said.

GRANDFATHER

To tell how my Grandfather came to be such an influential presence in my early life is to reveal a convoluted sequence of events over many years that sadly reveals human frailties of stubborn suspicion, resentment and unforgivingness.

My Grandfather was of that unfortunate generation who were destined to fall foul of two World Wars. In the first he fought with his two brothers. He survived; they did not. He persevered after demob to build up his own successful business and happily marry only to find the Second World War comes along and ensnares his only son in its foul embrace – but not until after there was some estrangement between father and son.

My grandfather was born and brought up in Blackborough, a grim coal mining town in the North Midlands. His escape from the pits was enlistment in the army at the outset of World War One, at the end of which he determined on a better future for himself. He would make a good livelihood from coal, but by delivering the stuff, not heaving it from the bowels of the earth. Life was good. His business prospered from one cart and a struggling horse to a fleet of delivery lorries. His wife, a quiet, dutiful woman, presented him with his only child, a son, my father, and they prospered even through the years of depression. "People will always want to be warm", he would say, thoroughly disapproving of those, now matter how impoverished, who avoided the middleman by nightly scavenging for coat bits on the slag haps of the gloomy landscape.

But he found his son reluctant to inherit the family business mantle. The boy had long suspected there was a world beyond the grit, dust and colourlessness of the restless clanking and hissing industrialisation of southern Blackborough and took himself off to what he saw as the bright lights and vitality of London itself. His father blamed the newly opened Picture House in Blackborough and his son's enthusiasm for reading. In London he became a waiter in a grand hotel and then moved into the kitchens as a trainee chef – and he met his future wife, my mother, who was an apprentice designer working on the refurbishment of the most expensive suites at the hotel. The couple journeyed North to 'meet the family' and confirm the news of the engagement but they received little welcome. They were met with resistance and suspicion by his father and she was seen as compounding the offence by appearing as posh, over-educated for a woman and having far too much of her own mind. His mother, far from in good health, was quiet and submissive but, in private, gentle and sweet with her prospective daughter-in-law. Any indications that the parents would travel 'down South' for the wedding were abruptly quashed by the father. The young couple returned to London, all meaningful contact with his parents effectively broken – only the formality of Christmas and birthday cards and the occasional letter. No wedding present wended its way southward, nor formal recognition of the birth of a grandson (that was me).

Along came World War Two, my father enlisted, my mother moved out of London and to a rented house in Surrey from where she worked as a freelance designer, until the birth of my little brother (more of him later) when she was forced to manage solely on my father's soldier's pay. Times, she later assured me, were hard. But to get harder. Soon after my brother's birth came the telegram, 'Missing in Action' to be followed by the seemingly inevitable confirmation of her husband's death.

The practical solution was frighteningly obvious. An old by now widower on his own in a house too big for him in industrial Northern England, a young widower struggling to manage with two young boys … all that was needed was a catalyst. And that was formidable and outspoken Great Aunt Philomena.

My grandfather's sister was as much a victim of circumstance in the First World War as anyone. She was deeply affected by the death of her two brothers. Already inclined that way in her adolescence, she took more and more strongly to religion, becoming a devoted Roman Catholic and, so my mother told me, close to taking the veil had not her mother been taken down by heart trouble, not having truly recovered from losing two sons, and both she and her father needed looking after, a duty too readily accepted in those days by the many young women left in spinsterhood by the sheer unavoidable shortage of young men, resulting from the carnage of war. My Great Aunt still clung to her churchly devotion, became a pillar of that community, Bible reading, Sunday school teaching, Church committees and good works. She was tall, slim, stoical, curt and unapproachable, strict and unforgiving but, my mother said, a truly good person who fell into chaste and celibate love with every young priest new to the parish. And it was Great Aunt Philomena who got straight to the point. Her brother, an old man, needed company and care : his daughter-in-law and her children needed security and a home. And that was it. One Autumn day, inevitably grey, we turned up at Grandfather's front door, three huddled figures, a pile of suitcases, a teddy bear and a much treasured, battered, fading red working model fire engine, apprehensive of our new life.

A strange menage, then, awkward, strained, its creaking cage lubricated by the oil of politeness and civility. Nobody said what they felt, nor felt they could say what they wanted to. We were in awe of grandfather; we were in *his* home and our presence tolerated for expediency's sake and because Great Aunt Philomena would frequently appear from her solitary life in her small rented terrace down the hill to make sure, in best headmistress terms, that all was in order.

But then – and I said there would be more of him later – there was also my little brother, Paul.

Looking back on it now, I am reminded of the Disney film that took my imagination at the time, *Peter Pan* and his depiction of Tinkerbell. A story of frightened children and pirates and death and crocodiles and kidneys and fighting – and, in the middle of it all, this tiny darting and skimming figure of bright whirring light, here, there and everywhere, impudent, uncaring for convention or the status quo, heedless of propriety or accepted convention, mad cap, enjoying total freedom.

That was Paul. And his greatest advantage was his instant rapport with his grave and unbending grandfather. And it was easy to see the reason for this bonding.

Paul would clamber onto his Grandfather's knee and sit confidently and comfortably settled against the old man's rising and sinking chest. He would even toy with the old man's fob watch and chain. To even the most casual observer, the physical likeness between these two was amazingly striking. Both had the wide forehead that tapered down abruptly to a pointed chin, faces almost invertedly triangular in shape. Two pairs of large, dark, soul-filled eyes. Small downturned mouths. Over all, a serious, almost mournful expression but for the pair of indecently large jug ears and the two wild shocks of hair, the old man's white and wavy, the small boy's dark and shaggy. But there was one more feature in common. Their identical smiles. Great, beamy revelations of even white teeth (Grandfather's not his own) and their spreading grins transformed their entire faces, forcing the cheeks into plump ruddiness, which compressed the eyes into a squinty glint, the foreheads clear of frown, where the ears perked up, alert in a canine fashion and, I swear, the wild hair bristled into a broom shape. Heads on one side, they looked like a couple of carefully depicted clowns, the impression being emphasised by the sight of my brother's skinny white bony knees and legs emerging from his baggy school shorts and hanging down to ankle socks and boots which looked a good four sizes too large for him. They were truly a matching pair.

And they had a mutual love for fun, the sillier the better. Paul would rush home from school each day, straight to his Grandfather, almost inevitably with a new joke. The old man's immediate reaction was to guffaw wheezily at the proffered witticism – the wheeziness increased as time passed until it became a fit of phlegmy coughing that was out of his control and necessitated a clawing for a handkerchief that he kept tucked inside his grey waistcoat. But after the choking guffaws came a considered appraisal of the quality of the joke. A mark out of 10 would be pronounced, almost always in excess of five. And a reward would follow for the joke teller. This came in the form of Pontefract cakes, the old man's one and only obsession. He had stacks of boxes of the things on his chairside table. A joke scoring five or six would mean one Pontefract cake; seven and above, two liquorice dishes – but, as my brother solemnly assured me when I asked him what he would get for a 10 out 10 joke – "There's no joke as good as 10 out of 10. It is not possible." I grunted disconsolately. My take on all this was that I didn't like liquorice anyway, so, who cares? That wasn't true.

Jokes only scored under five and received no reward if they were deemed too rude, i.e. referred to private body parts or items of ladies' underwear or were obviously an ineffectual concoction devised desperately by the boy on his way home purely to earn a mouthful of liquorice.

So the pattern of after-school jokes and sticky black reward went on even after Grandfather had retreated, by now wheezing and coughing constantly, too frequently finding it difficult to breathe, permanently to his bedroom. He existed in sick room isolation, only ever formally encroached upon for the mid-afternoon noisy joke share. The scramble of school boots up the uncarpeted wooden treads of the stairs, the unceremonious bursting open of the bedroom door, the piping rendition of the joke, the guffaw dissolving into a thick, grizzly cough and the clatter again as the small grinning figure skeltered down to the kitchen to announce the result of the joke fest – one thumbs-up if it were 5 - 6½ and two thumbs if it was 7 or above – and always the beaming smile smeared with the dark stickiness of Pontefract.

One night I was awoken by movement on the landing and a slit of light under the bedroom door. I shared a room with Paul. He was undisturbed. He could sleep through anything. I tiptoed out onto the landing. Mother was there in her pink candlewick dressing gown carefully closing Grandad's bedroom door. She glanced at me. "Grandad's not well. I've rung for the doctor. You go back to bed. Everything's all right." I hesitated. "Go on. There's nothing you can do."

Later I was awoken by a commotion downstairs. I crept to the top of the stairs. In the bright hall light below was Mother with Aunt Philomena and Father Nolan. They were in a huddle whispering. Mother was fully dressed. I shivered and went back to my room.

I must have dozed off for suddenly my mother was sitting on my bed, leaning over me. Grey morning was slanting through the clumsily drawn curtain. She was shaking my shoulder. She told me, subdued and solemn, that Grandad had gone in the night. I was to come down to the kitchen. Put my dressing gown on. And don't disturb Paul.

Downstairs was Aunt Philomena and Father Nolan. The plan was to see Paul off to school as if nothing had happened. He never expected to see his Granda in the morning anyway. Then, by the time he came home 'everything would be done' as Aunt Philomena put it. By this she meant the laying out. Mrs Doherty from the corner shop was the one for this. And after school Paul would be told. I was also to go to school. I'd serve no purpose by hanging around at home. Aunt Philomena's mind was made up. I didn't really want to protest.

I couldn't settle in school that morning and the prospect of double Maths in the afternoon was not to be relished. I asked to speak to the School Secretary and it was agreed I could go home at lunchtime.

The house was quiet, a strong sense of order. Mum hugged me. She looked tired. Mrs Doherty had been, done what was necessary and gone.

Father Nolan looked at me. "Would you like to go and pay your respects?"

I hesitated and looked to Mum for guidance. She went to speak but Aunt Philomena moved in.

"Of course he would. It's the thing to do." I again caught my mother's eye.

"It's up to him", she said.

Father Nolan said quietly, "We'll come with you." He rose to his feet.

Mum moved to me and squeezed my arm.

It was the first, and as yet the only time, I had seen a dead person. And it was not alarming. The bedroom had been cleared of all clutter, tidied and cleaned. Gone was the jumble of medicines on the bedside table, the water jug and glass, the alarm clock, the rolled newspapers; gone the dressing gown over the bed head, the walking stick propped up on the wardrobe, the old photograph albums and – yes – someone had disposed of all the packets – new or opened – of Grandad's Pontefract cakes. The old purple eiderdown had gone from the bed, messily plumped up as it always was, and the tartan rug. Just a polar white sheet covered it now, pristine, creaseless, carefully arranged, pulled up neatly to his chin. And there he lay, his face composed into unnatural seriousness, eyes closed. He could have been asleep but he wasn't. Someone had brushed his hair flat.

I didn't know what I would feel or how to feel it – but I felt so strongly my grandfather's total absence, as a simple statement of fact. The mask that his face presented was as alien to me as the neat austerity of the cleared bedroom. Where there had been a clutter of Pontefract cake boxes there were now, either side of the bed on the small chests of drawers, lace doilies and two neat matching vases of flowers.

Down in the kitchen afterwards, it felt strange to be sipping cups of tea and chewing pieces of rich fruit cake. Aunt Philomena had insisted on playing on the record player in the corner of the room, a selection of suitable records. We had just come to the end of Ernest Lough's rendition of 'O for the Wings of a Dove'. She had selected Kathleen Ferrier's 'What is Life for Me Without You?' and was leaning over to change the discs when she froze.

"What's that?" she queried.

We all were still, listening intently.

There was a noise, a footfall directly above in Grandad's room. Then another. And another. Mystification bound us into silence.

Mother spoke. "What time is it?"

She looked at the mantle clock and rose to her feet. "It's him. It's Paulie. He's home from school. We didn't hear him above the music."

"Shall I go?" Father Nolan rose to his feet, crumbs of cake falling off his broad black cassock.

"No." Mother was firm. "It's for me to go."

She moved towards the closed door, but it was too late. School boots clattered down the wooden stair treads. As she reached for the door handle, the door burst open and she had to jump back.

A small figure burst into the room, satchel swinging, black hair as wild as ever. Dark solemn eyes. He steadily proffered two bony fists, thumbs upturned,

"He loved it", he said. "He gave it a ten."

And his face exploded into a familiar transforming grin, a sprawl of firm even teeth that would have been as white as snow but for a film of glistening black Yorkshire stickiness.

GREAT AUNT MAY

Life changed irrevocably for Alice on her tenth birthday. Great Aunt May was due to pay a visit, as she had done on all of Alice's birthdays, but nobody had thought to warn Alice of the significance of this year's visitation.

Great Aunt May was a shadowy, diminutive figure who had become a decided presence in Alice's young life – her 'visits', infrequent and irregular, had punctuated her childhood. They were an 'event' in the humdrum, underprivileged lives of the family of six in their unremarkable, world-weary, two-up two-down, privy out back, terraced house in Stockport. But they seemed to have significance only for Alice, one of the visits each year inevitably coinciding with her birthday. For Alice there was always a present, an item of impractical luxury rather than of use – a lace edged, embroidered handkerchief smelling of lavender, a small empty scent bottle of blue glass with a silvery metal screw top smelling of lavender, a plump, blue velvet pin cushion – again that whiff of lavender – a hat pin with a glass bead at one end. All these Alice kept in a special box concealed for safety and, with special permission, in the bottom of her mother's old wooden wardrobe that took up far too much space in her parents' bedroom. On rare occasions, she was permitted to examine these items, sitting cross-legged on the rag mat, her skinny back leaning against the warm, unpolished dark brown of the wardrobe. It was the waft of fading lavender that she always associated with the lifting of the lid of her box of Treasures

Alice was kept home from school on the days when Great Aunt May came to call, even if it was not her birthday. This was a privilege accorded to none of her brothers and sisters and Alice inwardly relished this fact,

Part of the ritual of each visit was a catechism that Alice was subjected to. She would sit on a hard, upright chair facing Great Aunt May, white blouse, a cameo brooch at her throat, a dark cardigan, and was as attentive and polite as she had been instructed to be.

Great Aunt May always asked about Alice's dreams. These were not her aspirations for the future, or girlish fantasies that occupied her vacant waking moments, but the images and sensations that, unbidden, invaded her sleeping hours. Her mother sat alongside her, prompting the replies to Great Aunt May's gentle and persistent questioning – it was part of Alice's undertaking always to relate details of her dreams to her mother. It was only later that she discovered that her mother had diligently and without exception made written accounts of these nocturnal experiences,

Too often the dreams were wild, violent, distressing. Alice would sob them to her mother. Fires, storms, floods, eruptions, catastrophes of such a scope and nature that her child's sense of recall, choice of words and experience could only partially deal with. Sometimes there was deep sadness in calmer dreams – sickness, exhaustion, slow engulfing tears and death : rarely was there warmth and happiness, comfort or colour. Those were the dreams, few and far between, that Alice loved and longed for. Then there were the visions - strange, fantastic, nonsensical to Alice - that Great Aunt May took particular interest in. She put aside her teacup and saucer. She leaned forward, eyes glistening, the colour in her cheeks deepening, her breathing faster and less shallow. Alice told her of flying unassisted through white clouds, of swimming deep and green through endless oceans; of exotic creatures – dragons, eagles, snakes, angels and devils; of stones, rocks, jewels, piles of gold coins; of burning crosses, savagely swinging swords, roaring cannons; of snow and whiteness and gentle, soothing ice-cold, of eyes and smiles of evil and red claws and sudden rays of blinding white light.

By the age of ten, Alice found her dreams were becoming more alarming, far more vivid and disturbing. And some of them had a relevance she had previously never experienced : a sudden upheaval in the night, excited, sweating and terrified, arms threshing about to ward off falling black beams and bursts of searing flame, awakened possibly by the noise of her own voice (shrieking the name of her best friend Colleen as her sister Sheila grimly reminded her, having been disturbed from her own night's rest). This preceded by two days the death of that best friend in the Stockport rail disaster of 1951. Her little cousin Brendan's fight against polio and lung congestion was lost the afternoon after she awoke weeping with sadness, her body icy under the heavy eiderdown, her pillow damp, her head full of graveyards and strutting, gigantic, wildly pecking scarlet birds. Gently awakening from a deeply satisfying experience of sparkling summer seas, gliding galleons with bursting white sails and golden masts, smiles and white clothed tables laden with mounds of exotic foods, heralded the otherwise unannounced but very welcome arrival of her mother's favourite brother, Uncle Wilfred, a merchant seaman who hadn't set foot on English soil for some five years.

All these relayed in great detail and with total earnestness to Great Aunt May who became at once upright, alert and whole authoritative. "The time has come", was all she said.

Literally within minutes, Alice had on her coat and felt brimmed hat. Mother loaded her with an old shopping bag and two large brown paper carrier, heavy and bulging to breaking point. Mother tucked her treasure box under the girl's right arm and Alice and Great Aunt May moved to the front door.

"Now, you be a good girl", cautioned Mother. "Do as Aunt May tells you."

It was Mother's clumsy hug and a brisk kiss on her cheek that was Alice's final memory of life with her family in Stockport.

And so began her existence – 'life' was hardly the word – with her Great Aunt, three rooms over the shop in Ashby-de-la-Zouche : a shoe shop, seconds bought from factory back doors and peddled on at bargain prices to a grateful local community of farm and factory workers. Great Aunt May would never condescend to explain matters of her private life to her acquaintances and customers, but would drop sufficient judiciously selected hints that they could put two and two together for themselves. They concluded that Great Aunt May's new companion was her niece from up North, a dull, simple minded girl, more of a burden than a helpmeet to the shoe shop keeper. In fact, the reverse was true. Alice worked hard in the flat and behind the scenes in the shoe shop, a high price to pay for virtual imprisonment.

Gradually, the situation became clearer to Alice. Great Aunt May saw herself as keeper and guardian both of the girl herself and a family tradition that had swept Alice into its embrace. It was 'the gift' bestowed almost haphazardly throughout the centuries on women of direct lineage. It might miss one or even two generations. Before Alice, there had been Aunt May's mother's sister, Hermione Bolsover. So, even though 'the gift' might be dormant for many decades, the responsibility for dealing with its emergence was perpetual. Each generation produced its Great Aunt May to watch and wait and then pounce at the appropriate time.

Alice's time had come early. The upsurging power of her dreams – her future thoughts – had coincided with an abnormally early puberty. Thus was she swept away to a restricted and solitary life where her dreams could be less and less a response to external influences and more an irresistible condition of her extraordinary state of instinct and perspicacity.

She, with Great Aunt May's guidance, saw her dreams as an unpredictable condition she could live with but it was like an open wound vulnerable to infection, microbe infestation that could kick off into crises that would threaten physical and psychological well-being. In her case, these microbe invasions resulted from her proximity to other people. Something, anything that could carry on the air, through the ether, the telepathical instincts even, between them could occasion in her deep or trivial reactions that informed on, illustrated or predicted their lives. There was an enjoyable side to this, knowing the outcome of a turning point in a life, whether joyful or sad. But a darker, more sinister aspect of her powers emerged. On one rare occasion she chose to warn of what she had seen : Sally, one of Aunt May's more timid, quite impressionable shop girls, she advised not to take a train journey to Birmingham, the Bank Holiday weekend; she had foreseen death and shattering machinery. Sally went by coach and was killed in a multi-vehicle road accident. Alice realised the possibility that her dreams did not necessarily reflect the inevitable, but could also have a malign influence on the outcome. She could be the cause of future events – her dreams not merely predictions but a force emanating from her, governing the future. And worse, with that awareness came another – that her contact with the future could not be terminated by the predicted event, not even if it were death itself, She felt herself being drawn to Sally through the shock and distress of the terrible accident to what lay beyond, a massive truth that was never intended for the human mind, one shadowy glimpse of which would tilt consciousness and rationality off balance, inflicting on her a mental overload that could result only in insanity.

Her fears and, worse, the awful tension of not being sure of the nature of her powers worked on her like vitriolic acid on a fragile copper plate. She withdrew into her tortured being, dreading the self-imposed isolation of her waking moments and terrified of surrendering to the uncontrollable nightmare landscape that was her sleep.

It was thus that we found her. Aunt May had been rushed to hospital and quickly died of a heart attack. It was as the solicitors of May Veronica Beauchamp that we were summoned by Sheila, her great niece, to look in on the shop and Alice immediately, whilst she set out from Manchester to take over from her Great Aunt It was her 'duty', she said.

Alice sat in the corner of her aunt's sitting room. Hollow-cheeked, hollow-eyes, dark half moons under them emphasising their watery greyness and the gaunt boniness of the sockets themselves. Hair straight grey and glossy, shoulder length and straggling finely. Thin lips pale and working soundlessly. It was almost painful to observe the intensity of her glassy stare as she noted every detail of the floral wallpaper on the wall opposite, every fibre of her being straining to avoid acknowledgement of the least whisper, movement, breath, emotion or thought of whoever was present in the room with her. Her neck and shoulders were rigid with tension. The white slender fingers of both hands writhed in anguish and despair in her lap. At her feet, an old box upturned spilling out its contents – a faded grey handkerchief, a cheap blue glass bottle and a tarnished hat pin.

There was a faint smell of lavender.

HARVEY

Harvey was sitting quietly at the table in the living room reading his comic when he heard a loud knock on the kitchen door, the slam of the door swinging open heavily and his Uncle George's voice, "Hi, Sis. Where's his Lordship?"

His mother responded in gentler tones. "He's in the living room waiting for you."

"Right – no time like the present."

"Can you stay for your tea?" she asked.

"No … bit pushed for time. It's Wednesday evening. Club night. Thanks anyway."

It was the turn of the living room door now to burst open.

"Harvey, me beautiful boy!"

His uncle stood in the frame of the door nearly filling it. A large figure in a smart striped suit, colourful tie (Flashy! Dad would say), sparkling tie pin, a tight shirt collar restricting his stout red neck, his round face flushed and sweaty, dark hair slicked smoothly back, and his teeth, which could give him an almost goofy appearance, fully revealed in a sudden beaming smile, like a light going on in a darkened room.

"Your mam tells me someone's got an interview."

Harvey nodded.

"At Birkenstall's. On Friday morning?"

Harvey nodded again.

"Well, look who's come to help you – aid and assist!" He threw his arms wide open in a theatrical gesture. "OK, m'lad?"

Harvey nodded.

Mother's voice floated through. "Have you time for a cup of tea? A sandwich?"

"No, really Norah. I've just called by." His eyes were steady on Harvey's upturned face. "I've not got time now," he said, "but tomorrow, same time same place. We'll get you ready for this interview. Jobs for life at Birkenstall's, if you get it – correction, *when* you get it. You and me, unbeatable team. Now, tomorrow's Thursday, interview Friday morning. What time?"

Harvey went to reply but his Mother's voice came first. "Nine o'clock."

"That's good. He'll be first for the day. So listen, nephew. Tomorrow, you do two things for me. Get together everything you'll be wearing. Jacket, shirt, tie. Shoes – clean them. Second …" He looked intently at Harvey. "Get your hair cut. Nice and short. Parting. Brylcreem. Oh, and there's a third thing. Your application form. You've handed that in?"

Harvey nodded.

"A week ago", came Mum from the kitchen.

"I want you to write down everything you put on that form. Mr Birkenstall will use it to find questions to ask you about. Your schooling. Exam results. Interests."

"Fishing and Boy Scouts", added Mum.

"Good. Fishing and Boy Scouts. Anything else?"

Harvey opened his mouth to reply.

"No – not now. Have it ready for tomorrow. And we will have a rehearsal … yes, a rehearsal. I will be Mr Birkenstall. He's a hard man – knows what he wants and makes sure he gets it. Doesn't tolerate fools. He'll expect the best."

Harvey's stomach butterflies were restive again.

"And that's what we'll give him. OK? Tomorrow."

A call from Mum. "You'll stay for your tea tomorrow?"

Gerry adjusted his already immaculate tie and spread the fingers of both hands across his ample stomach.

"If you insist – and if it's worth the eating."

"You cheeky beggar – you'll eat what you're given, our Gerald."

Gerry leaned over to Harvey in mock confidentiality. "Take it from me, young Harvey. Never have an older, bossy sister. Bane of my life."

"I heard that", from the kitchen.

And he was gone. The room seemed larger, lighter and the dust started resettling.

Mum called from the kitchen. "Harvey, love. Lay the table for tea. We'll look you out a decent shirt afterwards."

. . . .

After tea the next day, Gerry announced, "We'll need the front room, Norah. OK?" He walked through and returned. "And the upright chairs." These he seized on in each hand, and disappeared into the hall. "come on, Harvey", he called over his shoulder.

When Harvey reached the front room, he saw one chair was placed at the far end with its back to the fireplace, the other facing it almost at the opposite end of the room. Gerry stood by the fireplace, open hand on the back of the chair, the other placed imperiously on his chest.

"Now. I'm Mr Birkenstall – Mr Horace Birkenstall, JP – over here, behind my large mahogany desk. You go out and knock on the door. I shall bid you enter and you come to the other chair and say clearly and with confidence, 'Good morning, Mr Birkenstall. I am Harvey Bailey for my nine o'clock appointment.' OK?"

Harvey nodded, shuffled out of the room and stood quietly in the hall. He raised his clenched fist to knock but hesitated. Gerry's voice boomed from within. "Come on, lad. When you're ready."

Harvey knocked twice, pushed open the door and peered around.

"No. No. No." Gerry's head shook vigorously, his double chins quivering, even his stomach seemed to judder with disapproval. "No – that's no good. Don't apologise for being here. Look, watch me. You come over here and sit down. See it from Mr Birkenstall's point of view. I'll go out. When I knock you shout, 'Come in' or, better still, 'Enter'. Then watch me – watch and learn." He went. The door was shut firmly behind him.

"Right? I'm coming." There was a pause then several loud knocks and – before Harvey could say a word – in stepped Gerry, beaming with confidence, head aloft, chest out. He closed the door firmly behind him, stepped behind the interviewee's chair holding it with both hands as if it were a lectern, cleared his throat volubly and pronounced with clear enunciation, 'Good morning, sir. I am Harvey Bailey come for my 9 o'clock appointment'."

There was a dramatic pause.

"D'you see how it's done? Confidence is the watchword. Show him how much you want to be there. Now your turn."

. . . .

And that was the start of a long and involved evening. 'Diction' was a word often used and 'presentation' but always 'confidence' and 'smile, smile, smile'. Harvey's cheekbones ached. His haircut was approved as was his jacket, shirt, tie ("Rather dull", concluded Gerry. "Must be one of your father's") and the polished shoes. And every answer to any possible question.

Finally, Mother entered with some timidity. "Have you not finished yet? You'll wear him out."

Gerry sighed greatly. "I think we're done." He ruffled Harvey's hair. Harvey felt like a nine-year-old. "You'll be OK, Harve. First job out of school. Always a big ask. Just remember, big Mr Birkenstall is looking

for a good lad   he wants you to do well. And I'm sure you will Norah
– " He turned towards his sister. "I'll pick him up in the car at 8.30."
He glared pointedly at Harvey. "Prompt. I don't trust buses that time
of the morning. I'll be on my way to the Bank anyway. See you then.
OK?"

And he was gone.

....

And it was these events of the previous evening that churned
around in Harvey's brain as he sat erectly outside Mr Birkenstall's
office at five to 9 the next morning. His right fist clenched and
unclenched in his lap anticipating his knock on the door. 'Confident
and assured', he heard the echoes of his Uncle's voice.

But events took their own turn. The door opened and a somewhat
stern voice said, "Do come in."

He obeyed. As the door swing shut at his back, he watched Mr
Birkenstall move decisively to behind his desk. He sat down.

"Take a seat", he directed. There was, as Gerry had predicted, an
interviewee's chair facing Mr Birkenstall's large mahogany desk and the
great man himself.

Mr Birkenstall had a long mournful face, a bald head with a fringe
of white hair around his ears and strongly contrasting black bushy
eyebrows. He smiled unconvincingly, his teeth somewhat stained. His
metal framed spectacles perched low on his beak of a nose glistened as
he lowered his head to look at the paper he held at desk level before
him.

He began, his voice refined and cultivated, "Bailey … Harvey
Bailey. Now let's see." He ran his eye up and down the document in
front of him. Harvey recognised it as his application form. Answers to
anticipated questions tumbled around in his mind. His heart beat hard.
His temple throbbed. His palms sweated. His throat and lips were dry.

"Well … Mr Bailey. I see you offer two referees. One from Mr
Pugh, your Headteacher. The other from Revd Jenkins, St Barnaby's
on the Hill. Very good. I should tell you I spoke with Mr Pugh on the
telephone. We are acquainted, Council work and such. He is pleased to
recommend you." He glanced at a second piece of paper. Handwritten
notes. "Hard working. Sensible. Respectful. Helpful. Good exam
results. School Certificate. I enquired further and he referred me to a
Mr Jarvis who was, I believe, your form teacher and … er …
Mathematics … in your final year."

He looked up at Harvey and raised an enquiring eyebrow.

"Yes, sir", Harvey had found his voice and - yes – it did sound confident.

"He also spoke very highly." He lowered the papers to his desk and flattened his hands on to the green blotter. "Ah, most satisfactory."

His smile – stern and hesitant until now – broadened into something almost welcoming and relaxed. "Most satisfactory." He doffed his glasses with a swift movement of his right hand. "Very good." He rose to his full height and moved around the desk to tower over Harvey. "I should like you to start here at Birkenstall's as a Trainee in our offices as soon as can be arranged. See my Secretary on the way out for all necessary arrangements."

He proffered at the level of Harvey's head an extended long, lean white hand. The nails were highly polished, a large gold ring glinted before Harvey's eyes.

The boy stumbled to his feet and inserted his narrow fingers into the huge enveloping grasp.

"Well done, Mr Bailey. Welcome to Birkenstall's."

Harvey freed himself from the firm grip and just stood there.

"That's all. You can go now."

"Yes, sir." Harvey's voice had deserted him – it was a hoarse, stuttering whimper. He scuttled for the door, opened it and stumbled out – all confidence gone.

A stentorian voice came from within.

"Close the door, boy."

He clumsily seized the door handle and pulled it toward him.

"Yes, sir", he croaked and was aware of tears coursing down his cheeks.

HE WHO IS MOST TIMID

Many many moons ago, in a land far distant, in a remote mountain kingdom, lived a maker of rich tapestries and a weaver of fine silken cloths. His name to us is unpronounceable but, were we to translate it, it could read, 'He who is most timid'. For he was a timid man, a very timid man and everyone knew him to be the most timid man they had ever known. He was a small man, delicate of feature, fragile in structure, shy of nature. Most things in life terrified him - thunderstorms, fast flowing water, the howling of wolves at night, a sudden loud knocking at the door, the billowing of his bedroom curtains in the moonlight, the unexplained creakings in the beams of his wooden roof when all else was quiet. But above all the greatest fear he had, of all the fears he had, was that of spiders.

And this was unfortunate - for the kingdom in which he lived stretched across the floor of a mighty valley and at the end of this valley, deep within a towering mountain, dwelt a kingdom of spiders.

The two kingdoms kept a wary distance each from the other. The humans fled from the spiders with ostentatious fear and loud cries, or they attacked them with savage blows and deluges of water. The spiders did their scavenging as discreetly as possible but found it difficult to resist the lure of the humans' homes - the novelty of crannies, fissures and cracks, water pipes and plug holes, the sweet smelling spice shelves and the warm airing cupboards.

But even the most timid tapestry maker and weaver of silks has a heart and is capable of falling in love. And this he did, with the beautiful daughter of the wine merchant who plied his trade several streets away in one of the city's grandest squares. But the vintner's daughter was a proud and haughty girl, as proud and haughty as only a woman blessed with remarkable beauty can be. And she scorned her timid suitor. She could only truly love a man who had no fear. But even the most timid of tapestry makers and weaver of fine silks who has a heart can also show true determination and stubbornness and he vowed to conquer his fears and return to the wine merchant's daughter with his suit.

One by one he set out to banish his fears; he stood naked in thunderstorms and hurled hostile words at the skies; he swam the heavy swollen fast flowing rivers and shouted defiance through the forest darkness at the howling wolves; he installed a tinkling bell to avoid loud knockings at the door and wooden slatted blinds so that his bedroom curtains did not billow in the moonlight and, in the silence when the roof timbers creaked, he would rush up his loft ladder, flaming torch in hand , to defy any evil spirit that might be invading his home.

But there were the SPIDERS. This would be a longer job. First he was not to panic and leap screaming on to a chair, gathering the hem of his gown around him. Then he was to stand or sit silently and watch the spider's smooth and steady scuttling until it was out of sight or, if he encountered a spider trapped in a sink or his bath or running across his sleeping bench, he devised a cunning plan to deal with this intruder. He had to hand a delicate crystal bowl and a large pomegranate leaf. He deftly placed the bowl over the spider then slipped carefully under both the wide smooth pomegranate leaf and gently took all to the window where he could, with one swift move, release the spider into the magnolia bush that grew beneath the sill.

And strangely, through patiently studying the small creatures, he learned to admire them and their ways - though he knew he would never truly welcome the touch of these specimens.

He had conquered his fears - and the whole world knew - and the wine merchant's proud daughter had no reason to resist her father's wish that she marry the now not so timid - some said, not at all timid - maker of tapestries and weaver of fine silks.

Meanwhile, in the spider kingdom deep in the mountain at the end of the valley the Spider King was having to deal with his own proud and haughty daughter. He had arranged a marriage, a most desirable alliance between two warring spider kingdoms, but his stubborn, strong-willed daughter resisted. She would marry a rich husband, of course, and one of a noble royal family - but not this one who was old enough to be her father, was fat and bald. She was worth better. And unable to sway her father who, himself, was unswerving and implacable when his mind was made up ("And he wonders where she gets it from", said the Spider Queen with a knowing smile to her ladies in waiting as they sat spinning delicate webs in the fading light), the Princess Spider decided to run away, out of the spider kingdom into the mountains to seek her fortune beyond the reach of the eight podgy and hairy arms of her ancient betrothed.

As chance would have it she came, distressed and weary, to the home of the no longer by any means timid maker of tapestries and weaver of fine silks. Distraught and careless, she found herself trapped by the smooth side of his marble washbasin. He saw her, she froze. He gulped and steeled himself. He reached for his crystal bowl and pomegranate leaf and nimbly trapped her, only immediately to release her into the magnolia bush. There she swiftly encountered outriders of her father's vast personal bodyguard who had been dispatched to find her, guard her and lead her safely home.

The tapestry maker and weaver of fine silks retired to his sleeping bench, unaware of the momentous service he had performed for the King of the Mountain Spiders. He had thoughts only of his dearly betrothed beautiful daughter of the city's grandest wine maker.

The King and Queen of the spiders rejoiced at their daughter's return. In their joy, all thoughts of a fat old husband was, for the moment, dismissed and she recounted how she had been saved by a kindly mortal and placed in the safety of a magnolia bush. The king dabbed away a tear. He thanked the God of all Spiders that his daughter had fallen under the protection of the rarest of all beings - a human who did not hysterically fear spiders but had the circumspection and magnanimity to preserve and protect even alien life. Such a being must be honoured. He issued an edict. Tribute must be paid. The King, his Queen, armies and subjects would journey at once to the home of this most magnificent of human kind to make obeisance in his very presence. So, in their vast hordes they set out.

And this is how it came about, that the maker of tapestries and weaver of fine silk , whose lack of timidity was known throughout the whole Valley Kingdom was found straddled across his sleeping bench, his frozen limbs twisted into grotesque knots, his dead eyes wide and staring, his mouth agape, his face contorted with fear.

When they moved his body - which was not easy as his bent limbs and torso had part petrified into rigor mortis - a single spider scuttled from beneath his nightshirt and instantly vanished into a narrow crack in the wall.

"A single spider", scoffed the beautiful daughter of the wealthy vintner. And she was glad. The fate of a woman whose betrothed met a sudden and unexplained death was to be robed in black and entombed alive with her beloved one in his sepulchre. "See how timid he really was. He has not kept his side of the bargain. Our betrothal is null and void." And she swept grandly from the room knowing that, as a maiden publicly deceived, humiliated and betrayed by her acknowledged suitor, she would succeed to nine tenths of all his worldly goods.

And the Spider Princess? It did not take long for the softness of her father's heart to harden again and she was despatched to marry her old fat husband. The Kingdom has never been big enough for both of them, mused the Queen Spider biting off the end of a thread as she finished her latest web.

MISS HENRIETTA MAPLEY

There were moments when Miss Henrietta Mapley sincerely wished she had never become involved in the blasted affair. When she had first received the invitation – or was it a notification? – from SPANC – S.P.A.N.C. – she felt quite flattered. She had over the years achieved something of a reputation as a local artist. Self-taught, she had developed her skills over the years and, usually encouraged by family and friends, begun to display her pieces when the opportunities arose – displays at local galleries, the Art College, libraries, the local theatre – even at commercial galleries where some of her works had fetched encouraging prices. But that was a rare occurrence. There was no living to be gained from it. She had to stretch her pension to afford her artists' materials.

Now S.P.A.N.C. – the Society for Promotion of the Arts in the Northern Counties – proposed a comprehensive display of local paintings all over the area in whatever venues they could appropriate. She was invited to show a selection of her works at Fullparton Village Hall – that was the next village – on Friday and Saturday the 14th and 15th of May, between the hours of 10 am and 6 pm. She would share the venue with a Cora Teasdale-Hawkins of the Beva Galleries, Little Morton. Henrietta knew of this woman but had never met her or seen her work. People talked of her in awe.

It was proposed in the letter that she, Henrietta, attend a meeting of the Fullparton Village Hall Committee to arrange details for the display – at 2 pm on the following Wednesday. She was given a phone number to confirm or change the arrangement. She was to speak to the Committee's Secretary, Mrs Blanche Shone. This she had done, and the meeting was arranged.

It took her a mere ten minutes to reach the designated Village Hall. The road outside was deserted. It was a pleasant day, clear and warm for early Spring. She left her car on the road and made for the front door of the Hall. The building was of timber construction, looking, she had to admit, rather run down and shabby. She pushed open the door and entered a narrow dark corridor. On either side were closed doors but directly ahead was one half open and there was a welcoming light beyond. She headed for that.

She entered the main body of the hall. It was plain, grimy cream walls, frayed and holed bottle-green curtains at the clouded windows that ran the full length of either side of the hall. The lights were horizontal fluorescent suspended by dusty cobwebbed chains. At the far end of the room were two unprepossessing brown wooden trestle tables set out with row of chairs behind. At the centre sat a man, his shoulders hunched, writing determinedly on some pages on a table. His head bent forward revealed a white bald dome with a fringing of wild bright ginger hair. To his right sat a woman, round faced, rosy cheeked, dark curly hair. She looked up and saw Henrietta. She stood and smiled pleasantly. "Ah, Mrs Mape-ly", she said. "Do come in."

Henrietta approached the table. The man still looked down. Quietly she corrected the woman. "It's Miss", she said. "Miss *Map*-ley. But please call me Henrietta."

"I am Blanche Shone", came the return. "We spoke on the phone."

There was a pause. The Secretary looked sideways at the man whose pen movements did not falter. Henrietta shifted her handbag from one hand to the other.

"Er", the Secretary muttered. She coughed emphatically. Another pause. The man looked up, straight at Henrietta. His face was bony and pale. The watery faded look of his eyes was emphasised by the strong lenses of his rimless glasses. His mouth was small and pursed. He was expressionless.

"Quite", he pronounced, as if the word had significance. "Quite."

He planted his hands, long white skeletal fingers splayed, copiously dappled with ginger freckles, Henrietta noticed, on the table and heaved himself to his feet. He was very tall, his narrow frame swamped in a loudly checked Harris Tweed jacket. A broad green and brown striped tie hung from his prominent bobbing Adam's apple.

The Secretary spoke. "This is Miss Henrietta Mapley, Mr Chairman."

"It is indeed. It is indeed. Welcome, Miss Mapley. Please take a seat." He wafted his right hand to indicate a chair alongside where Henrietta stood. Henrietta sat. He surveyed the room from his considerable height. "I declare the meeting open", he announced. "And the time is …" He consulted a large watch on his left wrist.

The Secretary cut in helpfully, "Four minutes past two", she said.

"14.04 hundred hours", he corrected. Let us commence."

With an impressive sigh he sank into his chair. The Secretary discreetly bobbed into hers. Without glancing to his right he intoned, "And the purpose of this extraordinary general meeting?"

"To discuss arrangements for the SPANC Art Display on Friday and Saturday the 14th and 15th of May."

"Indeed." He looked around. "Have we any apologies to announce?"

The Secretary handed him a piece of yellow A4 paper on which there was a typed list.

"Now, let me see. Commander A Boggins. He is still incommoded by a broken leg?"

"Yes, Mr Chairman."

"Right. Mrs M Blaxby."

"Arrival of a new grandchild. Little girl. Six pounds, seven ounces."

"Thank you, Madam Secretary. Mr. P. Everton-Stuff."

"Not available Wednesdays."

"The Revd Peter Georgeson."

"Officiating at a funeral."

"Mr C Furridge."

"It's his funeral."

"Just so. Miss G Munsch."

"Her dog is unwell and cannot be left. I have a letter of explanation."

"Later. Later. So, we are all here. Let us continue."

"Do we have a Quorum, in order to proceed?" The Secretary looked anxious.

"This being an extraordinary general meeting, there is provision, should the matter in hand be of suitable gravity and urgency that proceedings may continue unabated. This being at the discretion of the Chairman of the Committee or any other senior officer thus designated."

The Secretary leaned forward. "Art?"

"I permit matters to proceed. Please minute accordingly."

"Yes, Mr Chairman."

The Chairman leaned back in his chair and removed his glasses. His eyes over-brimmed. Henrietta feared a deluge. "We need to confirm the details with you. You have read the mission from the Society?"

"I have", confirmed Henrietta.

"Then, that would appear to be that. We would all appear to be in one accord. However …" He paused grandly and replaced his glasses on his beaky, freckle splodged nose, "there is one matter of concern. The Village Hall Committee's Hospitality Manager. She is unable to be present today. We have been informed of her apologies. But Madam Secretary, you say we have a letter."

"From Fraulein Munsch. Yes, I have."

"Then, please acquaint the Committee with its contents." Again he sat back. This time his eyes closed. Still no liquid was displayed.

"Dear Committee. I cannot come to your meeting tomorrow as my dog is ill. Not Maximillian but the other one, Johann. He has a disorder of the bowel so cannot be left for obvious reasons, nor in the garden as he will leap over the wall to Copper's Wood and will be shot if the farmer sees him. I will meet the artist lady at my house. Tell her to knock on the front door or come round to the side gate. Do not open this or the dogs will run to the pub across the road. Just call out, 'Hello. Hello. I am here. Where are you?' Yours faithfully, G Munsch (Fraulein)

"Thank you, Mrs Secretary." The Chairman looked pointedly and at length at Henrietta.

"This is our dilemma, and we do trespass upon your good nature and toleration in order to effect a compromise solution. Will you be prepared – nay, even happy – to call personally on our Hospitality Manager?"

"No problem", responded Henrietta placing her handbag with both hands firmly across her lap as a clear indication that she was about to stand up and depart.

The Secretary rose swiftly to her feet. "I will point out the cottage to you."

Both women stood waiting for some response from the Chairman. Crestfallen, he sighed deeply, airily wafted both his enormous hands and proclaimed, "I call the meeting to termination ..." He stopped and looked at his watch. "The time is 14.10 hundred hours."

"Ten past two", breathed the Secretary in whispered exasperation.

Henrietta was only too pleased to leave the fusty hall and, after receiving directions from the Secretary who displayed an obviously apologetic demeanour, she drove off through the village and easily found the designated cottage with its large dark wood front door. She knocked several times, each time more forcibly than the last. No reply. She followed the unevenly paved path round to the left of the building and her way was blocked by a chest high solid wooden gate. She peered over it and called out. Instantly there was a rush of loud threatening barking and two enormous black dogs appeared in a feversome rush. She stepped back almost losing her footing on the rough surface of the path. The dogs leaned their enormous front paws on the gate and barked with considerable animation at her, their heads bobbing, their eyes wide, white teeth flashing, pink tongues lolling, drool and spittle flying. She heard a voice, husky, determined, "Get down, you slobby animals. Down. Get down." The dogs disappeared and were replaced by the head of a woman, gnarled, dark skinned, thick lips, grey hair pulled back tightly from a wide forehead.

"You are the artist woman." This was a statement of fact, not a question.

"Yes, I am."

"Good. You to go front door. I will let you in. No worries. Dogs will be in the garden." The head disappeared.

Henrietta did as she was told. Eventually she heard movement from the other side of the door which creaked open and the same head appeared in the gap.

"You come in. Follow me." The woman's lips were deep coloured and fleshy, her teeth uneven, her nose negroid in that it was so broad, her eyes dark and shaded by copious grey eyebrows.

Henrietta followed her, through a dark, low-ceilinged room that was unbelievably cluttered with too much furniture and piles of belongings – books, cushions. The figure led her through another door into what turned out to be the kitchen. This was more brightly lit, the light streaming in through two windows and the upper half of a stable door which was open. The woman stood here, keeping an eye on the dogs outside whilst intending to have a conversation with Henrietta over her left shoulder.

"I am Hospitality Manager", she said forcefully. "I will see that …" Her head turned rapidly away, and she yelled out into the garden. "Maximillian. Don't you dare. Mutter is watching you. Down." She turned back, flushed, firm eyed. "He is nearing that damned wall. As I say, I will do refreshments for you. First there will be tea and coffee with sugar." And again, Henrietta saw only the back of her head. "You damned hunde. I will kill you." She again faced Henrietta. "I will have to go. You stay here. Don't move." And she instantly swing open the lower half of the door, exited and slammed it shut behind her. The noise of the screeching woman and the barking dogs grew more distant.

Henrietta looked around the deserted kitchen and her heart sank. This room was in disarray. The sink was piled high with dirty dishes, the windowsill was cluttered with grimy containers for kitchen cleaners, old milk bottles, a cracked jug and a neglected and dying, blackened pot-bound plant in a damaged pot. On the floor by the sink, a sack of potatoes, pulled open with much cluttered vegetables spilling on to the quarry tile flooring, the customary red of the tiles buried beneath layers of dirt and dust. There was a fridge, far from white, its door stained with splashes of food and spills from its filthy Formica top, On the floor near this, sheets of yellowing newspaper topped with bowls obviously intended for the dogs. Two floral bowls, wide and shallow, almost clean, containing drinking water. Two metal bowls, crusted with ancient remnants of dry meals, blackened chunks of meat and biscuit spilling over on to the paper. Her observations were interrupted by the reappearance of the now panting woman.

"The beggars. I now have them chained. They will subside. But Maximillian is not well. He is pooping everywhere. Even in here if I let him."

Henrietta smiled weakly. Not that it would be noticed, she thought to herself unkindly. She wanted to go. "So, you will be able to handle the food then?" The very thought made her shudder.

"I will be OK. You don't worry. I have help from WEE women."

Henrietta frowned. "WEE women?" she asked.

"Yes. WEE women. W.I. women. They help."

"Oh yes, I see. Well, it's very good of you." There was an awkward pause. Henrietta looked at the sink. She was frightened the woman would offer her a cup of tea or something. "I am afraid I have to make a move", she said. "It's very good of you to spare the time."

"It is no worry", came the reply. The woman advanced on her and held out her right hand to be shaken. As Henrietta reciprocated, she was left with the unedifying image of the dark, wrinkled claw, etched with grime, the long yellowing nails rimmed with black gripping her tiny, delicate pink fingers.

She regained her car, her head now full of misgivings. Her paintings surrendered to the dust and dirt of that drab hall. Her patrons – as she liked to think of them – confronted with that dilapidation, compounded by the dubious catering offerings of a mad German woman who had just left off her ministrations to her out-of-control diarrhoea-ridden dog.

"I will bring my own sandwiches on the day", she said to herself. "Safe in Tupperware. And a mini flask of hot sweet tea."

HOME

He promptly shifted from slouched to alert position in his favourite armchair as he heard a short sharp ring on his front door bell, the scratching turn of a key in the lock and the call, "Coo-eee – it's only us" in an all too familiar voice.

Such an incursion into the quiet sedateness of his domestic life only a short time ago would have aroused in him feelings of resentment – even dread. But things had moved on and he found himself gently smiling as he folded over his newspaper and made to rise to his feet.

The Hurdley sisters, Molly and Dolly, had now become an, at first tolerated, but now almost welcome part of his everyday life.

Retirement had occasioned him to look for a home – his first real home-of-his-own, it must be said. His childhood he had spent either in short term foster care or more lengthily in a children's home. In his mid-teens he had found (or had it been found for him?) employment in the hospitality and catering industry. He was a trainee in a large city hotel – at first a bellboy in perkily tilted pillbox hat and a natty tight waistcoat with shining brass buttons, then a kitchen hand and soon a trainee waiter (silver service and all). The hotel was his home – a dormitory and 'facilities' to share, meals in a room adjoining the kitchen – all taken care of. Work mates came and went; privacy was at a premium, personal security hard won.

As he moved up the ladder, matters improved. As a senior waiter, he achieved his own room – lockable! Long hours, short holidays (when he did not know what to do with himself), the hotel was his world. A big step, then, to seek promotion elsewhere, but this he did with much stomach-churning anticipation, and he moved to a large country hotel as Assistant Junior Restaurant Manager – again, a residential post. And there he settled, adjusting to rural remoteness and peace and quiet. He hastily ran to Restaurant Manager and was head-hunted to an even grander establishment, with royal connections, where he moved into Hotel Management – by now with his own bedroom, sitting room and bathroom (a modest suite, you might say). But always food from the kitchens – sumptuous leftovers mostly, but he had learned how to cultivate the chef, deal skilfully with outrageous annoyance and temperament, so that he was always 'looked after'. "I always look after, Signor, is that not so?" Even meals to his quarters on a tray on his days off.

But he had never had a home – until retirement required him to look for a flat – he found the prospect of occupying an entire home too daunting. Thus his purchase of a lease on No.2 Mulberry Gardens.

The Hurdley sisters owned the large Edwardian building which they had split down the middle. Through the stone porch, an enormously heavy front door, into the grand tiled hall. To the right on the ground floor, the sisters' living accommodation, up the grand staircase to their bedroom (presumably – he was never privileged or presuming enough to confirm this), again on the right of the building. To the left, off the hall, was his front door leading to his flat – a large living room (a big bay window looking over the front garden and drive), a generous sized bedroom to the rear and small (it must be admitted) bathroom and kitchen. But it suited him. Above him there was another flat of similar dimensions, he assumed, access to this via an outside staircase to the side of the house. Whoever occupied this accommodation was exceedingly discreet; he never saw and rarely heard them.

Truth to tell, he, at first, was at a loss with his new found independence – dealing with gas and electricity meters, finding provisions for himself, operating alien appliances such as a washing machine, even a hoover, discovering access to a TV and learning to cook.

This encouraged a certain dependence on the kindnesses of the sisters and they happily responded. Hence their coming together, hence their familiarities, hence the ready access to his home with their own front door key. (This convenience was not reciprocated – he had ready access to their more palatial apartment, but only following a discreet knock on the door and an appropriate wait for the door to be unlatched form the inside.)

"Coo-eee – it's only us", Molly's voice. High pitched and somewhat tremulous. Dolly's was deeper, more purposeful. "We've got something for you, through the post."

He took a nervous gulp of air. He knew what was coming.

Not long previously the sisters had described – well, in truth, Dolly had described, she was the proactive one, the mover – what would be good for him.

"Companionship, my dear", affirmed Dolly. "That's what. Isn't that so, Molly?"

Molly blushed, flustered as ever. "Well, I … that is … well …"

"Quite right", boomed Dolly. "See here." And she waved before her a copy of the local paper, the Durnham Herald, folded in half. She plopped the paper in his lap. "There we are. Pages 8 and 9. Classified and Personal Ads. Look carefully."

Molly tried to be helpful. "It's outlined in red."

"Quite so. There. Right under your nose."

He peered forward to see, squinting for he was without his reading glasses. But Dolly was impatient. She whisked away the paper. She stood over him, a lofty, confident figure. She smelt of carbolic soap and starch.

"Personal Ads. Men Seeking Women. Women Seeking Men. Men Seeking …" She paused. A slight cough. "Er … Men. Needn't go on", she finished.

"No, indeed not", bridled Molly revealing just the slightest bit of backbone. She visibly blushed, her wite churls bobbing with some agitation.

Dolly had recovered. "Men Seeking Women. See?"

He looked up at her, his usually mournful eyes taking on the aspect of a rebuked dog – probably a Spaniel.

"Just the ticket. We'll set you up in no time."

"I suppose it's worth try." He was not averse to the idea, but understandably cautious. Life had so far offered him little opportunity to indulge in a developing relationship. There had been some fumbling encounters with female members of the hotel staff – well, several actually he thought, trying to be fair to himself – but never with a guest, he remembered ruefully – that, however tempting, would have been beyond the pale.

"Well worth a try", Dolly confirmed. "Now, Molly, you have your pad and pen."

"Yes, dear." Molly perched herself daintily on a chair next to the table. "Ready to go."

"Right." Dolly planted herself heavily down on the plump cushions of the settee, her navy-blue trousered legs unfemininely splayed. "Right. Now, let's see. We'll follow the wording of most of these adverts. Er … 'Good looking bloke, young, fit body, social animal, up for anything would like to meet young, fit bird not just friendship, definitely more. Must be into house music, 18 – 30 holidays. Durnham.' Well, I got most of that. Now, let's see. Ready Molls?"

"Yes, my dear."

"Right. Um. 'Good looking bloke. Young. Fit.' Not sure about that …"

"What about 'pleasantly featured'?" ventured Molly, a rare moment of excitement in the wafting of her ballpoint pen.

"I'd like to plump for 'handsome'. What do you think, Molls?"

"Oh … well … I …"

"Too strong, is it?" She stared forcibly at him. Their eyes met, hers peering and searching, his widening and not a little startled.

Her firm, aquiline nose wrinkled as her eyes narrowed in concentration.

"Yes … I think we'll get away with that. Put down 'handsome', Molls. I don't think we're violating Trades Description." And she barked a sharp laugh of self-satisfaction.

"So … Handsome. Now 'Fit'." Another pause for perusal. "Molls?"

"'Slender'?"

"Too close to 'skinny'." She eyed him candidly. "Not much meat on you, is there? But you're not scrawny. How about 'lithe'?"

"Oh, yes, 'lithe'. I like 'lithe'." Molly's curls bobbed frantically. Hie felt quickly crossed and uncrossed.

"Molly", warned Dolly. "Yes … 'lithe'."

Molly's pen went swiftly to the page.

"Now – 'up for anything'." Dolly harrumphed disapprovingly.

"Perhaps just 'seeking friendship'", offered Molly hesitantly.

"A bit namby-pamby", retorted Dolly. "I think he'd like more than just friendship. Hey?"

He felt suddenly he wasn't even here. His life was in their hands. He felt he should say something. But his moment passed.

"I think 'Romantic'. Yes, 'romantic'. Tasteful yet meaningful."

Molly almost hurrahed. "Ooh! I *love* 'romantic'. 'Lithe *and* romantic'." Her pen glided gleefully over the paper.

"'Young … young and fit'." Again the piercing stare. A meaningful pause. A deep breath of decision. "Put down, Molls, 'Seventy years old."

Molly almost rose to her feet. "But, Dolly …"

He squirmed awkwardly. He had only just retired. His change of sitting position was of itself a protest. Dolly rose to her own defence.

"Hear me out. Hear me out", she said. "I'm bending honesty here for strategy – tactics. We put down his real age, and … well … that might misfire. But put down 70, which he patently isn't," He and Molly both subsided with no little relief. "and imagine the pleased reaction of those who respond to this advert. Beyond expectation. Much *younger* than they thought! Off to a good start." A pause. "Write down '70 years old'."

Molly's pen met the paper with far less conviction. "If you say so", she murmured to herself. But Dolly had A1 hearing.

"I do", she insisted bluntly.

After that, the exercise became much more matter of fact and to the purpose. Dolly realised she'd gone too far, perhaps. Molly felt sulky and subdued.

He just wanted to get the whole wretched business over.

They listed his interests, which was *not* house music and holidays of dubious intent. It was agreed Molly would type out the final copy and take it to the Newspaper Offices on the next day when she intended to exchange her library books in the centre of town and he would reimburse her on her return when the Herald's reception clerk had confirmed the cost.

There was a distinctly subdued air as the sisters withdrew.

And now … "Coo-eee, it's only us."

"We've got something for you. Through the post."

Dolly waved a large brown envelope. "It's from the Herald", she trumpeted. "On to the next part of the exercise", she enthused.

"Isn't it thrilling", cooed Molly.

He felt slightly sick, the result of a simultaneous sinking feeling in the bowels, excited fluttering in the heart and in the brain some despair that it was all out of his hands anyway.

CHILDHOOD or A MOTHER'S DILEMMA

I love my boy, I really do
Flesh of flesh of mine
When dark clouds rob the skies of blue
I know my son will shine

For my only son please be assured
I tend his every need
Provide maternal bed and board
Pursue the mother's creed

His good is my every concern
At work or rest or play
From me life's lessons he can learn
On me depend alway

I love my son – I say again
As he sallies forth – my dear –
E'en though he may meet grief or pain
With me find refuge here

I l love my lad, hear me protest
And so do year on year
Strive to give him of the best
With smiles, never show a tear

Life ebbs and flows, he comes and goes
As independence beckons
"We must refrain and give him rein"
That's what his father reckons

Love him. Do I protest too much?

Pick clothes from where they fall

Have his meals timed for such and such
Always at his beck and call

Love him? I do. I do my best
Stock the larder full all year
Treat his friends like welcome guests
Whenever they appear

I try to love. Hear his dad say
"Show the lad the door
There's only so much you can do
After all – he's 34!"

I OWN A DOG

Well, that is the confessional manner in which I intended to begin this piece.

I own a dog – well, a bitch really. It amazes me how 'dog' – and, even more 'bitch' – are derogatory terms for fellow members of the human race whom we find reasons to despise. The animal kingdom should sue – what's wrong with being a dog, a bitch, a pig, a rat, a cow, a slug? For work to be a banker, an estate agent, a politician, a journalist etc. Supply your own.

Anyway, back to my intention to admit I own a dog and have done for six years since I inherited her and she me.

And I should be able to claim ownership on so many grounds. I am older – she was seven then and I was … well, as I say, I was older. I am bigger – not surprising, imagine owning a domestic pet bigger than me. I am male and she female. Now I know that in these PC days, we all at least have to appear to cling to the fallacy of sexual equality, and I am just coming round to accepting that. But in a relationship between a man and his dog, there surely can be no doubt of sexual superiority (just where this argument leaves a woman who claims to own a male dog, I leave to your own prejudices).

So I have age on my side, size and sex. And intelligence. I am of the human race, she is merely canine – her skull designed by a God who decided there was less room needed to accommodate a canine brain. I should be winning hands – or paws – down.

Then why does it not work out like that?

Just guess – who finds whom to be at whose behest? Who takes on the responsibilities whilst who takes the opportunity to exercise self-will at every opportunity? Who, the moment a door is left slightly ajar or the fraction of a second when a back is turned, heads for the hills and is not heard from again until the phone rings and a voice enquires, 'Have you lost a little ginger dog? Well, we've got her here (name and address supplied). Could you hurry? We're meant to be going out.'? Or on one occasion, 'We've got to go out. We'll shut her in our garage. We'll phone you later to collect her.' One woman was out walking her three dogs. On returning home, she found she had four. It is not my dog who has to set out in the car to retrieve me!

It is up to me to respond to her habits and needs. To decipher the meaning of a whine or a whimper. Is it a biscuit, or a strange sound she's heard, or someone passing by outside, or the desire for a stroke and a fondling of the ears, or the need to go out into the garden? If it is this last then I have to make sure I listen for the clear intimations that a prompt re-entry is required. This is a sharp, repeated, peremptory yap – far from the mock angry bark that is sighting of the postman, milkman or paperboy – or next door's cat – or the bitch across the way (another dog, you understand). No – this is a cool, collected passionless yap – an assertion of personal rights and superiority. The yap will cease when I answer the door. If I have been prompt enough she will sail past me without recognition. Am I deemed to have been tardy, she will grumble disconsolately as she goes. But, should she consider that her period of yapping has been prolonged beyond what can reasonably be accepted as tolerable, she will walk past me growling, will reach the hall door, turn and yap twice in admonishment, and then go out.

If this narrative is beginning to sound whining and self-pitying, then I admit – it is and is intended to be so.

She rules the roost. I trail behind – metaphorically speaking – trying to keep up.

A fussy eater, she will deign to partake regularly of a certain brand of dog food – that is, until I go to the Wholesaler and stock up with a good supply. Then she won't touch it, and I'm off again to the supermarket to buy a selection to tempt her on a trial-and-error basis.

I feel I'm getting it all wrong. Perhaps it's the fact that I inherited her that's the trouble. If I'd *owned* her (that word again!) from day one, then maybe I'd have stood a chance of gaining the upper hand. But one change of ownership (i.e. she moved in on me), she saw immediately how the land should like, took advantage of my general natural naivety and began as she intended to go on.

The die was cast.

I should have gone to Carol. She is the master – I hesitate, for obvious reasons to say 'the mistress' – of taking on other people's dogs. The Barbara Woodhouse of Penyffordd. But her charges are exorbitant, necessary to support her extravagant and wanton lifestyle. By day a meek and demure optometrist's operative – by night the raving Queen of Broughton high life, leading wild congas of lasciviousness and debauchery around the Tesco's carpark as the night shift at British Aerospace emerge eagerly for their midnight break. (But I promised never to mention this to anyone.)

But back to me.

Self-pityingly, I am reminded of the old Music Hall song – the large man dominated by a small woman.

"Isn't it a pity that the likes of her should put upon the likes of him."

The real pity being that 'the likes of him' is me, and the 'likes of her' is a tiny, cute and utterly irresistible bitch – in the true sense of the word.

I WRITE

I WRITE because there's a sheet of paper on the desk
I WRITE because that paper, between the feint grey-green
Parallel lines, has challenging spaces of clean fresh-snow white
You can read fresh snow fall : the purposeful
Footprints of the postmen and his cycle tracks; of the
Mother walking her pin-point small child to school.
The sweep of the neighbour's car tyres : the shamrock
Padding imprint of the dog studying a trail with
His bewildered ice-cold nose, and a disorganising
Slurry where he has spotted a bird and scrambled
Wetly and icily after his prey, in vain.

I WRITE because there is a pen in my right hand
(yes I do write with my right, use my right hand
To write : it seems right so to do!)

And the pen is capable, when applied, of glorious
Swirls of blue-black, curls and coils of
Blue-black, wide strokes, hyphenetic dashes
And long fine lines, firm long fat lines.
And it is capable, when directed, of organising
These shapes and swoops, the squiggles and angles, gaps and
Spaces, into elaborate codes that link the imagination,
The brain, the coordination of limb and digit, plastic
And nib, into meaning and even thence to voice and sound,
Energy, influence and power.
That is why I WRITE
It's as simple as that —
OR P'RAPS NOT!

WORDS

If only words were like those garden seeds
You buy in dainty paper packs
And carelessly scatter, water well
Then sit back and relax

Eventually they will spring forth
Like beans and peas in serried rows
A host of golden sentences
Of sparkling poetry, maybe prose

See – a clump of metaphors in swaying bloom
A clambering vine of apt analogies
A surge of prolepses struggling for room
And all around a swarm of glistening similes

Hyperbole flushingly pink and overgrown
Irony shading her face with rampant leaves
Scarlet rhetoric upright and aloof,
Silver shining brackets of parentheses

And circumlocution coiling coyly round the trunk
Of woody emphasis' powerful firm-barked hunk
The purple papery petals' prolific permutation
Could only spout from multi-stemmed alliteration

Whilst zeugma's duplicitous display of doubt faces
Confuse malapropism's misplaced lacy expression
As bold sarcasm, defiant, kicks o'er the traces
Silenced onomatopoeia sinks gracefully into grey depression

Loathe to end this dream of burgeoning
Literary growth, I am
But cold reality dawns
and I see it is a sham!

If only … ah, if only.
In truth, inspiration's at a low
Fine words won't come and thoughts refuse to flow
The consequence of this all too well we know

The glint of disappointment in the stark and withering stare
Of she whom we must all obey –
Our reverenced Lady Chair!
Note the respectful tone in which these words are said

The downcast eye, deferential nod of the head
When we present before
The blankest white A4
And in halting whisper say
'

Sorry, Madam Chairperson.
Couldn't think of owt to say'.

For we have sat upon the barren shore
Where nothing can be grown
Parched sand drying moisture's balm
Unyielding rock, impermeable stone
The circling birds of prey in glowering skies
Have heard their croaking and despondent cries
Above our dismal selves, bereft and lonely
Heard their fateful message,
'If only … ah, if only
If only … ah, if only.'

INAPPROPRIATE GIFTS

With one enormous, nostril reverberating grunt he snored himself awake He gazed blearily around the sunlit room and carefully focused his eyes to read the mantelpiece clock – ten past 10. She was almost one hour overdue. Waiting for her, he had dozed off and now felt quite irritated at this change of routine.

Almost immediately he heard the familiar rattle and scraping of the front door being unlocked and opened. He sighed and relaxed.

"S'alright, Mr B. it's only me", she cooed. "Bit late, I'm afraid. How are you this morning?"

He sensed her enter the room behind him, the oozing smell of her usual flower-mist perfume. Stiffness in his neck and shoulders forbade him from turning to acknowledge her, so she walked around into his line of vision. "I'll get a move on." She smiled at him – her face over made-up, her long silver earrings swinging, her unnaturally white and even teeth revealed. "Are you alright? It's Tuesday", she said, "so it's downstairs and a quick flick round the bathroom. I've brought that spray polish I'll need so will settle up before I go. Do you want a cup of tea now? Or perhaps later when I've done a bit. I'll start with the bathroom …" and she disappeared.

This is how it always was. She chattered aimlessly and pointlessly on – giving him little opportunity to respond. And, in truth, there was little he felt inspired to respond to – a long string of her life's minutiae, half formed thoughts, gossip, unorganised flashes of memory. Nothing consequential or inspiring – just tittle-tattle, superficial verging on the meaningless.

She reappeared. She had doffed her red quilted coat, disposed of her wicker shopping bag and donned bright pink rubber gloves.

"Sorry I'm so late. Bit of a hold up in the High Street. You remember the bookshop – been empty for ages – well, they're doing it up, scaffolding all over. Gonna be a betting shop, I'm told …" He was frowning. She encouraged him. "You know, opposite the chemist, Mr Solomon. I always go to him. He's been very good to me and the kids over the years, so helpful and friendly. I know Boot's is bigger and nearer the car park but they don't know you the same in Boots. Mr Solomon's a real gent. I suppose he'll be retiring soon. Such a shame.

Well, I was coming through the High Street and there was lots of noise and commotion, people running. And just ahead of me all the scaffolding came crashing down. I slammed on the brakes. I thought my end had come. Couldn't see for dust. What a mess! Cars buried under them metal pipes. We just sat there. All of us. Then the police directed us up that hill by the theatre – you know, Market Street? I could hear ambulances as we was moved on. I was quite shaken. Nearer to death than I've ever been. I'm all right now. I stopped on the way up the hill, near the church, got out and took deep breaths. It'll be on the local news later, I shouldn't wonder. Still, none of this is getting the bathroom done."

She disappeared.

He would have responded. He would have felt like scoffing at her. Nearer to death. You're nearer to death now than you were then. We only have one death and yours isn't for a while. Death is never ambiguous. It's unequivocal and definite and comes when it comes, no matter what might happen on a Tuesday morning. What would she make of that?

Later she disturbed his reading of the paper when she brought him a cup of tea.

"I'm ready for this", she said. "Strong enough to stand a spoon in. And lots of sugar – for me", she added, "not yours. I know you don't on medical grounds. You help keep my conscience free, having no biscuits either. An inch on the hips, isn't it? I suppose your diet's quite healthy really – no sugar."

She paused, unusually for her, to take a gulp of her tea. He took the opportunity. "Talking of which", he said. "There's a package on the hall table for you."

She lowered her cup. "I know what that will be." She disappeared. He heard her voice behind him, the rustle of a paper bag. "Thought so", she said. "More chocolates."

"Another present from a friend", he said. "I daren't eat them."

"Getting to be quite a regular thing." She reappeared before him. "Are you sure?"

"You're doing me a favour. Removing temptation."

"Well, in that case."

"Otherwise, as the Irish playwright said, the only way to remove temptation is to give in to it."

She put her head to one side and looked at him. "Er … yes", she offered. A pause. "Well … must get on", and she was gone.

She sang as she worked and clattered about in the kitchen. He tried to return to the newspaper but he realised that soon the hoover would start up and, as always, she would raise her voice to chatter over the noise.

He remembered the morning when he had a phone call from the Supervisor at Social Services to say that Gloria would not be in for a few days, at least. It took him a moment to realise who Gloria was. It was Mrs Beamish who came to clean for him. Thank God they had never got on to first names. She had on first meeting announced herself as Gloria Beamish. He had welcomed her as Mrs Beamish (they had shaken hands) and she called him Mr Brough though she would inevitably have been aware of his first name, Duncan. Over time she had familiarised his name to Mr B, and once or twice he had modified his address to Mrs B – a slight comfortable jest between them – Mr & Mrs B.

Her temporary replacement had been a squat, dark haired woman – business like and not a little officious. She announced herself as Jeanette and determinedly called him, without consideration, Duncan. He never felt easy with Jeanette, who attended him for over a week. She said little but what she did offer was usually instructive and intrusive – advice about his choice (Mrs Beamish's really – he felt offended on her behalf) – *her* choice of cleaning materials, even her quality of work.

One morning she advised, "Gloria will be back on Thursday. Family problems, she's had." She leaned towards him, a move intended to convey confidentiality but succeeding in appearing merely threatening. "It's her son", she hissed. "He's attempted suicide. He's all right, apparently, but it was touch and go at the time."

That sealed his disapproval of Jeanette. It was none of her business to relay to him Mrs Beamish's unfortunate circumstances. In fact, as soon as she'd gone, he found himself slowly going from room to room checking things. He found he didn't trust that woman.

Mrs Beamish had turned up on Thursday at the normal time. She appeared her normal self – perhaps a little tired around the eyes, not quite as breezy? It could have been his imagination.

He did have something to offer her : a happy coincidence? "It's a box of chocolates", he said. "A gift from a friend – but I daren't touch them. You'd be doing me a favour."

She took them. "As long as you're sure. It's *The Bill* on tonight. Me and John loves The Bill. A cup of coffee and a chocolate – or two – or three", she added, smiling.

"You're welcome", he said. That had been the first time he had handed her one of his inappropriate gifts.

After that it did become something of a habit, when he was making out his weekly shopping list for his daughter-in-law, Jenny, for him to add at the bottom the four letter C.H.O.X.

After all, he didn't have that many friends to call and leave him inappropriate gifts.

IT TURNED OUT WELL

It was while I was waiting with idle pen and blank sheet of paper for my muse to strike, pre-occupied as I was with matters of perpetuating pedestrian domesticity, that my muse did strike by pointing out the blinding obvious - that my passage to aptly tackling this week's topic was clearly indicated within the intricacies of those very domestic problems no matter now mundane and unpromising they appeared to be.

Let me explain.

Two problems have reared their heads or, more appropriately, crept gradually and slug like into the fabric of my unremarkable existence (there was a third, just as irksome, but that remains, to-date, unresolved; perhaps I'll write about that next time!)

Firstly, on 20th November 2009, I ordered in the presence of a charming, eager to please salesman (are there any other kind?) some furniture from a firm specialising in Mobility products. I paid a sizeable deposit and was promised delivery before Christmas. Can you guess where this is going?

January 25th 2010 I telephoned the firm to see where the furniture was. Delivery within two weeks, I was assured, but no explanations. Two weeks later, no furniture, I phoned again. Delivery in two weeks, I was assured. I asked to speak to a Manager. She was not available but, I was curtly told, would only tell me what I had just been told. I made a separate call to speak to the Customer Service Manager. She too was unavailable but would call me back immediately.

Two weeks later no furniture, no returned phone call. My concerns that the firm had gone out of business were allayed by sight of prominent advertising in the national press. So, I acted.

I contacted my Bank to claim back my deposit, paid, wisely with a credit card and, acting under the guidance of Trading Standards, I sent a recorded delivery letter to the firm, claiming they had defaulted on our contract and stating they were obliged to return my deposit within 10 working days.

Immediately, I had a phone call that my furniture was ready for delivery; but I insisted they deal with the letter. Yet another phone call. They would be in the district next Monday, 1st March, and would deliver. Said no, respond to the letter. Monday 1st March the delivery van appeared with furniture. I refused delivery. Within half an hour a call from Tim Hedgcock. So sorry, very unhappy with the way I'd been treated, unacceptable, would I accept delivery of furniture on Friday 5th March, no more to pay, just for cost of deposit? Apologies. Apologies.

Meanwhile, on 9th January 2010 a huge crack appeared across a large pane of double-glazed window (caused by the intense cold?). I phoned my insurance provider to make a claim. They have my House and Contents and Motor Insurance and have had for well over 10 years. I was told I had <u>no cover</u>. I was in touch with an insurance company who handled business for the provider I was dealing with. I had to get in touch with the provider and within two days was granted *temporary* cover by the insurance company. No explanation was offered, no outline of the implications of the significance of *temporary* cover, certainly no regret expressed or apology.

I thought it best to extricate myself from the whole sorry shambles – especially if I wanted peace of mind when taking my car out on the road – so I cancelled with them and moved to a firm recommended by my erstwhile teachers' trade union. Currently I am refusing to pay cancellation fees to the insurance provider that severely, I feel, let me down although they did honour the claim for the window.

And here is the pay-off.

Furniture at less than half price.

And my new insurances, with a reputable firm, costing me £400 less in annual premiums. (It really must pay to Go Compare the Meerkat dot.com.)

As this week's title so appropriately indicates,

It turned out well.

IT'S A BOY

(2005)

A Saturday morning like no other. Trussed up in my school uniform, freshly cleaned and pressed. A new white shirt already chafing at the neck and firmly tucked into my trousers' waistband. A tie knotted and re-knotted to my mother's satisfaction. Thick layers of black polish over the scuffs and scratches of my school shoes. Standing in our front hallway, upon pain of death if I spoil the effect. Eyes to the staircase at mother's excited call from above.

"We're ready."

To my right, my father as awkwardly dressed as I – new suit, shirt, tie, shoes. "None of that top hat nonsense", he had determined.

Mother appeared in pink frock and coat, large fuchsia concoction of straw, feathers, flowers and netting on her head, her beaming face outstripping the ruddy glow of her ensemble. And behind her, in a billowing descent of white cascade and froth, was my sister Alice. Her wedding day. The normally dull hallway – respectable brown carpet, woodwork and fawn, modest wallpaper – glowed brightly with the morning's light reflecting off the lacy white expanse of her crinoline and flowing veil. I looked at her and had to acknowledge that, in spite of the restraints and indignities of this day being heaped upon me, for a bride she looked a bit of all right.

Mum turned to Dad. "Well, Ronald?" she asked, her eyes watery and glistening.

Dad breathed deeply. "By 'eck", he said.

The front door opened briefly and he was gone.

"Mum?", pleaded Alice.

"It's all right, love. He's so proud of you. He's just gone out for a walk."

Fast forward a couple of years. It was the phone call we had been waiting for, from the hospital. I was glad. Now I could be released from my homework (a rare dispensation). My sister Alice had produced her first baby. "It's a boy. Seven pounds, two ounces", said Mum as she, Dad and I reached for our coats and set out for the hospital.

At the entrance to the room Alice was in, Mum instructed, "Ronald. You stay here with Andrew. I'll just go and check." She disappeared through the pale blue door. A pause and Clive, the new father, appeared. "It's a boy", he said, flushed and excited. "Come see, granddad."

We entered the room. Alice was sitting up in bed, a bundle in her arms, Mum perched on the bed beside her.

"Isn't he lovely", said Mum. He wasn't particularly. Bright red, matted black hair, his white face scrunched into the only frown of dissatisfaction in the room. All else was beaming smiles. Dad ushered me in front of him, his hands gripping my upper arms, his warm breath on my right ear.

"Look, Dad", breathed Alice. "Say hello to your grandson." Dad's hands tightened around my arms. "Colin Ronald Smithson", she beamed.

Momentarily Dad's grip tightened like a pair of vices, then release and a draught as the door behind me opened and closed.

Mum and Alice smiled at each other.

"He's so chuffed", said Mum.

"He's gone out for a walk."

Time passes. Colin Ronald has just had his seventh birthday. I am at home, a rare occurrence since I started working in London. But a very sad one. Mum has died.

She had developed an adverse dependency for Rennies – they were everywhere, kitchen cupboard, her bedside table, next to her armchair in the living room, the car glove compartment, a packet in each of her handbags. Dicey digestion, she had decided. Part of growing old, was her diagnosis. But she was wrong. A visit to an oncologist had confirmed the worst and in spite of an operation that was successful in removing part of her bowel, the cancer had prevailed and she had lost the fight.

Dad had remained stoical and taciturn, dealing correctly with all the formalities of the situation he now found himself in.

The church service and cremation had been as soothing and seamless as one could wish. Dad had welcomed Alice on his arm and behaved with a decorum that was not without awkwardness and tension. "He's bearing up well", observed Aunty Vi solicitously.

We returned to the house. Thirty people expected for a spread. Alice's friend, Zena, was seeing to things. She had a qualification in catering and food presentation. She turned to father. "A cup of tea, or something stronger, Mr Wrigley?"

Father looked at the large white tea pot with small green ivy leaves that she held, one hand on the handle, the other on the spout. Mother's best china tea service, her treat for their silver wedding, never intended for use but because she always wanted one for best. The cups and saucers, the milk jug, sugar basin and teapot had been used never – until now. The pot glistened and glinted as it shifted in Zena's grip.

Dad turned and left the room. I moved to follow but Alice lunged forward and seized my arm. Zena muttered, "I'm sorry".

Alice looked at us both. "He's just going out for a walk", she said.

. . . .

Colin has moved up to senior school. Same uniform as mine, all those years ago. I'm working back in the home town again.

It's January. One of those days of the clearest blue skies, small pristine white scudding clouds, and the brightest sunshine that is remarkable for its total lack of any warmth – the winter air is nostril-pinchingly, mouth-dryingly, eye-wateringly, ear-nippingly, bitterly, bitterly cold. I gaze out of the window, glad of the close proximity of the humming radiator to my office desk.

The phone rings. It's Alice. "I'm glad I caught you", she said. "It's Dad. He's been taken ill. He's at the Prince of Wales in A&E at the moment. Can you get there?"

The drive across town was uncomplicated. There was even a parking space near the hospital entrance. But nevertheless it was too late. I missed him by some ten minutes.

Alice met me in the corridor. "He's gone, I'm afraid." She looked very pale, her eyes wide and dismayed. "Apparently he collapsed in the park. They got him here pretty quickly but there was not much they could do. He didn't regain consciousness."

"In the park?" I asked.

"Yes."

She moved towards me and held both my hands in hers. She smiled softly in spite of herself. "He just went out for a walk", she said.

JOYCE MARSH'S BROTHER

Joyce Marsh always felt she had lived in her brother's shadow, even though he was younger than her, by two years – well, 22 months and ten days, to be exact.

She always remembered him as an imposing presence.

Her first memories were of a larger-than-life, plumply fleshed, constantly writhing baby, propped up on cushions on the floor, his back against their father's worn armchair. She had her duty, to play with him, occupy him (a new word to her at that time), look after him. And that had not proved too difficult for he was an easy-going creature, a quick smile, plump hands that would readily grasp and play with anything; content to sit where placed, she now reflected, no signs of a desire to stir to alternative positions or to attempt a move to other places.

So he had always been there. 'A big lad', was the common verdict : thick set, stocky legged, chubby arms, a round belly, moon faced, his eyes reduced to dark pin pricks with the weight of flesh around them. His generous mouth was always at the point of smiling but was past that point on the presentation of any edible item. He loved food – in copious amounts, it soon transpired.

There was not much money in the home. Dad was unskilled and therefore poorly paid. He would turn his hand to anything with, consequently, long hours for little return. Mum found jobs, mostly cleaning, sometimes child minding, anything to which she could trail along Joyce and her brother. Whilst they were below school age. After which fate dealt a kindly hand. She was taken on by the local fish monger cum greengrocer. She learned how to prepare fish – skin, bone, fillet, slice – and became quite expert. The fruit arrived fresh and early every morning. She was able to prepare it, help serve it and the fruit and veg and clean her slab by mid-afternoon, then could be off to collect the children from school. It all fitted in well.

But the true benefit was her access to foodstuffs that she could acquire cheaply. For Hedleigh – that was her burgeoning son's somewhat grandiose name – had to be kept supplied. His appetite was formidable. But with a diet predominantly of porridge, left-over and damaged vegetables and fish scraps in various guises, bread, margarine and sometimes jam, she could keep him and the family nourished and satisfied.

She would see her two waiting patiently in the playground as she appeared at the end of the school day. Hedleigh, dwarfing the slender but, oddly, no shorter figure of his attendant sister. Both would smile readily on sighting her. Joyce would run over, hand slipped into her mother's, her head leaning into the warm wool of the woman's coat. Hedleigh would wait to be approached, his smile broadening as his narrow eyes moved towards his mother's swinging handbag, anticipating the emergence of perhaps a couple of grapes, a spongy apple, a plum or two, even a scrubbed if tired looking carrot. Friday was a special day – mum's pay day. There might be some squares of chocolate or a few toffees, coupons allowing of course.

Time moved on but Joyce never lost her role of responsibility for her younger but bigger brother. He did give some cause for worry. He displayed such inertia, such lack of initiative, such placidity He was easy for her to handle, so affable, so cooperative. But he was always there. Just me and him, she mused wistfully, without bitterness, when she observed the other girls of her age in giggling, garrulous gaggles setting off down the pavements away from school.

There were lengthier times when she had sole responsibility, usually during the school holiday when Mum and Dad were at work. She had to find places to go. Hadleigh had a limited attention span. They exhausted the attractions of the park – not difficult, an area of scruffy turf with rusting, dilapidated children's swings, a broken roundabout and a leaning climbing frame (not designed for Hedleigh's bulk), nor was he interested at all in clambering upwards and hanging upside down by the crooks of his knees. Joyce smiles now at the comic possibilities of these highly unlikely manoeuvres all those years ago.

Once a year around Easter time came a fair to the town. The two siblings were forbidden. "There's not very nice men there", their mother would warn opaquely, perhaps making the prospect of a visit there even more enticing.

So they went.

They couldn't afford to go on anything but enjoyed the experience of wandering between the rides, the gaudy, brash but tatty and rundown amusements, the ear-splitting clatter of the rides and the tinny amplified music, the loud raucous shouting and joshing of the hawkers, the sickening but alluring stench of frying onions, boiling sugar and uber-sweet candyfloss. Hadleigh would just stand and stare, having to be hauled away by his impatient carer.

On the periphery of the site there were various even more shambolic and less prominent stalls. One of them was a small stage in front of a shabby marquee which displayed a large cloth awning painted with gothic script in white and gold, 'M.W. Freak Show' below which were luridly technicoloured depictions of the bearded lady, the man with three eyes, a boy with no limbs, a sheep with two heads. Joyce looked on with wide-eyed apprehension. But Hadleigh had spotted a black painted board propped up almost carelessly in front of the stage. Emblazoned upon it was the invitation to take part in an eating competition. The prize – free goes on the fair ground rides (it didn't say how many goes nor for how many people). Joyce found herself in a very unusual situation – suddenly and swiftly Hedleigh had gone from her side. She just caught sight of a flapping of canvas at the side of the stage as he disappeared into the marquee.

She followed and found him in the dark gloom, the smell of Brut heavy and something rotting, her brother talking with extraordinary animation for him to an elderly olive-skinned woman. She would have been attired as a traditional fairground gypsy but for a rather splendid fur coat embracing her hunched shoulders.

Hadleigh turned to his sister, face flushed, voice unsteady with excitement. "It's jam sandwiches", he gasped. "All you can eat."

The old woman looked sternly at Joyce. She was obviously trying to make sense of the situation.

"I'm his sister", said Joyce, trying to appear confident and in control.

The old woman spoke in an unfriendly way. Almost with a hiss. "He wants to compete. How old is he?"

"I'm old enough", blurted out Hadleigh. And with his bulk in that stale-aired gloom, he might have been.

"It costs threepence", continued the woman.

"Well, we haven't got that", Joyce spoke in emphatic conclusion.

The woman looked from girl to boy, then back to girl, then focussed on the boy, her sly eyes widening. She saw her opportunity. She was seeking to entertain, after all, attract the punters and their money. Her freaks were not doing so well at present. The three eyed man had another hangover – the third this week; and the bearded lady had had to go home to his wife who was in troublesome labour. And suddenly she had presented to her the possibility of a fat boy who could eat anything and everything and would take on all comers in competition. Admission six pence. She looked at the moon face, the glowing cheeks, the broad smile, the wobbly belly … it was worth a chance.

"Come back this evening", she said curtly. "Let's see how much he can put away." She saw the girl hesitate. "I won't charge you", she added. "Not kids, I won't", as if needing to excuse her generosity even to herself.

And that was how it all started. Hadleigh was a great success that evening. Effortlessly putting away the unappealing dry white bread and meagrely smeared red jam sandwiches. No competitor could come near him. He gobbled and gulped and gurned, grinning at his audience, sunk eyes glinting, bulging cheeks flushing red. He wore a bright blue and white checked cotton shirt and a large white collar with a red and gold spangled kipper tie. The crowd roused him on. He leaped around the stage applauding himself with his enormous fleshy hands.

Joyce stayed in the marquee. She had already lied to her parents to get Hadleigh out in the evening – a walk in the park, she had said. Her parents, worn down after a hard day's work, had swallowed it – almost as readily as Hadleigh did all those piles of jam sandwiches. She could not watch his performance; afraid it would be more disgusting than she could bear. But Hadleigh eventually blundered backstage, the jam and crumbs clinging to the sphere of his lower face and chin, giving a gloss to his child-like demeanour. "Look", he spluttered, holding out his upturned school cap full of damp and glistening copper coins. "They threw us money. There's more. Mother Whitcombe's got more."

Then suddenly he stopped, subsided, head against one of the posts supporting the marquee, paused and gave an enormous belch. "I feel better for that", he apologised. "But let's get home. I need the lav."

And that was, as Joyce remembered, how it had all started.

Mother Whitcombe had come into their lives and Hadleigh had entered hers; gradually Mum and Dad were impressed by her fur coat, her constantly updated expensive coiffure and her conviction that Hadleigh had a future with her.

And, as so it proved. He worked with her on her sideshows, his speciality being the Fat Man Who Could Eat Everything. Once on the circuit he learned as an insider of the real possibilities of entering competitions and the professionals who prospered from them. He joined their ranks and travelled firstly all over the country and then abroad. The family got cards and phone calls from all over, including

America, Russia and Europe. Burgers, Hot Dogs, Pies, Eggs, Pizzas – but nothing sugary, that was dangerous, so he was warned after coming second in a cupcake consuming competition in Dallas. Sugar was poison.

Once again, this year he would be coming home for Xmas with her. Mum and Dad have long gone. She is now widowed, and her children have moved away. He, a solitary figure, will arrive in this year's smart car. Now, physically, a shadow of his former self. His lifestyle some years ago had caught up with him. Arthritis of the jaw, the threat of tissue damage during the stretching of the walls of his stomach. A far less robust figure he now presents, cautious in movement, his face gaunt, his frame much slimmed. And food? No longer the smile and the eyes lighting up. He eats what he needs, changing from what he can eat. For Christmas dinner she will do boiled fish in a bland white sauce with boiled potatoes and boiled veg and almost as a jam pudding will be crustless white bread in warm milk with a hint of cheap red jam.

JULIAN

The sun was hot – the sky high and wide and blue – full, fluffy cream-foam clouds moved slowly across it. To the left the towering white of the Kentish cliffs and to the right the glistening wrinkles of the warm summer-tamed sea and straight ahead, stretching forever into the ebb and flow of the intense heat haze, the stippled freckled browns of the empty pebbled beach – empty but for a single figure in the distance, a figure made uncertain by the corrugating waves of the skirling air – a dark figure coming and going – the ghost of a boy, the shadow of a man. She could not make up her mind.

The phone call had come on the Wednesday morning, very early.

"Julian has disappeared."

It was her mother sounding tired and anxious. The urgency of the call was underlined by its early morning timing.

Felicity herself was barely awake. "Hi, Mum. What do you mean?"

"He's vanished. We've not heard from him for ages. His phone is down and I can't get any sense from his friends in Hall."

Felicity's brain was clicking awake by degrees. Her brother Julian at the end of his first year at University. She remembered her own end of first year. Party after party, each one overlapping into the next. She saw Julian curled up on somebody's sofa, dead to the world, before being woken up for the next shindig.

Again the strained voice. "Felicity – it's not like him. No news for so long. And your Dad's very worried. He wants to get up and go to Canterbury, but that's totally out of the question – so soon after his operation."

Felicity felt her options fall away. She knew what she would have to do. "Felicity – please."

"You want me to go to Canterbury."

"You know I wouldn't ask normally, only – I can't leave your father. And you're only in Ashford."

Felicity tried to stifle a sigh of exasperation but was only partially successful. A pause. "OK, Mum. I can get away today." (She was a freelance journalist so most of her time was her own.) "I'll give you a ring when I've found him."

"Oh, Felicity." Her mother's attempts at thanks were stifled by sobs. Not like her, thought Felicity. The whole family was acting out of character. Dad ill in bed, Mum in tears and Julian out of his mind, no doubt, on the floor of some student digs somewhere – a girl's room, if he's had any luck, she conjectured ruefully.

She reached Canterbury after stopping for breakfast en-route. She found his Hall of Residence quite easily, part of the prominent University campus on the hillside above the city.

The place was buzzing with end of term chaotic activity – students and harassed parents scurrying everywhere with suitcases, boxes and trunks. She made her way up to his room. It was locked. She stopped a burly, red faced youth in his tracks. He put down his suitcase and grinned affably.

"I'm looking for Julian Richards", she said, indicating with an awkward hand movement the brightly coloured door marked 79.

"Julian? He's already gone."

He reacted to the all too obvious look of disappointment on her face. "Tough luck." His friendly grin broadened. "Tough luck on one hand", he added, "but good luck on the other. Here I am. The name's George – George Ralph. And once I've dumped this" (he nudged the battered suitcase with his trainered foot), "I'm free for the rest of the day." His thick eyebrows arched questioningly and he leant his head to one side. Felicity couldn't help be amused but she forced a frown and hissed sternly, "I'm his sister'.

The boy straightened up. "Now that's my tough luck." He reacted to her air of no-nonsense. "Try down the corridor, Number 70. That's Mike's room. He'll know more than me."

"Thanks." She smiled gratefully and turned away.

A loud knock on Door 70. She felt relieved. There was movement within and a male voice, "Hang on".

The door partially opened and a tousled head appeared at knee height. Beneath a mop of thick dark hair, a pair of bright blue eyes – decidedly blearily – peered up at her. "Yeah?"

"I'm looking for Julian Richards. I'm his sister." She felt that detail would prevent any further misunderstandings.

"Ah", came the knowing reply. "Hang on." The door closed and after a slight pause was fully opened. "Sorry about that. You caught me out." He was bare chested and hastily doing up the waistband and flies of his jeans. "Come in."

The room was in a state of disarray. Boxes. Books. Bedding. Cases. Clothes. The window was open so it smelt quite fresh.

She perched on the end of the bed as Mike – for it was he – gave her the story.

Julian had opted out. He had abandoned his course of lectures before Easter, had officially withdrawn from the university and had – in Mike's words – 'bummed around', staying here and there, sleeping on friends' floors, using the Hall's facilities surreptitiously, working at a couple of part-time jobs – lunch time barman at the 'Dog and Thistle', evening waitering at the local Italian. He spent much of his day sneaking into lectures in the Arts Faculty – History of Art and English. He had tried to change courses, from Economics, but couldn't swing it. Wrong A-levels. He was in the Uni's Theatre Group, run by the Students' Union. He still had his membership. But – and this was Mike's exact words, "He's not a happy bunny. He's changed. Very intense and very touchy. Moods – up and down. No middle way. Either on a high or way down."

His face brightened and he swiftly stood up. "I know who you need to talk to. Hang on."

He reached for a denim jacket draped over the open wardrobe door and plunged into an inside pocket for his phone. After swift movements of his thumb on its face, he raised it to his ear.

"Hang on", he said to her. There was no reply. His frown deepened. "Oh sh …" He glanced at her. "Sorry – it's just that …" His face cleared. "Oh, thank God you're there. It's Mike. Look, I've got Julian's sister here. She's looking for him. Would you? That'd be great. I'll tell her. See you."

He lowered the phone.

"That's Gracie. She is Julian's most recent. Lucky she's still around. She's coming over. She's the one you really need to talk to. She won't be long." He looked awkwardly around the room. "I would offer you a coffee but I haven't got any, the milk's gone off and I've packed the kettle. But I have got this." He reached beneath the chair's cushion and produced a torn roll of Polo mints. "Help yourself." He tossed them to her.

It didn't take long for Gracie to arrive. A tall, slim girl of stunning beauty. Long straight fair hair, wide grey eyes, high cheek bones, full lips. Gracie! She moved with grace, almost gliding in a flowing summer dress and flat slippers. She sat next to Felicity on the bed. Mike obviously sensed the oncoming intimacy of close women's talk. He moved to the door, an electric toaster in his hand. "Won't be a sec", he said. "I've got to return this to ... to someone." He smiled gently and was gone, firmly closing the door behind him.

Grace spoke in quiet, measured tones and Felicity gained a clear picture of Julian's recent months.

He was very unhappy with his University life. More and more disillusioned. More and more resentful. He had put up with two terms of Politics and Economics, but his heart wasn't in it. All his friends came from his social connections – the Drama Club, Film Society and the local Art College. His official studies became an intrusion on what he really wanted to do.

"And he couldn't do anything bout it. We wanted him to go home and tell his Mum and Dad. Take time off. Re-sit A-levels. Apply for another course but ... well ..." She obviously felt very discomfited. "I don't know ... Can I be frank? You won't be offended. It's just that things are not good for him now. We're very worried." Felicity held the girl's gaze. She was almost crying. She continued. "I don't know if I ought to."

Felicity tried to reassure her. "You can't stop there. We both want what's best for Julian."

The girl smiled gently. "Oh, Julian. We don't call him that. It's Jules." She looked away, breathed deeply and took the plunge. "It's all tied up with James", she said.

She must have heard Felicity's sharp intake of breath. James. This was the last thing she expected, here in the disorganisation of the featureless University cell, here on the bright summer morning, here from this cool and deliberate girl.

"James." She involuntarily repeated the name.

"I'm sorry." The girl was almost whispering as she turned back to her.

"He's told you about James", Felicity said quietly.

"At times he spoke about little else."

It was early afternoon that Felicity found herself hurtling along the motorway heading for the coast, following the signs for the port of Dover. As the girl had revealed confidences with Jules, all had fallen into place for Felicity.

James had died at the age of 15, buried under a cliff fall a short distance east of Dover. St Margaret's at Cliffe. He was her brother, younger by five years and Julian's older by five years. The accident had happened in May and Julian was due to start at James's senior school in the September. This was what was planned and this was what happened. She was 20, away at University and somewhat removed from the true effects of the tragedy at home. Julian was soon to be 11 and lived closely with the consequences, the complication for him being parental attempts to protect him in the aftermath, partly by leaving an awful lot unsaid.

Life went on. James had gone but was still omnipresent – his bike in the garage (Julian would grow into it), his pictures on the stairs, his coat and scarf in the hall for so long afterwards, his favourite bean bag in the sitting room, his rugby boots in the utility room on the folded sheet of yellowing newspaper, his shower gel in the downstairs cloakroom, and in the bedroom he shared with Julian – everyday. The neatly made single bed, never disturbed; its red Arsenal crested duvet cover; his certificates for achievement – rugby, judo, swimming, academic studies – maths, debating – on the striped wallpaper; his rugby ball, sports bag (Julian will be able to use these), his dressing gown – red again – on the back of the door, his clock radio, his Arsenal rug, posters, clothes in the wardrobe, hairbrush, comb and gel on the chest of drawers, faded, worn teddy bear in Arsenal scarf on the pillow. Julian shared all this – together with the unspoken expectations that James would now never aspire to. James showed promise that still had to be fulfilled. And Jules was there to do it – in his own eyes as much as in any others. Good exam results (equally in Maths and Science), good sporting prowess, good all round.

"So you are James Richard's little brother? Let's see if you're as good as him."

And Julian was – in any way he could be. He disappointed nobody. And nobody directly said a word. Julian obliged, without question. Until …

Until he couldn't take any more, concluded Felicity, as she swung her car into the car park at the top of Dover's cliffs. She approached the cliff walk steps that descended steeply to the beach and held firmly to the comfortably sturdy handrail. Luckily she wore sensible shoes for driving; these stood her in good stead now.

Finally she reached sea level, the crunching pebbles of the beach. And away to her left, the distant undulating figure of … it had to be Julian, back to the cliffs, facing the incoming waves. It was difficult to tell. Was he stepping towards them?

She lunged forward, stumbling on the yielding, uneven surface of the stones, the sun behind throwing a grotesque shadow ahead of her.

She called his name, but her voice seemed lost in the vast emptiness of the air.

Eventually, aware of an approaching person, he stopped and turned towards he. She kept on running.

"Julian", she gasped. She was breathless. "Jules. It *is* you."

He squinted his eyes, behind his dark framed spectacles, into the sun. "Good God, Flea." He waited until she was quite close, grinned and lapsed into an unerringly accurate impression of Humphrey Bogart. "Of all the beaches, in all the world … what the hell are you doing here?"

Panting, she looked first at him and then the encroaching waves. "Julian … you weren't …"

He laughed scoffingly at her, then down at the water, shifting pebbles, his scruffy trainers.

"What, me? Don't be so bleeding ridiculous! On such a lovely day as this?"

"It's just that …"

She stared intently at him. So tired. His face gaunt and drawn. He'd lost weight. He looked grubby and unkempt. His glasses were thick with dust. He needed a shave. His hair, no longer close-cropped, hung in thick auburn waves over his forehead and his ears, covering the nape of his neck. It framed his face, making it appear unnaturally pale, slender and delicate. His eyes, looking directly into hers, were big, dark and wary.

"Are you all right?" she asked. It sounded lame.

"That's a big ask", he retorted. "Define your terms – 'all right'."

"Don't try and be clever. We've all been worried sick."

"I'm not going to …" He glanced meaningfully at the sea. "You stupid bat."

"I know. I'm sorry." She wanted to hug him, throw her arms around him, but something, perhaps the fact that he towered over her, prevented her. "I know. I've spoken to Mike and to Gracie. I think I'm beginning to know. It's all about James, isn't it?"

He looked steadily at her, very knowingly. "No. It's not about James. It really isn't. Now it's about me. It has to be about me. I'm moving on, Flea. It's time I moved on. At last I've got my own future planned. And it doesn't involve immersion in the old briny." He smiled at her but his eyes were still so sad. "I've come her to say 'goodbye' to Jamie. So long and farewell. And …" He stepped forward and put his arm around her shoulders. "And, as you insist on interfering, big sister, you can help me ... tell Mum and Dad I'm going to Drama School. It's all arranged – and they don't do Maths and Economics there."

She put her arm around his waist and rested her head against him. The sun went behind a cloud. In the sudden cool glare, they shivered.

"That's what big sisters are for. I'll give you a lift", she said.

JUST NOT FAIR

It's just not fair! she said
That I've got ginger hair! she said
And do not say it's red
It's not
But a sheer and awful carrot
Like the plumage of a parrot
And if matters could be worse
Than confessing woes in verse
My hair is frizzy too
A busy, fizzing, fuzzy frizz –
Which I iron out in vain.

For the slightest hint of rain
Will respring it back again
To tight spirally
Freaky fiery
Copper wirey
Twisted fizzy busy frigging fizz.

And I've freckles and pale skin
When the sun is out, I'm in
Whilst my friends are basking sharks
I am skulking in the dark
Though jeans and cardigan would work, a
Better bet would be a burkha
And I'll cover the whole shambles
White skin, freckles, ginger brambles
Might as well vanish in thin air
Not that anyone would care
It just isn't, isn't fair!
It just REALLY isn't fair!

In a fit of petulance and rage
Hurls down her magazine
Which opens at a page

Where brown bloodshot eyes appeal
Flakes of scaley skin revealed
Rotten teeth, a sparse and scrubland patch
Where there ought to be a thatch
Of glistening black and richly oiled
Luxuriant fronds of blackly coiled FRIZZ

As she moves to go away
One well pedicured foot is placed
Firm and squarely on the face
Of the dying leper girl
Blood red scarlet painted nails
But you should hear the wails
That's a hideous shade of red
Oh, I wish that I were dead!
Then the foot in tantrum twists
Tears the OXFAM page to bits
And just flaky scraps lay there
In hot richly perfumed air
Now – that really isn't fair!

LAST REQUEST

Sheila heard her mother put the phone down in the hall. "Who was that on the phone, Mum?" she called.

Her mother entered the room looking not a little flustered and rather too flushed. "That was Auntie Bessie." Her voice was humourless and emphatic.

"Is she OK?"

"Oh, she's fine," came the knowing reply.

"But you're not", enjoined her daughter, guessing what was coming.

"No – can't say I am. Guess what. She's come up with another last request."

"Oh, for heaven's sake. How many last requests can one woman have?"

It was all the fault of the British Legion. Auntie Bessie had been part of that stalwart association for many years – rattling collection tins and carrying banners at Remembrance Day ceremonies – ever since her uncle had been killed in action. A ready social life had been provided for her in her widowhood and all was well until she went on a Wellbeing Course over a long weekend at a large hotel in Llandudno (out of season, of course). There she experienced Yoga, various craft workshops, self-improvement and discussion workshops even healthy mind and cooking demonstrations – and, so it turned out above all, a lecture entitled *Worldly Confidences in Later Years* by a lecturer in Psychology from Bangor University. He had introduced, to Bessie at least, the concept of a Bucket List.

Bessie beamed happily on her return home. "A bucket list", she announced, "is something you make out before you kick it – the bucket, that is."

She was a small woman, sturdy, self-possessed, perfectly capable, living independently in her own home, confident and assured – a long way from any bucket, one would suppose.

But a Bucket List she would make and each item she would announce to the family and totally expect action thereupon.

There has been her last visit to the seaside – Blackpool – a final chance to go to the top of the Tower and witness the splendid view. The outing had frankly tired her (no-one knew how many years she had in excess of 90) and she fully omitted to take into account her fear of heights. At the top of the Tower she refused to leave the confines of the lift and in a distressed state had to be despatched immediately down to *terra firma* where she took refuge in a nearby café being plied with hot, very sweet tea and a supply of Gypsy Cream biscuits until her family party rejoined her. Then straight home.

She had afterwards set her heart on a last Messiah at the Phil in Liverpool. The journey there in her great nephew's white van had been uneventful but she found the concert over-long and her seat unkind to her aching back, arthritic elbows and cracking knees and she demanded to be withdrawn, much to the chagrin of many other audience members and the conductor himself who looked imperiously and disdainfully down on her long before the Hallelujah Chorus which, she complained on the way home, was the only bit she really wanted to hear and why hadn't they played it earlier?

Her last had been another disaster – totally predictably – as had her determination to take a final stab at Zumba classes and to take up Archery – indeed, after her efforts Health and Safety moved in and the activity at the local Community Centre was closed down.

"So – what is it this time?" asked Sheila.

"She wants to meet Wayne Silver."

"Who?"

"Wayne Silver – you know, the singer and dancer, was a judge on 'Strictly' and was 'I'm a Celebrity' in the jungle. Well, he is appearing at the Empire Theatre in Liverpool. The British Legion on her behalf got in touch with the theatre and apparently it's all arranged. Sounds like a publicity stunt to me. She's to meet him at the theatre a couple of weeks before the show opens for a meeting that will be covered by the local press – the Echo, no less – and – here's the best bit – we are to go with her."

"No way", interrupted Sheila.

"Oh yes way", returned her mother. "It's all arranged. Our names are on the invite. And if I'm going, so are you."

"But Mum …"

"But Mum nothing. We are going."

And it was all arranged. A taxi into Liverpool and back. An afternoon meeting with the great man, public interview, spend time with the national celebrity. It was all arranged.

Sheila came that day. Crammed in the back seat of a piddling local taxi with her mother and Auntie Bessie's best friend, Mavis

Beardsmoor. Auntie Bessie sat grumbling in the front – anywhere else in the car, she claimed, would make her car sick. They were deposited at the theatre, ushered with little ceremony into the grand foyer and thence into a side room where they sat for a short while in folding bright canvas chairs surrounded by boxes of confectionery, crisps, chocolate bars, crates of coke bottles and lemonade – it was obviously a store room, the only noise being the persistent humming of three large, American-style, maroon and chrome freezers.

"It'll be worth it", confirmed Auntie Bessie with invincible stoicism, "if it means we can meet him."

Eventually the door was flung open and they were allowed out. Auntie Bessie was finally presented in front of a large poster for Wayne Silver's new touring show '50 Shades of Adonis'. The rest of the family was moved to one side, from where Sheila could see all that happened.

The arc lights bleaching all colour out of Aunty Bessie's pastel dress and jacket and her straw hat : the jostling members of the press – all two of them; and the photographer, an ancient, white-haired wheezing man with a large, old fashioned camera and an assisting youth, spotty face, lank hair and enormous ears who looked as if he'd sneaked out of school for the day.

Then a commotion outside, the doors flung wide and in swept the man himself. Taller than Sheila had anticipated – and older. His narrow-lined face caked with orange make-up, black eye liner sinking his eyes into their sockets, full lips unnaturally red and two rows of technically enhanced enormous white teeth, positively glowing almost radioactively. He wore a turquoise satin shirt which clung unflatteringly to his gaunt upper torso and low-slung tight trousers in embroidered denim. Cuban-heeled boots, red leather, were what gave him his unexpected height, Sheila observed. On these he tottered.

He posed dramatically, gesticulated wildly and called for 'Nathan'. "Nathan, darling. Where are you?" Sheila could see vivid streaks of lipstick besmirching his teeth.

Nathan appeared, as tall as Mr Silver, equally as skinny but with a thatch of virulent black hair and glass frames with sequins. He had a floral smock-like blouse in puce and tight jeans, orangey-yellow canvas shoes with winkle-picker toes.

Mr Silver leaned towards him and hissed – "Who's the old girl?"

From nowhere, in smart tuxedo, a mustachio-ed, portly gentleman appeared, presumably the Theatre Manager.

"Mr Silver. Mr Silver. It's our pleasure. Our pleasure entirely, sir."
He indicated Aunt Bessie and the gigantic poster.

Wayne Silver persisted in a further hissed aside to his assistant.
"Come on Let's get this over with."

Instantly his scowl vanished and his teeth beamed in insincerity as
he turned his full attention to the Manager.

"Sorry, Gerry Darling. Lovely to see you as ever. And this …" He
paused dramatically and threw back his head, hands aloft, as if
discovering a beautiful flower for the first time. "And this must be …"
He leant towards the ever-attentive Nathan and hissed, "What is her
bloody name?"

"Bessie", hissed Nathan back. "Bessie Something or other."

The red lips parted. The teeth flashed. "Bessie. Bessie, darling. My
greatest fan."

Without further ado, he placed himself beneath the poster for his
show. "Ready for my close-up", he quipped in a shrill, exalted voice.

The photographer raised his camera. The spotty youth gaped
uselessly.

A frozen pause. Bessie wide-eyed, mouth agape.

Then, "Wait. Wait. Oh my God" from Mr Silver. He flapped his
hands, a kind of effeminate panic. "Nathan. Nathan. What have you
forgotten? What, my treasure?"

Nathan stared aghast. A long pause.

"The flowers, my little dove. The flowers."

From somewhere – Sheila didn't see where – was produced an
enormous bouquet of flowers – every colour under the sun. Passed to
Nathan, this was soon placed into Mr Silver's outstretched hands.
Sheila noted the bright orange nail varnish. 'To match his face', she
thought viciously.

"These", Mr Silver said surveying Auntie Bessie's diminutive figure
"are for you". And he dumped them into her arms, swamping her in
trembling blooms.

He turned towards the camera, posed expertly – all teeth and smiles.
The camera clicked – and clicked again – and clicked again.

"Thank you, darling", shrieked the great star and suddenly he and
Nathan and the reporter were gone. The large glass doors swing
forwards, the photographer plumped his heavy camera in the grasp of
this pimpled youth and the manager discretely withdrew.

Mother firmly said, "Let's get back to the taxi."

It was two days later when Mother returned from a further visit to Auntie Bessie's. She took a pile of copies of the Echo. On page 3, the photograph of Wayne Silver beneath the poster of his new show at the Empire, the word 'Adonis' clearly visible. And alongside him an enormous bunch of flowers amongst which, if you looked carefully, could be seen the profile of a stunned and amazed elderly lady – barely visible.

"Well?" asked Sheila, as her mother entered the room.

"She's OK. Loved it. That huge bunch of flowers. No vase big enough. She's plonked them in a bucket on the sideboard."

"And Mr Wayne Silver?"

"Oh, she loves him. Such a very, very nice man, she says. So very nice." There was an awkward pause. "And guess what…"

Sheila stiffened in her …

"She's thought of another last request."

But Sheila was up, out into the hall, grabbing her handbag from a low stair, her coat from the hat stand and went through the front door with a speed that would have done credit to the great star himself. Mr Wayne Silver, such a very, very nice man?

A LAUDATION TO BETTY, GILLY AND INGE

It was a happy accident
(Though some may say quite silly)
That 80th birthdays should coincide
For Inge, Betty and Gilly

And birthday wishes did abound
On that I will not linger
Taroo-la-lay Oh frumptious day
For Betty, Gilly and Inge

240 candles they were lit
Balloons, streamers and confetti
To celebrate the natal days
Of Gilly, Inge and Betty

At which of these three Wordsmithesses
Will excellence point the finger?
Which will be our 'poetess laureate'?
Will it be Gilly, Betty or Inge?

For one has tales of swimming far
After plunging off the jetty
The waterlogged struggles, a fight for life
That was Gilly, not Inge nor Betty

And one breathes poems Wordsworthian
With the beauty of a lieder singer
Of flowers and trees of birds and bees
Not Betty nor Gilly – but Inge

Then one has humour, wry and keen
With quips we'll never forget
A sardonic look at life's vagaries

Not Gilly, nor Inge, - but Bet!

Which has the Wayward Factor X?
Is it Inge, Gilly or Betty?
It takes a braver man than me to decide
For I'm too much a wetty!

Tis insidious to choose 'A Best'
Let joy reign unalloyed!
Let's celebrate, we've got all three
Inge, Betty – and Gilly Boyd.

LEFT SHOE

Our Albert was off to Secondary school
And we knew there would be trouble
He's the untidiest beggar in the world
His bedroom is a bomb site plus rubble

In Primary school he could be contained
They only had one little shelf
And on that went all their daily needs
He could manage that, just, himself

Senior school's a different kettle of fish
You need not one bag but three
A bag to hold books, a hold-all for lunch
And a duffel for games and P.E.

On the first day of term Albert swaggered away
He'd insisted he'd go on his own
'I'll be all right. You see if I'm not"
Said Mum "We'll see – when he gets home"

Mum had made Albert's favourite tea
And exactly at quarter past four
She heard a noise at the garden gate
Then Albert burst in through the door

His Mum looked down at Albert's feet
It was just as she had feared
"I know it looks odd" our Albert said
"But my left shoe just disappeared

"To catch the school bus dead on time
This trainer I had to borrow
But the P.E. teacher, Mr Pugh,
'll help me look for my shoe tomorrow"

His mother took his duffel bag
And said "I'll wash your kit"
She loosened the cord and looked inside
And Dad said "There's not much of it

"There should be shorts and a tracksuit top
Rugby shirt and a gym vest too
Now you've only got one such
When this morning there was two"

And so it went on day after day
And no left shoe appears
And what came home in the duffel bag
Could keep Oxfam supplied for years

Next day Mum cried out "What has happened now?"
Albert limped badly up the path
She ran out full of doubt and fear
Then stopped and began to laugh

"A teacher lent me another left shoe
It's such a prat I feel
It was Madame du Pont who teaches French
It's bright red with a four-inch heel"

Next day Dad said "I can feel a draught
Albert! Come in and shut the door"
But Albert's left foot clad in running spikes
Had nailed him to the parquet floor

The fourth day's shoe was bright yellow and red
With bells a tinkling feature
The toe curled up where a note was pinned
'On loan from the Drama Teacher'

The duffel bag was like a lucky dip
Yielded contents without warning
Mum washed and pressed all unfailingly
To return them clean in the morning

Mud caked rugby shirts for the 1st XV
Navy shorts and sweaty socks
Speedo trunks and blood-stained vests
And a well-used cricket box

One night emptying the duffel bag
Mum pulled out her hand with a 'Ah!'
Midst the shirts and shorts and stinking socks
She discovered a white sports bra.

Mum worried. Not a wink all night
She confided "I did feel a fool
But how did he get a white sports bra
When he goes to an all-boys school?

LESSONS

I was quite young, still at school, when I came to the conclusion that there are three kinds of lessons. There are those you receive officially and compulsorily in school, day after day after day; there are those you receive unofficially, also in school, usually whispered from behind hands or in skulking groups behind the bike sheds, traditionally, or in our case in untidy, disorganised groups outside the gate, waiting for the school bus; then there are the lessons that life dishes up – circumstances you meet, unpredictable and surprising, but the truest of all.

I remember the one I got from Dad one Saturday afternoon after he'd returned from the supermarket with the weekly shopping in the boot. Mum had called me down from upstairs to help unload. I dawdled, of course, quite deliberately, hoping that by the time I got there Dad would have done it. But this time, no such luck. He had been distracted into getting a bucket of hot soapy water and a cloth and was cleaning the muck sprayed up from the road onto the wheel hubs and sides of his car. "Before it dried on", he always said. We lived in a farming village and the local farmer paraded his herd through the main street. A combination of their droppings and a hefty rain shower would easily mess up any passing vehicle.

I lifted the load from the boot and reached for the first handful of bags. Dad appeared red-faced and panting at my shoulder.

"Leave the two blue bags", he said. "They're for Gran. I'll run them over later." Gran lived in a small bungalow at the other end of the village. "Put them on the back seat", he directed. I lifted them out of the boot Dad paused and looked at me earnestly. He glanced at the blue bags. "Remember what we talked about the other night? About Gran and what's gone on? It's called Alzheimer's", he said. "I'm no expert. It happens to some older people. I suppose it's a kind of tiredness, things wearing out. They get confused and unsure of things." He moved away, his hands and the cloth he held dropping foaming liquid into puddles on the drive. "It usually starts with forgetting things – names, places – things." He bent to peer inside the driver's window. "Damn", he said. "Now where have I put the blasted keys?"

He stood up abruptly and looked me full in the face. He was a fraction ahead of me. I smirked at him – it was a facetious facial expression I had been working on since I'd discovered sarcasm. "Really, Dad. *How* old do you have to be?" A soaking soapy cloth hurtled through the air and splattered across my shoulder.

"Not too old to remember where your backside is when I want to give you something a good kicking", he retorted, grinning. "Now, get those bags into the house!"

......

I never really wanted not to visit Gran. She was only a short distance away, no effort at all on my bike after school. But I suppose it was rather boring – actually that sounds a bit cruel. Say, 'uneventful'.

The bungalow's old-fashionedly furnished – no, say 'traditionally' patterned carpets, patterned wallpaper, patterned curtains, cushions, antimacassars – all in shades of beige and faded pastel colours. The furniture, the picture frames and that of the large mirror over the brick fireplace, the doors, windows all dark wood.

I used to go to mow the lawn at the back, maybe once a week, Spring through to Autumn. I always received a lovely welcome. I went round to the back door, propped my bike up against the now disused coal bunker (she had installed gas central heating), knocked on the door and went in. "Gerald!", she would exclaim. She was invariably sitting in her favourite easy chair, usually with a book. "Is it that time already? I'd quite forgotten you were coming."

"It's Wednesday, Gran."

"Of course it is. Give me a moment." There would be some idle chat unadventurously covering the same ground. School. How's Mum and Julie (my sister)? I always fed her back the same information. She never seemed to tire of it. To her credit she steered clear of other family endearments – how you've grown! What do they feed you on? Must put manure in your shoes! AND she didn't expect me to kiss her. I'd put an end to that when I was about 13 – and not too graciously, Mum always reminded me!

And so I went to mow the lawn, the clumsy green electrically-driven machine being kept in the garden shed.

It was a day such as this when my earnest mowings – I loved achieving the striped cricket pitch effect (well, kind of!) – was disturbed by an awareness that there was a voice behind me. I released the hand pressure on the handle of the mower and turned to face the head of a stern-looking woman peering over the hedge of the adjoining property.

A round face, compressed lips, glinting tortoiseshell glasses, double chin, a tightly curled helmet of greying hair.

"Young man. I couldn't make myself heard. Have you to go on much longer with that awful din?" I didn't know what to say. "Well? How much more do you expect me to endure?"

The question seemed pointless to me. Any fool could see I hadn't far to go. "I'm sorry", I muttered. "I won't be long now … er … Miss", I added almost automatically. Suddenly I was back at school being admonished by a teacher.

"Miss?" There was a note of scorn in her voice. "Miss? I am <u>Mrs</u> McReady and you are shattering the peace of my afternoon."

"I am sorry." I was totally at a loss. I was only mowing a lawn.

"And well you might be. There are laws you know. The Highways and By-ways. Local Government Regulations. Bylaws. There are times when the operation of machinery is allowable – subject to horsepower and decibel rations – usually during the working day – industrial and agricultural machinery. And from the noise you are making, such is yours. I advise you to acquaint yourself with such bylaws – you will find the Shire Hall an eminent locality for such determinations – and aim to abide by them. Then no further action will be taken."

I just stood, dumbfounded and open-mouthed. I noted bright red flushes appearing on her cheeks.

"Well?"

"Er … yes .. Miss…is McReady. Yes."

"Very good. You can carry on." And she was gone.

I took no little pleasure in returning Gran's mower to full roaring life. "Silly old fool." (Actually, what I really thought was ruder than that.) If it was up to me, I'd go over the whole lawn again. But that might ruin my stripes.

And so Mrs McReady appeared on the scene – well, at least, on my scene.

I mentioned the encounter to Gran as I had my customary glass of milk and clump of chocolate digestive biscuits before setting out for home.

"I've just been told off over the hedge by a Mrs …"

"McClintock", interrupted Gran. "She's just moved in. She's rather domineering. Makes her presence felt."

"Bossy – and very loud. She needs her decibels checked."

Gran cocked her ear in my direction. "Sorry, dear. What was that?"

"Nothing. Something she said."

"No doubt she means well", said Gran. "But she does get on your nerves."

And there the conversation ended. But also there the trouble began.

Julie and I gradually became aware that something was afoot. More and more frequently we were asked to go and call on Gran. At first we were give lame excuses to go. The lawn needed cutting more frequently (I was never again reprimanded by Gran's imperious neighbour). The hedge clipped. The weeding done. Shopping delivered. Julie had hoovering to do. Bedding to change and carry home for laundering. Kitchen floor to be washed. Windows cleaned. Sometimes, trivially, a book to be returned, a magazine; and we were never sent together. Always at different times so that the family – together with Mum and Dad's separate evening visits – were in more frequent and longer contact with Gran. And always the question after each visit. How did you find her? Was she all right? No sign of anything unusual? Once Julie let slip that Gran had her cardigan on inside out, the label exposed. Julie had helped her put it right and they had laughed together, relaxed and genuinely amused. But Mum had shot off in her car. "Tell Dad, when he gets home, where I've gone."

Julie and I knew we were in a team keeping close watch on our subject. We were mystified. "She really seems all right", said Julie. "When we're with her."

"Yes, she does", I confirmed.

But there were anomalies.

Mrs McReady – or Mackintosh, as Gran had called her to me – or MacDonald as Julie fed back, was reported to live with her niece – or daughter-in-law – she had no children of her own, related Mum. She's never been married, Dad got from the wife of a friend at the golf club. "Gran's getting very confused", said Dad.

And then came the gift. I saw it first. A large ceramic pot – pearl bluey grey background with a circle of dark blue dancing figures in flowing robes, gazing steadfastly over their shoulders, hands intertwined. They danced amidst floating blossoms, their boldly depicted feet on spiky petrol blue grass mounds. They looked Greek to me, Classical Greek, like illustrations in an ancient history book at school.

Then the pot – or jardiniere as I later found out – stood resplendent and enormous, rather dwarfing Gran's modest side table set under the window of her sitting room.

"It's enormous", I said to her, somewhat in awe. "Where did you get it from?"

"Mrs Mackintosh", she said. "She brought it as a gift. Wouldn't take no or an answer."

"What? That bossy old bat?"

"That's not nice", gently reprimanded Gran. "She means well. She can be quite nice."

I couldn't hide the disbelief on my face.

"She brought it around this morning. She said her husband had never liked it and had suggested she bring it for me."

"That's very generous", I said. It looked to be quite an expensive item.

"They're having a clear out. Moving to Austria … or is it Australia? She never stops talking. I get quite confused at times."

Mum was all ears when I got home. "Mrs McReady … "

"Mackintosh", I corrected.

"McDonald", chimed in Julie.

"Is going to Austria?"

"Or Australia" I added.

"And gave Mum this bowl?"

"It's getting worse", Dad murmured.

Thereafter gifts continued to appear. Vases. Ornaments, kitchen utensils, cushions, a shower cap, a pair of garden shears.

"These from Mrs Mackintosh", she confided to Dad one evening. "I sometimes go round for a cup of tea – she is most persistent – and I always come away with something."

Mum heard this and was alarmed. "You don't think – oh, no – it can't be – you don't think Mother is helping herself? She does seem so confused about everything."

Mum decided to act. "Sean", she said to Dad. "Come with me. You can call in on Mum and make sure she's OK. I'll go straight round to Mrs McReady …."

"Mackintosh", from me.

"McDonald", from Julie

"Enough of that!", from Dad.

Mum continued. "Thank you. I'll go and call on her and find out what's happening. She must notice things disappearing. Now, where have I put my handbag? Sean, where are the car keys?"

And they left, slamming the front door behind them.

It was Mum's decisive action that sorted it all out.

Her knock on the front door of Gran's forceful neighbour was followed by a long pause before the door opened. The tall forbidding woman filled the door frame.

"Yes", abrupt and unwelcoming.

"Hello", said Mum. "I'm Sheila Ransom. The daughter of Mary Smith, your neighbour." No response. Just a blank stare. "Your neighbour. Next door." Another pause.

"I know who you are. You took me by surprise, that's all. I was expecting my husband. He's due home from work. He's our Ambassador in Austria. Still, never mind. Do come in."

She led the way through to a large well-appointed sitting room. "Take a seat. We will have morning coffee. Do you like digestive biscuits. We have ours imported."

Mum involuntarily checked her watch. It was 4.30 in the afternoon.

"It is good to see you. I have so few visitors. Have you brought your invitation?"

Mum was silent. Nonplussed.

"Never mind. It's not essential. Though it is desirable. Emma will be here directly. She is my … er … granddaughter, on my sister's side. Staying here whilst her marriage breaks up." Mum waited patiently whilst the tall woman paced the room, somewhat absent-mindedly, Mum thought. Suddenly the pacing stopped. "There is something you can do for me before you go." She was next to a small occasional table and she reached for a silver cigarette box that had been placed on it. "This box", she continued. "We've had it for so long. I'm very tired of it. I can see you like it. I want you to take it. Find it a good home."

She turned to Mum and dropped the object abruptly in her lap. "There. Now, about this table lamp …"

She was hauling the plug from the wall when another woman entered the room. Small, blonde-haired, a comfortably rounded, pleasant soul, calming demeanour. Very business-like.

"Good afternoon. I'm sorry, I was in the garden, didn't hear you arrive. Marjory, shall I help you with that? I think it had better stay where it is, don't you, my dear? It looks so nice there."

And this woman – Mrs McReady's niece, daughter-in-law, whatever – took control. She politely and firmly asked Mother to leave and promised soon to get in touch with her through Gran.

"Your visitor has to go now, Marjory. She has pressing business. But she will come again."

"If she's invited", returned Mrs McReady.

The blonde woman smiled at Mother as she showed her out. Her smile smacked of a kind and sweet disposition.

"You see how it is. No, keep that for now. It makes life simple", as Mum proffered to her the shining cigarette box. "We'll sort it out later."

And that is how it is", concluded Mum over supper that evening. "It's all Mrs McReady – and that *is* her name! She is the confused one, the one losing touch with reality. And her forceful, domineering attitude to Gran – together with her confusion and forgetfulness – makes Gran seem uncertain. And we were all reading it wrongly. Poor Gran. She had started going for tea at Mrs McReady's just to keep her out of her own place."

"And the gifts?" asked Dad.

Mum looked over to the cigarette box on the sideboard. "We'll give them all back. In secret. To Emma", she said.

She quickly surveyed the table. "Oooh", she said. "We've not yet had our pudding. I almost forgot!"

LINDA

First of all came Maisie
As fresh as any daisy
Long blue-skied days when
Clouds at worst were hazy
Blonde curls, green eyes
'Twas no surprise
She was about to drive me crazy

Unlike Dorinda Ball
Who really did appal
To show her pants
To all the lads
Did handstands against the wall

Sweetly Maisie blushed
As home from school we rushed
Just us alone
I'd walk her home
My first big serious crush

Much later would come LINDA

Katherine stood tall and lean
An academic's dream
I met her at a Debating Comp
She captained the opposing team

Our A-levels were the same
We saw them as no game
We became buddies at our studies
Success would be our aim

We worshipped Jean Paul Sartre
Adored Chopin Sonata
Saw art-noire films in black and grey
Endured many a grim avant-garde play

And atonal chants by Camerata

At the end of our sixth form days
We went our separate ways
North East went she and old Dundee
South West I plunged in a daze

But I was closing in on LINDA

Like no-one I had ever met
At Uni there appeared Antoinette
Short and round, of thought profound
Long flowing robes that swept the ground
And, boy oh boy, she'd been around
Came all the way from London town

She was up to date with every trend
Tantalising titbits without end
Musicians fab; artists hip
Spliffs to jab; discs to flip
The Stones, The Who, the latest craze
Shrimpton, The Crew, Modesty Blaise

She strode
I stumbled in her wake
But after a year a sudden break
She appeared in October a different take
She had lost a lot of weight
Her razored hair blonde to the roots
A mini-skirt and kinky boots

She'd only come to collect her stuff
She's bailing out, she's had enough
She'd opted for a brand-new start
Fashion Studies at St Martin's School of Art
She'd gone. The scent of incense snuffed

And who would take over her rooms?
LINDA!

LUCK

Luck – bad or good – came in many different shapes and sizes in the trenches. Although he did not realise it at the time, Corporal Sydney Grieves' luck had been good. He had been designated as sentry outside the Guard Room.

First there was his surprise at the nature of the Guard Room. Rid your minds of any picture you might have of a type of prison cell. This was a room at the end of a corridor on the ground floor of the dilapidated French chateau in which they found themselves billeted. The room was high ceilinged with ornate carvings and cornices; the walls were covered with lush fleur-de-lys papering, now torn, faded and flapping. There was an elegantly carved marble fire place, blackened with careless misuse, over stuffed with coils of rusting barbed wire to prevent any escape attempt. There was a tall window, panes shattered, barred with narrow beams of old wood, haphazardly but firmly nailed in place. The floor was of stained and battered wooden blocks. There was a narrow, collapsible camp bed – tattered blankets, a discoloured pillow – against one wall and a simple upright wooden chair near the fireplace. That was it. Sparce, unwelcoming and bleak. The entry door was heavy wood with extravagant carvings and a large brass handle. There was a prominent lock from which protruded, on the outside, an enormous black metal key.

It was Sergeant Blackman who had introduced him to this place. The Sergeant, though normally officious and unfriendly to his lower ranks, had taken a shine to Sydney Grieves for no other reason than it transpired they hailed from the same town in South Eat England. Sydney had him to thank, he believed, for his second stripe.

"This is it, lad", he had said. "He is to be kept in here throughout the Court Martial and … er …" He paused, "… afterwards". It'll be your job to guard him night and day. You'll position yourself here." He indicated with his large, thick-fingered hand the area immediately outside the door. There was a trestle bed and a chair identical to that within the room. "Of course, there is to be some relief for you, but it will be irregular and infrequent." Sydney could not hide his displeasure. "Sorry, lad", continued the Sergeant. "It's the best I can do."

The regiment – or, should we say, what was left of it – was for a spell well away from the front line, enjoying the period of respite, chance to relax, take baths, repair clothing and equipment. Even get bored. The luxury of that! The only fighting here was that arising from disputes over the endless card games and accusations of cheating. Sydney would be separated from all this. On duty! But the Sergeant had pointed out the advantage of his situation. "This will be your contribution to the problem of the prisoner. It will end after the Court Martial. The others? Well … if things go against young Davies … then they will play their part." His voice faded away. But Sydney knew the drill. From them would be chosen the eight required to form the firing squad. He, at least, would be spared that – if it came to that, of course, he hastened to add to himself.

Ironically, it had been whilst he was gathering his kit in preparation for his extended stay outside the Guard Room that Davies had been installed. When Sydney arrived and took up his post, the Corporal outside the door departed with much haste and little ceremony. Sydney put his stuff on the camp bed and went to the door. The large key was in place. He carefully turned the handle and pushed. The door did not budge – locked. The soundless ease with which the handle turned indicated the lock was well oiled. There was a spy hole in the door, a hole bored through covered with a flap of heavy sacking. He lifted this and peered through. The coarse canvas felt rough against his skin : the pungent smell of oil was acute. Davies sat on the chair against the wall by the fireplace. His head rested against the faded wallpaper. His lips moved silently. His eyes were closed. Sydney recognised him with something of a shock. A bulky youth, ruddy faced, a shock of honey blonde hair. It was Cowbury. Private Davies was Cowboy, the tall lumbering figure of fun who had become a recognisable character in the camp. Ungainly, clumsy, dark eyes, much taller than those around him. Sydney, always from a distance, had seen him as somewhat simple minded – sent on errands by the others, like an eager to please young golden Labrador. Timid, cat-called, always grinning affably. Apparently, rumour had it, he had tried twice to gain enlistment into the army. Fibbed about his age. His height had belied his 14 years – that and his bulk and his prematurely broken voice, rough and deep throated. Also, ironically, about his height - he had dipped his knees at the measuring stand and just got in at maximum height. Not that the recruiting staff really cared. Consequently, none of his uniform fitted. His sleeves were too short, his breeches left his knees uncovered though he was taught how to tie his puttees so that this was not evident. He had no army boots but continued to wear what he wore on his home farm in the Welsh hills – until the death of a guard R.S.M. had made available boots that would suit him. A kindly nursing sister, treating a gash in Davies' forehead, saw to that.

Now he sat alone in the faded splendour of his chateau salon, head pressed to the wall, silently mouthing who knew what.

So Sydney was privy to the comings and goings of the next few days. Various officers, the M.O., the Chaplain, on one occasion the Colonel himself, and also on a single visit a Sergeant and his Lance Corporal assistant both from the Pioneer Corps, both skilled in Carpentry. The significance of this last visit was not lost on Sydney; they were covering all eventualities. In all this, Sydney was successfully dispatched; he stayed respectfully outside the door, to attention, saluting when required, but never seeing Davies and certainly not able to communicate in any way.

On the day of the trial, Davies was escorted by an officer and two military policemen past him and off down the corridor. An attempt was made at a marching contingent, but Davies's ungainly, bumbling efforts in the centre did little to add to that impression. It felt strange to Sydney, standing there, with the large wooden door swinging open.

It was Sergeant Blackman who kept Sydney abreast of the details of the Court Martial. He reported that all seemed to be going well for the lad: his simple nature was on view to all, his affability, his eagerness to please. And there were 'mitigating circumstances' (the Sergeant emphasised those terms carefully – obviously an expression he had picked up from his unofficial sources.) The lad had been twice wounded, a slash to his forehead and a bullet wound to the thigh. He had been caught by an exploding shell – ironically, friendly fire (he had wandered off when he shouldn't have) and had been hospitalised for some time, delirium, shaking and deaf, but eventually deemed fit to return to duty.

"It's his wandering off that's the problem" confided the Sergeant. "He tends to do it now ever since he was in the field hospital. Add to that he now can't hear one hundred percent. His mate says in the lulls of battle – when the firing is distant and the shelling – he hears things. The wind in the hills, the sheep – when the land's as flat as a bloody pancake and no sheep for miles, not even in the farm yards anymore. God knows what the blazes is in that. The lads lay bets. Rats say some. Horses, says another. Flat on the floor, sobbing out his eyes.

Eventually he gets over it and lies on his bed, but they know, next opportunity he'll wander off." The Sergeant paused at length. "And that's what he can't do. Put himself in danger and those sent to get him. And what if he's captured? Not that the Krauts would get much out of him." He allows himself a quick smile. "No. But this time he didn't half go on a wander. Brought back miles by the Military Police. Came to the attention of H.Q. Has to be dealt with. Seen as cowardice and desertion by the gold braiders. So, now see where he's landed himself."

Davies was finally delivered back after the verdict. "Guilty" one of the Military Police mouthed to Sydney.

"But with mitigating circumstances" confided the other as they locked the door and set off down the corridor.

It was Sergeant Blackman who awoke Sydney in the middle of the night. He stood over his recumbent body, his face grotesque and demonic, lit from below by his swinging oil lantern.

"Stir yourself, Corporal", he said. He was officious, business-like. "It's come. The big push. We've to move forward at dawn. All of us. All armed. The medic. The cookhouse. Pioneers. All of us. They will come and get Davies, then you report straight to the Company. I'll see you there." And he was gone.

Barely had Sydney risen to his feet when the Military Police arrived with torches. "You can go, Corporal. Leave him to us." One of them reached for the black handle of the key.

Sydney set off down the corridor, through the spacious entrance hall and out on to the crumbled terrace and steps of the chateau. It was surprisingly light out there, the moon full in a cloudless sky. He was impressed with how cold it felt. At the foot of the steps were two horse drawn vehicles. One enclosed, at the rear an open door with a small barred window. A Military Policeman stood quietly by. The other a flat cart. The horses moved restlessly. The drivers were in place, whips idle in the still air. On the flat surface of the cart stood a man carefully lowering a ground sheet tactfully to mask the load of the cart – a long, square object, the light colour of newly sawn wood of its construction startlingly white in the moonlight. Securely its lid was in place, the unsophisticated carving of a simple cross upon it, the heavy screws proud, waiting to be twisted in pale.

A shift of the ground sheet and it vanished into darkness.

MADGE BRIMBLE

Madge Brimble knew she was running late. She had risen at her customary respectable hour, had dallied over a leisurely breakfast (a mistake now, in retrospect), had taken time to read her paper (delivered at an early hour during term time as Wayne, her paperboy, had to complete his round before school), not even looked at the Crossword (save that for later) so running on time. BUT, then her sister Beryl had telephoned with yet more and lengthening divergent problems – trivial matters but obsessively dealt with now that she lived alone and had too much time on her hands (her husband had finally left her, but that's not our concern at this moment). Beryl had droned on and on; Madge pictured her narrow pinched lips confiding confidentially into the telephone mouthpiece at the other end.

And now, rather abruptly, having engineered release from her sister's continuing tales of woe – somewhere between the unreliability of her grandson and her suspicion of next door's cat terrorising Popsie, her miniature poodle – she rushed upstairs to her bathroom mirror. Her anxious face gazed back at her – pale blue eyes startled, her mousy hair whisping out of control. Mind you, she always appeared to be in a state of worry. Her face was puffy and permanently flushed – to do with her blood pressure. She nervously applied lipstick to her full lips and padded powder on to her cheeks, chin, forehead and nose in a vain attempt to counter her naturally ruddy bloom. Too late she spotted that her unsteady hand had sprinkled a fine dusting of powder on to the bodice of her navy-blue dress. A less particular woman would have probably cursed, looking skywards to reproach the gods themselves. Madge saw it as a justified result of her meandering morning activity and rushed down to the hall where she kept a clothes brush in a small drawer of the ancient brown wooden coat stand.

She looked at her watch. Now she really was late and – horror of horrors – she would arrive late, puffing and panting after a desperate dash on her upright cycle through the quiet morning village. Her ringing of the front doorbell of the grand house would shatter the peace and silence the hushed chatter of those already present at the meeting. Mrs Buck, Lady Mershe's companion and housekeeper would admit her into the hall and show her through to the Salon. She would enter and all heads would swivel in her direction, all eyes alert and inquisitive, all sedately sitting contrasting reliability with her quivery and fussing entrance, her full head of hair even further unrestrained, her floral scarf at her throat and her shining leather handbag flapping untidily.

Her words would stutter out. "I'm so sorry … so sorry … Lady M … so sorry … a bit of a family crisis. Oh dear!"

All heads turned towards the formidable Lady M (this was how she was familiarly addressed, but Madge felt that, in her current circumstances, it perhaps sounded a trifle impertinent and not a little flippant).

The Lady spoke, rich voice and gracious, "My dear Madge. Do come in. We have hardly started. See. There is a seat by the window. It is good to see you."

The other members of the Wilton-under-Wychwood Ladies Guild stirred restlessly as Madge edged her way to the proffered chair. It was the one always assigned to latecomers, it being a particularly uncomfortable piece of furniture, all hard wood and no padding, not in any way suiting the normal posture of a seated form, and it was, as Lady M had indicated, by the window, subject to draughts through the gaps in the frame of the high sash windows.

"Thank you. Thank you, Lady M. So sorry." The aged chair creaked as she sunk heavily into it.

Madge had ended up in the situation that every member – some sixteen of them – of the aforementioned Ladies Guild tried desperately to avoid. They all knew the consequences of late attendance – not a fine or a reproof – nothing like that : not even a critical comment in the minutes. But being absent in that gap between the gathering of the on-times and the formal start of proceedings. When the void would be filled by idle chatter and the inevitable object of that very daintily expressed gossip would be – what else? – the absentee herself. Madge could imagine it.

"Now", from Lady M. "Are we all here?"

The silent response to her enquiry would be answer in itself.

"Then who?" Her majestic head would slowly revolve, surveying the assembled company. "Let me see." A long pause. They all knew who was missing, but it was proper for Lady M to make the realisation and then pronounce the conclusion. "Ah … dear Madge Brimble. Have we had an apology?" This directed to her small, mousy Guild Secretary, Dorothy Brambleigh, who briefly returned to her writing pad, fluttered its blank pages and looked up at the 'grande dame', her face registering sad regret and the shake of her head and slight shrug of her shoulders conveying a silent negative response.

Madge imagined what would happen next.

Lady M, "For me, that's not like Madge. So rarely absent, if at all. Surely she would keep one informed." A long pause. "Perhaps Miss Buck took a call. But no, she is punctilious about passing messages on. Dear me. Quite perplexing."

The assembled company exchanged knowing glances. They held their peace. Who would provide the cue? Madge could anticipate all this in her imagination as she pedalled frantically towards the Hall.

Lady M, "Dear Madge."

A voice from the gathering, cut glass, refined, "Such a nice person …"

"Indeed." Lady M rose to full voice. The brakes were off. "Indeed, such a very nice person – but …"

And the gossips would be unleashed, led by the Lady M, and all Madge's shortcomings and failings and guilty what-she-thought-was-secret and eccentricities and peccadilloes were up for grabs – like grain thrown down for eager hens to be pecked at and fought over and scattered and consumed and relished, little by little bit.

As Madge had made her way to the high window chair proffered by Lady M, she wondered which bits of her had been forensically examined. She would never tell from the stillness of them seated around her, not even from their pursed lips, puckered foreheads, sidelong glances of their narrow, pale faces.

But it was these opportunities that were regularly seized upon, because of lateness and absence. And she had been as guilty as the rest.

How else would she have known of Emily Page's tendencies to solitary drinking; of Doris Blackwell's daughter being taken into care, formally adopted and now never referred to; of Celia Hardcastle's desperate cheating, never spoken about until now, in the Wilton-under-Wychwood Annual Fete and Produce Show Baking Competition, her offering from Harrod's; of Topay Inkerton's shady past as a show-girl (and was that all?) is past her Soho at the Windmill; of Colleen Ramsey's dismissal from her post as Head of Languages in a top Girls Boarding School after a nervous breakdown; of Madeline Brough's brother's incarceration following the Great Train Robbery in nearby Buckinghamshire; of Denise Fould's disposal of five – or was it six – husbands.

It was that word 'But'.

The starting gun to the gleeful gossip and spite race …

"Such a nice person … but …"

Ah, well thought Madge. Lady M herself was never late and certainly could not be absent – she had after all the power to cancel the meeting. Now, that would be a meeting worth going to … perhaps the murky and unobtrusive Mrs Buck be prevailed upon.

MAKING SENSE OF MRS HEDGE

"It makes <u>me</u> happy."

Beryl Hedge peered directly at me over her half-moon glasses. Her eyes were pale blue-grey and piercing. Her thin lips were compressed into their customary tight, down turned semi-sneer. Her hollow cheeks pinched with red. She had mouthed the words emphatically, giving each syllable full weight. Her chin jutted out, dimpled with determination and resolve.

"I suppose you'd better come in."

I closed the front door behind me and followed her across the deep carpet pile of her dark hallway to the quiet of her warm lounge, lit only by a number of low table lamps.

She sat in her accustomed wing backed plush armchair. She smoothed the folds of her skirt with elegant gesture of her slender white hands. I sat opposite her on an ancient threadbare settee. A large black cat shuffled away from me in a leisurely fashion.

"Would you like a cup of tea? Coffee?" She inclined her head questioningly. She interpreted the ensuing pause as a declination on my part. "Rum or sherry?"

"Not for me, thank you."

She took a deep breath. "I suppose you've come to tell me off." Her voice was light, cultural but to the point.

"Not at all", I replied.

The widening of her eyes indicated that she didn't believe me.

And she was right not to.

My wife had waited by the partially opened curtains of our sitting room for the police to depart. Their car had sped swiftly away. Miss Hedges' front door had been shut firmly. My wife turned and looked at me. I was simulating disinterest behind a fully opened newspaper.

"I think you ought to go over and check she's all right."

I lowered the paper and gave her an appealing look.

'She's on her own. Go on. She'll respond to you better than to me. She doesn't like women. Someone's got to talk to her. It can't go on."

The pale grey-blue eyes were unrelenting in their gaze. The voice was as precise as ever. "Well, why have you come if not for that?"

"We're … that is, Val and I were concerned about you. Alone here."

"Alone … but not lonely." She blinked and removed her glasses. "There's a difference between solitude and solitary."

I didn't want her to start playing word games with me. That was her refuge at times of difficulty. And I wasn't sure of the distinction here, anyway.

There was a faint attempt at a smile from her. "That sounded rather pompous", she acknowledged. "I think I could do with a drink. Join me."

It was an order rather than an invitation. She rose to her feet – a slight figure but not lacking in authority.

"I shall have a G and T" she confirmed. "And you?"

"Whisky, please."

There was silence whilst we nursed our drinks, silence but for the restful ticking of the large ornate grandfather clock and the stretching and purring of the several cats around the room.

"The police were very polite, considering", she said, taking a further delicate sip of the liquid from her cut-glass tumbler.

"Have they decided anything?"

"No further action", she said, "as long as it all ends here."

"And will it?"

I would have welcomed an instant decisive "yes" but instead there was a meaningful pause then a tentative "Yeeeees" I felt she could almost have added "I suppose so" with a note of reluctance.

"It must end here and now. You know that." I was testing the water. She did not take kindly to ultimatums.

She scratched agitatedly behind her left ear then stretched her slim pale fingers as she lowered her hand to her knee. Almost a feline gesture. The ice cubes clinked in her glass.

"To tell the truth", she stated quietly, "It's all becoming rather boring."

"Not for the people who received them." I was growing in confidence now that she was displaying an unaccustomed acquiescence.

She looked directly at me – alert. "Oh, them", she said dismissively.

"Yes, them." I was in no mood for anything from her other that an indication, no matter how slight, of regret, even apology, though the latter was most unlikely. "There has been a great deal of hurt."

"There has been a great deal of truth", she returned forcefully.

"Truth can hurt." Anything I said now seemed pointless, platitudinous. The least hint of self-reproach on her part had disappeared. She took a huge, unlady-like swig from her glass – an inelegant throwing back of her head. She even licked her lips.

"To quote Mr Eliot -", she obviously felt she was now on firmer ground. "Mankind cannot bear too much reality."

"Or words to that effect", I corrected her. It was a game we sometimes played. Exchanging literary quotations and correcting each other. It was like challenging unfamiliar words in Scrabble.

She stood up abruptly. Her now empty glass was abandoned, rolling on its side, on the cushioned seat of her chair.

"Now is not the time for this", she said. "I want you to go."

"And what shall I tell Val?" I rose to my feet, towering over her.

"That I will survive. That I am perfectly O.K. Come over, both of you, tomorrow. I'll have gathered my thoughts by then and you will."

"We will."

She led me out into the hall and opened the front door. As I paused close to her, she added "Tomorrow morning......for coffee. Perhaps stay for lunch." Then firmly she gripped my arm. "You will come. That's a promise."

I glanced down and smiled in confirmation. Her eyes looked up, pale, pleading, streaming with tears.

"Tomorrow, for coffee", I said.

The door closed swiftly and firmly behind me.

And that was the last I saw of her. The police were there again the following morning, investigating her death this time and its cause. She had been spotted slumped on the floor by the milkman passing her kitchen window.

It now makes sense to Val and me. This delicate, refined lady, an ex-deputy headmistress of a select girls' private school – aloof, withdrawn, almost hermetic – particular, cultured, erudite, artistic without family or friend in the world suddenly found to be the author of a spate of the most vile, offensive, obscene poison pen letters that, for some time, had plagued the community, causing distress to and the fracturing of families and relationships, on delicate, lilac coloured, lavender scented paper penned in a carefully italicized hand, the envelopes franked at all times of the year with stamps of bright colourful Christmas issue.

No ... we could never make sense of Miss Hedge.

MEMORY LANE

Ceri Jenkins settled herself into the proffered armchair, positioned her open pad upon her knee and sat poised with her HB pencil. She focused on the old lady siting opposite her. The room was cluttered in an old-fashioned way, cosy but organised. It was warm after her brisk walk there through the January cold : there was a noticeable smell of lavender (furniture polish) with an underlying scent of cats. Indeed there were two cats curled up in the chintzy covers of the two-seater settee. Since she had arrived they had studiously ignored her.

The elderly woman opposite her smiled encouragingly. "Well, dear?" she questioned. For the first time Ceri felt apprehensive.

"I've a list of questions, I'm afraid."

"Of course you have." The smile did not waver. "Fire away."

Both knew the purpose of Ceri's rather formal visit. She was a student at the local tech following courses in Advanced English Language. She was working with others on a project in journalism and they were preparing to publish (that is, write and print the text for) a magazine. Mrs Black, their tutor, had arranged for interviews with members of the local community. Ceri had been assigned to Mrs Mavis Dugdale – or had Mrs Dugdale been assigned to Ceri? Her brief was an article on local history.

"Well," Ceri felt her full confidence returning – the homeliness of the setting, the gentle features of the elderly interviewee, her softly permed whit hair, her delicately pink complexion, her fluffy knitted cream cardigan. She had even left on her floral apron. She wore blue fleecy slippers. Ceri cleared her throat. "Well. I am writing a piece" (that sounded good, she thought, very professional) "about some aspects of local history – the social side, the community, changing attitudes, what is different – that sort of thing."

Mrs Dugdale sat perfectly still, her gaze intent yet relaxed. Her hands were folded together and composed in her lap. The cats slept on.

Ceri continued. "I propose to entitle my article, "Down Memory Lane". She breathed in intending to continue but involuntarily paused.

"Memory Lane", echoed Mrs Dugdale. There was a note of enquiry in her voice – her eyes widened, her back stiffened, her hands moved abruptly, claw-like, to grip the arms of her chair. She moved her feet to implant them firmly on the floor as if to stand up "Memory Lane", she repeated. She smacked her hands together in an enthusiastic, forceful clap. "Ah! There I can help you." She stood up. The cats looked up at Ceri and rose to alert positions, legs stretched, backs arched, tales erect. One of them hissed. "My dear, I can help you." The woman moved decisively to the door but, as quickly as she had done so, she abruptly stopped, turned and faced Ceri. "But not now, my dear. There is something I must find. I've put it away safely … but where? I must think." Her hand was on the door handle. "I must find it." She looked Ceri full in the eyes. "And you must go now and come back." She disappeared into the hall and Ceri heard the front door being opened, the rattle of the dangling safety chain. The old lady's voice floated through to her. "I shall phone Mrs Black to arrange a convenient meeting. All right, my dear?"

And Ceri found herself clutching her pad, pen, coat and briefcase, out on the path between neatly manicured flower beds. "Goodbye, my dear." And the door closed behind her. Two cats stood by the wall, gazing intently at her, their tails swaying.

Back at college, Mrs Black put it down to the eccentricities of old age. They would have to wait to hear from Mrs Dugdale. If there was no response, they would come up with a Plan B. "Don't worry, Ceri", she said. "There is a myriad of alternative strategies." But Ceri was nonplussed. What had she done wrong? She half hoped for an alternative strategy.

But within days there was a phone call from Mrs Dugdale and, without consulting Ceri, Mrs Black had accepted a further interview. "Mrs Dugdale seemed very enthusiastic", offered Mrs Black to a rather subdued Ceri – but there was a distinct lack of conviction in Mrs Black's voice.

Still, Ceri found herself once more at Mrs Dugdale's spic and span house. "Come in, my dear. Come in." Mrs Dugdale was animated, her eyes sparkled, her cheeks tinged with red. "Come through", she invited. "We're in the dining room today."

Ceri followed her through. the room was all patterned wallpaper, dark curtains, an oak dining room table and chairs, a heavy carved side board with a large mirror above it. She caught a full reflection of herself, looking nervous and diminutive she thought.

Mrs Dugdale continued with a sweeping hand gesture over the full extended table. "Look what I have dug out for you." There was a generous spread of old photograph, yellowing newspapers and typed

A4 sheets. "Now – let's really go down Memory Lane. Look at this."
She held up to Ceri's gaze an old photograph of an antique street sign.
A black border, a white background and, in quaint but firm lettering
the words, 'Memory Lane'. For the next hour or so, Mrs Dugdale was
totally and confidently in charge, sifting volubly through the paper
evidence on the table revealing the reality of what had been Memory
Lane.

Lord Brocklebank had been the influence in the area. He occupied a
grand home just on the edge of the small town and seemed to control
almost everything. Much of his wealth came from his husbandry of the
woodland on his estate which necessitated the movement and export
of sizeable amounts of timber. With the coming of the railways he had
organised a branch line which skirted the town and arrived at a small
terminus just outside his estate where he had built a station platform
that enabled the wood to be shunted up on to a level suitable to the flat
trucks of the train for easy loading. The line was also eventually used
for a shuttle service that would ferry, in one or two carriages, the local
townsfolk into Ashford especially on market days. In fact, in effect,
Lord Brocklebank's private railway.

An unadopted, unsurfaced, somewhat rutted and pot-holed lane led
from the town, parallel with the railway, to the station platform. It was
truly unadopted – used frequently by pedestrians and summer visitors –
just unnamed.

"But then came the War, my dear." Mrs Dugdale had until now
scarcely paused for breath. "That is, the First War – or the Great War –
they didn't know it was to be the *First* War. And the Brocklebank
Terminus took on a new role. It became a point of departure for all our
lads going out to fight. They would assemble at the terminus – lines of
them with their cases and bundles, cocky comments and daft, broad
smiles – with their wives, families and girlfriends all standing by,
fighting back tears, arms around each other, waiting for the shuttle.
And it would come. You'd hear it chugging closer and closer – steam
hissing, the crash of metal, the screech of brakes. And the lads would
file aboard – not always in coaches, sometimes standing in trucks. Not
a long journey into Ashford. And off they'd go to much waving of
hands and handkerchiefs – a chorus of jokes and callings-out. A flurry
of smoke and steam, and flecks of soot falling like black snow. Then
that awful silence when all folks could do was walk home – down the
well-trodden unadopted lane, back into town.

This happened again and again — a rallying point for our lads from all over the county. And, of course, for the many families and wives and girlfriends, this was the last they ever saw of their men.

Flowers were left tied to the wooden railings and supports of the platform. Scarves, shawls, ties, bowler hats — many mementoes, each with its own memory, tethered to the old wooden beams and uprights. It was a place of pilgrimage, especially when the war news was good — and more when it was bad. Groups of people — mostly women but some men, the old and the too young — gathered, huddled together, even sang hymns and popular sad songs. This one day — and no-one knew from where — appeared this sign." She went back to the photograph in her hand. "Someone adopted the lane. Memory Lane. They had hammered the sign to the platform itself."

Mrs Dugdale for the first time paused and looked down at the photographs on the table. Her eyes glistened with tears. She sifted through the photographs of groups of people, the women in ankle length dresses, boots, waisted coats with pleated skirts, hair rolled up, straw hats, the men with flat caps and bowlers. Little girls in frilly pinafores : boys in breeches, dark socks and boots — also with manly flat caps. She selected one picture. "See that?" She whispered, "That is my grandmother as a young girl. That is the day she bought posies for both her brothers — as she did for many, many years."

Ceri was stilled with awe. How pointless and facile — even facetious — seemed to her now her glib, cliché references to 'Memory Lane'. How could she do justice in her writing to this?

She felt the friendly and comforting touch of Mrs Dugdale's hand on her shoulder.

"Goodness me", came a whisper from quite close to her right ear. "How I can talk. I'm parched. Come through to the sitting room. I'll make a pot of tea. I've done some baking. Do you like Victoria Sponge? Go through. You can keep Bertie and Polly company — though no doubt they will be asleep." And they were.

MICHAEL

Matthew was alerted by the sound of the telephone ringing in the hall. He paused to hear the soft soles of his mother's slippers scuffle across the parquet flooring below. The ringing stopped. Her voice sounded indistinctly and he heard the receiver being put down.

"Matthew?" she called – her soft voice betraying sounds of urgency and excitement. "Matthew? That was them. They're at the Peterborough Service Station. They'll be here in less than an hour."

He felt old frustration tighten within him. On a good day it would take him well over an hour to get from the Manor Park Services to home. Mother's wishful thinking was foreshortening the journey.

He was aware of her heavy breathing as she hauled herself up the stairs. She stood panting on the landing.

"Matthew, where are you?"

"I'm in my room", he replied.

"Well, I must get ready now", she stated. "I shall be needing the bathroom."

He found her on the landing. Her rounded cheeks were flushed with the exertion of the climb. She was clumsily removing her apron, catching its shoulder straps on her glasses, disorganising her softly permed white hair, one arm pulling the garment over her head, the other steadying herself on the stair-rail.

"I'll get out of your way", he said. "'Ill go to my place of exile." A light-hearted comment but with a point.

"You'll be all right." She looked at him directly in the eye. "It's only for a few nights. It was your idea."

"I'm teasing you." They both knew it was more than that.

"Oh, damnation and curses." This was very strong language for mother.

He shifted his full holdall from one hand to the other. "What is it?"

"It's the joint", she said. "I've forgotten to switch the oven on."

"I'll do it on my way out", he offered.

"Do you think lamb is all right?" she worried.

He felt his impatience surge. "We've been through all this."

He remembered their earlier conversation when Michael had announced his visit by letter. His mother had talked it through with Alice, her younger and very supportive next-door neighbour. Alice was a small woman – "Petite, Matthew dear", she opined in her fussing way – platinum blonde hair, tightly curled, bright red lips, heavily made up eyes and a succession of brightly coloured cardigans.

"Alice says …" Mother began. So many of her opening conversational gambits began this way. "Alice says …" Alice was an authority on everything in his mother's eyes. "Alice says goat. She says they don't eat beef because it's sacred, and not pork if they're Muslims. I thought chicken but it's a bit ordinary for such an occasion. And not fish – it's rather smelly. So goat."

Matthew did not enter the debate. He always came a poor second to Alice in domestic mattes.

Not unexpectedly, Mother could not get goat in the local Co-op. She confessed in a relieved tone. "I wouldn't know how to cook it anyway." Delia Smith was no help either.

"And do you leave the horns on?" Matthew's sarcasm went over his mother's head – but only for an instant, then she grinned. "Don't be daft!"

"What about lamb? It's close to goat."

Mum paused. "I'll ask Alice." The peroxide dwarf had won again.

In the kitchen, holdall in his left hand, with his right he turned on the oven. He waited to hear the whoosh of the gas ignite inside. On the worksurface was arranged in water filled saucepans all the vegetables prepared for a traditional roast lamb lunch – peas, carrots, potatoes and sprouts.

His mother had, of course, first asked Alice. "Alice says yams, sweet potatoes and …" She paused and consulted her scribble in the small notebook she carried with her everywhere, a much-needed aide memoire in her advancing years, "and plantain."

Again the Co-op was of little help. Alice had driven her there : they often shared shopping trips. They had consulted a supervisor, a rather gruff young man. "Hardly out of school", Alice had concluded.

"Sorry, madam. No yams or sweet potatoes. No call for them in Thetford. And plantains …?" His confidence eluded him. Alice was as helpful as ever. "It's like a banana", she prompted, refusing to accept the uselessness of their mission. "But kind of hard and unripe." A helpful shop assistant overhead them. "We've got three", she asserted, "green bananas. I've just put them up." And she shot off to return immediately with a large bunch of the wildly green curving fruit Mother was too polite and confused to demur. "Oh, lovely", she said. "We'll take them. Thank you so much." Alice tactfully only sighed and bit her lower lip.

When he'd arrived home from work, Mother still appeared to be fretting over the vegetable choice. "Look, Mum", Matthew offered his too often spurned advice with caution. "Go for a traditional roast. Michael will love it after so long abroad and ... Kisoo ... Kishtoo .. Kish ..."

Mother took out her notebook and flicked over the pages. "Kishtutseeba. I wrote it down", she announced proudly. "Well, Kitshtut ... whatever ... will eat simple vegetables, I'm sure."

Mother closed her notebook. "Yes. That's what Alice said."

Matthew closed the backdoor behind him, walked across the backyard, stepped easily over the low fence onto next door's drive and let himself up the metal folding step into Alice's pale yellow and cream touring caravan. This is where he would stay during his younger brother's visit. The caravan had a musty air – a combination of the winter's damp and the recently prolonged application of warmed air from a large calor gas heater. He would open the window to reduce the fog. He put down his holdall and sat beside it on the bed. He felt the quilting of his sleeping bag under his hands.

It was not without relief that he had consigned himself to the caravan. It was Alice's suggestion, of course. "Alice says", this from his mother, "it makes sense in the circumstances."

At least he would be free of the chaos that would inevitably ensue in the house. It was a modest three-bedroom semi – one in a long line of identical constructions that serried both sides of Turnpike Drive. It would have to host his mother, who had moved from the main to the smallest bedroom – and that's exactly what it was, room just for a single bed and little more. Mother's room she had given over to Michael and his wife, Kishtutseeba and the baby. And his room, the other double, was for the three other daughters and the maid.

His mother had acquired these much longed for grandchildren suddenly and without prior announcement. "The grandchildren I've always wanted", she breathed rapturously, firing an unintentional barb at her other unmarried son – unintentional but no less hurtful for that. And the news *had* been unexpected, unheralded.

Many years before, in dubious circumstances, Michael had left hurriedly for a career in capital venture in Kenya. A good looking, youngish man, he had been advised before going out there to take a wife 'for reasons of propriety, he being of the white community'. The scandal of Happy Valley still loomed large amongst the ex-pats. He had turned to his girlfriend of long standing, Judy, and they had set forth, unceremoniously, with the intention of an African wedding, safari honeymoon et al. The family heard little of Michael after that – just cards at Christmas and the odd uninformative tourist postcard of Kenya. All through his father's illness and demise and his mother's growing infirmity, Michael remained aloof – seemingly unaware of his family's decreasing fortunes and the necessity of their considerable downsizing to 49 Turnpike Drive.

Matthew had unquestioningly assumed responsibility for helping to look after both his parents, somehow juggling his accounting job at a local engineering works. Michael had, over the years, become a remote figure. Until the letter arrived.

Michael would be coming over for a visit. And in a flash was recorded his history of the past years. His marriage with Judy had not lasted. She had taken up with the manager of the International Bank where she worked and Michael had remarried, to Kishtutseeba. She was of the well-educated middle classes and had also a promising school teacher. They had had in remarkably quick succession, two daughters and finally, after a lapse, a son. Michael wanted to bring his son, named David after his grandfather, home to meet his family.

Mother was shocked at all these sudden tidings, stunned, tearful, then delighted, wet-eyed and elated. And earnest preparations began for the visit. Loads of food, new towels, pillows, blankets and two Z-beds and a folding cot. An equally thrilled Alice took charge. Mother seemed younger with all the excitement and got out long overlooked items of family history, photographs, certificates, school books etc etc. The house was cleaned and polished as never before.

"Your dad would be so proud", Mother enthused – far too often for Matthew. He retained his controlled and sardonic exterior but inside resentment grew.

Mathew cooed teasingly. "Uncle Matthew", she crowed. "sounds good – *Uncle* Mathew. Two nieces and a nephew."

"Yes, Grandma", he returned tersely.

"There's a problem", she said. "Shall I be Grandma or Gran – Granny or Nana? Or will there be an African word for me?"

"Ask Alice", he muttered to himself as he noisily folded his Daily Telegraph.

"I want to be a Nana. That's what Alice is called."

He was startled by the sudden movement of the caravan door and realised the wind must be getting up as it slammed shut – a good opportunity to get the van aired. He rose to his feet to tackle the tightly shut windows.

He did not know how he would face his brother. Michael had always glided through life with a confidence and carelessness that Matthew did not have. Michael was tall, fair skinned, a shock of dark wavy hair, slim, deep eyes with luxuriant lashes that (Mother said) 'any girl would die for'. Matthew favoured their father's side of the family, average – average height, nondescript mid-brown straight hair, rather podgy face, pale eyes and a somewhat flushed countenance. Michael had swaggered through school where Matthew had plodded. Michael had swept on to University but, typically, not stayed the course : Matthew had become a trainee in an accounting department.

On unexpectedly leaving university, Michael had been found a sales job in a local car franchise firm. He had become a great favourite with the Italian brothers who managed it and, without apparent conscience, become involved in some very dodgy arrangements with government grants put in place to boost the fortunes of the car retail industry. The firm had gone into liquidation prior to a court case involving fraud charges. The Italians incurred long prison sentences – hundreds of thousands of pounds were involved. Michael was to a degree exonerated because of his youth and inexperience, and his father's exemplary reputation in the local community, but he still went to prison for a short while.

His father was broken, lost his confidence, his business acumen and reputation undermined, and never really recovered before his illness hit, polycystic kidney disease. Michael left prison, disappeared from view until announcing from Kenya his arrival there with Judy – working with contacts he had made one can only guess where.

Now he was triumphantly returning home, a successful businessman with his family *and a servant*. Matthew's distrust and resentment had been kept in check by his brother's remoteness and geographic distance. He knew how deep his feelings went. He could not trust his reaction to his brother's arrival and customary splendid nonchalance.

Eventually he returned to the house. His mother, dressed in her new royal blue dress and matching jacket, her hair immaculate, make-up applied, even deep red nail varnish, was in the dining room laboriously folding white linen table napkins. Her hands shook with apprehension. "I can barely remember how to do this", she said.

Matthew sat in the lounge and looked at the paper when there was a knock at the front door.

Mother almost squealed and pushed her chair back nosily. "It's them. It's them. Matthew, you go. Answer the door."

As he crossed the hall, she was already at the mirror patting her hair, brushing beneath her eyes with her red tipped fingers.

He swing open the front door. I hope he's grown fat and bald, he thought.

But the face that met his was rough-skinned, a full dark moustache, heavy eyebrows. He took in the navy-blue uniform, the two-way radio on the chest.

A deep voice, serious and respectful. "Mr Watkins … Mr Matthew Watkins?"

Mother froze. Her hands to her hair. Her face drained of colour.

Matthew nodded.

"May we come in, sir. It's bad news, I'm afraid. There's been an accident."

MIRABELLA

Ever since she could remember, Mirabella had been aware of the existence of three three wish-fairies though, in fact, she had only ever seen two of them.

Let me explain.

Mirabella had fond, fond, ever more distant memories of those times, as a little girl, she would be nestled down on her mother's knee, comfy against her mother's ample form, secure within the embrace of the engulfing, generous padding of her fleshy arms. Mother would tell her of the three wish-fairies. These were – or had been – small china statuettes of elfin like creatures, slim and elegant white limbs, perched on top of red with white spots toadstools, each dressed in lilac, embroidered flower petals, with hats of inverted foxglove trumpets. Their eyes were downcast, their cupid bow lips delicately pursed. They were on the narrow shelf over the small Victorian fireplace in her mother's bedroom and Mirabella would remember the rich rose-in-bloom wallpaper, the ridges of the deep pink candlewick bedspread, the glistening satin of the leaf green eiderdown.

"Tell me again, Mummy", she would insist, burying deeper into the fond embrace, "about the three wishes, and why now there are only two wish fairies."

"Well", sighed her mother, enjoying the re-telling almost as much as her small daughter. "Your Mummy and Daddy rally wanted to have a beautiful little girl that we could call our own and we waited and waited."

"For a long, long time," chimed in the little girl.

"For a very long, long time", confirmed the story-teller. "Until your Mummy decided to make a wish with the wise fairies. She took one carefully in her hands and quietly breathed her wish to her. Then she gently kissed her."

"You wished for your own little girl."

"For our own little girl. And ...", the woman paused expectantly.

"And it worked!" her daughter exclaimed in a joyous whisper.

"Yes, it worked. Along came our own dear, sweet little Mirabella."

"Who", prompted the little girl with persistence, "who ..."

"Who we loved and loved and still love and love with all our hearts."

There was a pause.

"That is me", said the child.

"That is you" came the echo and the cuddling grew stronger and stronger. The child looked at the shelf, at the two fairies.

"So why are there now only two fairies?" Though, really, she already knew the answer.

"Because a fairy can only grant one wish and when this is done, the fairy has to fly away back home."

"To Fairy Land?"

"To Fairy Land. Now ...", the mother's grip relaxed. "Time for bed."

Over the years, Mirabella got used to tiptoeing into her parents' bedroom to gaze enraptured at the two silent, unmoving wish fairies, but her instincts told her that any further wishes had to be about really important things, not used for what she wanted for her birthday, or where to go on holiday or anything like that.

One day she returned home from school (her best friend's mother had dropped her off) and the front door was opened by her Aunty Pat. She was her father's sister, small, slim and blonde – the precise opposite of her mother. Mirabella was surprised.

"Come on in," said her Aunt. "I've got you milk and biscuits in the kitchen."

Mirabella pottered through the lofty hall, over the black and white ceramic tiles. "Where's Mummy?", she asked, dropping her satchel on the floor and shrugging off her school coat.

"Mummy's not very well. She was at the shop this lunch time." (Daddy had a hardware store in town. Aunty Pat worked with him, did the books and accounts.) "She felt ill, so Daddy took her to hospital. That's where she is now, with Daddy."

Mirabella was not unduly alarmed. She knew Mummy could be unwell and she knew hospital was a good place to be. Hadn't she had her tonsils out and been told not to be a fool? And hadn't the nurses and doctors been so kind and friendly? "Daddy will stay with her until she is settled for the night. Then he'll come home. But that may not be until after your bedtime."

And that's how it was. Aunty Pat tucked Mirabella up safely in bed, read her a short story as it was rather late by then, and left her in a deep sleep.

So deep that she did not hear the disturbance in the early hours of the morning, when her father finally let himself in through the grand glass panelled front door, did not hear the m… (Aunty Pat had been waiting up for him), the scraping of chair legs on the kitchen floor, the hot sweet tea being made, the rattle of cup and saucer, eventually the deep, choking sobs.

Next morning, Daddy and Aunty Pat looking disassembled in their dressing gowns, she was told she would not be going to school that day and Daddy would stay home from the shop. Gradually, that Mummy would not be coming home, that they all had to be brave, that Mummy had gone to heaven to be with Granny and Gramps and Uncle Bob.

"And with Fluffy?" came the innocent enquiry. Fluffy was her guinea pig that had died some months earlier.

"And with Fluffy," confirmed Aunty Pat quietly. Daddy turned away, fumbling for his handkerchief.

Time passed as time does. Aunty Pat moved in to look after her brother and her niece. It was a largish house. The downstairs rooms had lofty ceilings, ornate cornices, tall windows with sweeping draped curtains. Up the majestic oak staircase to a broad landing, four bedrooms and a bathroom.

The time for Mirabella's 8th birthday was approaching, the first since her mother had gone.

"We must do something special", said Pat, speaking out of the girl's hearing.

"Think we will", smiled her brother. "I'll think about it."

And he did. A traveller came into the shop who dealt with far more than the workaday supplies that Marabella's father usually required. He had a catalogue and father spotted a device for inflating balloons with helium and a range of balloons also.

The plan was made. A party – with floating balloons – one enormous pink one for Mirabella (her favourite colour) with a large figure 8 emblazoned in gold on the sides.

The day arrived, as did a gaggle of children, mostly girls. Each child was greeted with a balloon and shown into the sitting room. Aunty Pat had devised some balloon games, but fate took a hand. One of the girls inadvertently released her balloon and it floated to the high ceiling. There was no way to get it down. The string attached was too short. The little girl wailed. Someone's mother went over to pet and console her. A boy, with a wicked smile, saw the opportunity. He grasped another boy's balloon, pushing his victim over, and released it ceilingwards. There was a joyous gasp and soon all the balloons rose one after the other and wafted gently above their heads. There was just Mirabella left clinging onto her enormous pink globe, its golden number eight catching the light. They all stood expectantly looking at her. A shadow of anguish flicked across her face, then she smiled, sweetly raised her hand and with a wafting gesture released her balloon also. There was a spontaneous cheer and round of applause. Aunty Pat and the other mothers thought it was time for games and tea in the garden and quickly the room emptied. The balloons gently and silently bobbed overhead.

Dad, later that evening, after the guests had gone, devised a way to clear away the balloons. One of Aunty Pat's finest knitting needles duct-taped to a broom handle. He pierced the balloons one by one and with each explosion a wrinkle of coloured rubber and string fell to the floor. Mirabella stayed his hand; she wanted her balloon to stay aloft. "Forever," she said. Dad relented and set too clearing up the mess on the floor before his sister's cats choked themselves whilst playing with the remnants.

Forever is not long. Soon the pink balloon lost its glow and its surface became a kind of froggy skin. The golden letter 8 lost its shape. "I think she's dying," mused Mirabella.

"Deflating," said Dad. Next day, whilst Mirabella was at school , Aunty Pat applied the knitting needle to the final balloon. If Mirabella ever noticed it had gone, she never said. Perhaps she spotted the remnants in the swing lidded bin in the kitchen.

Mirabella had a major problem in her life. It was her hair. Tight dark curls. "Part of your Italian ancestry," joked Dad.

"A painful nuisance," agreed Mirabella and her Aunt after her hair was washed and had to be attacked with brush and comb. Pat was breathless, her niece in tears. It could be said, it all come to a head with some unkind teasing at school. "Gollywog head" sneered one of the boys. That was it. Mirabella stared at herself in the mirror of the dressing table in her father's bedroom – her angry face, her red weepy eyes, her unruly black curls. She went over to the wish fairies. This was important enough. She gently lifted one up, whispered her wish closely to it, a feather kiss at the top of its head and down again. She left the room, far from convinced.

Next morning, once her father was in the bathroom, she slipped inside. On the narrow ledge there was … only one fairy. She whooped for joy and skipped happily downstairs.

And it worked.

Next time Aunty Pat went to tackle her normally unyielding locks, she anticipated a tug on the comb but paused. "This is easier than I thought I'd find. If I wasn't so sure I'd say all this hair is unravelling." And over the weeks it did, never becoming what you'd call straight but far easier to deal with. Thus enabling Mirabella to have it effectively trained into a style and framed her wide, round face to far more pleasing effect.

Time passed – as time will.

And Mirabella, now in secondary school, came home with the news that for the celebration of the school's centenary, each school year could choose an event of its own. Her year were going to hold a dance in the school hall. Food, drink and a DJ, special lighting, the lot.

Aunty Pat and she devised what her outfit would be. Her aunty, luckily, was a deft seamstress. Luckily, as Mirabella's generous physique (she'd taken after her mother's, smiled Dad proudly) often required clothing made to order. They decided on a kind of shift dress, just above the knee, with long sleeves. The material was a shiny silver with silver sequins. They would buy silver tights with scarlet red shoes and an Alice band and a neat little shoulder bag with a diamante clasp. The excitement was tangible.

Dad, very proud, delivered his daughter to the school where she was soon engulfed by a phalanx of squealing girlfriends. They disappeared into the Hall. Dad drove away. She would be brought home by one of the mothers who was arranging the buffet.

The Hall was as they'd never seen it before. Fairy lights, festoons of tinsel, the flashing lights at the disco desk, long tables of food and snacks and cans of soft drinks, chairs all round the walls and proudly suspended in the centre, one of those balls covered in multi-faceted small reflecting glass pieces; it revolved slowly, sending flashes of light, glittering snowflakes around the room.

The dancing started, the boys at one end – more athletic gyration than dance. The girls at the other, bobbing up and down in huddles. Gradually the two groups began to close in. Couples began to separate from the two throngs. Mirabella was right at the centre to the room, momentarily isolated. Then came a guffaw of laughter from behind her, where the boys were. Some of the girls giggled.

A rough boy's voice. She turned and he was pointing at her. Mirabella. Mirabella!" he called. "Hang her from the ceiling." Cheers from his cronies. A gaggle of girls swooped on Mirabella, surrounded her, mother hens, sweeping her to safety in a far corner. "Don't take any notice", they cooed. They sat her down. "You leave her alone, Gary Smallwood", cried one girl threateningly.

"Sir. Sir!"

A male member of staff entered the fray to sort it out.

But Mirabella's night was ruined. She retreated to a nearby classroom and sat being comforted with plates of food and cans of Coke. "That Gary Smallwood's ignorant. Pig ignorant", said one girl.

"He's been sent home", said another.

Arriving home, Mirabella tried successfully to hide her earlier distress. Her aunt put down her flushed face and flustered demeanour to the exertions of the evening and the cold night air. There was little surprise when she opted to go straight upstairs. Dad didn't even stir from behind his newspaper in his favourite armchair.

Once in her bedroom, her tears of anger really flowed. She felt awkward, her dress too tight, her head band ridiculous. She tore it off, hurled it across her room and stared into her mirror. Red-rimmed eyes stared back. She put her hand to her face – bright red nails, short stubby fringe, rolls of fat around her waist. There was nothing else for it. She kicked off her somewhat scuffed shoes and went swiftly to her father's room. She seized the remaining wish fairy, held it close to her face and almost growled, "I want to lose weight. This is my wish. I want to lose weight." Then a desperate, "Please" with an anything but gentle kiss.

Once in bed, surprisingly quickly she fell asleep, not even aware of her aunt coming in to check she was all right.

Next day was Saturday. She slept in, waking when it was fully daylight. She hadn't even closed the curtains.

She sat up. She felt drowsy, hot, sweaty. Hardly surprising, she thought. She pushed back her covers and lowered her legs over the edge of the mattress. She paused and took a deep breath. She took stock. She couldn't feel the pile of her bedside rug under feet, let alone whether her slippers were there. She eased herself forward, for a moment felt unbalanced, then comfortingly, the ruffled wool against her toes. No slippers. She pushed herself upright and unwittingly propelled herself so that she fell against a chest of drawers near the bed. She held it firmly. She felt desperately thirsty. She made for her bedroom door. It was as if she was walking in slow motion – the ground a gentle sensation under her bare feet. She reached the door and held gratefully on to its handle. The door was already open.

The landing was deserted. The house seemed empty. She had no idea what time it was. As she tried to cross the landing, losing control as she reached for the banister. She felt very strange, light-headed. Would she faint? She breathed deeply. No. Her grip on the banister rail steadied her. She edged herself towards the top of the stairs. She'd feel better when she had some breakfast, a cup of tea. She found herself groping her way downstairs, holding firmly to the banisters, hand over hand, like climbing a rope only pulling herself down. She supposed she was awake – not having one of those floating dreams.

She reached the hall floor breathing quite heavily from the exertion of her descent. She steadied herself against the newel post. She had anticipated the startling cold of the tiles beneath her feet, but it was not there. She let go of the bannister and felt herself gently plunge towards the open door of the sitting room. As she passed through, she tried to grip the door knob but failed and plunged in.

At the time, Pat was in the kitchen when she heard a muffled, plaintive cry. "Aunty Pat. Aunty Pat. Help. Help me."

She stopped what she was doing. Paused. It was Mirabella's voice. Seemed to be coming from above.

Quickly she left the kitchen and went to the foot of the stairs. There it was again. "Aunty Pat. Help me." She was undecided – from the sitting room or upstairs?

She went to the open door of the sitting room and glanced inside. Nobody. She moved quickly up the stairs. Paused on the landing.

"Help me, Aunty Pat."

Now the voice seemed beneath her. Under the floorboards? Ridiculous. She tried each of the bedrooms. Mirabella's was empty, her bed clothes thrown back. The bathroom? No-one.

The call again. "Aunty Pat." Surely at foot level. It couldn't be, she thought, but looked in the airing cupboard anyway. She stood at the top of the stairs.

"Aunty Pat."

It *was* downstairs. She rushed down to the hall, stopped and held her breath.

"Help me. Please."

It had to be in the sitting room. She burst through the door. No-one. The room was empty ... a slight movement above her head drew her eyes upwards.

She gasped. There, against the ceiling, the pink night gown billowing gently, her arms airily wafting, her round face waving softly from side to side, her dark hair tightly curled as of old, her rounded limbs shifting and nudging the cornice, her plump hips now above the picture rail. "Help me. Please. Aunty Pat."

There must have been a slight breeze as her body floated away from the upper window.

The aunt stretched her arms upwards. Her eyes met those of her niece.

"I'm here. Don't be afraid. I'll help you", she said, trying to sound reassuring but inside was thinking, But how the hell do I do that?

From somewhere inside her subconscious came the image of a large pink floating balloon with a golden eight emblazed upon it.

Later, up in the main bedroom, the air was cool and still but what Aunty Pat had not noticed in her hurried perusal of the room, the narrow shelf was empty – the third wish fairy had returned home, her purpose fulfilled.

MY SISTER

To get anywhere near even a vague approximation of the truth about love would require more than a lifetime of close study and an even longer period of close-up experience. And all this has to start somewhere.

In my case, it began with my sister.

They are strange creatures, older sisters. They inhabit a different world. They drop in and out of yours with casual indifference – usually causing trouble, telling tales on you, bribing and blackmailing you to lie on their behalf and intimidating you with a gaggle of similar minded girlfriends who laugh and sneer at you, especially at any efforts you make to form a truce with them, let alone establish cordial relations

"Just go away and play."

The great mystery is that any member of the male gender could make a successful approach to this hostile exclusion species; an even greater mystery is that he should want to. Spend time with my sister? Voluntarily? You must be joking.

But times change.

I and my two considerably younger brothers became bemused spectators at what was beginning to happen, storing our observations and forming a collection of generalities as to what might be suitable behaviour if even, God forbid, we should feel it appropriate to approach girls other than with a white flag of surrender.

I suppose my sister could come under the heading of 'reasonably attractive', even if she was far too short – certainly attractive when compared with one or two of her coterie of friends. I would never have perceived or admitted this at the time but, on reflection, I suppose it is true.

We heard about her boyfriends rather than had face to face encounters, except for one or two who appeared self-consciously either totally submissive and respectful or acting artificially and unconvincingly confident in our front room.

They came and went, when and how she welcomed or dismissed them. They were all much of a muchness – mostly school friends from the local sixth form – but there were exceptions.

One was Denzel.

He had prematurely left the 6th from and didn't seem to do anything other than play bass in a local skiffle group. He was tall, gangling and specialised in being untidy. A mop of straw-coloured hair (don't forget, those were the days when retired Colonels deluged the Daily Telegraph with letters of disgust at the unruly - in their eyes - mop tops of that emerging group, The Beatles. Denzel's smile was crooked and his teeth healthily white but uneven. His eyes were a bright blue, his eyebrows askew and his complexion a disorganised jumble of freckles and blotches of vigorous acne. His clothes consisted mainly of voluminous checked shirts, a knotted kerchief at his neck, below a prominent and knobbly Adam's apple, baggy jeans (none too clean), brightly coloured socks, not necessarily matching and worn sandals. Either this was a carefully cultivated look or he was bonkers (presumably the latter as he was going out with my sister). He sat sprawled on the settee, long thin legs splayed out, puffing on a roll-your-own cigarette carefully pinched between thin nicotine stained fingers, the nails of which were elegantly long and filthy.

What a catch!

Mum and Dad tried to conceal their horror, thus denying my sister the outraged reaction that I suspect she was seeking. Denzel lasted a good while before he was dismissed form my sister's courtly retinue. We thought she just wasn't really into skiffle and hanging around the front of the stage night after night in local clubs pubs and the Lane End Palais.

Between boyfriends was when my sister commandeered the use of the phone. This clumsy, large black contraption was kept in those days on its own well-polished wooden side table in the hall. There was usually a fight not to respond to its clamorous ringing, especially if there was a good programme on the television.

Between boyfriends was when my sister sat at the foot of the stairs to do her homework, balancing her books on a tea tray. We would hear only one and a half rings from the phone and then her voice as she answered it. Then would follow either a long conversation which interested us not at all or a very abrupt call of "'S alright. It's a wrong number." There were lots of those. They were people wanting to talk to Mum and Dad but who, if they were attempting to do so, would occupy the line and block out my siter's anticipated caller. It took Mum quite a while to tumble to that and, after a brief but animated exchange of views, my sister retreated sulking to her room for several days and I, who was inevitably sent out to answer the phone even in the middle of

Wagon Train or *The Adventures of William Tell* and had the job of informing many enquirers that she was not available. I got my own back on her for disturbing my viewing and invented reasons for unavailability – she was having a sulk, squeezing her spots – they got more and more unpleasant according to how miffed I felt, until of course she sneaked to Mum and I was forbidden to employ any such lurid inventions. "Just say she is doing her homework".

"Yes, Mum."

"Or else", would mutter my sister, razor in one hand, a tube of dermatological cream in the other.

All this until Brian appeared. Tall, fair-skinned, dark-haired, with the good looks of what was termed a matinee idol in those days, he slipped in almost unnoticed. He was respectful and polite, well-spoken, didn't sprawl or smoke, had finished his A-levels very successfully, was pursuing a degree in whatever subject was needed to become a successful Civil Engineer AND came from a posh part of Chester. He turned out to be 'the one'. He was never dismissed. And stayed the course, even surviving the evening when he was accosted by my sister's diminutive brothers, wide-eyed, determinedly demanding of him, "Do you love her?" The grim set of their jaws and their physical hunch in preparation to pounce if he gave the wrong answer, produced an assured, "Yes" accompanied by a scarlet blushing. From Dad came wild swipes at small heads with his rolled-up newspaper and abrupt dispatchings to bed.

And, as I said, all this was teaching us young males to reach various conclusion about love and its truths. Actually, if I'm honest, it led to greater confusion.

We first know that the ball was in the girls' court. That you approached as the lesser being and hoped for the best. Above all, we believed that we had to be better off – and more sane – than those who chose to pursue our sisters.

Though I will add that Brian remained in the picture for over 40 years, until death did them part.

I MET MY WIFE AT THE AIRPORT AND THE SMILE WAS WIPED OFF MY FACE BY SOMETHING SHE SAID!

He lowered himself sedately onto the railway station platform and immediately saw his wife rushing towards him through the noise of the carriage doors slamming, the bustling shadows of fellow passengers, the white billowings of steam.

"Oh, there you are, my dear. I'm so pleased to see you."

Any smile that might have lurked there was instantly wiped from his face. That she had come to the station to meet him, moreover that she professed pleasure in seeing him, spelled trouble.

"How are you, dear?"

A peck on the cheek.

He stopped, lowered his suitcase to the ground and transferred his briefcase to his right hand.

"I had to come and meet you – to warn you."

The station platform was darkening in the winter afternoon, the gloom competing more and more successfully with the guttering dirty yellow light of the spluttering gas lamps.

"Mother has arrived. No warning. She telegraphed ahead at the last minute. She wants us to meet her new companion. I think she wants our opinion."

He showed no reaction, just lowered his briefcase to balance on his suitcase.

Relief showed in her voice. "Well, good for you. You took that very well. They'll only stay for a few days, Mother said. I think there's some tension. Miss Pinkerton turns out not to be a cat person and Mother loves beyond care Whimsy, Mimsy and Mr Proudfoot – "

"Whom, of course, she has brought with her?"

"I know, my dear, but don't start. Anyway, that's not all. Cook is unwell and has gone home for a few days to her mother's. Which leaves yours truly to do all the catering. I know, dear, but there's no

---

alternative. Anyway, Vanessa is also home and I had hoped she'd be a help – she did after all do Cordon Bleu in Switzerland – but she's gone into one of her famous glooms. I don't know which side of the family she gets it from. Certainly not mine – although there was Great Aunt Hester and that incident with the caddy and the number five iron in Aberdeen – but she recovered from that, eventually, after treatment, which is more than could be said for the poor caddy. Vanessa's been let down by Charlie – you remember Charlie Carruthers-Windrush – who was meant to be taking her to Maisie Simpleton-Barrack's engagement bash at Flukesbury Hall at the weekend but he's called off for some rugby championship or other at Twickenham – or Wimbledon, which is it? – so Nessa can't go without a beau. There is Hamish McNirtle at Heversham Towers but he's such a bore, and he does have ginger hair, and will take any favour from Nessa as an indication of undying love since what happened in the boathouse at Lady Marmsbury's, so he won't be suitable at all, and he will wear a kilt which is all right until the Gay Gordons gets really lively and then – well, we all saw what we saw on New Year's Eve. Daphne Pilkington still can't entertain even the thought of hearing a skirl on the pipes without recourse to wavering knees and an attack of the vapours. Though I said to her that she'd seen all those statues in Rome two summers ago, so what was she expecting?

"Oh yes, and the ceiling in the west wing has spring a leak again. Owen and the gardener's boy are attempting a temporary repair but I'm not happy with him up on the roof – he is over eighty and has got weak ankles. At least Brindsley won't be home. He spoke on the telephone and he decided to give his Grandmama and her 'bloody pussies' as he calls them - he's very much your son, my dear – a miss, so he'll stay with Ferdy Crabbe-Streeting for half term.

"So, apart from that …

"Oh, I had to get rid of Molly from the scullery. The stupid girl was in hysterics. Apparently, she's convinced herself she's with child after being locked in the cupboard with Arnold, the under-butler, playing Sardines at the servants' Halloween Party. She's gone shrieking off home and word has come via Agnes Morgan who had it off Miss Simperton at the Post Office that her father is coming to sort it all out and Arnold is worried because he's heard that Molly's father is the Blacksmith from Nestling-under-Whitwould and is seven feet tall and a champion fairground pugilist but I said not to worry because you'd be home to sort it all out. Oh dear!"

She stopped and looked over her shoulder. "There's Marion Soulsby and that awful sister of hers. She's bound to spot me and insist on coming over. Then I'll have to invite them to tea to meet mother. Hold this."

She whisked her compact from her handbag and got him to hold its mirror in a position where she could catch what bleary light there was to check her make-up once she had lifted the brim of her hat and bared her small even teeth back at her own reflection.

"There. That will have to do."

She snapped her compact and bag shut, straightened up and turned to face the Misses Soulsby. He paused and blinked as the two ladies in question disappeared behind the ticket barrier.

"Well, I say. Of all the nerve. They're going. Snubbed by the Soulsby's. Can this day get any more fraught? Well, my dear …"

She turned back. But he'd gone, literally in a puff of smoke as the last carriage door slammed in the noisily departing 4.10 p.m. for Shoeburyness.

All that was left, in a pool of grudging amber gaslight, was a suitcase, a briefcase and a tightly furled umbrella angled across them both.

NEVER AGAIN

Never again –
On Thursday mornings –
Never again.

The 10 a.m. trudge to the flat plastic wood-grained uninspiring plane of the workroom table surface.

The black wrought metal of the hardly upholstered chair frame.

Never again – the anxiety of the reluctant Muse to confront the terror of the blank sheet of paper. The anguish of selecting the right words necessarily in the right order.

The trepidation of anticipating the receptiveness or otherwise of the audience.

Never again – the uncertain determination to bring them to laughter, tears, empathy, indignation, concern – anything but polite indifference.

Never again. Never again.

Not now I've had sight of how different Thursday mornings can be.

Soup – hot, homemade, rich and depth of flavour soup.

And cake – tea or coffee – more cake – conversation, idle and careless, then more and more cake. And comfort, embraced by, cosseted in, calm and warming homely domesticity, thick, swaddling cloaks, woollen shawls, hot water bottles, feather pillows, duck down duvets. Think dens, nests, hideaways, burrows, sets, think Messrs Mole, Badger and Ratty.

This is what Thursday morning could be – should be – but won't be.

For see – the soup brewer, cake baker, home keeper, coffee percolator, tea masher, lace maker, world comforter, toast butterer, domestic goddess – won't be there.

She'll be at the brown / black table in the beige room on her black hardly upholstered chair, flicking the barbed tip of her flashy and lashing metaphorical whip, driving weak words before her like a literary chariot-riding Boudicca, ploughing Moses like, parting a Red Sea of writers' reluctances (and, in doing so, mightily mixing up her metaphors).

So there is no choice.

Never say never again.

But take some comfort at least in the 11.15 or thereabouts cup of tea and proffered biscuit (oh! where is the cake, cake and more cake?) and beneath her steady gaze and eagle glinting eyes, bow your head and write.

But, perhaps, on the way home in desperate tribute, buy a tin of Cross and Blackwell's Leek and Potato, heat it up to scalding to disguise the thin and weedy flavour, and a plate of Mr Kipling's metallic factory fondant, far sweeter than sugar was ever meant to be.

But it won't be the same.

Nor can it be – never again.

NICKNAMES

They called him Jack Clark because that was his name. He was their teacher of History. He was never given a nickname.

Teachers who are not nicknamed are a comparatively rare breed. There are two types of teacher who do not earn the somewhat disrespectful familiarity of an invented soubriquet – the very popular teacher who is respected and he who is disliked and feared, even despised. No attempt at familiarity is deemed appropriate here. Jack Clark was certainly not of the former designation.

Lean and crabby, steel grey hair sparsely plastered back from his domed forehead, gaunt cheeked, a thin top lip slashing severely and horizontally beneath his narrow hooked nose, a chin that protruded unnaturally and when he smiled, which was rarely and to chilling effect, the mere humourless parting of the blue-tinged lips, he revealed small, even teeth irretrievably stained a khaki yellow by his heavy smoking habit.

His classroom was No. 11, at the end of a long corridor, and was a place of uneasy silence, the smell of chalk dust, stale tobacco and fear. Boys sat cowed in serried ranks of ancient, stained wood and metal desks. He prowled between them, his black academic gown threadbare and shades of deep green, brushing against their shoulders and bowed heads, a waft that disturbed the stale air with faint waves of acrid seat, fusty dampness and, in the lessons immediately after lunch, traces of pungent beer and sometimes a recent cigar.

Jack Clark would have been viewed with suspicion and dislike simply because of his unapproachability, his sarcasm, even hostility, his humourlessness, his unnecessary strictness and unerring ability to turn History lessons into lengthy endurances of tedious note taking and rote learning. But what relegated him to the ranks of those hated and despised was that which above all offends the sensibilities of the young, before experience teaches them that it is an inevitable fact of life, and that is unfairness.

Jack Clark had his rules, you see, which he deployed callously and deliberately. But he never outlined what those rules were. A circumstance arose where he had to assert himself unavoidably at the expense of a boy's dignity and self-respect, then he would apply one of his rules. It would be inconsistent with, even contrary to, others of his rules but there was no chance of appeal for the rules, as I said, were never delineated so there was nothing tangible to appeal against.

His decision had been clearly stated.

"But, sir ..." was the instinctive protestation.

"Those are my rules", he would hiss.

Further protestation. "But that's not fair, sir" would be greeted by a hefty swipe across the head or a vicious pinching of an ear. An appeal for 'fairness' was heard rarely in Room 11.

Jack Clark had decided expectations from each pupil. The brightest had to perform well and, providing they did so, had a relatively easy time, struggling with some success within his narrow and arid world of dry-as-dust text book readings and parroting recitals, by heart, of lists of historical dates.

Middle-of-the-roaders had to work hard to avoid weekly detentions or the completion of hundreds of punishment lines, seemingly endless repetition of a singularly elaborate expression of a rare historical fact – page after page after page often completed, by necessity, in the cold light of dawn having left the warm comfort of bed some hours earlier than would be normally expected.

The dim ones? For them there was no hope. Berated and beaten by him on the knuckles with a heavy ruler, they sat at the front of the class - "So I can keep my eyes on you" - suffered the constant indignity of the loud pronouncement of their always low marks and their weekly commitments to detention for failure in omnipresent tests and poor homework results. Their only consolation – and it was not inconsiderable – would be their exclusion from his classes as soon as selection was made by him of those who could move forward to Year Five public exams. He would tolerate no boy who might present any risk of failing the History exam. They were out. He jealously guarded his 100% pass reputation. If he allowed you to stay with him, you were guaranteed a pass. A pay-off for years of discomfort and harsh treatment at his hands.

And this is where Gerry Ralph fell foul of him.

Gerry Ralph could ordinarily have had a relatively easy time in Jack Clark's classes. He was very bright, presented a smart and respectable front, produced all work diligently and on time but, more, had the presence in school that Jack Clark totally approved of : upright, clean living and a first class sportsman – Captain of rugby, cricket and swimming, member of the gym squad, a fine marksman in the CCF and a renowned golfer. Even more, his father was a School Governor and his mother not distantly related to the royal family, her brother an 'Honourable' something or other.

Gerry's failing in Jack Clark's world was his sportsman's instinct for fair play.

Gerry had an unexpected friendship with, and admiration for, one of the least able in the History class. A giant of a boy, a wild crop of dark hair, cheeks of red, raw and crustaceous acne, he sat lesson after lesson at the very front, his large figure crammed and bent incongruously into the confines of his minute, in comparison, desk and chair. He squirmed and sweated and faintly groaned and winced at the insults and punishments repeatedly heaped on his head.

Gerry knew that this pupil had the physical prowess of a more than capable rugby forward and the capability to rise from his incumbent posture and, with one swift movement, heave scrawny Jack Clark through the air and out of the closed History room window. But he knew this could never happen and he grew to resent more and more the injustice of it all. He was reminded of an elephant in a circus ring and, ironically, in one of Jack Clark's lifeless accounts of life in Elizabethan England, they had met up with the cruel pastime of bear-baiting – their History text book contained a rare illustration at this stage, the gigantic magnificent beast set about by lean and vicious snarling dogs. This brought the whole situation searingly home to him. He came to suspect that the scrawny and angular master took a special delight in subjugating the cowed form of the normally towering and lowering boy.

Jack Clark overstepped the mark. The class came straight on to him from a PE lesson. He always insisted they arrive at his classroom on time and well presented. He would inspect them, that their hair was tidy, shirts tucked in, ties neatly tied. He latched on to the state of their hands. Were they clean after the demands of rolling around in the dust of the gym floor, handling the heavy equipment? He snarled at George's friend that he should show him the state of his finger nails. The other boys were busy copying out a chapter of their textbooks. Gerry had paused and was watching. Jack Clark's long, nicotine-stained fingers seized his friend's fleshy paw. "Look at the state of those nails!", he hissed. "Filthy. You only need one of these." He reached in the breast pocket of his worn and faded Harris Tweed sports jacket and produced a nail file. "It works like this." He secured the boy's outstretched forefinger, moved the file as if to clean beneath the boy's nail bed, instead, inserted the pointed tip of the file and thrust it deeply into the soft pink underflesh of the boy's nail. Gerry heard the compressed gasp of his friend, saw the shuddering of his body, the blood drain from his face. Jack Clark moved quickly away. Tears welled in his friend's eyes, his heavy lips gaped in shock as a large blob of bright red blood splattered onto the open white page of the book in front of him.

Gerry was transfixed by what had happened. The victim, as he hunched his shoulders and sank his head towards his desk in humiliation and pain, tentatively edged his injured hand into his blazer pocket. The rest of the class scribbled industriously on, unaware of what had happened.

After than, Gerry Ralph was a thorn in the side of Jack Clark. He became the enigma that that man and his indiscriminatory rules could not deal with. He was the bright and able pupil who would fail in History. He would pass everything else with flying colours in the classroom, on the sports field, everywhere, but would fail in History. There would be no credibility if Jack Clark refused to accept the boy in his exam class. So he would finally lose his 100% pass rate The smirks (after years) would pass from face to face of his common room colleagues. Even the Headmaster would be guilty of an unguarded smile when he announced the exam results at the staff meeting that inaugurated the new school year,

Jack Clark had offered his apologies that he would be unable to attend this meeting, for personal reasons.

NIGHT DREAMS

Over time, the feeling increased,

Firstly it was a mere apprehension, then a growing misgiving, gradually a fear and now a tangible terror. More and more he fought, at night, against falling into sleep and being absorbed, swamped in the same recurring dream. No – now it was stronger than a dream and had become an all-embracing positively physical sensation.

And it always began the same way.

Suddenly, in his sleep, which had become deep and profound, he realised that indeed he was asleep and dreaming, bogged down in a turgescent numbness, a weighty drowsiness, and he was sinking, gently but inevitably, through a dimly translucent gloom. But it was the extent of his drifting descent that he feared. He prayed that he would reach the ultimate depth of this watery, stygian, half-lit netherworld and, even in his aged and feeble physical condition, be able to use a suddenly discovered strength in his emaciated legs to thrust himself upwards, fighting the panic in his throbbing chest of an overwhelming suffocation, a knowledge that he was close to drowning, upwards to the surface when he would burst into body-wracking gasps of relieving night air and lie gasping on his unyielding pillow, exhausted, staring wide and wild-eyed at the shadowed pale ceiling tiles of the hospital ward around him. In his immense relief, he shouted out, a rasping, loud, animal, primaeval roar. Then he lay still, breathing heavily, alarmed by his own desperate outburst.

There was the clatter of shoes on the dull and stained parquet flooring and a face loomed closely above his own.

"What on earth are you doing?" The nurse's voice was a harshly emphasised whisper. "We have no time for this kind of behaviour. We have other people to consider. You are not the only one, you know." He felt himself shaken roughly. "No, settle down. Go to sleep." Spittle splattered on his upturned face. "I've got better things than pander to the likes of you." The face with its unconcealed annoyance disappeared.

He froze. But suddenly his chest heaved and he gulped in the stale air of the ward. He realised that in his anxiety he had stopped breathing. His pale gnarled fingers clawed at his loose sheets and seized clumps of the coarse material. He was suffused with a strong feeling of relief. Once more he had survived the nightmare – the ending he had most feared. When his feet would reach down to push up from the depths but would encounter nothing, no resistance, no end to his descent, and he would continue to sink into deeper darkness, total airlessness and … he could only but acknowledge the inevitable. "At my age", he reasoned, regaining some clarity of thought, "what else do you expect?"

He could move his head but little. However, propped up on his pillow he was able to swivel his gaze to his right and see the nurse at her workstation, glaringly illuminated directly from above by a single yellow downlight, pouring over her computer screen and keyboard. She paused, looked up directly in his direction. Was that really a vindictive glare in her eyes, or merely the momentary reflected flash of light from the metallic frame and glass of her spectacles, polished to sterility?

His gaze returned to the grey shadows directly above him. Now he would force himself to a stillness of the mind, lying, his eyes held open, dry and sore, reddening and stinging. Anything was better than yielding to sleep again. Even the long, still hours until early morning's increasing activity edged the ward back into predictable, monotonous, daily routine. The noise, clatter, voices : the movement, disturbance, the busy-ness and silence-breaking sense of purpose. Now he could sleep – well, at least doze – the agitations around him preventing his surrender to the deep, deep sleep of soundless solitude that he dreaded most.

He allowed his lips to curl into a grim smile and he breathed steadily, pushing away the certain knowledge that again night would come.

NOT GUILTY!

Six times the words arrowed across the courtroom piercing with a kind of violence the still, close, expectant air.

Six times in the abrupt stentorian delivery of the foreman of the jury, an elderly man of undeniable military bearing, cropped grey hair, clipped moustache, tight double-breasted navy-blue blazer, indecipherable heraldic badge on breast pocket, a tie of regimental stripes. The words like bullets fired from a rifle.

Six times, each verdict was endorsed and re-endorsed, each time more emphatic, less disputable. And after the sixth time, an achingly stunned silence – but for the gentle sobbing of a well-groomed young woman in the public gallery.

"That's his wife", whispered a close observer of the scene. "No – his daughter", came the muted response.

The accused – though now the acquitted – stood without motion or expression. His fine features remained unperturbed. His steady gaze met a point somewhere in the middle distance, as all good actors are trained to do. Look for Row J and glance gradually from left to right and you will appear to be taking in all the audience. Today is like that. The muscles in his face were under total control, even the nervous twitch in the hollow of his cheek that is so effective in camera close-up for revealing a repressed indication of stress or lack of control. And the hands, which can be such a giveaway (every accomplished actor knows exactly where his hands are and what they are up to at any given moment), hung loosely at his sides denoting calm and confidence. All in all, a superb performance.

Which continued soon after on the steps of the courtroom. The undulating crowd of press and paparazzi seething at his feet, he maintains his stance, almost aloof, measured, a hint of the world weary as he issues unhurried platitudinous utterings about forbearance and justice and understanding.

"What's next for you, then, Josh?" A coarse and clumsily shouted question from one of the rough-voiced clambering press pack employing the disrespectful familiarity of the abbreviated form of his first name.

The aged actor breaths deeply, the nostrils of his classical aquiline nose constrict effectively. "No", he confides in almost hushed tones, "I must get back to work." He turns to go.

A short distance from this hubbub, through a side door kindly pointed out by a considerate court official, exits another figure. A woman, middle aged, her head swathed in a fading floral scarf loosely knotted under her chin, obscured as if trying to withdraw inside the fur collar of her somewhat voluminous beige coat, her scruffy shoes flat and sensible, her gloved right hand gripping the handle of a shopping bag, incongruous and shocking in its vivid scarlet colouring. She keeps closely to the high stone wall as she moves away, anonymous and furtive.

The elderly actor is now within the safety of his black Rolls Royce. His wife, the elegant young woman, who has staunched her tears and re-established her composure, and he sit at opposite ends of the richly leathered bench seat. In the city traffic they acquire the same anonymity as does the shabby woman with the scarlet shopping bag. The news will not have broken yet. The crowds hurrying alongside the Rolls, briskly jolting against the plodding woman, will not have the renowned veteran actor and his reprieve brought to the forefront of their minds until they reach home and turn on the day's headlines.

The actor arrives at his house with no delay, through the grand automatic gates of his estate. At the pillared front entrance he dismisses his driver for the rest of the day and, without thanking him or waiting for his wife, he sweeps up the stone stairs and enters through the heavy oak door, across the marble tile hall, straight on up the curved wide staircase to his bedroom. No pause in his progress as he simultaneously manages to release his tie and shrug off his Saville Row suit jacket, ostentatiously lined with gold and bronze satin. These he drops carelessly on a chair. He moves through to his bathroom, stooped at the scallop shaped hand basin and splashes vigorously and copiously cold water over his face. He buries his head in the lavish pile of a luxuriant white face towel and retreats to his bed where he suddenly sits, huddled and ungainly, shaking and deep breathing uncontrollably, face still pressed into the towel, his long grey hair, usually and familiarly to his many fans swept back in firm waves, now dishevelled, moving in wafting disarrangement in time with the shuddering of his head and hunched shoulders – his whole being.

The woman has found her seat on the commuter train to her home station some twelve miles out of town. The carriage is surprisingly empty. She glances at her watch. It is earlier than she thought. The length of that day's hearing and the overcast nature of the winter afternoon had made it seem much later. She realises she is ahead of the rush hour. She presses herself into her window seat, her bright red bag bundled into her lap. It is her plan, once at her home station, to indulge in the not inconsiderable expense of a taxi to her outlying address. Although not the subject, so far, of press publicity, she is known locally to have been involved in the recent court proceedings, even to have been instrumental in their instigation, and now she can anticipate the blame and the pointing fingers. A taxi will see her swiftly back at her small terrace. She will retreat to her back kitchen. She will keep the curtains drawn, avoid electric light and use a couple of candles she has bought for the purpose. She will not draw attention to her presence. People will think she is not at home. The storm will break around her in the darkness with the lightning features of news bulletins and scary headlines. People will see her and judge. She is too terrified to cry.

But she has her bag packed. In the dead of night he sister will come to collect her, her luggage and the cat's bed. Rosie, her brindled moggy, the love of her life, has already been spirited away to safety. She will stay with her sister for as long as it takes. She and her sister know the truth, although her sister always thought her involvement in the whole awful business was inadvisable for exactly the reasons that have now transpired, the acquittal. And her disappearance with her sister out of the back door through the darkened brickyard and along the deserted rear alleyway is most timely. She will not hear the smashing of the glass of her front window, the clunk of the half brick on the carpet, the jeering cat calls of 'lying bitch' and worse, the hiss of the spray paint as 'bloody bitch' is scrawled across her white front door, lettering the same colour as the shopping bag now rocking on the back seat of her sister's small car.

There is another woman with her bags packed.

The actor's young wife, his third to be exact, stands in the doorway observing her husband's quaking, huddled form crouched on the bed. He senses her presence, rises stiffly to his feet, dropping the white towel in a huddle on the deep emerald green carpeting of the bedroom floor. He straightens his back and tries in vain to regain his composure and dignity. In vain because, despite his efforts with unsteady hands to sweep back his unruly swathes of silver hair from his brow, his face, though stiff and immobile, is stained with strands of brown, trickles of black descending from his eyebrows and eyes. He attempts a smile, his teeth beautifully even and artificially whitened.

She looks at him in scorn. What a performance, she thinks. But, my God, he's wearing make-up! The pathetic old fool!

She says, her voice cold, imparting information like a tannoid voice at an airport. "Dinner will not be long. Take your time." She cannot help adding. "Smarten yourself up. You look a mess."

The note of relish is evident in her voice. She leaves the room and pauses on the expanse of the carpeted landing. The house is bathed in light.

She has her plans. A packed bag. And her mother, younger than he, will pick her up later, by pre-arrangement. It will do his cause no harm now if it leaks out that they are separating. She knew it would be inevitable, especially if the verdict was 'Not Guilty'.

OUT OF SIGHT

They say 'out of sight is out of mind'
They also say that love is blind
But surely something here's not right
For being <u>blind</u> is out of sight
Being in love is out of mind
And prone to every raging kind
Of madness, passion and confusion
Which leads me on to this conclusion
The rarest love can only be had
By those who can't see they are totally mad.

PAIN

Pain – a warning bolt up to the brain
That tells you – don't do that again!
And, if you really won't refrain,
The result will always bet the same,
That stern assault upon the brain.

That stern assault that we resent
As if the Gods themselves are bent
To plague us with malign intent
When really it's a message sent
By nerve – to brain. A warning – pain.

And so at night we lie awake
With needling sharp or throbbing ache.
At least pain-killers we might take
That may or may not our pain slake.
A silent prayer we're bound to make,
'Let burning rings of anguish break'.
But e'en as fervently we pray
To take this bane of life away
We know that it is Nature's way
That pain is natural, and must stay.
So much to gain
From having pain,
That warning bolt up to the brain.

But, while accepting that is that,
I won't put down the welcome mat
But lock the door and hide the key
No matter how well meaning pain is meant to be.

PARENTS

On looking at the title for this week's writing assignment, the first thing I did was get in touch with my Muse. She was surprised not by my getting in touch but by the fact that she was not met by my pathetic and hysterical pleadings for help – ideas and inspiration – with frantic nods towards the ever-encroaching deadline. No, I informed her, you can have the week off, which was very good news for her as she was besieged by requests for help from her sister TERPSICHORE, the Muse of dance, who is constantly occupied by the insuperable dilemmas of a certain Anton du Beke and is presently in daily attendance on him at the *Strictly* studios. When his ministrations to his competition partner threaten his back, his knee joints and his sanity, TERPSICHORE is at her wits' end and her sisters flock to her aid, even if their dancing and coordination skills are as dire as those of his designated partner.

So, off she's gone. I just don't need her. PARENTS! What a doddle for a school teacher – like asking Ruth to write about THE SALLY ARMY, or Fred on 1939-45 AIR WARFARE, Eirys on PATAGONIA or Carol on MARMITE and Iris on LIVERPOOL CHILDHOOD.

Parents. How frequently is the dire boredom of Speech Days, Sports Days, Carol Concerts, ghastly Parents' Evenings enlivened by contemplation of the reality that is PARENTS. The ones you met before and can anticipate, from the pleasantly welcome to the obnoxious and disagreeable – and the novelty of those you are yet to encounter. And suddenly seeing where the pupil has originated and why he or she is like he or she is. The endless fascination – and the entertaining gossip in the staffroom next day. Unexpendable fodder.

Sometimes the whole picture fits.

Take the DRUMMONDS – brother and sister, 13 and 15. Megan and Sam. Apart from their sex, they could be identical twins, even in the body shape. Generously rotund. Worryingly overweight. Round, jolly, beamingly ruddy faces, a profusion of mid-brown curly hair, bright blue eyes, equally laid back to the point of complacency and totally non-academic. Enter Mr and Mrs – farmers – and we have four peas in the pod. (How can a wife look so like her husband?) The four sit in a row, patiently waiting their turn for the next teaching member.

They are silent, unmoving, uncommunicative but for a large box of Jelly Babies passing continuously between them. Podgy fingers pluck the minute bright-coloured confection from the yellow box and pop it between fat pouty lips. Pass the box on. Now it makes sense, the weekly note from Mum explaining that Megan and / or Sam cannot do PE and / or Games and Swimming today. The sports staff are relieved, their main problem being the unavailability of sports wear to fit the burgeoning frames of this perfectly pleasant but utterly indolent duo. Sam couldn't even be inveigled into 'putting the shot' on Sports Day though, rumour had it, he could carry a full-grown sheep under one arm at home.

Barnaby Savage's mother always came, but not for several years as Mrs Savage. During his six years in the school, Barnaby's mother had adopted the use of four different surnames, three through marriages and one other a less pleasant re-nomenclature. "And Mrs Brooks-Peterson would definitely like a word with you", said the School Secretary. "I haven't got a Brooks-Peterson in my class". "No – it's Barnaby Savage's mother." "But she was Mrs Waterman at the Carol Service." "Well, she's Mrs Brooks-Peterson now, and this time it is marriage." Barnaby himself was totally self-adjusted. Tall for his age, slim and good looking – popular with the girls – a boy of considerable charm. Perhaps he was cushioned by the fact that his mother's changing partners became progressively wealthier – as did his mother. And each school holiday indicated a stay abroad in their chalet in Switzerland, a condominium in Florida, an island retreat in the Caribbean. And what was half term but a chance for a shopping spree in London, or Paris, or New York? Barnaby was an industrious boy who saw that responsibility for his future lay in his own hands and, as he was inevitably at school anyway, he might as well benefit from his incarceration and leave with some good qualifications – as long as it didn't interfere with his social life – setting academic work to be completed during the school holidays was an utter waste of time. Books would just add unnecessary weight to the parents' initialled in gold, calf skin luggage.

Fourteen-year-old Nigel Brunstrom arrived mid-year. A quiet boy, soon popular with his peers, he blended in. Then we spotted the name of the new Police Chief for North Wales – Brunstrom. The truth was out. "I didn't want everyone to realise", he confided. Whilst his father's eccentricities attracted more and more attention in the media – his obsession (at the cost of all else, it would seem) with correct procedures and swift and smooth passage for all on the A55, his preoccupation with minute details of protocol (so what if seaside towns were gradually yielding more and more to the workshy and the drug addicted?) – whilst all this was progressing, Nigel kept his head down and worked hard. But academically he struggled. His father presented himself – tall, angular, bony faced, a reedy, expressionless voice – at appropriate events. We never met the mother but I did see Nigel a couple of times at the local Tesco pushing a full trolley for a rather slight, somewhat haunted looking woman, whom I took to be his mother.

The father was officious and clinical when discussing his son's progress. He seemed to quote from some educational manual. With 'quotients', 'percentiles', 'progress benefit factors', 'propential marginal targets', text-book language without any text. Instinct prompted that the son needed protection from this thin-lipped, humourless progenitor. Humane intercourse was impossible. God knew how the merest whisper of criticism of the child would be interpreted and acted upon at home. Not for a minute, physical reproof, but worse … uncomprehending mind-gaming, the unforgiveable error of falling short.

So the parents entertain and inform but sometimes you get too close.

Rory Stewart was a small blond-haired boy, well below the average 11-year old's height. I first encountered him when he auditioned for the Junior Play and, in the role of a cheeky young street urchin, he seemed ideal. Except that he never arrived at the designated time for rehearsal. "Anyone know where Rory Stewart is?" Inevitably the reply, "He's having a kick about on the playing field." He was obsessed with soccer. The school's game was rugby but he was fully involved at evenings and at weekends with the local town soccer team boys' divisions. He was hauled in to rehearsals where he behaved genially if with little obvious conviction until finally he gave a scorchingly effective performance, word perfect, inventive, clear, vivid and assured. After the last performance, his mother appeared backstage. Herself diminutive and blonde, a pretty face, a genuine warm smile. "He done well", she mocked. "He did", I assented. She expressed true gratitude that he had found a worthwhile outlet other than the hitherto exclusion of all else but soccer.

Once he was in the Senior School, I often met Rory's parents at Parents' dos. The mother friendly and pragmatic, the father equally lacking in height, more reserved and monosyllabic : dark hair swept back, steel rimmed glasses, always a smart, expensive suit, shirt and dark tie, immaculately manicured nails, I noticed, as he made frequent and copious notes at parents' evenings, not often connecting with his cool grey eyes.

In English lessons, Rory chose to sit always at the back, his work cautious and unconvincing. Disappointing from one who showed such promise in the school play. Writing a story, for him, meant three quarters of a page of awkward, stilted narration – generally unconvincing and without flair. Until the occasion when he handed in his homework books and I found three sides of writing. It was an interesting story, full of convincing detail, authoritative and about soccer. A boy failing in a team who was placed in goal for a practice by default, found his strength and went on to prosper. I held him back after class to emphasise how pleased I was with his effort. "I didn't think we'd be allowed to write about soccer", he said. And thereafter that's all he did. But the stories, though inevitably repetitive, were good and got better.

Apart from the plays, I saw little of him unless he was in my English class until, at the age of 15, I became his form teacher and got an overall view of his progress. He was just holding his own and heading for a fair spread of GCESs. He was still by far the smallest in the class, of boys and girls, and had two close friends who towered over him and shared his persisting enthusiasm for soccer. His lack of stature did worry him. He was losing credibility with his age group on the soccer pitch, but he was well established in the school.

It was at this time that his parents split up. The father left the marital home and now his parents came separately to events, two separate interviews on Parents' evenings about Rory's progress. It was odd but tolerable.

GCSEs came and went. Rory entered the Sixth Form – Business Studies, Sociology and Sports Studies. I saw hardly anything of him but learned from his next-door neighbour (a Maths master) who had anxious representations from his mother that Rory was sometimes excluded from the under-18 football team and was experiencing some isolation from his friends. They were pushing the boundaries, getting into pubs and the local seaside night spots with an over-18 policy – Rory wasn't. Also they now saw nothing of his father who had re-married.

It was one morning in Spring, a gentle sunny day, welcome after the rigours of a hard winter when, in the staff room at an 11 am coffee break, the Headmaster interrupted the comfortable murmurings of idle conversation with a sharp rapping of his teaspoon on the rim of his cup. An abrupt respectful silence. This announcement – a particularly sad one, he forewarned; he regretted to announce that the previous evening Rory Stewart's mother had returned home to find that he had hanged himself from the bannisters in the hallway. He was dead before the ambulance arrived.

The funeral was held two weeks later on a school day early afternoon.

Provision was made for a few to attend from the school. The Head would remain behind and hold an all-school assembly in honour of Rory. The Deputy Head would represent the school together with four selected staff – I was one, the Maths teacher neighbour another – and a small group of Rory's sixth form friends (their parents would meet them there).

The ceremony was cold and bleak without any redeeming features that could introduce any relief to the dark atmosphere of the proceedings. Even the floral tributes – red and white wreaths for Liverpool FC and the inevitable white and blue carnation footballs – seemed a trite mockery of the unrelenting gloom of the day.

We stood quietly awaiting the start of the service. A noise behind which must be the family entering the rear of the church. I glanced around and in full view were Rory's parents : the father - glacial eyes straight ahead, unblinking, body erect, dark suit, black tie, face taut, cheek muscles pulsating. But his mother – it was as if the tsunami of grief had, in sweeping over her, forcefully hurled her bodily against an unyielding wall and left her breathless, battered and saturated into an unnatural paleness, all colour and strength drained from her. Dressed in black, her face seemed to hover in mid-air, the eyes in staring bewilderment of intense sorrow and blank incomprehension, her features sunken as if outlined on a pale balloon that had gradually been deflating leaving the previously pretty plump features to harden into cruel defacing lines that etched sorrow into the soft flesh which could never be removed.

It was not until the coffin passed us, being borne gently out of the church on black-suited shoulders that I saw, amidst the family floral tributes, someone had placed a pair of used football boots, not in an orderly fashion, neatly parallel, laces arranged, but as if they had been hurriedly dropped in the hall as he came home and the door slammed safely behind him. And wisely, whoever it was, in view of their final destination, had left them caked in dried earth.

PARTNERS

Elizabeth Pennyfeather awoke earlier than usual to an immediate knot of anxiety in her stomach as the day dawned on her that it was Thursday – the first Thursday in the month – the day of the regular Tea Dance in the Village Hall. A gentle, retiring person, she did not relish the obligatory enjoyment, the enforced gregariousness of these occasions, but her attendance was a duty, an obligation to William, her twin brother, who provided the music. He was the self-styled M.C. (or D.J. as he preferred to be called) and she went along to help with the 'setting up' – the sound equipment, speakers, boxes of LP records and decks.

And once all the equipment was in place and tested, and enough of the dancers had arrived and William had adjusted his gold bracelets on his wrists and his large black plastic shades on his forehead and set the stylus down on the spinning grooves of the opening waltz, she had little excuse other than to step out from behind his desk of decks and inevitably indicate herself available as a dance partner.

And it was always the same.

A Waltz – and up would step Mr Rosebury from Smithy Cottage at the end of the village. Tall, thin and stooping, grey faced, grey hair, half moon glasses perched on the bridge of his beaky nose from the end of which inevitably hung a generous droplet of mucus, and a creeping, gradual semi-smile that revealed rows of unnaturally white and even teeth between narrow, downturned bluish lips. His Harris Tweed sports jacket was worn and smelt of grilling bacon and dogs, his faded, limp, badly knotted tie hung discouragingly down and the points of his striped shirt curled dispiritingly up.

Luckily at these events conversation during the dancing was discouraged by William's habit of keeping the music turned up very loud out of respect for the poor hearing of most of his elderly revellers. Occasionally, Mr Rosebury's lips moved in a mournful drone but all Elizabeth could do was nod politely in acknowledgement and smile.

The Gay Gordons – and up would pop, on nervous twinkling feet, Cyril Bartliff from the flat above the corner shop. A slight, energetic man – extraordinarily slim from a diet almost exclusively of baby food. He always wore his chalk blue pinstripe three-piece suit that betrayed its age through lapels far too wide and trousers somewhat too flared; a gargantuan knot in his wide tie of some glittering blue and silver floral brocade-type material. His hair carefully bouffant and too freshly blonded for a man of his certain age, and no close scrutiny being needed to become aware of fastidiously applied makeup around the eyes, with blusher on the cheeks and lips. He added the flourish of delicate little jumps and skips to the steady pacing of the Scottish dance whilst he la-la-ed along with the melody and emitted high squealing whoops of delight at regular intervals. Elizabeth looked about her at the stomping formation and grim concentration of the dancers. The Village Tea Dance Gay Gordons were hardly that, but Cyril Bartliff most emphatically was.

Then the Jive, which she dreaded most. For up loomed the towering, elephantine bulk of Bradley Cumberstone, the erstwhile village postman who, since he had retired form his daily twelve-mile expeditions of cycling and foot slog, must have added a good six stone to his already substantial seventeen stone frame. He always wore his greying hair cropped short above his fleshy florid face and the same vast scarlet red shirt. Elizabeth somewhat unkindly reckoned he looked rather like one of the many imposing cylindrical post-boxes that he had daily spent so many years of his life unloading. He obviously had a wide range of garishly coloured bow ties for he sported a different one for each dance session, even being known to change ties between dances. Every Christmas he had two bows – one a black background offsetting green and red springs of holly, the other green sporting tiny gold and silver Christmas puddings. Bradley Cumberstone loved to jive. He threw back his head, hunched his shoulders, curled his upper lip in true Presley fashion and span alarmingly around the floor passing Elizabeth's delicate hand from podgy paw to podgy paw with startling alacrity. As with so many weighty people, he was impressively light on his feet. Elizabeth noted that, for his extraordinary size, he had very small feet and the manner in which his black trousers tapered from his voluminous waist down to his dainty black patent leather shoes created the impression that he was dancing on points like some inflated wildly coloured whirling dervish ballerina. She thought of the hippos in *Fantasia*. The disadvantage being that as he whirled, ducked and dived, his scarlet shirt clung damp and sweaty to every contour of his rolling body and a sudden movement of his head would release fine sprays of sweat to refresh those within close proximity, i.e. Elizabeth.

For the Quickstep and Foxtrot, Elizabeth required a manly partner to hold her firmly and lead her purposefully through the intricacies of this dance's rhythm and this she always got this in the box square shape of Mrs Hortense Weatherfield ('HW' to her friends). She would grasp Elizabeth with emphasis, state deeply and brusquely, "I will be the man", and whisk her away to the middle of the floor. So unerringly efficient was the support and guidance offered by the bulky Mrs Weatherfield that Elizabeth coped confidently with the 1-2-2's and the sudden changes of direction required by the dance in spite of having any sight of the dance floor and its occupants totally obscured by the enormous cushioning of Mrs Weatherfield's mountainous bosoms, one on each side of Elizabeth's head. Mr Weatherfield, a man of fragile build and insignificant stature but nevertheless a splendid sidesman in the Church always demurred from attending these occasions. Elizabeth saw, even though she could hardly see anything at all, exactly why.

Then, one day, the Viennese Waltz. Elizabeth normally shrank to William's side to avoid the continuous rumbustious twirlings of this dance but on this occasion she was waylaid. A tall, dignified figure in superbly tailored linen suit with neatly knotted striped tie on an immaculately white shirt, slate grey hair curling in a leonine manner from a wide tanned forehead, sparkling grey / green eyes and a hint of a knowing smile teasing his firm well-sculpted lips.

"May I ...?" His voice was low and purring, his hand firm in hers. He smelt of an attractively spicy aftershave and fresh laundering. "I'm a newcomer but I do love the Vienna Waltz." His one arm around her waist and the other hand gently but decidedly attached to her left, she felt his confidence and expertise give wings to her feet as she span this way, then that around the floor. Occasionally their eyes would meet; his gaze was direct and humorous and a wide smile would emphasise his nobly sculpted high cheekbones and rows of firm white teeth, undoubtedly his own.

The Interval followed the Viennese waltz, a necessary breather during which he settled her in a chair near the door (to catch some of the afternoon's cool breeze), fetched her a cup of tea and chatted, mostly about her, she remembered later – he communicated a genuine interest in her somewhat humdrum existence, reacting to her revelations with gently mocking wry comments and that same inviting smile and warm gaze. She hardly noticed the passing of time but suddenly there was Amanda Plassy, the wife of the retired village doctor. "Ah, Colonel Kiggell." Amanda was an organiser, loud, forthright, smacking of hockey team captaincy, healthy living and cold showers. "Latin American next", she announced. "May I?" The Colonel rose, inclined his head ruefully to Elizabeth and was whisked away on to the floor. The Colonel glided silkily into the Samba, his gentle gaze transfixed by the braying hectoring energetic lips of Amanda's bony, narrow face. Elizabeth was in turn scooped up by Dr Plassy and resigned her feet to many minutes of being trampled under the clumsy efforts of this dull, ungainly man.

Eventually the Last Waltz was announced which was Elizabeth's signal to call it a day. She plumped behind William's desk, sorting out the many tea cups and saucers he had acquired, cleaning up his chocolate biscuit wrappings and sorting LPs into appropriate sleeves. The Waltz ended. People headed for the door. Elizabeth emerged from under the desk where she had been returning LPs to their carrying cases. A huddle of people around the exit – a few stragglers sitting gossiping, reluctant to draw the event to its conclusion. No sign of the Colonel. Elizabeth smiled. Maybe next month … but she never saw him again.

PIPPI

Well, I am on edge. And Mum is on edge. Dad is too – you can tell by the way he subtly extends his working day arriving home just in time to stop his evening meal spoiling. Terry keeps his head down and spends even more time – is that possible? – with his computer in his attic bedroom. Even the dog is affected.

She is the one – Pippi, her name – who really benefited from Gran's arrival to live with us. Previously her week days were composed mainly of long periods of isolation. We all went off to work and school. Mum popped home at lunchtime (she only worked in the medical practice – administration manager – in the next village), and then a lonely watch until mid-afternoon when we came clattering back from school. Suddenly Gran was there virtually all day and every day and Pippi readily adopted her newfound compatriot. She was given a bed in Gran's bed / sitting room but usually lay at Gran's feet, her shaggy black and white head heavily across Gran's instep.

But once a fortnight – when Gran is particularly on edge – Pippi senses that a form of separation might be the better part of valour – and retreats to her old daytime habit of lolling in a comfortable chair in the window of a front bedroom, watching the world go by – not much of that in a sleepy English village – barking and whining at the postman, any passing tradesman – and hurling herself excitedly downstairs when members of the family return home. She lumbers enthusiastically around any and all pairs of legs in the Edwardian tiled entrance hall, the fronds of her plumed tail waving frantically to and fro.

At times of stress though, Gran takes a back-place in Pippi's attentions : the canniness of canine instincts.

Gran's move to live with us has, in all other aspects, ben a great success. Left alone after Grandad died in their small bungalow some distance from us, anticipating future likelihoods, she moved into what perhaps rather grandly was termed 'a granny flat'. One of the large rear ground floor rooms of our grand Edwardian house became her bedsitter and the adjoining structure which had housed a dental workshop in former times, equipped as it was with heat, light and plumbing, became a reasonably sized kitchen and a bath --- er, more correctly – a shower room. So Gran had a fair modicum of independence should she require it, but was readily part of family life. Apart from the mutual attachment of woman and dog, her continual presence in the house offered definite reassurance in a quiet rural location, as well as there always being someone to take in deliveries, pay the milkman, host the window cleaner and gardener etc. etc. It was good when you were home from school unwell, to have really maternal sympathy and instant attention. Even if you were a captive audience for colourful accounts of the good old days and Grandad's youthful escapades. When we were younger, she sometimes read to us – Gran was not without literary aspirations.

But once a fortnight came the stress – Gran was on an edge, elements of which she generously distributed to all the family.

She became positively reclusive but we felt the tension. We were urged to quietness first thing in the morning when preparation for school etc would normally have occasioned a healthy hubbub. Hisses of 'quiet' and earnest 'shushes' were quite daunting. "Don't disturb Grandma!" Had she been up late at night again, her head bent over her writing desk, a lone figure in the pool of yellow light thrown by her reading lamp? She would appear at the kitchen door, her grey hair dishevelled, her cream candlewick dressing-gown firmly if unevenly belted, her eyes dark rimmed and strained. She took in the busy scene. A pause. "I'll come back later", and she was gone. Pippi pressed herself under the kitchen table, curled up, her tail covering her black nose.

In the evening, Gran would be uncommunicative and restrained at the dinner table. She would pick at her food, refuse pudding (normally her favourite course). She would make an unenthusiastic attempt to join those settled in the sitting room afterwards, but she would stare vacantly at the television, sigh deeply and dramatically, her hands moving constantly and restlessly over her lap. She would haul herself to her feet – ignoring, "Are you all right, Mum" from her daughter and leave the room. Then she would reappear, sit and tut in an annoyed and annoying manner at whatever moving picture was displaying itself, and then, again, up rather clumsily and off. Eventually she would fail to reappear and would remain incommunicado until breakfast next morning, even failing to be tempted by the proffering of a late-night hot chocolate or comforting cocoa.

This would go on until Thursday when we knew, in the evening, the cloud would have been lifted. Gran would be Gran again and she would sit in the kitchen as Mum prepared the meal, a sweet sherry to her lips, a hairy contented black and white head in her lap.

"How did it go?" Mum would routinely enquire, a little tentatively.

Gran would take a gentle breath of contentment. "Not bad at all", she would say quietly. "I truly think they quite liked it." There would be a pregnant pause, an invitation for Gran to proceed. "The Secretary was really appreciative – she always enjoys description, nature, the countryside. The Vicar's wife dabbed her eyes at one point. She's so very sensitive. I think it was the description of the moss of the crumbling green stone. That got to her." She half smiled with quiet satisfaction and took another sip of sherry.

"And Amy Turkington?" This question from Mum was inevitable. But we really had to know.

Gran straightened up. "She looked down her long nose, said something about it being 'quite effective if a little predictable and clichéd", but 'something of an improvement' then she went on to read her effort, a blinking sonnet, wouldn't you guess? Which was absolutely marvellous – very, very good. She gave us all a copy to keep."

She finished off her sherry in one swift swig. She stood up. Pippi, her head suddenly dislodged, looked up in surprise, her dark eyes moist and doleful. Gran stiffened her spine, threw back her shoulders. "But I'll show her. *I'll* do a poem next time. There's plenty of time. Two weeks. I'll show her. I'll show them all. Now, shall I lay the table?"

We heard the determined, almost warlike clatter as she tackled the cutlery drawer in the dining room. With one thought we looked apprehensively at each other. We had ten or eleven days; then, as another Thursday approached, we would have to endure Gran's preparation for the next meeting of her Writing Group.

Pippi, following Gran, not quite wagging her tail, padded optimistically out of the room.

POST-IT NOTES

He gently eased open the drawer and looked down into the honey wood interior containing a generous scatter of small squares of paper – a disorganised patchwork of pastel yellow, pink and green. Some were curling at the edges, beginning to coil – all were marked with dark scrawled lettering. The solemn look in his hazel eyes beneath the furrowing of his brows was a marked contrast to the wistful smile that gently formed on his lips. He ruminated on the strangeness of Post-It Notes being totally an accidental invention. He'd read it somewhere, he couldn't remember the exact details, but it amused him to think that someone somewhere had made millions from what looked like oversized pieces of sticky confetti.

He focused on some of the words penned clearly on the notelets. Coffee. Kettle. Glasses case. Milk. He wondered what an outsider would make of them. Perhaps they aided a student learning English as a second language who used them as a vocabulary broadening exercise – or a child learning to recognise and spell the names of everyday objects. His smile faded quickly away as the reality of their use coldly returned to his memory.

They had been his mother's idea, born, as many good ruses are, out of necessity. Dad was beginning to have good and not so good days. "He comes and goes", Mum had said. Words would fail him in mid-sentence. He'd go upstairs or into the garden but quickly return to her. "Peg", he would ask. "What was I going for?"

She started almost innocently labelling the kitchen cupboards to remind him of the contents. If he went out to make a pot of tea there would be door slamming and cursing as he trawled the cabinets and drawers for required items. Pride forbade him from asking, yet again, where she kept the teaspoons. The Post-It Notes imprinted with neat lists indicated the presence of tea bags, tea cups and saucers, sugar etc. etc. It was some time before the need for milk did not obviously guide him to the fridge.

Philip, a teacher, lived away and only came home during the school holidays. His first memory of seeing a plethora of Post-It Notes around the house was one Christmas. It was one of Dad's good days and he could see the funny side of the unusual Christmas decorations – yellow, blue, pink, green rectangles dotting the house. At that stage they were mostly bearing instructions – reminders to turn off the TV, check the kettle had water in it, lock the front door.

They became a family joke on Christmas Day. One of Mum's small presents on the tree was a bundle of Post-It Notes. She giggled and Ben, the youngest of the children and the least reverent, grabbed the notes, distributed them and everyone scrawled on them and stuck them needlessly around the room. A pink 'Mum' was stuck on her forehead – as if anyone could forget who she was! A yellow note identified the Christmas tree. Someone stuck a blue 'Toaster' on the television. Ben spent the rest of the day with a green 'Bum' on the back of his trousers and Aunty Alice, Mum's sister, good naturedly sported a white 'Old Bat' on her lapel.

Towards the end of the day, Dad went into the kitchen to make a cup of tea – but he eventually gave up in exasperation. He sat, quiet and withdrawn, on an upright chair by the sideboard, a bright pink 'Dad' stuck on his left shoulder.

Philip didn't come home again until Easter. His phone calls home echoed with Dad going rather than coming. But mum was all right. She had Alice and her husband Jim, and Philip's sister Jenny and her Brian. He sensed the difference as he entered the front door. His mother's welcoming hug had just that note of urgency, was just that little too prolonged. "How's Dad?" he asked.

"Not so good today." She released him and stepped back. He saw a blue 'Mary' on the front of her cardigan.

He walked into the sitting room. Dad sat in his favourite chair gazing wide eyed at the animated and garish children's cartoons on the TV screen. He turned as he noticed the two figures entering the room. He pushed himself quite readily to his feet, smiled towards them and offered his right hand. "Come in", he said. "And what can we do for you, young man?" Philip froze. A slight, sharp intake of breath.

Mum spoke. "This is Philip, dear. He's home for Easter."

"Of course it is." Dad's voice was irritable and hurried. "Come in and sit down."

Philip quietly shut the drawer, the memory of that moment bringing a sharp stinging sensation to his eyes. He found it even more painful to dwell on the halting conversation that ensued from that moment – his father obviously having no idea that he was talking to his older son but valiantly trying to maintain polite pleasantries. He knew, though, to call the woman in the room 'Mary' - when she was facing him and close enough for him to decipher the lettering on her blue tag.

During the Summer term, Philip made an effort to get home for several weekends and, unusually for him, for all of half term. Dad's bad days now far outnumbered the good. "He comes and he goes", reported Mum in all of their frequent phone calls. "Alice and Jenny are a great help." And, of course, it was just after one weekend when he couldn't get home – right at the end of the summer term – so many reports to do, admin, end of term activities – that he received the phone call from Jenny. Dad had finally gone. Gently, in his sleep.

"I'll be home immediately", he said.

He had almost forgotten the Post-It Notes until some weeks after the funeral. After Dad's passing, Aunty Alice had moved in with Mum and she had surreptitiously, gradually removed the pastel squares and placed them in the drawer. Philp had discovered them by chance whilst looking for any of Dad's belongings that needed disposal.

He left them there, except one.

A bright pink square, in Ben's black scrawl, 'Dad'.

That reminds me, he thought.

PROBLEMS, EH?

(2005)

"Problems, eh?"

The voice, suddenly close to my left ear, hauled me out of my reverie. I was perched on the front garden wall beneath the 'House Sold' sign, agitatedly if mindlessly swinging a large bunch of keys backwards and forwards between my hands. Problems preoccupied me. Today we were moving house which presented anticipated problems that either materialised or didn't, and unanticipated problems that seemed to have equal effect were they trivial or major. My current problem had veered from trivial to significant a while ago, and was rapidly acquiring the designation of 'major'.

"Oh, sorry", I said. "I was miles away. I'm waiting for the removal men. It's well overdue – all my earthly goods somewhere on the road between here and Ashford." I extended my hand. "Brian Morgan", I offered. "Your new neighbour."

"Gideon Browning." He looked at me with large sombre eyes. His whole face was careworn from the furrowed brow beneath the bald dome of his head to the fleshy, wobbling chins below his full, downturned mouth. "It happened to us", he continued. "We lost a wheel. Everything spilling out onto the road. I walked with my eldest four miles back till we found it. Had to leave him there to protect the load. I came back with blankets. Three days before repairs could be done. All that time my boy stood there with a garden shovel. Me and the girls journeyed there and back carrying necessaries for the wife. Let's hope you've broken down nearer. And the weather's changing. You can feel the wind coming off the sea. Which will mean heavy rain, if I'm not mistaken. And fog following. That'll bring the chill in."

He was only serving to add to my concerns. It was already late on a Friday afternoon. Phoning the removal firm's office had proved fruitless. All we could do was wait – though sitting twitching on the front wall would not help hurry events along.

"All our pots and things were broken when it lurched over – lots of damage. It all had to be unloaded onto the road to repair the wheel, then back in again. It was dark by then. People came to help and we lost a couple of chairs. My eldest needed eyes in the back of his head."

But my gaze was attracted to movement at the end of the road. A big white van, the logo of a large chess piece in red and sweeping black lettering.

"Ah, there it is", I said. "Excuse me. I'd better go and alert the troops." I ran up the driveway. "I'll tell my wife it's here." I turned to smile and wave but he'd already gone.

. . . .

Frances, my wife, was successfully and efficiently directing the removal men as they came in with box after box, item after item. The garden table and chairs had ended up in the kitchen and I had decided to unlock the shed at the bottom of the garden realising that, before long the lawnmower, garden tools etc would be requiring a home. Light was failing and the shed was situated beneath mature trees at the far end of the long garden right up against the tall hedge that separated us from next door. I put down the two plastic chairs I had carried and contemplated the large bunch of keys in my hand. One of these must be for the shed, I reasoned, and I began the process of selection and trial, without success. I tried to hold the keys in such a way that I knew which I had tested and which I hadn't but this made the turning in the lock difficult and the gathering gloom did not help. In my increasing agitation I quietly cursed.

"Problems, eh?"

The gloomy voice seemed startlingly close to my ear. I jolted nervously.

"Oh, hello. Mr Browning. I didn't see you there."

His long face seemed suspended over the hedge, the shadows deepening his eyes and emphasising the heavy bags beneath them. His cheeks seemed even more hollow. The shading under his chin blended into the almost black foliage of the hedge. It was as if he was floating in space.

"It's the keys", I said. "I'm trying to unlock the shed. There are so many of them."

"You want the shed key?" he returned. "It's hanging on the shed. See? Up to your left? Just underneath the overhang. No, more to your left. That's right."

I had my hand on the key, silver and well oiled. It easily turned in the lock. "The bane of my life, keys", I said. "I'm a teacher. Seem to spend my entire time locking and unlocking things."

"Never troubled me. Never had anything that needed locking away. Possessions, valuables only bring care and trouble. You get so frightened of losing them, it takes all the pleasure out of having them. If you've got nothing then you've nothing to lose and no jealousy to rouse in other folk, no envy, no ill feeling. Covetousness is a sin."

I swung open the shed door and found the light switch.

"Look at that", he said. "Dusty cobwebs, broken flowerpots and a broom handle. Carefully locked away. Daft, isn't it!"

He had a point. I turned to lift the chairs. "Well, thanks for pointing out the key …" But he had gone, just dark shadow where his face had been.

……..

The next morning was grey and overcast but we were too busily employed inside to care. We had two days to devote entirely to unpacking before grandparents were due to turn up with the children, the dog, a cat, a rabbit and a stick insect. As the cooker we had brought with us could not be connected until Monday (unless we paid triple time to some local electrician), I had undertaken to erect our barbecue on the patio just outside the conservatory. The first home cooked meal in our new home would be chargrilled – or most likely well and truly charred – sausages and burgers with a bottle of good red wine.

As I fiddled with the many components of the barbecue, trying to align the various slots and apertures so that they would take the, by now, quite rusty bolts and nuts, vague memories of my tribulations in putting this apparatus together when I had first purchased it a couple of years before became far clearer. I remembered Frances ushering the children away from where Daddy, with fiercely reddening face, was volubly damning the whole concept of 'home assembly' and determining to do horrible things to people who were no doubt paid a fortune to design those blasted fiddly contraptions that have a built-in resistance to ever allowing themselves to be constructed with anything approaching ease and that there most probably aren't the right number of bolts and nuts in the pack as it was most probably made in Hong King anyway with Oriental inscrutability … I twisted the nut, the bolt slipped and two pieces of sharp metal gripped and threatened to sever my right forefinger. I swore loudly and vehemently ..

"Problems, eh?"

"Oh, Mr Browning." I smiled weakly towards where he was peering over the adjoining wall. "Not my forte, this kind of thing."

"Strange contraption", he affirmed.

"Just a barbecue." His large eyes stared down at me, grey and watery, no indication of any kind of understanding of what he was witnessing. In the grey light he looked quite pallid, beads of glistening sweat breaking out on his top lip and wide forehead. "Our cooker's not plumbed in yet", I added in explanation.

"Oh, a stove!" he said. "Take some heating up, that will, what with the weather on the change and rain due. Hard to find dry fuel in this weather. You just get low embers and clouds of smoke from the damp. You'll be lucky to get anything cooking on a day like this. You'll need skill and patience. And something sturdier than that", he added as parts of the structure slipped from my grasp and noisily clattered with metallic rasping to the stone paving. He paused and sighed deeply and discouragingly. "I don't give much for your chance of a hot meal ..."

"Brian. Brian. Could you come here?" Frances' voice broke in on his monologue.

"Hang on", I called. I lowered what had not yet fallen from my hands to the ground. She appeared at the door.

"It's our next-door neighbour called round." She went in and I rose to my feet.

"Excuse me, Mr Browning."

But he had gone.

Inside the kitchen stood a woman, middle-aged, blonde, jeans and bright sweater, big blue eyes, full even smile. She couldn't have been any more strongly contrasted to Mr Browning.

"Hello, I'm Brian. Pleased to meet you."

"I'm Eve." We shook hands warmly.

"Eve has come round", interjected Frances, "to invite us in for a meal this evening."

"Any time", said Eve. "When you're ready. It'll be Chilli, in the oven, so will keep. We'll eat when you appear." She eyed the disconnected oven,

"That's great", I returned. "Thank you. I was just setting up the barbecue. Or trying to. Your husband, quite rightly, didn't give much for my chances."

She looked at me blankly.

"Mr Browning. Gideon. He could see the trouble I was having." I held out a rusty bolt in the palm of my hand.

"Now you've lost me", she said. "Sandy's away playing golf. Our surname is Bessley. Mr Browning?"

"I – it doesn't matter. Someone I bumped into. Took it for granted he was from next door."

There was an awkward pause.

"Anyway", she breezed, "I'll get out of your hair. See you this evening. Anything I can do, just call. Frances has got my number. Don't work too hard. Bye." And she turned into the hall.

I never saw Mr Browning again. Frances teased me and 'Problem, eh?' passed into family folklore, dolefully muttered whenever even remotely appropriate.

And years later, when I'm out in the garden, struggling with the lawnmower, rebuilding the strimmer, fighting with a bicycle repair or muttering curses over a football that's mown down a section of my bedding plants, I still half expect to sense that pall of gloom that heralds the lugubrious observation, "Problems, eh?"

RAIN or SETTING THE SCENE

I should have ordered rain
And had the mean and biting Winter winds
Deliver looming grey and slate black clouds
To weigh down low upon the scene

I should have ordered rain
To plunge dark into puddles of liquid steel
Reflecting with an absurd cruelty
The pointless powerlessness of sudden loss

The hunched and huddled mourners become
Ridiculous bats suspended in gloomy serried rows
Inverted they stretch anguished, black and skeletal claws
Desperate to root again in grounded earth
Like sight distorted through the swelling lens of tears
The wind sweeps corrugations through the surface of these molten
mirrors

I should have ordered rain
Instead the sky is pale and bright, a cool, blue light
The clouds new-minted in this sudden Spring
Are frisky white and carelessly gambolling
Long shadows fling themselves across the rich brown of the mounded
earth
Across the burgeoning new green blading of the tousled winter grass
As the early Sun boats promise of his Summer warmth to come

By penetrating the dark protection of my winter coat
The careful severe knotting of my solemn scarf
And suddenly makes their clamping and confining weight
Unnatural and resistible.
His brilliance shatters to a million blinding shards
The watery prisms of my brim-full eyes
So that I cannot see —
But in my mind I can,

The frank amusement of her sudden smile
Enjoying the irony that
In seeking so precisely to set a suitable scene
Somebody failed to order the rain

I feel myself allowing myself to imitate her sudden smile
So palely, wanly emulate the mischief in her sudden smile
The dark clouds lift so slightly from my dull and clenching brow
So minutely lessens the constricting, knotted sorrow in my throat
The leaden gloom in my aching chest

For the first time since -------
I take a deep reviving gulp of cool and sun warmed air
I should have ordered rain
But I didn't
And now
For the first time since -------
We can smile again.

RAINDROPS AND ROSES

Late Summer – a family bar-b-q to celebrate Granny's 80th birthday. Suddenly the bright afternoon is converted to one of ominous darkness, the heavens open and pummelling, saturating chaos descends. The women flee to the garage carrying anything that is perishable in the torrential downpour – they stand in steaming huddles in the semi-darkness, dripping and shivering, clinging to sodden plates of quiche and sandwiches, bowls of diluting trifle and fruit salad, papier mâché'd clumps of 80th birthday cards – and one even with an indignantly saturated and quivering toddler whose vibrant face paintings have dissolved into Jackson Pollock squirms of bright primary colours on his white skin : in the Wendy house are crammed far too many moaning and bickering children in their dresses or clinging summer shorts : the men brave the torrent to squirrel away through the French windows into the brimful conservatory and sitting room all cushions and upholstered furnishings. Whilst Granny, wheelchaired and alone, wheel rims staunched in sudden mud, beneath a golfing umbrella, mournfully surveys her battered slice of pink birthday cake and the beaten blooms of her prized rose bed, pink and yellow petals battered into the dark soil by the unforgiving hurtling gobbets of heavy rain.

Whiskers on Kittens

Those are what you see in stark close-up as the family cat, having o'er leaped the sofa's headrest, with a banshee shriek, sinks his claws into your head and left cheek. That damn child, how many times does he need to be told not to tease the animal with his humming and flashing light sabre? The pain is excruciating : the blood spurting over your new white shirt and the hitherto pristine expanse of your cream and taupe brocade three-piece suite is disastrous. The cat, with his whiskers, has disappeared from the room.

Bright Copper Kettles

The trouble and effort to keep them bright. They hold a position of prominence on the Welsh dresser in the large entrance hall. A wedding gift from her mother, they are a family heirloom destined for our oldest daughter. "I don't want them", spurns Emily, dashing past on her way out to school. Meanwhile, they have to be kept shining against the event of the unexpected arrival of Granny, who lives just not far enough away. I grumble as the onerous cleaning chore looms ahead.

"I saw on telly" announces Emily (which is unusual as 'telly watching' is un-cool for someone supplied with elaborate computer access, iPod facilities and Blackberry in her own room). "I saw on telly a programme where a little old woman called Aggie, and a big fat old woman with uncool white six-inch heels and a bleached blond Amy Winehouse beehive cleaned some copper kettles. It was all home made and bio-sustainable. They mixed bicarbonate of soda with lemon juice and olive oil and salt. Dead easy. That's what I'd do." And she flounces off to a sleep-over with Heidi-Jayne and Maisie Sunflower.

I tried it. It worked – for a while. Then the tarnishing re-established itself. "I saw on telly …" same voice, same unlikely source of information, "to prevent tarnishing on a bread oven door in East Anglia, the team used goose grease" and she was gone.

Heaven help me, I tried goose grease. It worked but it stinks. How do you remove blobs of goose grease from bright copper kettles? Emily hasn't seen that programme yet.

Warm Woollen Mittens

A nightmare from my childhood and from my Granny who, brought up in times of dire austerity, would waste nothing so that we were less likely to want anything. This determination culminated in her unravelling every warm woollen item of clothing and reconstituting it with the ferocious click of her knitting needles, into a serviceable accessory or garment. Hence into annually produced warm woollen mittens for all her grandchildren – including me as a lanky thirteen-year-old. They were inevitably too small and multi-coloured and, in contact with the smallest amount of moisture, or worn once in the snow, lost all tensile strength and hung like incongruous, crocheted bags from one's wrists. They were then disposed of in school wastepaper baskets. The rest of the winter our blanched and blotched knuckles froze. We always claimed we'd left our gloves at school, so we never got a new pair.

Brown Paper Packages Tied up with String

Now we turned to Grandpa. We children were evacuated to live him once the phoney war had scared mother into acknowledging reality. And we received regular parcels from our uncle who was with the RAF in Cambridgeshire where sweet rationing was not a problem. These packages would arrive – imagine today's pizza boxes, but deeper – brown paper packages tied up with string. And we children knew what lay within – chocolate bars, nougat, toffees, marshmallow and Barski's Nut Crunch – billed as real Mounty Food – he gets his man with this. But Grandpa held the parcel and his obsession was the string. He had jars of the stuff in his shed, wound into tight balls. Waste not – again. The string binding each parcel had to be minutely unknotted, with the aid of a penknife (the blades for removing stones from horses' hooves, a kitchen fork, a bradawl and a pin). This detailed work which seemed to take forever. We children hovered outside the kitchen door, salivating, our stomachs churning, a growing conviction that if it took any longer the treasures inside would perish and subside into staleness and mould. The string removed, the brown paper would just as carefully be preserved into immaculate concertina folds and Granny would emerge with the revealed treats for long overdue distribution – though we could only eat one item a day. For me, string and brown paper reads exasperation and frustration.

These are a few of life's plain simple things
When the Dog Bites
Now, here is reality. That's what dogs do : after the doe-eyed whimpering, the seemingly supplicating droop of the head, the soft panting and the elevation of the front paw – that is what they, with canine cunning, do – and that's what reality does – BITES.
When the Bee Stings
Ditto – but then the bee does – is that true? Silly bee.
When I'm feeling Sad
Which is most of the time
I simply remember life's plain simple things
And they think I'm going mad.
The moral of this, don't take advice from a novice Nun who thinks that the sensible thing to do during a violent thunderstorm is to bounce up and down on a bed with six spoiled, over-privileged brats spouting meaningless ditties. Julie Andrews – may you be forgiven!

RED

There is always
One drop of red
One splash of red
One splatter of red
Required to start a war
Even the start of
That War to End All Wars
That War that will be over by Christmas

And that one drop, splash, splatter
Is promptly added to by others
And the splash becomes a puddle
And the puddle a pond
The pond a trickle
The trickle a flow
The flow a gush
The gush a pool
The pool a lake
The lake a flood
Always of red

Look – in the amber grey of a winter
afternoon dying
And you will see rising from the scarlet sea
The dark shapes of the fortifications
That support the oppressive stone walls
of the keep
That mightily surrounds the soaring structure of four towers
They have their own savage history of bloody execution
Rising into the yellowing murk of the
decaying day's skies
Their pale walls reflecting the fading light
appear white
Against the dour glowering dullness of
the threatening clouds

A light breeze springs up
In defiance of the still life of the scene
But instead of the gentle sound of rippling
over the red surface
(indeed there is no rippling)
Hear the faintest whistle of the wind
hissing between the regimental
arrangement of the carefully planted slender
stark dark upright stems
The almost silent tinkle, distant china teacup
and saucer rattlings of the curled crimson
ceramic petals
For the scarlet spread is of poppies
Thousands upon thousands upon thousands
Each glinting with artificial bleeding gloss
Unyielding to the breeze
Unbending even to the fitful movements
of the strands of a century of time
Each one a death
Each one a tragedy
Each a bleeding wound in humanity
A stigmata gouged into the sanctity
of life itself

And the crowds will come and say
"Cor, look at that, our Wilf
How many's them?"
"More than we'll ever be able to count."
And they'll go away

Leaving the red flood
As a stain on eternity
That began with one spot
A single spot of red.

SESTINA

I write because there's a sheet of paper on the desk
I WRITE because that paper, between the feint grey-green
Parallel lines, has challenging spaces of clean fresh-snow white
You can read fresh show fall : the purposeful
Footprints of the postmen and his cycle tracks; of the
Mother walking her pin-point small child to school.
The sweep of the neighbour's car tyres : the shamrock
Padding imprint of the dog studying a trail with
His bewildered ice-cold nose, and a disorganising
Slurry where he has spotted a bird and scrambled
Wetly and icily after his prey, in vain.

I WRITE because there is a pen in my right hand
(yes I do write with my right, use my right hand
To write : it seems right so to do!)

And the pen is capable, when applied, of glorious
Swirls of blue-black, curls and coils of
Blue-black, wide strokes, hyphenetic dashes
And long fine lines, firm long fat lines.
And it is capable, when directed, or organising
These shapes and swoops, the squiggles and angles, gaps and
Spaces, into elaborate codes that link the imagination,
The brain, the coordination of limb and digit, plastic
And nib, into meaning and even thence to voice and sound,
Energy, influence and power.
That is why I WRITE
It's as simple as that –
OR P'RAPS NOT!

SEVEN DEADLY SINS

Sorry, I've not been able to write anything for this week.

Can I just explain why not?

The problem is in the title – requiring some experience of a Deadly Sin.

I am a person just not given to sinning. I lead a clean, pure life, untrammelled by deviousness or misdoings. I like to think I positively exude goodness, love of my fellow man (and woman), trust, serenity, kindness and charity. I take great Pride in my essential saintliness. Sin is no part of my existence. So how then can I write about it?

I hear my voice in the past telling my students – always try and write about something you have experience of. Now, I must respond to my own wise advice. But, how to get experience of sin?

What are the Seven Deadly Sins? I sat down and wrote out six. It's like the Seven Dwarves, isn't it? Everyone can get to six – but seven. Impossible. There's always one missing. Apparently it's usually Bashful. So it is with the Seven Sins. I turned to Google to discover two things. Firstly, Envy was the sin I failed to identify. Secondly, there are Eight Deadly Sins, but one is so similar to Sloth – or is it Slothe? – I really couldn't be bothered to find out. Too much effort. Well, it is so similar to Sloth, such a fine distinction, that it rarely achieves a separate identity.

Anyway, now I had my seven and a new determination to set out to experience them one by one.

I would start for practical reasons with the physical, tangible ones.

Avarice. Immediately my mind went to the renowned Ebenezer Scrooge, sitting in his counting house counting all his money. That is what I must do. Realise all my savings into coinage – bright shining new coin – and count it, sit amongst it, pile it on my bed and sleep under it, strip off my shoes and socks and paddle in it. The image was so inviting.

I telephoned my bank. A very polite, well-spoken lady told me my call was very important to her but all her colleagues were busy at the moment and I was in a queue and she was so grateful that I was prepared to wait – and wait – and wait. She kindly played me some orchestral music that sounded as if it had been hand recorded in a lift at John Lewis's some years before. Again and again, how important I was, how sorry her colleagues were and how good it was of me to wait – here's some more of the awful music. I could feel my temperature rising. Anger welled up. But then – after only 35 minutes and 14 seconds – a voice. It was Mary and could she help me?

She seemed not a little phased by my request. All that money in brand new £1 and £2 coins? She suggested I contact my local Bank Manager, make a personal visit, pre-arranged. To cut a long story short, this I did. I think he enjoyed the novelty of the enterprise brightening up the otherwise grey prospect of his day-to-day office life. An excuse to get out the old armoured van from the garage behind. A mini staff outing, in flak jackets and helmets, with a police escort (by now he was bristling with enthusiasm). He could see the coins delivered to my front door with pleasure in a few days' time (how much time did I have?)!

I returned home. At least Sin One was under way. Now Sin Two. Gluttony.

This proved to be much easier, aided and abetted by the time of year and the results of the economic crisis. Shelves in the supermarkets were groaning with unsold Xmas food stuffs all rapidly approaching their sell-by dates. One penny Xmas trees? A pale boast against what I got my hands on. Trolley after trolley-load of tins of Quality Street, packets of mince pies, Xmas puddings and cakes, dozens of selection boxes, foil wrapped chocolate tree decorations, Father Christmases, marzipan, crackers and fruits, After Eight mints, red mesh stockings full of boiled sweets and liquorice All Sorts. You get the idea. I would go home and start on all these – dirt cheap – no need to buy real food this week. Whilst waiting for my Avarice to show up I contemplated Sin No. 3 – Lust.

Normally I would have been a little daunted at pursuing this particular peccadillo but with the general air of excitement I had begun to generate – and with my ever-increasing sugar rush – I felt my misgivings fade away.

But how?

I needed lycra-d women. Leotards. Sweaty headbands. Leg warmers (do they still wear them?) Hot pants. From somewhere distant, my 16-year-old self was beckoning me. I admit with shame I drooled melted chocolate. A clammy chocolate Santa wilted in my hot hands.

How? When?

There is the W.I. Hall, Mynydd Isa. The ladies of that august organisation have regular Healthy Movement Sessions. The windows are easily accessible. I checked the local paper. The sessions were twice a month - the next not until January 26th. Too late.

I spotted the ad. Zumba Classes in St Dieniol's Hall in Mold. Weekly. Thursday evenings. Women only. Perfect. But risky. The idea of being found guilty of peeping-tommery. I felt my ardour chill.

There must be something easier. Although perhaps we should suffer for one's art. But prosecution and a court appearance and a first and suspended sentence at best, then inevitable relegation from Wayward Writers – all my efforts in research of the Seven Deadly Sins wasted? No – not worth the risk.

I ruminated as I unceremoniously stuffed marshmallow snowmen into my mouth.

Inspiration!

The bloke who came to trim my hedges told me that the property behind was newly occupied by an attractive young couple - "She's a real looker", he confided – who had filled their sizeable conservatory with gym equipment. I knew that if I got on to my shed roof and parted the greenery, I would get a splendid view! Allowing that she was probably at work all day, her exercise bouts would take place in the evening. From my conservatory I would easily see if there was a light on in there and I could make for my shed roof. I could nip next door and borrow their ladder. The plan fell into place.

My evenings were spent in my unheated conservatory, stuffing myself with mince pies and Xmas puddings, bitterly regretting the time I was not spending gloriously counting all my new shiny, freshly minted coinage that had by this time been delivered.

But there were new worries there too. The antiquated heavy blue armoured van with *Securicar* emblazoned on the side and filled with security figures in flak jackets and helmets and movements of bundles marked with prominent £1 signs into my house had attracted considerable attention, not least from a gang of Irish tarmackers at the top of the road who leaned interestedly over the handles of their spreading tools, puffing on half-consumed cigarettes and glancing significantly at each other. I sensed the vulnerability of my piles of treasure.

The coins were packaged in square packs, tightly bound in plastic. In order to disguise them, I arranged them into a larger oblong shape – about two feet high – draped this with a dark brown sheet and placed a couple of magazines and a vase of flowers on top, hoping that to a hurried balance through the window, it would look like a kind of coffee table. Even so, I resolved to sleep at night on the settee to be extra secure.

But the evenings still had to be spent in the conservatory.

Thus it happened – the light went on. I dropped my half-consumed Xmas tree shaped toffee bar and went into action. The next door neighbours were out so I unhooked their ladder off the wall anyway. Across the frost encrusted lawn. Up the ladder, onto the sloping icy shed roof. I knelt precariously and parted the stiffly frozen fronds of the hedge. There was the conservatory, fully illuminated, gym equipment but no sign of human life. I held my breath, ready for Lust.

It was a long wait. Nothing happened. No-one came or went. I felt keenly the cold cutting wind coming driving from the hills across the valley. The freezing damp on the roof melting in contact with my knees and lower legs seeped into my trousers. My ankles stiffened. My unprotected hands were stinging with cold, my fingertips going numb. The hair on the back of my head bristled at the blast of the wind. My eyes watered. My nose ran. My lips trembled and my whole body started to quiver. Not Lust but the cold. The fog on my breath steamed up my glasses.

Then – movement. A figure entered the lit arena. Fumbling, I cleared the mist from my lenses and saw – baggy beige shorts, think white hairy legs tapering down into incongruously large white trainers. A string vest stretched over a distended belly, stooping shoulders, puny arms, the dome of a blad head shining in the electric light, clumps of grey hair around the neck and a glum, sullen expression on the old man's fleshy, flushed face. There was one thing I had anticipated. A sweaty headband – bright turquoise and none too clean.

I slumped on to the damp cold of the roofing felt, lurched to the ground, abandoned the ladder and slunk indoors. Failure. Cold, shivery, sickly with chocolate and marshmallow, I sank on to the settee. Defeated.

Now what of tomorrow? Two problems. First, Wayward Writers with an empty sheet of A4 – and what to do about leaving my coin treasure trove unprotected?

There was a solution. Dorothy, my ever-helpful next-door neighbour. In her mid-eighties, carefully coiffed white hair, small delicate frame, always in pearls and pastel twin set, alert blue eyes behind fine silver rimmed glasses.

I phoned her shouting (she is deaf) I explained as much as I dared. Could she housesit for me tomorrow morning? Something of value to be protected. Straight away, "Yes, of course. 9.30, then."

I sank onto the settee's cushions and prepared for a long, uncomfortable night. My stomach growling from its eccentrically rich sugar diet, shaking from the effects of a severe chill, the beginnings of a cold – and the experience of defeat.

9.30 a.m. – the ring of the doorbell. Dorothy bustled in, all 5' 1" of her, a bundle under her arm wrapped in what looked like a faded duvet cover. She required no explanation.

"So, that's it", she said curtly, eyeing the brown draped box. "Get rid of those books and flowers", she ordered. "Put the sofa cushions for me to sit on." I did. She sat. she burrowed into her bedding bundle. This'll set me up". She produced a thermos flask. "Camomile tea", she explained. And a packet of strong mints. She placed these on the settee within reach. "Now." She burrowed again and out came a large dark rifle and what looked like a small black knitted bag. She noted my surprised look at the rifle. "Don't worry. It's loaded but the safety catch is on. I borrowed it from my grandson last night. He's in the Argoed Cell of the Flintshire Division of the Welsh Volunteer Army. He won't need it till the weekend."

She fumbled in the knitted bag and produced a ball of wool, a white wad of delicate lace-like construction and her crochet needle. "It's a layette for our Alicia's new baby." This in her lap she took both hands to the black knitted bag, stretched it out, raised it into the air and pulled it down over her head. It was a balaclava helmet – the kind with just a slit for the eyes. She turned her head to look up at me. Her blue eyes glinted with a hint of steel. She mouthed something but the thick wool mesh obscured the meaning. There was an awkward pause.

"Well, I'll be off, then. Thanks again." I reached for the door handle. "See you later."

I was almost out of the door. Her voice came clear and decisive. I turned. She had lifted the balaclava clear of her jaw.

"I'll need you back by 12.20. I'll need to go home, for *Loose Women*. Then me dinner before *Neighbours* at 2. Then a quick cup of tea and a nap before *Alan Titchmarsh*. Don't forget." And the black wool mesh gag snapped down again with impressive finality.

So that's why I couldn't decide on a Deadly Sin to write on. My investigations are still 'a work in progress', you might say.

But I know what Envy is. How I envy all you who obviously have no trouble in sinning and have something to write about.

And if anyone's got any suggestions about Lust, I'd be ever so grateful – If you've got room for 57½ chocolate Santas. There's a bite out of one of them.

SHORTS

It's been the same, the woeful cry
Since days of Primary School sports
"You must come, mum, and dad come too
But please don't let him wear his shorts."

At all costs cover up those legs
Were our unachievable thoughts
Over time the opposition grew
To father wearing any kind of shorts

We know a man cannot choose his limbs
And has to live with what nature wrought
But he could stop our faces turning scarlet red
If only he didn't wear his shorts

They've wickets lost. Stopped rounders games
And been seen in bowling greens and tennis courts
They emptied gyms and swimming pools
When exposed beneath a pair of shorts

Podgy, hairy, sweaty, a kind of marvel
And on one knee a pair of warts
That sprout ginger, copper wiry hairs
Which can't be concealed by a pair of shorts

For the family holiday this year
Preparations were frantic and so fraught
We raided father's own suitcase
And secretly took out his pair of shorts

And substituted alternatives
At great expense to us we had bought
Jodhpurs, lycra tights, denim culottes
Anything but father's usual shorts

We thought we'd won, with smugness smirked
But such victory is sweet and short
He appeared poolside in fluorescent pink trunks
Said, "I never did much like them shorts."

SMILE

No need to look far for signs of crisis
Patients all left to their own devices
Dereliction of duty and sheerest folly
Patients left outside lying trolley by trolley
It's 9 am in A & E
No patients will be seen till half past three
Oh, where are all the staff? Alas. Alack
When will all the nurses be coming back?
With beds unmade, dirty bedpans piling
The nurses are attending a workshop on 'Smiling'
While they practise their smiles, teeth bared, cheeks aching
They listen to instructions the experts are making
When you are checking a patient in,
Welcome him with a loopy grin
When you strip him for a full bed bath
Greet what you see with a delirious laugh
The greater the patient's pain and fear
The bigger your grin from ear to ear
Injecting a vein or stripping off plaster
Accompany it with demonic laughter
Always employ the most massive of smiles
When you're shaving their bits or treating their piles
And if you have bad news to impart
Do it with a giggle that comes from the heart
"This is going to hurt a lot", you say
With a chortled guffaw and a yippee-eye-yay
"Your grandpa's dead, better order a wreath"
With the widest grip – show 'em your teeth.
"Nothing more can be done. You're at death's door"
With a tee-hee-hee and a jolly haw-haw
"It's a serious op. You don't stand a chance"
Slap 'em on the back – do a merry little dance
And be especially jolly, really bright and gay
When they contract difficile or MRSA
In the operating theatres we have a special task

For you can't see a smile through a surgical mask
In fact the solution is quite apparent
We'll order some masks that are transparent
And as the anaesthetist's needle goes in
The last thing they'll see is his sweaty plastic grin.

And just as we've concluded the NHS blew it
Into the frame steps Patricia Hewitt
With her well-practised smile, humourless and cold
She proceeds to tell the nurses what they don't want to be told
That all the grinning from ear to ear
Has given the NHS its best ever year
No closures, no redundancies
No junior doctors forced to their knees
Applying for jobs that are already theirs
On a dud IT system – nobody cares.
Because they're all giggly, jolly and gay
All financial deficits have been swept away
Because of leadership – she's always been right
The future of the NHS is golden and bright
From the stage she smiles down, serene and sweet,
All the nurses gathered at her feet
She sees herself, Madonna, her smile beatific, caressing
She raises her dainty hand to give the crowd her blessing
But suddenly she's aware there is no a sound
The nurses' jaws drop, smiles fall to the ground
The rows of eyes before her are reddening with rage
And the seething crowd of nurses moves toward the stage
And what follows now is too hideous to recall
Soon all that's left is her smile, nailed to the wall.

SPRING

I can't claim to be 'dreaming' about Spring but allow me to offer a few 'thinkings' about her.

To use the vernacular – See? A quality pun already – vernacular, vernal (Spring), vernicle – please yourselves.

Stat again.

To use the vernacular, we always 'dis' Spring. We *dis*respect; we *dis*parage. Do Spring a *dis*service. Dissipate; distract from her, displace, disregard, disdain, discredit, discount. In all these ways we – proud members of an enlightened society – *dis* Spring.

We belittle her, diminish her, sentimentalise, romanticise, chocolate box lid her, sweeten her, pastel paint and prettify, we 'wander lonely as a cloud' through her, merry month of May her, sing carelessly of the flowers that bloom in her, a young man's fancy lightly turns to thought of her as sweet lovers love her.

What we have done to Spring! We have changed her very essence.

To truly appreciate the abomination we have invited upon her, we must go back in time.

When Winter had power.

When the year's end shrank into barren cold, increasing darkness and a surety of famine and pestilence. The sun's rays grew pallid and weak, the nights so long that there ever being another dawn became a remoter and remoter possibility – and come the dawn and daytime was dull and overcast, barely distinguishable from night. Sustenance, preserved in salt, ice or coagulating discolouring honey, or dried in the smoke of dying fires, was gradually and remorselessly used up. Despairing man turned to the remaining skeletally emaciated cattle and sheep, the ones to have so far survived, and what meat there was went first to the vulnerable, the infants, children and the aged who, even so, were unlikely to survive the penetrating winds, the foggy vapours, the agues of sicknesses of bone and belly that Winter's ministrations visited upon them. And the cold – the awful, penetrating pervasive, aching, rheumy freeze of the dark season. The cry was to the Gods. Why were they forsaking us? Why allow all to perish without light, without warmth, without love, without hope? All around disease, deprivation and death. Keep your eyes to the ground – to look up would be to see the end, and seeing it would bring it closer faster.

And then …

Spring.

A hundred faint indications at firs,t half hopes, half of half hopes that the Gods were relenting. A sun's ray here, a drop of melting ice there, a blush in the sky, a trickle in the river, a green blade, the paw mark and spore of a wild animal in the slushing snow, a bird's pipe, a gentle wind. Spring, at first, an anticipatory breath tightly held, lacking the confidence to reclaim itself without sufficient evidence that the Gods were withdrawing their malignity, that their decision had become irreversible.

And then the apocalyptic joy, the ecstatic thrill of LIFE AGAIN – the rebirth, revival, resurrection. The pain of the burst of warm fresh air into the crushed, starved, matted lungs; the agony of the blinding bright sunlight assaulting the pin-prick pupils of deadened eyes; the ferocious flavours of fresh foods on stale, furred, numbed tongues; the freedom of limbs from the parchmented cutting rough folds of the rancid, foul-smelling rotting animal skin coverings of the dark season.

Then the full SPRING; the dancing the crying the shrieking the feeling the holding the kissing the weeping the laughter the running the leaping the diving the swimming the awakening and never sleeping the feasting and drinking the hymning and praising and vowing and promising the racing the galloping the vaulting the flying, the ecstasy that is agony and the agony that is ecstasy. Not a fibre of being but alert, alive, tender to every sensation. A colossal oneness of passionate gratitude and intense relief.

That was SPRING.

And how do we greet her?

We clean the windows, de-tog the duvets, dry clean heavy winter coats, put away fur lined boots, drag out and oil the lawn mower, buy summer holiday brochures and seed catalogues, have the car serviced, leave the curtains and even the windows open that little bit longer …

And SPRING shrinks back into all the cute prettiness that we allow her, her essence diluted, her spirit broken.

ST SWITHIN AT THE OLYMPICS

Written on Sunday 15th July 2012 (12 days to go until …)

What joy! How gay! Such unalloyed bliss!
This very day – St Swithin's day is this!
White fluffy clouds and blue skies, oh such sights
Mean surely now it will not rain for 40 days and nights.
And storm drenched fears that threatened our great Olympic pride
Can happily and finally be firmly set aside.
Poor Usain Bolt was set to look a most ridiculous fellah
In flippers, snorkel, water wings designed by Paul McCartney's
daughter, Stella.
The King of Race-track Speed, soggy and sad'll
Be doomed to splutter his 100 metres in useless doggy paddle.
Perched on the top-mast board, his figure bronzed and toned and neat,
Tom Daly looks down in horror as the water laps his feet
While competitors in long jump, high jump, shot put and the hurdles
Just disappear defeatedly in splashing whirlpool gurgles.
The Navy's finest battleship that on the Thames should have its home
Finds itself adrift and floating somewhere above the Velodrome
Where St Christopher Hoy and cohorts give up on their cycling rally
With desperate last-minute rehearsals for an underwater synchronised
ballet.
And look, Seb Coe, like stormy clouds his features grim and dark,
Has converted the Olympian stadium into his own private Ark
And has loaded up 2 x 2 athletes from across the realm
Last seen sailing past Buck Palace with Boris Johnson at the helm.
Poor squirming Mr Buckler cowering before MPs he kneeled
The truth of the scandal at 495 can at last be revealed.
The shortage of personnel can hardly be blamed on him
He had to sack most of his staff when it was found they could not
swim.
So thank St Swithin with blissful heart for a blissful end to this story
As we turn our glad eyes London-wise to sunny Olympic glory!
CODA
My optimisms for St Swithin's Day on reflection make me wince

For there has been convincing rainfall on every day since.
So perhaps proposed changes to the Olympian motto will now be better
From HIGHER FASTER STRONGER
To DEEPER COLDER WETTER.

STANDING STILL

Standing still was the problem – stone still, statue still – not a twitch, not a blink, not a breath.

It was not natural.

In his village, amongst his people, no-one was this still. Only the dying and the dead and all who in the dark hours willingly journeyed into the state of half-death, which he now knew as sleep. And to adopt this stillness, the body was stretched out on the floor. The stillness he was forced to adopt was standing stillness which at home was the posture of death and danger – the hunter waiting, poised, under the natural concealment of the leaves and plants of the jungle, his outline blurred by the shifting dappled shadows, anticipating the nearness of his unsuspecting prey, when suddenly he would leap with poised blade or fang and the stillness would be shattered by furious roars, the commotion of struggle and the shrieks of pain and fear.

Otherwise, there was no standing still.

How his entire being resisted it.

But he had been told how lucky he was.

When he was called in out of the thickly muddied yard, the overseer's stick slashing across his back to make him move faster; when he was stood near the fusty smelling timber house wall; when the white face peered around the door frame, her eyes pale green and cold, a delicate white hand clamping a small muslin bag filled with sweet smelling flower heads and carefully selected spices to her nose; when she had stared at him, nodded slightly and withdrawn; when Mother Batthi had seized him firmly by the scruff of the neck, dragged him without ceremony across the wet soil and horse dung of the yard to the paved shade where stood the large wooden vats in which the coarser household linens were washed, steeped, battered and stirred. There, her unrelenting grip at the base of his skull, she had with her other hand roughly torn off his faded, rotting and stained calico shirt and breeches and hoisted him, his scrawny and wriggling ebony limbs, his narrow boy chest heaving, over the side into the lukewarm soapy water where she dealt with him like she would a rough blanket – pushing, pulling dunking and diving – until he swam in a brown cloud of his own relieved filth. She laid off. He stood chest deep in the murky soup, rubbing his eyes with his knuckles, his skeletal shoulders shaking with trepidation.

"You are a lucky one", she said and spat ostentatiously to ward off any evil spirits listening. "You are chosen by the mistress. Life will be good for you."

She pressed his forehead down on the rough wood of the vat's rim whilst she searched his black finely knotted hair for any signs of verminous life.

"Now, out!" she instructed. "And wipe yourself with this," a torn piece of a sack used for carrying the cotton. "No, through that door there." He turned to obey. "Boy, boy, cover yourself", and he wrapped the sacking around his narrow hips. Suddenly, in spite of his fear and the strange smell of soap that clung to his damp shivering body and the bruising pain at the nape of his neck and on his grazed forehead, he felt to a small degree at home – bare footed and only in a loin cloth.

Thus was he trained – bullied and beaten – in preparation for his new role. He learned to stand still for hours on end, stiff and erect, head slightly bent, unblinking eyes cast down, arms and hands extended forwards at chest height holding a weighted wooden tray. He became used to the aching pain that started in his forearm, moved to his wrists and fingers then upwards to his shoulders and finally, after many hours, to the slimness of the small of his back.

After several days of this, he was introduced to his uniform. Mother Batthi again, roughly dunked him. "You lucky boy", she intoned repeatedly. A mantra interspersed with copious spitting, "You lucky boy". She rubbed him with a large woollen cloth that was saturated in perfumes so sickly that he felt himself beginning to retch. Then a black manservant dressed in a frock coat of emerald green, with lace cuffs and an unwelcoming scowling face, helped him dress. A white shirt, fine smooth cloth, white stockings that had to be tied tightly to his lanky thighs, knee length breeches, thick and black, a rose-pink jacket, with a full skirt and an embroidered raised collar, a frilled choker tight around his neck, a white curled wig, its pony tail and black ribboned bow weighing heavily on his sore neck and a triangular pink hat to match his jacket. Finally stiff white gloves – and, most difficult of all, black shining shoes each with a sparkling golden buckle. He tried to walk, stumbled and fell. He would have been beaten but for care of his new uniform. He stood again. His feet protested at their cramped confinement. Never before had they known any restriction of any kind.

And so he learned to stand — hot, chafing, encumbered, imprisoned — for entire evenings at the Master's parties and balls. He was an ornament, holding out as an offering to all a silver salver of sweetmeats and sugary delights. The sway of people came and went — the swishing and scraping of the richest and finest cloths, the dazzlingly contrasting colours, the glint of jewelled rings and bracelets, the deep roar and shrill laughter of voices, the pale white hands of the ladies selecting the daintiest pink rose-scented cakes, the strong tanned fingers of the men seizing handfuls of sugar-coated almonds.

But, worst of all, these hours of still standing gave him time to think — to imagine, to dream and then to remember and yearn for the days when he knew his real world, his village, his mother, father, brothers and sisters — there were moments when he thought the intense sadness surging through his being would overcome the stiffness of his pose and the steadiness of his outstretched hands and their heavy load and all would be lost — bringing consequences to such awfulness that even he, who had already suffered such terrible things, could barely imagine them.

But always he heard his mother's warning voice — the last time he had ever seen her : that, if he heard the screeching of the flame bird that was not quite like the screeching of the flame bird and the high shrill whistling, then he should flee — run into the jungle and keep running until there was only the silence of the jungle. Then he should curl into a tight ball in the darkness of deep undergrowth and wait for nightfall and the break of the next day before cautiously, ever so cautiously — like a shadow — returning.

And he heard the shrieking and high piping and he fled — but not far enough and not for long enough. He had to return, not cautiously enough. Seeing his village burning ahead he stumbled forward and was trapped in strong olive-coloured arms, his face muffled in stale-sweat smelling robes, swung upside down until a violent jolt made him lose all contact with his nightmare and he sank into merciful oblivion.

He had heard the tales of the swarthy men who came silently in large, flat bottomed boats — who swooped unheralded and soon disappeared leaving an entire village in smouldering destruction, stripped of all life, save a few whining dogs, bleating goats, crying babies and whimpering small children. The rest had achieved that final stillness of death or had been spirited away, on the flat boats, down the river.

A sudden noise jolted him back into awareness. Someone had nudged her flowing golden skirt forcefully against his extended arms and almost overthrown him. He steadied himself and breathed deeply to ease his beating heart.

After so many months he had mastered the skill of still standing. Now his real fear was strong and immediate. The shoulders of his coat were gradually straining, the chest tightening. His white socks did not come quite so far up his legs nor his breeches quite cover his knees. There was a tell-tale length of jet-black wrists between the clean creamy lace of his cuffs and the stark whiteness of his gloves. And his shoes, the small prisons that his feet had never became used to, were cramping his toes more and more and rubbing his heels raw. He knew it was easier and cheaper to replace the boy rather than the uniform.

"You are lucky, boy."

He wanted to spit the dark spirits away. But he could not. He was not even allowed to blink.

He knew his luck was running out and he would soon move into an existence where he would long for a chance to stand still and have only the pain of hard, unyielding, unnatural shoes to fear.

TABLOID NEWSPAPER : THE EDITOR'S DILEMMA

Tomorrow's edition – preparations begin
Type setters toil, the print rollers spin
All the copy submitted is so dark and grim
I can't have this – no! Stop the press!
We'll sell no papers if we depress
To have bleak headlines will be a folly
Let's lead with something dafty but jolly!

Striking by one million workers
Calls to ban the wearing of burqas
Stop the dole for work-shy shirkers
Please, something else. Stop the press!
Posh Spice has designed another dress.

Refugees drowning in the Med
For Cancer patients, there's no bed
In Gaza no time to bury the dead.
Enough! Enough! Stop the press.
Simon Cowell's worth a billion – more or less.

Sex assaults from decades back
Civil war throughout Iraq
Fatal plagues of dope and crack
No! Something else! Stop the press!
Daniel Craig pictured without his vest.

Compulsory organ donation
Scotland becoming a separate nation
Austerity and rampant inflation
Need something else. Stop the press.
Jordan is getting bigger breasts.

Bombs and terror in the Ukraine

The ozone layer is on the wane
Tsunamis and earthquakes again and again.
Please, something else. Stop the press.
Justin Bieber is changing sex.

Pay sleazy bankers even more
Ignore the plight of the UK poor
MPs expense claims continue to soar
Search for something else. Stop the press!
Prince Harry comes out and wears a dress.

The North fires rockets at South Korea
Syrians flee from terrorist fear
Pakistan's bombs will soon be nuclear
Enough of that! Stop the press!
Minister fails primary school spelling test.

This wasn't how it was meant to be
When, with my first-class Journalism degree,
I set out in this Fleet Street biz
To tell it exactly how it is
With all the idealism of youth
To wave the flaming torch of truth.

That was a time I can scarce remember
The torch is now a smouldering ember
And truth whilst headlines deceitfully rage
Is a dying whisper on an inside page
But I've my own last headline – stop the press!
I'll gasp it with my final breath
"This world is in one Helluva Mess!"

TAKING STOCK

Margery Morris was jolted out of her mood of indolence and torpor as she slumped in front of an unremarkable Sunday morning TV debate between undistinguished minor politicians. It was a word one of those self-important, would-be-pundits used that had attracted her attention. A word she had been searching for to describe her own dilemma. The word summed it up perfectly. Marginalised. That's what she had become. Marginalised. She had toyed with Isolated. Victimised. Set-upon. Ignored. Over-looked. But none of these had truly suited. Yes – she had been *marginalised*.

The world had moved on, like a tidal wave sweeping round, but not quite able to swamp, a small island. She had to take stock.

Which is ironically where the true nature of her problem began to manifest itself. Her stock had indeed been taken. Boxes of the stuff, surreptitiously out of her rear store room. She knew she did tend to overstock and consequently had to keep a close tally on sell-by and best-before dates, and in her checking she became aware of gaps in her reserved supplies. At first she put it down to tricks of the memory – after all, she was not as young as she had been. But then, she noted, deficiencies became too substantial to be ignored. She had frequent recourse to her stock book and invoices and receipts and realised her stocks were vanishing.

She called in her daughter, Ruby, who helped her run her market stall. Ruby confirmed the worst and guessed that her mother's unsuspecting friendly nature was being taken advantage of. The police were informed (the market had its own designated officer – a female called Jo Summerfield) and Margery undertook to keep a watching brief.

It had not taken long to pin-point the suspect. There had been within the town a noticeable increase in immigrants from Eastern European countries. Young men (well, more like boys to Margery's maternal gaze), rather shabbily dressed, but with attractive Slav appearance – cropped blond hair, aquiline noses and clear blue almond eyes, tended to hang around the market stalls, chatting amicably in very broken English, often sheltering from the cold, she thought, and being helpful where they could – shifting boxes, moving stock, the like. The only return they seemed to expect being a kind word from the 'English Granny', as they termed her, and perhaps a handful of cheap boiled sweets – they particularly liked the brown and gold striped ones that were humbugs.

But boxes were disappearing and a whole scam was uncovered. Confectionaries such as that Margery sold had value in their own poverty-stricken countries as a form of currency. A rucksack full of sticky, acid coloured and flavoured boiled sweets could be readily traded for all manner of necessities. And how could border control challenge a traveller's apparent sweet tooth? For Margery a lesson had been learned, another element of trust destroyed.

Like her grandson.

Jack is slightly built, a thatch of red hair, dark rimmed glasses concealing a slight turn in his right eye – the doctors said it would improve with age. The boy had a wide winning smile. He was as skinny as a rake with seemingly enormous feet. "Just like his grandad was", beamed Margery, remembering faded photographs of a youth well before the war in torn ribbed sweater, baggy coarse cloth shorts, thick ankle socks and boots, laces trailing. The same smile, the same hair explosion, the same skinny limbs. Jack's smile had faded somewhat as he moved up to secondary school. And sweets began disappearing. Ruby had realised what was happening and had arrived one Saturday morning with a very despondent and uncomfortable looking Jack.

"Apologise to your Nan" she had ordered strictly, manhandling the boy far from gently with a firm grasp of his right upper arm. "Go on."

The boy was bright red by now, his full lips downturned, his chin angrily dimpled, his breathing deep and agitated. He looked down and muttered something. It could have been "Sorry, Nan".

"Now, go and wait for me outside", came the curt command. The small figure hastily disappeared and Ruby visibly deflated. Her shoulders slumped, she emitted an enormous sigh. "Don't ask, Mum", she said. "He's having trouble at school. Bullying. Ginger and Four Eyes they call him. The big boys. And Shrimp. There's most probably worse, but he won't say. He's been buying them off – with sweets that I've not bought for him. The Headmaster thought he was bringing them in and running an illegal tuck shop – they're not allowed sweets in school. But it wasn't that. His form teacher found he was trying to buy off the cat-calling and bullying. But he has to learn he was wrong, no matter what. But don't be too hard on him, Mum. His dad has had a real go at him."

Ruby knew that the last person to be 'hard on him' would be his Gran. She knew she could go off to do her shopping, leave him with his Gran and the right things would be said – no doubt with a shared chocolate bar and a cuddle. "But if he's ever caught half inching from you again, he'll be seeking out the school bullies as a gentle alternative to what he'll get at home." The two women exchanged knowing smiles and Ruby raised her voice. "Jack? Jack? You can come back in now."

But it did unsettle Margery more than she cared to admit. It all added to the feeling that life was moving on without her. She was being side-lined and – now she had the word – marginalised.

It was her parents who had taken on the stall after the war – when sweets came off ration and they were an indulgence that parents who were nonetheless cash-strapped would offer to their children. Mother ran the stall while Father, after active service, returned to his former job of driving for a haulage contractor.

Her mother rapidly became a prominent feature of the market. Her stall positioned just inside the market's main entrance was a magnet for all. They painted the frontage and internals in the primary pastel colours – sugar colours – sherbet pink, apple green, mint blue, lemon yellow – like a crazy collection of summer seaside beach huts. And above all, in liquorice All Sort shiny black, red, blue, green and white letters, 'SWEET THINGS'. Mother was like an all-year-round Mrs Christmas surrounded by her serried ranks of gleaming sweet jars and a counter piled high with garishly wrapped bars and tubes.

Margery learned how to help serve the customers and sort out the rear stock room. Eventually she herself, an only child, took over the running of the place, her own husband working on the buses, her two children looked after sometimes by child minders, other times in the stall helping out or under foot according to circumstances.

Times changed. Sweets changed. All pre-wrapped and packaged. There was competition with the supermarkets. Sales diminished and these were worrying years. The nature of the market hall was different. There was, in particular, an influx of Asian traders, firstly in stalls of fantastic bales of exotic materials for saris and curtain drapes; then foreign herbs and spices, strange breads and vegetables which became gradually more accepted and usual. Hardware, carpets and rugs, sandal-wood ornaments and fretwork small tables and screens. Smit, Jones, Hardcastle and Blackwood gave way to Singh, Murpur, Desai and Tikaram. But 'Sweet Things' persevered. Ruby came in and re-organised the stall, returning to the traditional jars and sugary offerings

– barley sugar sticks, hammer shattered slabs of toffee – creamy, nutty, treacly - sherbet dips, marshmallow cones. For a while, business thrived.

But times do not stand still.

Now, when a child appeared before the stall, wide eyed and yearning, it was more than likely that, with an imperious tug on the arm, mother would whisk him away, conscious of the possible effect on carefully maintained teeth and assiduously measured waistline. "A piece of fruit if you're hungry". Mr Desai's greengrocery had a display of individually priced and ready washed to eat apples, pears, small bunches of large purple grapes and bananas – "very customer friendly" he would boast to her, bowing ever so slightly. Christmas and Easter were still bumper times for her – selection boxes and brightly boxed eggs – which was some compensation.

But the Council busy bodies were as ever alert, up to date and interfering. They were considering a re-alignment of the market, a make-over, an updating.

"Our problem is", confided to her Mr Ogilvy of the Retail Street and Market Vendors Taskforce, "deciding on the prominence of pitch awareness on the market premises. The ambience we wish to achieve." He wafted on, "responsibilities to our healthy eating initiatives", "five a day awareness", "response to obesity concerns", "cascading down to street level our thrusting, dentrifical objectives as administered by our Public Health Company directives". The intention became obvious. Shift Sweet Things from its street frontage entrance gate prominence to somewhere further back – say where Maison Minx's Adult Books Films and Toys now skulked – all black, purple and gold – in the far reaches of the Market Hall's ancient brick work and iron girded vaulting.

Margery switched off the TV. A perky female presenter was introducing yet another MP to discuss yet another concern that bothered the Westminster Villagers far more than it did the life of his constituency.

In the sudden silence her had reached for the sheaf of papers on the cushion beside her. The forms were completed. All that was needed now was her signature. A stroke of the pen to bring to a conclusion decades of Sweet Things. She reached for her pen but her finger found a stock of liquorice studded with diamond hundreds and thousands. She looked at it fondly, bit off a sizeable mouthful and lay back. "There is still time for change", she smiled to herself.

TEACHERS

Teachers are generally a realistic bunch, pragmatic, down-to-earth, no-nonsense, honed on the frequent experience of having hopes dashed and illusions shattered. Except, noticeably, in one particular and peculiar area. They continue to believe that the rabble of recalcitrant, monosyllabic, uninspired and uninspiring 16-year-old, post-GCSE, potential school leavers will re-emerge after six weeks' holiday and the trauma of exam results as purposeful, mature, industrious, respectful, clean and tidy members of the Sixth Form. And weirdly, unbelievably and inexplicably, they tend to be right. Thus it is and always has been.

I remember my first days in the Sixth Form – never a more optimistic and fortuitous period in my school career. We had shaken off the herd mentality. Now smaller classes, more informal groupings, a dedicated Common Room – away with the old school blazer and into a suit, with a sixth form tie and a white shirt. And more – much more – an ability to concentrate on the academic subjects you are interested in, narrowed down from the wide spread deemed appropriate at GCSE level. I went from ten subjects to four, all of which I had some enthusiasm for, not the least being Art.

We met as a group – only three of us – before Mr Rees, the Head of Art. Rees Rees was his name, but generations before us, with an untypical lack of originality when choosing staff nicknames, had christened him Dai-Dai Rees.

He briefly laid out the prospects of our two-year study course. No surprises. Basically drawing, painting and pottery, with a side order of History of Art – essays and coursework. Then he added, "I am trying out something new this year. Once a week, for the first year at least, you will be attending the local Art College for Life Class. Tuesday evenings at 7 p.m. You will make your own way there – there's a bus from the town centre to the Heights. You, Crashley, will be responsible for the folder of paper you will need – and bring it all back clean and unsullied. The classes finish at nine. Any questions?"

"Yes, sir." (This was Andrew Parivs). "What do we wear? What I mean is, must it be school uniform?"

A pause. "No – I suppose not. But you must be tidy and acceptable. Don't forget, at all times you represent the school. Mr Braintree, who takes the class, I know well. He will keep me informed of your progress and the appropriateness of your behaviour and demeanour."

"Yes, sir."

Outside, afterwards, we expressed our ignorance – and innocence.

We'd no idea what our demeanour was nor precisely what a Life Class entailed.

"I've seen *Still* Life", proffered Adrian. (He was by far and away the most well informed and worldly of us - he had an older sister at University.) "It's all bowls of fruit and vases of flowers, chairs and folded newspapers. I suppose that's what it is."

We knew that formal part of the exam syllabus. "I don't see why we couldn't do that here", ventured Bob. A very preceptive observation in view of what was to follow.

A couple of days later, after consulting his sister, the oracle, Adrian came up with – "She says it could be drawing people, the human form – face or hands or feet." He looked down conspiratorially. "It could be nudes", he muttered, "but she says not for school kids. It'll just be people."

Tuesday evenings did not seem to offer a great deal.

Bob brightened the mood. "There could be girls there from the Grammar school", he said, hopefully.

"No way", grumbled Adrian. "If there were, we'd never be allowed near."

We grunted agreement.

Tuesday came. We stomped up the impressive stone stairway at the grand entrance to the Art College. Bob heaved under his arm the large cardboard art folder – or 'portfolio' as Adrian christened it. Inside the grand echoing entrance hall were clear signs leading to 'Life Class'. We went through hefty wooden swing doors with glistening dark green glass panes. A large, lofty room. Parquet flooring. A semicircle of easels and stools – in the centre a podium with a dilapidated sofa, half covered in some old curtains on top of which was a number of red and royal blue cushions.

Already some of the easels were taken so we moved to three alongside each other. A tall, thin bespectacled man, a lined pale face, a mane of white hair and a noticeable stoop approached. He smiled and removed his grey-framed horn-rimmed glasses.

"Ah – you must be the three from Roger Manwoods. Welcome. Welcome. We'll be starting any minute now." And he swooped away.

We simply proceeded to do what we observed the others doing. We clipped our sheets of paper to the board on the easel and lined up our pencils on the narrow ledge at the bottom. The general air was one of quiet purposefulness – we were awed into silence.

Then some movement. A door at the far end of the room swung open and a woman appeared. She was tall, her dark hair swept up into a bulky, untidy arrangement on the top of her head. She wore a loose, white with green flowers, satiny kimono and had pink fluffy mule-type slippers on her otherwise naked feet. She placed a packet of cigarettes and a lighter on a wooden, upright chair behind the podium.

Bob, who was next to me, flinched. "It's a woman", he hissed. "It's a bloody woman." I glanced at him. His round face, normally flushed, was verging on puce with panic. His circular national health glasses lenses glistened manically in the reflected neon light and the tight curls to his startlingly ginger hair positively glowed. "It's a woman", he gulped.

Adrian bent over and growled, "Shut up, you prat."

All three, we looked up slowly and observed what followed. The woman moved to the end of the podium. Facing us she shuffled off her pink slippers, her feet flat and splayed on the dark wood flooring, each toe resplendent in bright red nail varnish. She then, in a swift and simple movement, allowed her kimono to fall from her shoulders so that it flowed down her left hand into a cascade of shiny material on the dark floor. She was stark naked.

I heard, "Bloody hell", softly from my right.

In all honesty, I can't recall the next few moments. I think I went into a state of semi-shock. I just remember my blank stare and the impression of an area of blinding pinkness.

She moved unhurriedly to the podium, draped her kimono over an arm of the sofa. She arranged herself on the furniture, leaning on her right elbow, her weight mainly on her right hip, her left forming a mound from which her left thigh stretched over her right down to the cushions of the seat of the sofa where her left calf lay in front of her right, her left heel nestling neatly into the instep of her right foot. She was still.

Mr Braintree approved her. "Lovely, my dear. Lovely. Perhaps angle your head a little this way? Perfect. Is that comfortable for you?"

And he moved away from her leaving me, pencil poised, eyes wide, mouth dry and a little sweat on my forehead and upper lip, alone in my first encounter with a totally naked woman.

As my best friend Russ O'Connell said at the back of Double French in Lesson One the next day, "You mean naked – totally naked – you could see everything – everything? What was it like?"

But I couldn't answer that question.

My mind went back to the previous evening.

My eyes travelled between the model and the spidery sketch that I was unconvincingly scratching onto my paper. Suddenly Mr Braintree loomed behind me. His left hand firmly placed on my left shoulder, he leaned tightly into me, his face close to my right cheek. He reached over and seized my pencil in his wrinkled and bony claw hand. He held it delicately between thumb and two nearest fingers, his little finger raised as if, with refinement, drinking tea from a china cup.

"My boy, this of yours is such a sketchy outline. You've caught the angle of the head and the thrust of the shoulder but here there is no weight. Look how the right breast curves to the side – it pulls down – it is curved, rounded, so, it has weight." His pencil draughted in the shape with confident and effective shading.) "And the left hip is a sold curved mound of flesh. See how the weight of the thigh plunges down the curve of the knee." (Again the pencil expertly illustrated his words.)

For me, light was beginning to dawn. He was able to discuss the naked woman as clinically and dispassionately as if it were the body of a car he was considering or an animal lying in repose in a field. And he talked to me about rounded breasts, buttocks and thighs and curves. Adult to adult. He moved away and I breathed deeply.

That is why I could not tell Russ what it was like. That was grubby talk for schoolboys. I had moved on – adult artist and student artist, so I liked to think.

But I still had to live with the anxiety of what I would do if ever I encountered her in town. I would not know where to look.

APOLOGIES TO TEDDY BEARS EVERYWHERE

If you go down to the beach today
You're sure of a big surprise
If you go down to the beach today
Step carefully, it would be wise

For where there should be fresh air and peace
White scudding clouds, gently lapping seas
There's people and people doing just what they please
It's awful!

There's bar-b-cues with the stench of burnt chops
Big bold ladies who've decided to remove their tops
And transistors blaring out 'Top of the Pops'
It's awful!

Fat speedo-clad men displaying tattoos
Be careful! You can't just walk where you choose
The damp sand is littered with fresh doggy poos
It's awful!

The bikers who congregate round their bonfires
With smell of hot grease and highway-burned tyres
And rancidness as their leather clad flesh perspires
It's awful!

Spoilt children who scream and demand ever more
Candy floss and ice cream, crisps, sticks of rock by the score
Only then to be sick all over the floor
It's awful!

The lads brawl and shout, the girls watch and titter
The lads flex their muscles, the girls choose who's the fitter
The girls slurp their vodka, the lads neck their bitter

It's awful!

Some fool on a rubber duck drifts out to the ocean
There's screaming and sirens. Oh! Such a commotion
The rescue achieved with a great wave of emotion
It's awful!

Seagull flocks swooping low as they nick peoples' snacks
And there's nowt to be done to prevent these attacks
Insult added to injury, white slime lime plops down bare backs
It's awful!

Then coaches pull up to the top of the stairs
Old folk totter down in Derby and Joan pairs
Then bicker and curse, can't put up their deck chairs
It's awful!

Now the beach is more crowded than ever before
The sun's had enough. He decides to withdraw
In rush the clouds and a heavy downpour
It's awful!

My hotel room is the best place to be
With some Chicken and Chips and a nice cup of tea
Watch the 'Holiday' programme on a wide-screen TV
It's delightful!

So, if you're planning to go down to the beach today
It's an idea that's not very good
Instead of going down to the beach today
Try a picnic with teddy bears in the woods.

So if you're planning to go down to the beach today
There's still time to save your face
Don't go down to the beach today.
Go seek out some other place.

TEMPTATION

I must resist the temptation to do it
My doctor advised if I don't I will rue it
My bank manager agreed and offered his view, it
Would do me no favours should I pursue it.

My family piled in and added its weight
They say the prognosis will hardly be great
That I could end up in a terrible state
If I insist on indulging at my present rate.

I toss and I turn and lie awake nights
And should I drop off I have dreams full of frights
On the edge of a cliff when I'm so scared of heights
With no trousers in Tesco's and other such plights.

It started so innocently, who would have known
That something so small so great would have grown?
For each selfish indulgence I now must atone
But who can I turn to? I feel so alone.

My counsellor wept, didn't know what to say
The vicar said all he could do was pray
My psychic in a plasma fog faded away
The Salvation Army called it a day.

My greatest fear is that, should it expand
I'll lose total control as it gets out of hand
And if I should yield to its every demand
Then chaos and disaster will spread over the land.

So in dire desperation I'm resorting to verse
Can any of you help me break free of this curse?
To your wisdom and kindness I cannot be averse
Though I do not think matters can get any worse.

So I'd like to beseech you, each, every one
But an insurmountable barrier I know there is one
For because of my shame, as dark clouds shroud the sun
I can never reveal what it is I have done.

So —as you sit there agog, curiosities grow
Exactly what I am up to – Ha! Ha! –
You will never know!

THANK GOD FOR HARRY

It became a common pattern that in the large Edwardian town house on the outskirts of the city centre there were only two rooms in use most evenings. He sat in a corner of the large downstairs sitting room, alone at his desk by the light of a simple, large, red-shaded standard lamp – a pool of isolation in an expanse of gathering darkness. She spent time upstairs in the front, generously sized double bedroom – now occupied solely by her – perched on the velvet cushioned dark wooden stool in front of the antique folding mirrors of her matching walnut dressing table with its bow-fronted drawers and claw-footed legs. He was absorbed in his computer, the flashing screen giving his fleshy, sagging face a sinister glow, lighting it from below in a soulless blue. She leant towards her mirror, making the final touches of her carefully applied make-up, it being more of a mask as the years took their toll on the gentle folds of her skin and the hitherto smooth and unblemished nature of her complexion. She was not stupid. She realistically acknowledged the effects of age. But she was in fighting mode. Her figure she now felt was finally in contours. Trimmed with a fastidiously strict diet and a carefully planned exercise regime. She had now spent so much on flattering clothing and quite expensive accessories. Her whole life had changed since she had become a 'new woman' and she acknowledged that she had Harry to thank for that. Harry! She paused. Her right hand, patting her carefully curled hair into place, froze in mid-air. Ah, Harry! Soon she would be with Harry.

She rose, picked her handbag and tartan wrap off the large double bed, moved swiftly across the room to the door and was about to exit the room, her hand on the light switch when she stopped and so remembered the ring on the third finger of her left hand. She sighed with impatience, returned to her dressing table, dropping her bag and wrap on the bed as she paused and, with more impatience than ceremony, removed the ring with a vigorous twisting tug, placed it at the back of the top right hand drawer of the dressing table and reached for a small tube of matt velvet foundation cum concealer under a pair of black gloves in that drawer. Carefully she applied the cream to her now naked finger, deftly concealing the band of fair skin where, for many years, her ring had been. Her brow furrowed, her eyes narrowed in concentration as she took care to avoid getting any trace of the cream on her manicured dark red nails. With a slam of the drawer, she strengthened herself and now did leave the room, suddenly plunging it into darkness. She descended the carpeted stairs, quietly and soundlessly crossed the tiled hallway and out through the tall, wide front door, its stained glass panes catching both the indoor light of the porch and the orange glow of the streetlamps.

From where he sat he heard her exit, the closing of the front door, and the crunch of her footsteps on the gravel drive. He heard the car door thud shut, the engine purr into action and the crunching sounds as the car churned up the gravel as it revved into motion. Then, comparatively, there was silence apart from the more distant hum of cars on the street and the usual nocturnal disturbances of town life.

Again, keeping to the routine now firmly established, he barely noted that there had been no vocal confirmation of her deception either from her nor a response from him. The 'Goodbye', then 'See you', then 'I'm off's' had eventually terminated in mutual silence – replaced by footsteps across the hall and doors closing. Eventually he would go to bed in his own large rear bedroom and would sleep well. She would be there in the morning, without makeup, in a lilac dressing gown, for a cold breakfast punctuated with monosyllabic, eerily polite conversation, while he would render superfluous by turning on the bright, purposeful talk of Radio 4. But he would never fail to look for her wedding ring and there it would be sparkling on her ring finger.

But there was one aspect of the evening's routine of which she was not aware, he was pretty sure. He would give her about half an hour, then heave his ungainly bulk to his feet, stalk across the sitting room, on up the stairs to the front bedroom. He would quietly enter, strangely yet perhaps not using a torch for the intrusion, and go straight to her dressing table – directly to the top right-hand drawer. Previous careful searching had taught him exactly where to look. And there it was, an undeniable admission of what her intentions were that and most evenings. Her abandoned wedding ring. A cold metallic circle on its hard bed of dull, dark walnut. If he caught sight of the tub of formulation cream, it did not matter, its significance would not register with his male lack of imagination regarding its possible usefulness.

Carefully and quietly he pushed the drawer to. His shoulders stooped and his head sank forwards. In spite of their now customary aloofness, their gradual estrangement, the lack of the least vestige of warmth or care or consideration, this abandonment of her acceptance of any responsibility of being his wife really struck home; there was an ache in his chest, a tremor in his hands resting on the glass surface of the dressing table. Above all, he felt his age – unsteady and so very weary.

The round torch rolled loosely where he had placed it. Its beam of bright light distorted the dimensions of the room, shadows came and went, the wardrobe shifted, the curtains flared. He steadied it. Lifted it and shone it around. The room was as empty as if she was still in it, with him. All her personal effects in a stark, unforgiving clear white spotlight beam, each an indication of her betrayal.

He wiped the sweat forom his forehead. In vain, tried to set his parched lips with a dry tongue. He was hurting, deeply hurting.

He stumbled towards the bedroom door and out onto the landing. He desperately gripped the banisters and in doing so dropped the torch. He peered hazily down the stairwell. The carpeted treads came and went. He closed his eyes – deep breaths. Deep breaths.

Tomorrow! He knew what he would do tomorrow. Phone the one person he could rely on. His younger brother. He knew the situation. Always there to support and give advice. They would meet up for a lunch time drink. The very thought of it was consoling. Meeting up for a drink. He felt steadied. Thank God for brothers. He almost smiled. Good old Harry. Thank God for Harry.

THE BISHOP

From where he had parked his car, near the wooden hut signposted 'Village Hall', he could see across the narrow road a lychgate and, beyond that, a drive leading up the hill to the square stone tower of the old church itself, St Peter and All Angels. He was aware of two figures – men in dark coats – standing within the lychgate, another close to the tall hedge on his right and yet a fourth leaning on the horizontal bottle-green painted wooden panels of the hall itself. There was no movement from any of them. They all looked his way. Had it not been a bright sunny day, their presence, he remarked, could have seemed somewhat ominous.

He looked at his watch. He was in good time for the meeting. He relaxed in his seat and took a pause to reflect.

The Bishop had called him in. Lawrence was glad of that. The Bishop was newly appointed. Lawrence, a mere Deacon, welcomed the opportunity to meet him one to one, face to face. He had heard a lot about the Bishop – the youngest in the land, fast tracked up the ecclesiastical ladder through many urban parishes where he had had great success filling the pews, with new forms of service and ritual, lively and informal. Meeting him, Lawrence had reckoned, would put him 'on the map', so to speak.

The Bishop's Secretary had looked up when he entered her office, the Bishop's anteroom. "Canon Pennyweather", she acknowledged in a discreet tone. "If you wouldn't mind taking a seat."

Lawrence complied. He observed she was a diminutive woman of some incredible years, probably twice those of the Bishop himself, he mused. Neat and concise in action, she smiled briefly, raised the mouthpiece of her phone to her face and sat obviously attentive to a voice at the other end. She replaced the receiver. "His Grace will see you now", she said and indicated with her eyes the large oaken double door across the room from Lawrence.

"Thank you", he said. His voice sounded loud in the room. He rose and advanced, making for the large brass door knob.

The Bishop was already standing and walked forward to meet him, hand extended. "Welcome, Lawrence. Great to meet you."

So this was Bishop Wayne. Small, neat. Fair hair spiked not unlike a member of a boy band. He wore a purple cassock. His face was healthily tanned. His eyes a deep brown. "Take a seat, mate." He retreated behind his enormous desk. "Now, to the point."

Lawrence was required to go, on the Bishop's behalf, to the village of Upper Applebridge, some fifty miles south in the Diocese. In getting up to date with all his paperwork the Bishop had determined that somehow the parish had remained 'rather off the radar' as he put it. "We've got copies of the Parish Council meetings, of course", he said. "But it's all a bit vague, inconclusive. They seem to get away with blue murder. You look at these", and he pushed across his desk towards Lawrence a clump of worn and dog-eared files. "Lovely 'n neat", he went on. "Beautiful script – not typed or printed of course – fastidiously written but doesn't say a lot. See what you think."

Lawrence was to be the Bishop's observer at a parish council meeting and report back. "See what's going on", he instructed. "Y'see, Lawrence – er, Larry?"

"No, Lawrence, your Grace."

"I see, Lawrence." The Bishop did not look pleased to have to use the formal name. "Y'see, I feel we've got to make inroads into these rural backwaters. You can sense the inches of dust on everything. The wheezing organ (if it's played at all). The creaking doors – and the limbs of the old incumbents. The pews are empty", he said. "This can't go on."

Lawrence was fully aware of the young trendy Bishop's general intentions before he had attended the interview.

The Bishop talked on in the same mode. Lawrence watched him intently. The Bishop's mouth worked animatedly, his ultra-white, beautifully even teeth gleamed, there was a sparkle to his dark eyes. But the rest of his face was poker still. Not a twitch of the eyebrow nor a crease in the brow. No trace of a bag beneath the eyes nor a line from nose to sides of mouth. In spite of himself and his hearing the rumours, the conclusion Lawrence reached was alarming – Botox – the man had had treatment. It was true. And he also noted, as he departed when the Bishop came close to shake his hand, that healthy glow of his was not his own – make-up and, he felt a smirk of disapproval, eyeliner. Consequently when the Bishop turned his head to walk away, Lawrence was not surprised to spy an ear stud, nor to hear the valedictory "Tara then, laddie. Have a good one."

Luckily for Lawrence, at this stage, all he had to do was observe; it would be someone else's task, someone of higher rank, actually to move in and suggest the inevitable reforms – out with the pews, in with the screen and recorded hymn music, the karaoke style singing, the interpretative dance groups, the electric organs and guitar. Perhaps a visiting preacher in a red rose and acid green fright wig. No, thought Lawrence, no; his imagination was running away from him.

A tall, stooping figure emerged from the Village Hall and approached him with gloomy and unenthusiastic greeting. In taking the man's hand, Lawrence noticed it was damp and flabby, with a weak grip.

"Do come inside", said the man. He peered disinterestedly at Lawrence with sombre drooping eyes. Wisps of greying red hair swished unconvincingly down towards his bony nose.

"Thank you, sir", replied Lawrence and he followed the stooping shoulders. "Sit there." The man indicated on Lawrence's left an isolated metal and canvas chair. "For the time being", added the man. And he disappeared through a door at the far side of the hall near a small blue-curtained stage. In the middle of the hall was an assembly of small tables arranged to form a large square. Chairs identical to the one Lawrence sat in were positioned around.

The large room was intensely silent. Lawrence almost felt nervous. His right hand clasping his brief case was clammy with sweat. As the minute hand of the hall's clock clicked to the three, indicating it was 15 minutes past the hour, the designated time of the meeting, the door at the far side opened inwards and a line of people began to emerge and make their way and stand each behind a prearranged chair at the table. No-one looked at Lawrence. He may well not have been there. They all, with the minimum of fuss, sat, all but the tall stooping man with the gingery wisps. He looked over at Lawrence and spoke.

"Please come over to the table." Lawrence did so. "Be so kind as to take that centre chair." There were three unoccupied chairs just ahead of Lawrence. He did as requested. They all sat silently. Then the gloomy droopy-eyed man raised an enormous bony fist and rapped three times on the table. All rose to their feet, Lawrence a little after the others. "The meeting is in session" intoned the same man and Lawrence's eyes were attracted to the open door. Firstly appeared two enormous, thick-set, ruddy complexioned, shaggy-haired youths in tight dark T-shirts and jeans. They stood either side of the door where there appeared an elderly woman of commanding appearance, square faced, red pursed lips, startling black eyes, carefully applied pencil thin eyebrows, ink black hair tightly pulled back, With deliberation she went straight to the head of the table. Behind her a small figure, a woman, slight of build, in a floral dress with a white collar, white cuffs at her wrists, large pink-framed glasses and a mess of ginger curls for hair. She slipped tidily in at the chair beside her imperious predecessor who spoke grandly, "I call the meeting to order" and they all sat, one of the large youths crossing swiftly to pull out the chair of the imperious lady and settle it comfortably behind her so she could repose. He then moved with his brother – for surely, Lawrence decided, that must be the case – to sit on either side of Lawrence, who quickly became aware of the broadness of their shoulders dominating him and the tree-trunk thickness of their bare tanned arms restricting any movement of his own shoulders. His briefcase was on the floor to his right. There was no way he could get to it.

The imperious lady spoke again. "I declare the meeting open. Mr Purblind?" She inclined her head towards the gloomy man.

"No other business, ma'am. I suggest we move straight to the point. Consideration of the Bishop's proposals as identified in his missive from the Palace of the 14th of last month."

"Thank you, Mr Purblind. Is that motion carried. Will all in favour please indicate."

As one, all round the table raised a hand. This movement from the two hulks either side of him succeeded in subjecting Lawrence to even more pressure.

"Motion carried." The grand lady shifted in her seat so that she could view Lawrence directly. A cameo brooch sparkled at her throat. Her look was one of total disdain. "Canon Pennyweather." Her voice was clipped and authoritative. "You are here present as an emissary from his Grace, Bishop Wayne."

"Yes, indeed I am", responded Lawrence. He almost added "Ma'am".

"We are pleased to welcome you."

Immediately there was the thunder of knuckles rapping on the table's surface, a deafening round of approval from those assembled. Lawrence felt himself violently shuddering with the physical reverberations of the giants sitting closely either side of him.

The banging ceased. Lawrence became still.

"However, the Committee has reached a formal decision that the matter is to be considered and debated in a closed forum. Mr Purblind?" She nodded with deliberation towards him.

"Indeed, ma'am", said Mr Purblind. "It is incumbent upon me as Secretary of the Committee to request the departure of strangers."

Silence fell and Lawrence was stunned. He wanted to raise a protest but burly shoulders closed even more tightly upon him. He spoke up. His voice sounded useless and feeble. "But, I say … well … I really must protest. His Grace the Bishop …"

"Canon Pennyweather. We are *in camera*", intoned the Secretary who rose to his feet.

A clamour of banging on the table and a chorus of "Hear hear! Hear hear!"

A further protestation from Lawrence could not be heard. The clamour persisted. Lawrence felt movement either side of him. The pressure was being released. He felt he could rise to his feet. But a new sensation gripped him, literally. Firm pincer movements on the upper parts of his arms. He rose. He felt his feet leave the floor and suddenly he was up in the air, fiercely held, floating towards the outer doorway, which burst open before him. A blast of bright sunlight blinded his eyes, fresh air assaulted his face. He felt released, the earth beneath his feet and suddenly he was alone, the door slamming shut behind him. He was aware he was shaking, his upper arms ached with soreness. He breathed deeply.

A voice behind him. The grating of an opening door and a crunch as his briefcase crumpled at his feet. The bang of the door roughly being closed.

He looked around. The solitary figure was still there. Dark, inactive, dispassionate. Staring at him.

He stooped to reclaim his bag. Well, Bishop Wayne, your Grace, he said to himself. I don't give much for your chances here. As much hope, he thought inappropriately, as a snowball in hell.

THE BOAT

Throughout the years she had learned to hate the boat. And now she stood, on a bleak, grey windswept winter's afternoon, looking down at her blotched red coarsened bare feet standing on the sodden stained rotting timbers of the small jetty. The river was in full flood, dark, swirling, ominous – the boat juddered and bucked as it pulled on its tethers of coarse rope. A curious flat affair, broad of prow and of stern – mottled with damp and age.

The boat represented to her the unkindness of fate that had been her entire life. The large stones she clasped in either hand felt cold and very weighty.

She thought back to her grandmother who had taken her in suddenly and unexpectedly when the first signs of the plague – the scarlet ring rash, the sneezes and aching limbs – had shown in her parents. She, so very young, had been instantly whisked away to her grandmother's hut on the edge of the village. She had never been a welcome addition to her grandmother's lonely lifestyle – she, her cats and chickens – and she grew up in an atmosphere of quiet but persistent resentment.

But grandmother was not without enterprise and on her granddaughter's twelfth birthday she took advantage of an opportunity. The old ferryman lived with his wife and two sons, a little older than her granddaughter. The wife, never a strong woman, was finally confined to her bed. The old man and his sons would need looking to, food, cleaning, caring for, woman's work – her granddaughter was a strong girl, hardworking, no looks to speak of but brain enough in her head. That is what the old woman told the old man. And the girl moved in, tending the wife, working for the men, washing and cleaning – with her grandmother's parting advice always in her ears. That the old man could not go on forever. That local law and tradition decreed he would pass on the ferryboat and its business to his older son, as it had been passed to him. And that this son would need a wife. And there, living with him, would be a girl – hard working, not much to look at, agreed, but with some brain and broad child-bearing hips. Mind you be that girl!

The old man was in no hurry to pass on – either the ferryboat or his life. His wife soon died, which lessened the girl's burden somewhat as she settled into the routine of devoting all her waking hours to tending for the brothers and their father.

Human beings being what they are, it had to happen. The younger brother came sniffing around the girl's room, which was in a small lean-to – damp and bare – behind the cottage. He was wide eyed, dark eyed, lean faced, short cropped dark har, an angled smile, firm even white teeth. She found him irresistible. He laughed and teased her and tickled her and cuddled her and flattered her and charmed her – in her innocence she did not see where all this would lead until too late – and then it became the accepted thing that he would come to her at night when the mood took him, which was often.

But this was not as it was meant to be, she protested to herself. He is the younger brother.

The older brother was broad, fleshy in a white, unshapen way, hanging jowls, fat lips, small doleful eyes, a mop of ranging gingery hair, and a wit that was snail slow and as directionless as the flight of a moth.

And he would inherit the mantle of ferryman. Be that girl, her grandmother's words echoed down the years. And she was. She served the younger brother, but cossetted the old man, tended to his older son and became his wife. They moved into the old man's double bed – that was proper, in view of everything and all – and she lay for night after undisturbed night alongside the heaving, quivering, snoring mound of flannel-clad flesh that was her gormless husband who twitched and moaned and paddled in his sleep, but dreams could not have been the cause for he was too dim for them. And she heard, way after midnight, the returning, unsteady steps of his younger brother, flaunting at her yet another night spent at the ale house and later with one of the all too ready girls or even matrons of the village.

The father sensed his own failing powers and decided the time was right to hand over to his son – well, to a son. He recognised the woeful shortcomings of his older son and sought the advice of the local priest and, together with him, the permission of the local Lord to forgo the custom of local law and tradition, and pass the rights and holdings of the ferryman to his younger son.

The older son and his woman were to stay in the cottage, but under sufferance. The women's work was already clearly defined; the older son would labour for his brother and eke out scant rewards.

The younger brother would achieve the wealth of the rights of the ferryman – work that was not seasonal, was regular and independently paid – even with gracious tips if men and women of the gentry availed themselves of his services, either for the sake of recreation and variety or to avoid the tiresome detour to the ford some distance down river.

Then, it had to happen, human beings being what they are. The younger brother announced he would be taking a wife – a mistress for the house who would need waiting upon, who would have children to be waited upon, who would share with her husband the old man's double bed and all the laughs and teasing and flattering and charming and expertise of her new man,

So she stood on the jetty – morose and stubborn. In her hands the heavy stones, the last of those with which she had weighed down the boat within an inch of swamping, with which she had loaded the pockets of the old man's greatcoat that hung from her thin shoulders and shrouded in swathes her bony arms. She would lie in the boat, set it adrift and then turning, twisting, the bobbing and rise and fall of the shallow boat on the winter swelling river would force the water over the sides. The water would add its own weight to that of flesh and stones, and would take the craft and its willing burden down – down to where there was no loneliness nor self-pity, no injustice nor cruel fate, no laughter, no teasing, no touching and no charming.

THE CATCH

Tom, never the sharpest knife in the drawer
Took a while to see what other folks saw
That the reason he spent so much time by himself
Was because he'd been left alone on the shelf
Then the light truly dawned with a brilliance he hated
Why, all of his mates had just got themselves mated
And if he was to find himself a match
Have to transform himself into something of a catch
But how to do this, what was he to do?
Ideas sludged through his mind, like fish swimming through glue
He did of his best, worked hard for his pay
Then home for his tea at the end of the day
(Which he made for himself since his Mam passed away)
Bowl of porridge, some cheese, a few stale crusts of bread
Several tankards of beer, then away to his bed
Things had to change, he could see that right now
He knew what was needed, the question was how?
He'd have to go out when he'd done with his tea
Socialise in the evenings, be as smart as can be
In his suit, shirt and tie, then set out on his path
And if really necessary, might even take a bath
So he took down his suit, hoped it was still a fit
Took it out in the garden to air it a bit
Shook of all the dust and where spiders had spun
Flicked out the mothballs, scraped off stains one by one
Tugged and stretched at the creases as he pulled really hard
A cheer woman's voice floated across his back yard.
"What you up to, Tom? Beating up on a suit?"
He paused. He was breathless. Tom blushed to his roots
It was Josie, his neighbour, leaning over the wall
She could do this with ease, she was so big and tall
Her broad face in the half-light like a full moon it seemed
A glint from her glasses, her toothy smile gleamed
"Just trying to make this suit fit for the wearing
When I've got out the creases, mended some of the tearing."

"Oh come now then, Tom. That's no job for a man.
Here, give it to me. I'll fix it. I can.
Be like my Pa's Sunday suit. So spick and so span."
Tom paused. "Here. Hand it over. Oh, do come on, man!"
Next day brought it over. Said, "The best I am able."
Saw Tom's shirt and tie screwed up in the kitchen table
Seized them in her firm hands. "Glory, ain't they a mess
I'll take them and wash them and give them a press."
So it was three nights later, Tom, true to his word
Set out into the night, strutting like a cock bird
He was back rather early. She came over to enquire
Tom was sitting, head stretched back, in front of the fire
"What on earth?" she exclaimed. She saw he was not good
All down his shirt front was bright red gouts of blood
Tom's reply, it was muffled as he held to his nose
An old worn out tea towel to staunch the blood flows
"Tried it on with Ann Marlow. Put my arm found her waist
But she was then with Mike Parker. He thumped me in the face."
"You give me that shirt. I'll see that it's right.
In milk and saltpetre it'll soak overnight."
The next night Tom went out. Met with Angela Bride
Things were going well. They sat close side by side
Tom tried out his flirting but the sweet nothings he spoke
Just came out all wrong when they were meant as a joke
Angela Bride, she took umbrage and seizing his ale
Poured it over his head and ran off with a wail
Josie believed him when he said that what looked like a tear
Was merely a last trickle of the previous night's beer.
Bent him over the tin bath, carbolicked his hair
She dried it and trimmed it and combed it with care
His shirt, vest and tie she laundered and dried
And the following night he again set out with pride.

Her heart sank when he told her he'd took up with Big Bess
The blacksmith's stepdaughter shod a horse with the best
And when he had pressed his suit really too hard
She picked him up bodily and across the yard
She carried him just like an old sack of rye
And dumped him unceremoniously in Farmer Burns's stye
For what he came home soaked in, that and the stink

There was only one remedy of which they could think
To fill up the tin bath with water piping hot
And stick him right in it, his clothing, the lot
She fetched him fresh towels and whilst drying his hair
Whispered, "There is a solution" very close to his ear.
"I've got an answer. I hope you'll agree.
I thought that you might find a true match in me."
It took a short while for Tom to think matters through
For a woman like her 'twas the best he could do
As he put his arms round her, came one final thought
He had set out as a catch and had truly been caught.

THE DRIVING INSTRUCTOR

If asked to draw up a list of jobs / professions / careers / occupations that require an above-normal degree of inter-human intimacy, you might consider a doctor (Ear Nose and Throat – light; Gynaecology – heavy), a dentist, a masseur, fitness instructor, plastic surgeon perhaps – but would you include in your list a driving instructor?

Think about it.

Two people in an enclosed, confined space, mutually exploring a situation of ever-increasing stress and tension – temperatures, frustrations and humidity rising – contracted to stay thus for a whole hour, curiously detached from normal life, but subject to the conditions of the busy to-ings and fro-ings of unpredictable vehicular life outside their capsule. Bad enough if it's family or friends travelling together – is the car too hot, too cold? Is that a draught from the narrowly open window? Not that flaming Coldplay CD again! The smell of those Pickled Onion crisps make me feel sick. My leg's gone to sleep. Can we stop for a break? The dog's been sick – so on and so forth.

But a driving lesson – two total strangers in close proximity experiencing too much of each other, of their personalities, habits, temperaments.

I was reminded, when cleaning out my desk the other day, how at one time in my life, none of the above had occurred to me. I had decided in part to escape the tedium of a 9 – 5 office job, to train to be a Driving Instructor. Now, before me on my littered desk, I had come across the fading, creased cover of my first log book – listing times of appointments, clients' names etc etc.

It all came flooding back in technicolour detail, the first of my pupils.

14th April, 9 a.m. Mr Wayne Broughton. Aged 17, to be met at the Driving School.

He was easy to spot – a gangling youth in denim jacket and jeans, sitting with shoulders hunched and head bowed on the perimeter wall, swinging his lower legs and pounding his heels on the grainy brick work.

"Mr Broughton?"

"Yeah? Yeah, mate, I'm coming."

He clambered into the car – a smell of brash, cheap aftershave and peppermint.

"I'm your Instructor, Michael Brand." He didn't react to my proffered hand.

"Great. Let's get going, then. I *can* drive", he warned. "Me brother learned me, didn't he? Round the estate in the Fiesta – for years. And up on the moors at weekends. Reversing. Emergency stop. The lot. And three-point turns."

"Right. We'll still need to start at the beginning …"

"Yeah. I've got to learn to pass my test, innit? That's what my old man said. I got these lessons for my 17th birthday. That was yesterday so I'll show you what I can do."

"OK, but first …"

"Right. Ignition, into first and off."

We shot out into the traffic.

"Bleeding hell, them lights'll go to red" and we leapt forward through the light luckily still at green. Our speed eased.

"Mr Broughton", I said, gripping on to my seat.

"Call me Wazza", he said through gritted teeth as he concentrated on the road ahead. "Short for Wayne. All my mates do."

"Right – Wazza – I want you to turn left at the next junction and pull up, as soon as you safely can, at the kerbside."

These manoeuvres he completed with impressive skill and we sat together in the silent, stilled car.

"OK, mate?"

"Fine – as far as it goes."

I went on to explain that in these few minutes of 'expert' driving, car control, steering and gear changing, he had *not* used his indicator, rear view mirror, handbrake, seatbelt – nor had he kept to the 30-mile speed limit.

"Nah. That'll come", he grinned. "But I can double de-clutch."

He turned out to be the easiest pupil I have ever had to get through his test first time – less than three months into his eighteenth year.

16th April, midday. Miss Wanda Hetley. 24 years of age, to be met in the car park of Medleigh Gardens in the town centre.

She stood there, a vision in bright pink and fuchsia, tall, slim, flowing blonde hair, a skirt way above decency, displaying long tanned legs, perched on five-inch heels.

I climbed out of the car. "Miss Hetley."

"Hello", she purred. "You're dead on time. I like that in a man. Now, can I put this lot in your boot?"

Piled on a bench beside her was a collection of assorted carrier bags and hat boxes. "I thought if we met here I could kill two birds with one stone and finish my lesson at home."

I went to open the boot.

"Oh, and there's Poopsy too. He can go on the back seat – he's used to that."

A white miniature poodle looked balefully at me from where he was tethered to the same bench. I paused, "I'm not sure regulations allow ..."

"Oh, come on. He's no trouble, are you darling?" She scooped the animal up to lie across the generous proportions of her bosom. "You won't even know he's there." As she moved with him towards the car and me, the creature's bright black button eyes looked fixedly into mine and he sneered.

She climbed into her side of the car, I into mine. Both doors slammed shut. I was doused in an intense sweet florally citrus perfume – a truly pink smell. I was aware of nervous panting noises behind me.

"Right", she said. "No, I have driven before but it was a long time ago so I'm not strictly a beginner like I put on my application but let's pretend I am." The panting at the rear dissolved into a low, rumbling growl. "Don't worry. He'll soon settle. Won't you, my lovey?" She glanced over her left shoulder. "He doesn't like men", she explained. "Do you, Poopsy? I tell you what. Put your hand near him – let him sniff you. That usually works."

"But ..."

"Then he'll know you're friends. Go on. To please me."

Awkwardly, I did as requested, twisting uncomfortably in my seat. The fuzzy white head turned in my direction, the dark glinting eyes narrowed and his lip curled revealing a needle row of sharp teeth. "See. He's all right."

I managed to pull my hand away as the dog reared up, barking loudly and snatching for the tips of my fingers.

"Naughty Poopsy", she cooed. "I just don't understand it. Sit, now, sit", she commanded. But the hound stood there, nine inches of quivering defiance, teeth bared, growing deeply and horribly. "Oh, ignore him", she said. "That's best. He'll soon settle. Now ..."

She turned to the wheel, reached up and adjusted the rear-view mirror so she cold see to straighten her already immaculately arranged hair and check the perfection of her carefully applied make-up.

"Now, I know what's what." She looked down at the dashboard. "Well, most of it. What would you like me to do?"

I glanced down at her slim brown legs – her pearl grey shoes with their five-inch heels.

"Oh, silly me. I have got driving shoes. Be a dear. In the boot, you'll find my vanity case – it's pink. I'll change in the car."

I won't go into the contortions she went into to exchange her heels for flat pink brocade slippers nor the indelicate amount of stocking top and expensive silk underwear – pink! – that the shortness of her skirt inevitably revealed. Suffice it to say that her wretched dog did get a snap at me as I leaned back to place her discarded shoes on the back seat. She didn't seem to notice.

But she – every lesson in a pink haze of sweetness and never again with Poopsy in tow, but always with a boot full of shopping – proved to be a fast and proficient learner – her incentive being the sports car that her boyfriend would buy for her.

"When I pass", she said. "He's so generous."

I knew it would be pink.

April 18th. Miss Myrtle Coldstream. Age undisclosed (i.e. above seventeen) to be met at the driving school. She was not one of my regulars, though already a pupil at the school with one of our experienced teaches, Doris Brownlow.

She sat bolt upright in the driver's seat.

"Now, Miss Coldstream", I said, "according to your record I see you're moving very close to being able to take your test, in Mrs Brownlow's estimation."

She visibly bristled.

"Before we begin, Mr … er … er."

"Brand. Michael Brand."

"Before we begin, Mr Brand, I must make one thing clear. I am here under sufferance."

I was lost for words.

"I shall explain. I was insistent at the outset of my driving course that I should only entertain a lady driving instructor."

I observed her closely as she spoke. She looked determinedly ahead, angry spots of red glowing on the broad expanse of her cheeks. She had heavy brows, dark cropped hair, a thick neck and clenched lips.

Not a trace of make-up. A denim blue man's shirt open at the neck. A whiff of carbolic soap and TCP.

"But circumstances prevail against me. Mrs Brownlow is unavailable, for family reasons I believe, and so not to disrupt the routine pattern of my weekly driving practice, I have had to settle for you." She paused. "There is nothing personal in this, you understand. It is that I feel personally more comfortable in a situation – confined as we are – that is not trans-genderal."

"I quite understand", I responded.

Her large capable hands reached for the wheel, then her left moved to the gear lever. I noticed how brawny her forearm was. She oozed confidence and determination, forcefulness and physical strength.

"What we usually do is go down the High Street then left up on to the Webley Estate. There we practise manoeuvres." Her gaze on the bonnet of the car did not waver.

"I will be led by you", I concurred diplomatically. I felt I was in safe hands.

"Right", she said. She began very fastidiously. "Belt. Handbrake on. Rear view mirror. Wing mirror. Ignition. Depress footbrake and clutch. Into first gear. Mirror. Mirror. Indicator. Handbrake off. Move off."

The engine noise increased. The car moved – then the engine roared – the car shot forward and kangaroo-ed – she released the clutch pedal and depressed the accelerator simultaneously - and as we were hurled into the road, she emitted a high-pitched squeal, "Oh my God! My God!" she shrilled as she slammed down on the clutch pedal and brake. I applied the handbrake and leaned across her to switch off the ignition. She made another high pitched squeaky noise and shrank away from my outstretched hand.

"Mr ... Mr ..." she squealed. "I insist you stay on your side of the car. Mr Brand, your elbow is on my knee."

That lesson was abandoned. I never knew whether she ever passed her test, or even returned for another lesson. I was left bemused by the Jekyll and Hyde of Miss Myrtle Coldstream – from stern masculine capability to shrill female panic in the depression of a pedal. Startling and unnerving.

It was as I closed the log book that my eye caught the name of Basil Roundtree. Age 53. Meet at the Dalton Towers Hotel.

A tall, slim, distinguished gentleman. Dark blazer. White shirt. Striped cravat. Gold cufflinks. Greying, swept-back hair. Aquiline nose. Rather full lips. Discreet, musky cologne.

"Ah, my boy", he enunciated. "You hold my future in your hands." His tanned and well-manicured hands held the wheel gently. "I come to you desirous of the need to drive competently and convincingly – but not, you understand, to pass my test." He paused for dramatic effect. I was all ears. "Let me explain. In the life of an actor, there is above all one guiding principle. Be ready to be anyone, do anything. If a casting director – may the gods protect us from such abominable creatures – asks if one is capable of a certain skill – be it horse riding, scuba diving, sword fencing, brain surgery or taking wing – one immediately replies in the affirmative. Invariably one will never be required to provide evidence of the professed accomplishment. Although once I did indicate I was capable of high wire walking ... but we won't go into that. Suffice it to say, a double was found. Thus it is in this case with driving. 'Of course, you can drive', he said. No response from me was required nor was forthcoming. I have of course in my many screen appearances driven a car, or at least appeared to do so.. You will have observed this in viewing my films."

I looked blankly at him. "No. Oh well. Well, let me tell you, it is all smoke and mirrors. Half a car barely and front projection. But not for my current epic. I have got to drive. So, my boy, you have five lessons on five consecutive days to turn me into a second Stirling Moss." He smiled at me, his eyes drilling into mine, oozing charm. "A combination of perfunctory driving ability and consummate acting skills will see me through, have no fear."

Within five days, in his own way, he was able to display a degree of proficiency at the wheel.

At the end of each lesson he was whisked away by his chauffeur in a Grey Silver Cloud Rolls Royce.

As I squirrelled my old log book away, I sensed again the faint panic of close confinement which was the Driving School saloon car.

THE FALL

A cautionary tale about 'The Fall' that inevitably follows the deadly sin of Pride.

Tony's lying awake with a dreadful headache
On his mattress he's tossing and turning
Oh, his poor heart is thumping, his blood it is pumping
And deep in his guts there's a burning.
There is no ignoring wife Cherie's loud snoring
It's like sharing a bed with a tractor.
In a sweat-ridden haze he remembers the days
When there wasn't a single detractor
When the public applauded and everyone lauded
His triumphant success in the polls
Black, brown, yellow and white, centre left, centre right
He had captured their hearts and their souls.
How, only nine years ago, could he possibly know
("Things can only get better" they'd crowed)?
Truth would be the reverse, things could only get worse
As he rushed to the end of his road.
His heart bursting with Pride, Gordon Brown at his side,
He just failed to take warning at all
Of that canker within, that one Deadly Sin
That always comes before a Fall.
A wide smile, lobe to lobe, he bestrided the globe
He hobnobbed with the good and the great
As close as he can to the world's powerfullest man
And this what sealed his fate
Like a moth to a light, to a House that is White,
He was drawn – ah, alas and alack,
Like a moth to a flame, seeking prestige and fame,
He agreed to make war in Iraq.
Desperate to please, he fell down on his knees
And succumbed to George Dubya's seduction
"George, if you say it's true, then I'll say it too.
There **are** weapons of mass destruction!"

We are sadly aware of the death and despair
That he brought to that poor strife-torn nation.
The naïve deluded fool replaced Saddam's cruel rule
With just more strife and more conflagration.
Though a loud public voice said he'd made the wrong choice
He just jumped on a jet and was gone
To an inter-continental life with his 'First Lady' wife
To his best friend in old Washington.
"And there let him stay", the folks at home say
"We feel cheated and somehow suborned.
We had hoped for much more; remember the old saw –
'Hell hath no fury like a nation scorned'.
We will get rid of Tony and each cheating crony –
Blunkett, Mandelson, Prescott and Clarke.
We will wipe them away on the next polling day,
Leave Blair hugging his PRIDE in the dark."

THE FLATS

In the buildings where we lived
Me Mam, me Dad and me
My brothers five, me Granny too
The cat – me sisters three
It was a lovely block of flats
Built after Hitler's war
On a cleared and flattened old bomb site
To house the homeless poor
(that was us!)

Grand entrance hall, posh staircase too
All with a smart tiled floor
And narrow landings, spick and span
Each flat its own front door

The housewives with no front step to scour
Were not happy as you'd think
But polished and buffed the hallway tiles
Was like a skating rink

And us kids - well, we lost out too
No road to run and play
To plot and scheme, to fight and dream
To pass our livelong day

But in the flats, for safety's sake
In case of fire or flood
There were some back stairs builded in
Dark concrete and plain rough wood

So, at the front all glass and gloss
You'd mind your p's and q's
Whilst at the back on rough old steps
You'd be just how you'd choose

The lads would sprawl and fight and call
Eyz the girls with sullen face
In pencil skirt the girls would flirt
But keep them in their place

Bottles of brown were passed around
Matches flared and lit our smokes
With language crude, bawdy and rude
We sniggered at dirty jokes

Then cards came out, we gambled stakes
At Twenty-Ones, Poker, Whist
The cry of 'Cheat!' turned up the heat
Noses crunched with bloodied fist

The girls went, done up to the nines
On what they called a shopping trip
Came back with not one penny spent
Bags full with goods they'd nicked

These steps they throbbed with careless life
A culture all its own
Though hard and rough, the life was tough
We called the steps our home

And now I stand, my cup in hand
My grandkids at my side
In a loud crowd at safe distance kept
To see the awful sight

They've come with fuse and dynamite
Sixty years after my teens
To demolish the flats and that'll be that
Simply blast them to smithereens

Those tawdry steps will be no more
Gone all their tell-tale marks
Of ciggy burns, scuffs and brown ale stains
Faint echoes of boisterousness and larks

My grandkids' eyes are eager and bright
Agog with what they'll see
As the towers sink in a dusty row
There's a different meaning for me

It was life for us, we pushed our luck
As youth is doomed to do
Irreverent, loud, with no respect
Yet we were innocent too

We had no phones, no trolls, no drugs
No sexting, porn, no knives
And my heart sinks as the towers go down
With fear for my grandkids' lives.

THE GHOST WHO ATE UP COLOURS

The ghost who ate up colours
Has had her wicked way
Has written a sordid novel
One God-forsaken day
The title of this torrid tome?
I'll give the game away
It is foul – disgusting – degenerate
And called "50 Shades of Grey"

THE GREAT IDEA

An almighty crash of shattering glass. A weighty splash of water. A high-pitched wailing sustained scream. And then silence – total and unnatural.

It was Saturday morning and already light. The very moment she awoke, Frances was wide-eyed knowing that she had had the greatest idea ever – not just the greatest idea that an eight-year-old girl can have, but the greatest that any person living anywhere in the entire world has ever had. An idea that needed telling. Holding her breath, she listened hard. Someone was moving about downstairs and it would be Mummy, first up as usual. And she would be so pleased to hear this idea which would put so much to rights, solve so many problems. Frances was quickly out of her bottom bunk, into a pair of jeans and a T-shirt and out on to the landing. There she paused. She could hear the television in the sitting room below. That would not be Mummy. Some-one else was up. She flitted quickly down the stairs and went straight into the kitchen. It was deserted. A used mug and cereal bowl on the table – nothing else.

She crossed the hall into the sitting room. Sprawled on his back on the settee was her 11-year-old brother, Callum. Dressed only in boxer shorts and T-shirt, he had his head propped up on cushions, and was shovelling into his mouth spoonfuls of glistening, milk-sodden cereal from a bowl balanced precariously on his chest, his eyes glued to the riotous colours of Saturday morning children's TV.

"Where's Mum?" asked Frances. Callum gulped down more cereal and acknowledged her not at all. "Callum!"

Callum's eyes swivelled towards her. He looked half asleep. "She's gone to the doctors to get my prescription. She won't be long."

"Callum. I've had this brilliant idea." She moved towards him, propelled by her eagerness to tell someone, even Callum.

"You're in my way," he cried out. "Move! I can't see the telly."

She side-stepped swiftly and went on, "I've had this great idea."

"Now I can't *hear* the telly", he complained.

Frances glanced at the set. There was nothing worth hearing. Shouting, laughing, people being gunged, grimacing, gurning, silly hats.

"Fran." There was whine in his voice that was too familiar. "Fra-an." He swung the cereal bowl in her direction. "Get me some more. Nutty Crunch. Please."

She looked at him as he stretched his legs, pointed his feet and wiggled his toes. His toes were startlingly long and they folded and unfolded. He had the Mackenzie feet. Daddy had them and Moira, Callum's twin sister, had them. "Prehensile", was the word that Jessica, Frances's sixteen year old sister had come up with. "Like a monkey. You can use them like hands." They had nickname Callum 'Cheetah', which had been his dad's name at school.

The cereal bowl waved about under her nose. "No", she said firmly. "Get your own."

"Get lost, dwarf", she heard as she left the room.

There was movement in the kitchen. It was Mummy, flushed and slightly out of breath, at the table, riffling through her handbag, still in her coat.

"Mummy!"

"Hello, Fran. What are you up to? Had your cereal?"

"Mummy. I've had this brilliant idea ..."

"Hang on, love. Let me get through the door. Anyone else up yet?"

"Callum's watching TV. That's all."

"What about Daddy?"

"No."

"Be an angel. Pop upstairs to Daddy and tell him to get up. I'll put the coffee on. Tell him to move. The boys have got their rugby trials this morning."

"But, Mummy, I've got this idea."

"Later, love." She was moving towards the larder. "Be a good girl. Go get Daddy."

Reluctantly Frances turned away. She plodded upstairs and, on the landing, saw her parents' bedroom door was ajar. Daddy was sitting on the edge of the bed, his head in his hands. He looked at her blearily.

"Where is everyone?" he asked.

"Mummy's downstairs. She said get up coz the boys have got rugby and Callum's watching television."

"Right", he replied. "Tell Mum, I'm in the bathroom."

She longed to tell *him* her idea, but she would have had to go near him and he would have demanded a cuddle. Normally, she loved a cuddle from her daddy but not an early morning cuddle, when he was all soft and warm and lumpy but he would nuzzle his chin in her neck and his bristles would scratch and scrape too painfully and his breath would be dry and stale, like old milk. No, she wanted to tell Mummy first, anyway, then Mummy would be so pleased she would tell everyone else.

"Franny."

"A face poked out of the partially opened bathroom door – dark almond eyes and a bright towel coiled into a colourful turban.

"Franny – my favourite eight-year-old sister." This was Jessica. "Go and get Moira. She said she'd help with my hair."

Frances thought perhaps she could tell Jess. It concerned her, after all, *then* she could tell Mummy. She moved towards the bathroom.

"Jess, I've had this brilliant idea …"

"Not now, Fran. My hair will be too dry. Get Moira, there's a love."

"But Jess …"

"Get Moira!"

Frances turned and went into the large bedroom she shared with her sisters. Moira was a silent lump on the top bunk under a pink and lavender duvet.

"Moira. Moira." She reached up and tugged at the duvet. The lump shifted and a muffled voice grumbled. "Go away, it's still the middle of the night."

"No it's not. It's daylight. Jess says you're to come now. Her hair's drying."

A long growling sound from somewhere in the depths of the duvet. "Oh, God!" Another heave, this one positively seismic, and slowly and deliberately a foot emerged from the bottom end of the bunk. Another set of long Mackenzie toes flexed themselves luxuriously. A second long groan. The top end of the duvet lifted slightly and, in the narrow darkness of the gap, Frances could see the glint of eyes. "Tell her I'm coming", followed by a long sigh.

Frances left the room and knocked on the bathroom door. She knew better than to go straight in.

"Yes?"

"Moira's coming."

"Right."

Not even a thank you, thought Frances.

A figure loomed up behind her, pushed her to one side and plunged into the bathroom. Frances felt a warm wave of damp, perfumed air before the door slammed shut. Jessica would be the last to be told the great idea, she decided. Now for Mummy.

She set out down the stairs when she heard a determined knocking on the bathroom door. It was Daddy. She could see through the balustrade uprights, in his crumpled purple pyjamas, hammering with this fist.

"Who is it in there?"

"It's us, dad." Jess's voice.

"Well, come on out. You've had long enough."

"But, Dad …"

"I want to use the bathroom."

"But, Dad …"

"Now!"

Frances had crept back up the stairs to watch events unfold. It was like this every weekend.

The door opened nervously and Moira's face appeared. "We're doing Jess's braids. We can't stop now."

"I need to use the bathroom. Let me in."

Screams and cries and the door was swiftly closed. "No, Daddy. We're not decent."

Frances could see her father's exasperation welling up.

"This is a family bathroom, not a flaming hair salon." He stamped to the top of the stairs. "Magda. Magda!"

Frances looked down. Mummy had come into the hall."

"Yes, dear."

"Can you please get these two out of the bathroom?"

Mummy came straight upstairs, brushing past Frances with an affectionate stroke to the top of her head. She went to the bathroom door.

"How long are you two going to be?"

"We've only just started, Mum." That was Jess.

"We're having a crisis." (Moira). "A hair crisis."

"You can finish it off in your bedroom."

"No, Mum. We need the sink. It'll be ruined. Please, Mum."

Frances heard her Mummy say quietly but firmly to Daddy, "You'll have to use the shower room downstairs. I'll get your shaving things." She knocked on the door. "Daddy needs his shaving things."

Again squeals and shrieks. "No. He can't come in, Mum. We're not decent."

"No. I'll come in and get them. Unbolt the door."

The bolt scraped back and Mummy disappeared inside to re-emerge, her hands full of toiletries, a razor, a toothbrush. She dumped them in

Daddy's hands as the door shut firmly behind her. She called over her shoulder. "And get a move on if you want a lift into town. I've got to get Callum's prescription before the rugby trials."

Daddy looked at her. "His inhaler again?"

"Yes. He's broken another one. Fell on it. He's got a nasty bruise on his hip."

"God, he's hopeless."

Frances stepped to one side as her father squeezed past her in his descent of the stairs. "Out of the way, Pumpkin", he said. Frances stepped up to the landing. "Mummy", she said. "Can I tell you my brilliant idea?" Her mother looked down at her and smiled.

"Oh yes. Your brilliant idea. What's this all about, then?"

"Well. I've had this marvellous idea – in the night. You know what you said …"

Her mouth tensed and straightened up. "Wait a minute. Where's Ben?"

Ben was the baby of the family – not yet two years old and doted on, even by Rory, his oldest (14 years old), cynical brother.

Mummy dashed to Ben's room. Truly a box room – it barely held his large cot and a chest of drawers. There were toys scattered on the floor but no baby.

"Now where is he?"

She knocked again on the bathroom door.

"Jess. Jess. Where's Ben? Have you got him in there?"

"No, Mum."

Jess opened the door, her hair lank and dishevelled, braided on one side of her head.

"Where's Ben? I asked you to keep an eye on him. Where is he?"

"He's all right. I put him in his room with his toys. He's quite happy."

"Except he's not in his room now!"

"He'll be all right. He can't have gone far."

"You can be so selfish, sometimes. You only had to keep an eye on him." She turned from the bathroom door, which closed slowly, quietly and diplomatically.

"Frances. Check in your room. I'll look in the boys' room."

She pushed her way into that room. Rory was still an undisturbed heap on the top bunk under his duvet.

From her room, Frances heard Mummy pull back the boys' curtains so she could better look for Ben.

"Rory. Rory – have you got Ben in there with you?"

"What?" (Genuine surprise.) "Ben? As if!"

"Well, where is he then?"

"Oh, Mum."

"I can't see him. Anyway, it's time you were up. You'll be late for rugby. Come on. Now." And, as she left the room – "And when you're up, open the window. It stinks in there." She joined Frances on the landing. "No sign?"

Frances shook her head.

"Well. He won't be in my room. Daddy's only just come out of there." She paused and then leaned over the balustrade. "Neil. Neil!" she bellowed. Frances could feel the temperature rising. Daddy appeared at the kitchen door, half his face covered with shaving foam.

"Yes?"

"We've lost Ben. Jess left him in his room and he's gone. You'll have to look down there, even the garden, if you have to."

"He'll be in the house somewhere." A large blob of white foam splattered at his feet. "Probably upstairs."

"But I've looked everywhere. Oh no!" A sudden realisation propelled her into her own room. Frances followed her. "Oh NO!! Realisation realised. "Ben! No! Naughty!" The baby was sitting by open drawers of her bedside table enjoying the novelty of transforming her old cosmetics – lipsticks, blusher, powder, eye make-up, perfumes and creams – into wondrous playthings. She scooped him up and held him away from her, covered as he was in some of everything he had extracted from her drawers. Suspended in the air, dripping predominately with cold cream and face powder, Frances thought he looked like a miniature snowman melting.

Mummy was at the top of the stairs. "Neil, look at this."

"Where was he?"

"In our room. In my drawers again. Look at him. How could you? How could you lie there sleeping and ignore this? You'll have to come up and get him. Take him in the shower with you."

Inquisitiveness having got the better of her, Moira appeared from the bathroom.

"Moira. You go down and get me something to clear up with. Bucket of water, kitchen towel, some J-cloths, Mr Muscle – use your common sense."

Rory appeared and burst into laughter. Immediately he was handed the baby. "Take this CAREFULLY down to Daddy", Mummy commanded. "And get some breakfast. Have you opened the window? Good. Then get going."

Frances followed her mother back into the bedroom where she on the bed and surveyed the sodden mess on the floor. "Luckily most of it's on the rug which, thank God, is washable."

"Mummy. What about my idea?"

"There really is a time and a place, Fran. Just pop downstairs and get all the cereals out and some milk out of the fridge. I'll roll this rug up …" Again, Mummy's preoccupation discouraged Frances, but this time she felt definite stirrings of resentment and self-pity as she wandered off downstairs.

Rory was in the kitchen. The cereals and milk were on the table.

"Look at my shirt", he grumbled. "Soaking wet. Lipstick stains and I stink of perfume." He sat at the table, spoon poised.

Frances took her opportunity. She was fond of Rory, but somewhat in awe of him. He was the clever one – everyone acknowledged that. Fourteen going on 40, Daddy had said. Frances wasn't quite sure what that meant. She pressed on.

"I've had this brilliant idea", she said.

"No, you haven't", came the abrupt reply.

"I have", she protested. "I haven't told you yet."

"No, my sad little sister. You fail to comprehend my meaning. You are a mere girl. As such, you are unable to have brilliant ideas. They are for boys and men to have. Girls and women just follow along after making use of the brilliant ideas."

He paused for effect. Frances looked nonplussed.

He continued. "I elucidate. Ideas – like telephones, CD players, hair dryers, washing machines, iPods …" He paused. He could sense that his erudition was being wasted on his diminutive audience of one. He was right. Frances had lost track of what he was saying, but she was sure he was right, because everybody always said Rory was intelligent.

"Sometimes too much for his own good", Jessica had been heard to mutter.

And it was Jessica who now, with Moira, burst in on the scene, her glistening braids still yet unfinished. She waved her cell phone in her right hand.

"Just who I've just had a call from."

"Whatever", from Rory.

"Sarah Harrow" said Moira. "She wants us to meet up in town this afternoon and she wants to know if my 'cool' brother will be there."

Rory's neck and head pulled tortoise-like into his shoulders.

"And she doesn't mean Callum", added Jessica.

Mummy had entered with a full wastepaper basket. Moira chanted, "Sarah Harrow fancies Rory."

"Oh?" asked Mum. "Who's Sarah Harrow?"

"She's in Year 9. She's a girl with a *reputation*."

Mum rose to the bait. "What for?"

"A reputation" rejoined Jessica, "for having an appalling taste in boys."

"And she fancies Rory. And she fancies Rory", came Moira's chant.

Frances looked at Rory with his long angular face and mane of dark curling hair. She could never imagine anyone fancying any of her brothers.

Daddy appeared, draped in large white towels, carrying a pink, shining, polished, splendidly naked toddler who was crying pitifully.

"Take him, Magda. He won't shut up."

Frances had by this time inveigled herself into close proximity to her mother and was reaching for her hand but Mummy turned instantly and reached for Ben. His red eyes told the tale. "He's got soap in his eyes. Didn't you use the baby shampoo?"

Frances's lips tightened, her forehead creased into a deep frown, her eyes glared, her shoulders hunched. How could she compete? She hadn't broken her inhaler, or locked herself in the bathroom, or upset a whole chemist shop on herself or showered a baby with grown-up shampoo.

And she had another idea – bred not of altruism this time, but of anger and frustration.

She left the throbbing scene – wailing, arguing, protestations, accusations, teasing chants – and made her way purposefully through the sitting room, past the blaring television, to the open doors of the conservatory. She felt the cold marble tiles under her bare feet. Just inside the door to the left on a skeletal wrought iron table stood Mummy's glass globe vase, half full of water and sprouting three large white lilies. She encircled this with her arms and, staggering, reversed towards the doors, leaning backwards to take the whole weight of the globe. Then she closed her eyes tightly, took a death breath, and simply let it go.

The smash. The crash. The splash. The scream. The silence.

She stood stiff and still, her back to the sitting room. She heard movement behind her. Someone had turned off the TV.

"Fran. Fran. What's the matter?" Mummy's voice, concerned

"What on earth's happened?" Daddy's voice, perplexed.

"Franny." (Moira)

"Good one, Fran", Rory, impressed.

"What's she done, Mum", Jessica, gently

"Wicked", Callum, gleeful.

Now Mummy. "Hang on to Ben, Neil. There's glass all over the place."

Frances sensed her mother approaching and then saw her come into view as she moved to stand in front of her, looking down.

Don't be nice to me, thought Fran.

Mummy crouched before her, gazing intently into her eyes. Frances felt her chest heave, her eyes fill with tears, great sobs gulped from her. She couldn't breathe. Her Mummy placed her hands firmly on her shoulders and held her steady. Fran wanted to explain.

"Oh, Mummy", between gulps. "Mummy. I broke your vase. I'm sorry. I broke it." And she lunged at her mother in a mutual hug. "I'm so sorry."

Mummy muttered something about it not mattering but Frances knew it did. What matters, she thought as her tearful gaze over her mother's shoulder took in water devastation on the conservatory floor, is that she knew how to make her voice heard.

THE KING

King Biddulph the 14th of the ancient kingdom of Grand Acrimonis gently awoke from his deep, drug-induced night's slumber. He slowly opened his heavily lidded eyes. Even within the confines of the heavy drapery of his curtained emperor-sized four poster bed, he could tell that it was time to start his day. No matter how carefully the folds of heavy damask were arranged by his bevy of retiring servants, there would always be chinks that let in the odd glimmer of dull, early morning light.

In a leisurely way, but with an accustomed reluctance, he extended his podgy, immaculately manicured right hand towards the delicate, intricately carved ivory and brass handbell that rested on a small pedestal ideally placed for his outstretched arm. His plump pink finger and thumb gently caressed the detailed carvings on the cool white handle. His hand froze in mid-motion and slowly withdrew from its intended action. The King sighed deeply. He lay on his back and his whole body absorbed the sigh – its enormous mounds of soft velvet pink hairless flesh undulated visibly through the fine white linen folds of his nightshirt, causing a rippling sheen on the billowing surface of his creamily silk over sheet.

For the King knew that the faintest tinkle of that bell would start his day – that hoards of minions would, two by two, in orderly procession, descended upon him, provide for his every need – the Gentlemen of the Royal Bedchamber – in minute and particular detail attend to his very personal function, until he was fully presentable to start the day and be wheeled to the public chambers where he would breakfast and attend meetings and greet supplicants and courtiers and diplomats and politicians and orators and journalists and writers and fools and singers and all manner of obsequious lackeys. His world would be a mass populated circus until his evening commitments ended and he would retreat once more to his private quarters, and gradually, as his Bedchamber personnel performed each their tasks and withdrew, so peace and prayers for privacy would return. The last face he saw at the end of his day, bowed in humility with eyes downcast, was that of the Gentleman of the Bed Drapings who proficiently hauled together the weighty curtains, his final act being to place the small bell in position on its highly polished dark wood podium. The King breathed deeply in the familiar fusty air of his night-time canopy, feeling his sleeping nocturnal draught gradually overcome his gargantuan frame and his already wearied and befuddled mind. Slowly – gratefully, on this bed (in which he had been born and on which he will die) he sank into a delightfully lonely oblivion.

That was why he had had hesitated to touch the small bell.

Whilst the King lay, reluctant and undecided, way down in the bowels of the palace, in one of the honeycomb of rooms, most of them stone walled and windowless, paced in fevered agitation Master Valiant Crunt, until this moment, one of the lowest of the King's household. He was in a state of febrile apprehension and excitement. He felt he would vomit. His brow was damp with sweat, more of it trickled coldly down the small of his back, his legs felt unsafe and – worst of all – he held them out before him, thin and pale – his hands trembled.

It would all lead to nothing if his hands trembled. Perhaps it was the cold of the dark early morning in this stone cell. He pressed his hands tightly into his armpits for warmth and he perched on the edge of his roughly hewn wooden bed, pressing his thighs and knees together in an effort to convince his legs that, when he stood up again, they would have the strength to sustain him.

He knew what they were all waiting for : way above his head, in a world far too privileged for him to have any true concept of it, a small bell would tinkle. The signal would be given, echoing down the staircases of the mighty building, along the gangways to the subterranean servants' dormitories – and platoons of waiting King's gentlemen and King's gentlemen's gentlemen, and King's gentlemen's gentlemen's assistants and King's Gentlemen's Gentlemen's assistants' helpers would stir themselves in readiness, pick up their gear and tools of their trade, and take up, in respectful and earnest silence, their fore-ordained place on the multitude of stairways that ascended to the vaulted luxury of the Royal Apartments above.

Valiant Crunt was now one of those, and lucky to be so.

Born of impoverished peasant stock, his parents' seventh son, their thirteenth child, though only ten of those had survived beyond infancy, his mother had in desperation, had him smuggled as a tiny boy into the palace kitchens. Then he had earned his keep as a Small Scourer – squeezing his way into the confines of grease lined ovens, soot thickened chimneys, crusted drainage pipes, choked sewers, scraping and scrubbing where only one of his size could reach. Scratched, scarred and stinking, he would huddle down at night with the kitchen's dogs and cats : they were used for keeping down the vermin in these hot, steaming dungeons and he would have to fight them for scraps of food that fell to the floor, their only reward for the tasks they performed.

Good fortune smiled upon Valiant Crunt. Mistress Bessill, a cook whose speciality was preparation of fowl and game, took a liking to the boy – his dark curly hair reminding her of her own long-lost son – and he rose to kitchen assistant. He moved to a place in the subterranean dormitories – long dark and dank, stone rooms with serried ranks of crude wooden cots – where slept the other servant men and boys.

And then he discovered a strange phenomenon. There poor, uneducated, scraggy waifs, with their unhealthily pale bony angular limbs and coarse inarticulate tongues, their rough peasant manners and vulgar personal habits had the most astonishingly perfect faces, heads and hands. Their hair was beautifully cropped and combed, some into extravagantly opulent sculptured styles : or they had none at all but domes of smooth polished sheen. Their eyebrows were plucked and shaped – craftily coloured with paints and dyes. They had long, feathery eyelashes, lips plump and healthily red; those whose maturity warranted it had their jowls immaculately finely razored and scented with pomades and fine powders. Their cheeks were delicately rouged and artfully so, their cheekbones were pronounced and enhanced, the hollows beneath being effectively emphasised. And their fingernails! Meticulously shaped and filed, glossy with silvery polish and exotic smoky-hued varnish.

These hands were also healthily fleshy after careful massage and manipulation and were worked with ointments of fleshy tones that left them in strange ruddy contrast to the pallid narrowness of their stringy wrists.

But Valiant's perplexity at the strangeness of these weird and exotic creatures did not remain long unsatisfied, for he had inadvertently been housed with the lower order of those seeking training for occupation in the royal bedchamber – the apprentices to the helpers of the assistants of the gentlemen of the lord of the King's Bedchamber who were primarily concerned with the appearance of the royal personage. His hairstylists, wigmakers, cosmeticians, masseuses, tonsorialists, mani-and pedicurists. And, in preparation for all this and each his personal advancement up the ladder to a position of prominence in the royal boudoir, they only had each other to practise upon.

Valiant Crunt was a new face, a new head, a new bearer of ten finger and toe nails. He was leapt upon, preened and pampered, much improved and suddenly saw his way to the top.

Now, years later, he waited in a frantic nervous funk for the signal that the King had performed that morning's summoning tintinnabulation. He would gather his gear, take his place in the dutiful queue on the stairs and patiently wait for two hours of gradual ascension until being admitted to the greatest of all presences where he would bow deeply and scuttle forward, for the first time, to his personal territorial claim on the great geographical body mass of his mighty sovereign – his was the honour to attend to the nails, the quicks and cuticles, of the royal right hand.

Thus he could not afford for his own hands to shake nor for a bead of sweat from his brows to soil the plump pampered flesh of a royal finger.

The King's right hand would be his for as long as he pleased the King.

And that right hand now finally, after a sigh of resignation, reached again for the tiny bell.

THE LIGHTS IN THE WINDOW

The month - May.

The weather - mild and sunny.

The year – 1943.

The scene - the country village of Little Tiddlecombe-under-Wychwood.

Normally, a peaceful place, calm, placid, almost half asleep.

But on this particular day disturbance and perturbation, consternation and concern, a shifting population, elbowing, hustling, grumbling, pulsating ... and not an air-raid siren to be heard! So What?

Mrs Madge Baldray was the first to be alerted. Gently (but thoroughly) she was dusting her front main bedroom. Her bright yellow duster swished and polished. Aware of her advancing years and her retreating faculties, she kept in a wardrobe upstairs a second bank of cleaning implements – mop, dustpan and brush, dusters – she knew all too well her increasing habit of clambering up the narrow staircase, wondering briefly why she had come there at all, realising it was in order to do a bit of cleaning and that she had left all her cleaning tools in the understairs cupboard on the ground floor.

So had emerged her Plan B. First floor cleaning self sufficiency. However one faculty that was not failing was her hearing. She picked out the distant sound of old Bert Chitling's van huffing, puffing and coughing its way, much as Bert himself did, with exhaust popping and exploding approaching the village down Shooters Lane, a route he only used when trying to access or leave the village unnoticed. It was early afternoon and he was heading secretively home. She knew what that meant. She dropped her duster, swayed and fumbled her unsteady way downstairs as quickly as possible, hauled herself into her royal blue serge coat and faded felt hat, grabbed her wicker basket, purse and ration book and front door key and left the house. The aim of her mission was clear to her – but first she must contact her dear friend, Miss Molly Smaltering, who lived just beyond the crossroads.

Old Bert Chitling, as was customary during one of his not infrequent excursions, had left his boy apprentice, Cyril Peasegold, in charge of the shop. Cyril, a tall thin spotty youth with mournful eyes, goofy teeth and a beaky nose that constantly dripped, enjoyed the quiet hours of responsibility. Without old Mr Chitling to order him about he could enjoy a feeling of self importance and a time of serenity and almost total inactivity – for there was nothing to do in the shop as there was nothing to sell.

The shelves were bare, the white polished trays were empty, the metal hooks hung highly polished and useless, the marble counter top was glistening and unstained, the chopping boards had their ruts and cleaver scars newly scrubbed and the till was gathering dust in its inactivity. Nothing to do. The shutters were down, the *Closed* sign displayed on the door.

Cyril sat on an old stool towards the rear of the shop in the gloom (only one hissing gas mantle allowed by his glowering boss. "There's a war on you know"). He stared down into a hand mirror that he had found in a dresser drawer in the back room. He was practising facial expressions that he would use to impress the love of his life. He curled his top lip into a smile which he thought reminiscent of Humphrey Bogart. His eyebrows, puny and pale, he tried to form into an American gangster threatening frown. His pale eyes could not achieve a dark cow-like Ronald Coleman smouldering stare. But for a moment he could believe – Cissy Clement would surrender herself into his arms which for these purposes were broad and steely powerful (Jonny Weismuller).

Cissy Clement herself was down on all fours scrubbing the Victorian tiles of the vicarage hall floor. The ceramic surface glistened beneath a film of steamy water and carbolic suds. She heard the telephone ring in the vicar's study. She did not pause in her scouring movements – it was not her job to answer it. Miss Melody Psalter, the vicar's saccharine sister, emerged from the kitchen. "Oh dear. Oh dear." She mouthed, "So sorry, Cissy dear, to step across your beautiful shining floor. You're such a good girl. I'll be so very careful." She advanced cautiously, laying down sheets of newspaper before her. "So sorry. So sorry. No don't disturb yourself. I'll get by." Cissy scented lavish perfume as she wafted past, her full skirt brushing Cissy's cheek. "So sorry", she heard directly above her.

Melody Psalter spent her entire life in a state of perpetual apology, mostly to her brother Stephen, a large man of considerable self-importance, proud of his booming baritone voice which he deployed most effectively during church services when he bawled out the hymns and psalms, successfully drowning out the inaccuracies of his 87 year old choir mistress, Hermione Waterford, whose arthritic fingers failed to target accurately the keys on the church's ancient harmonium.

Cissy sat back on her haunches and listened intently to Miss Psalter's one sided telephone conversation. "Oh, it's you, Stephen … No, sorry, I was in the kitchen … Oh, really? … Yes, I'll do that straight away – Cissy can go. Yes, I know where the coupons are. Yes, dear, straight away. Goodbye … Oh, I'm sorry, I thought you'd finished … Yes, dear … I won't waste a second … Oh!" This last, a note of astonishment. Her brother had suddenly ended the call. Abruptly and thoughtlessly.

Cissy guessed what was coming. An errand to the shops for Miss Psalter. A pleasant break for her – and if it was to Mr Chitlings Butcher's shop, then there would be Cyril, tall and smelling of Brylcreem – but with that rather off putting leer, all teeth, twitching lips, mobile eyebrows, his pale eyes slightly crossing – somewhere between Lon Chaney Jnr and Buster Keaton.

"Hurry, hurry Cissy dear. I'm sorry to chivvy you along but the vicar is so insistent. Sorry, my dear. Are you ready?"

Cyril heard the grinding of gears as his master's van clunked to a halt outside. His peace and quiet was shattered. It would be all hell to pay now (he liked that phrase – Errol Flynn used it in *Guns Over Shanghai* with Rita Hayworth). Cyril was trying to grow a trim moustache like Mr Flynn but all he could manage was a cold sore and two white headed pimples. He rushed to the door, loosened the bolt and Mr Chitling burst in with a box in his arms.

"Quickly boy", he ordered breathlessly through his reddening puffy cheeks and his bristling grey Crippin moustache. "Quickly boy, before the hoards descend." And together they rushed in trays and boxes of the innards of sheep, pigs and bullocks. It was all the butcher had been able to get but he was confident of his customers' inventive capabilities in converting these unlikely ingredients into meals of varying degrees of satisfaction.

As quickly as they could, they would lay all the bloody, rubbery, jelly-like masses on to display trays in the window, would raise the shutters, open the door and … "Quickly boy", he admonished. Cyril fantastically saw himself and his boss, Major Herbert Chitling, preparing to meet an attachment of German Stormtroopers.

Madge Baldray and her thin whispers found Molly Smaltering was by now breathlessly more than half way down the hill into the village. From every house came women of all shapes and sizes, all coated and be-hatted, all with bags, baskets and coupon books at the ready. They barely acknowledged each other but plodded determinedly on. Cissy, younger than all the others, was gaining ground in the race. She hurtled past Mrs Baldray and Miss Smaltering. The former shot her a sideways glance of not inconsiderable venom, inwardly cursing the sturdy legs and stamina of youth.

"Ready, boy?"

Cyril nodded, glancing with satisfaction around the sodden masses of crimson and white flesh gleaming in the light of the now illuminated 4 gas mantles. "Yes, Mr Chitling", he affirmed, anxiously biting his bottom lip. He was nominally in charge of crowd control whilst Mr Chitling manned the counter and the till, slapping bleeding remnants onto sheets of greaseproof paper, hastily forming tight newspaper parcels and covering the keys on the till with blood-slime as he depressed them. Cyril knew the line of femininity would swing him aside as he would feebly protest, "Now, ladies … Please, ladies … Form a queue … One at a time, ladies." He would watch forlornly as Cissy swept determinedly past him. If he was lucky she would stamp on his foot, even if it was without intention.

The moment had arrived.

"Are you ready, boy? As soon as I raise the shutters, you unbolt the door and stand back." Cyril knew that that meant being flattened against the wall.

"Ready? Ready? Now."

Shutters up with a clatter. Dozens of pairs of hungry, piercing eyes gazed down through the glass at the suddenly revealed platters of animal offal suppurating in the sudden sunlight. Then the crush for the opening door.

"All this", thought Bert Chitling. "All this for the lights in the window!"

THE LITTLE TERROR

The air turned blue, the language rough
When Shaz told Gaz she was up the duff.
He spat out his beer and roll-up too
And asked when the little terror was due
Shaz wasn't sure, she hardly knowed
For the little terror hardly showed
"I'll see you then", as he left the house
Her old mum said "He's an idle louse.
"Just like all men. And, yer know, I'd rather
The little terror didn't have him for a father."
So alone Shaz was left - slowly inflating
In her dim jumbled mind slowly debating
The ups and downs of motherhood
Everything bad, nothing much good.
Her old mum said "It's not as bad as that
We apply to the council for a flat.
Grants for maternity, benefits they'll pay
Free teeth and glasses, and the CSA
With all the aid that charity's giving
The little terror will earn us a living."
Mum said "Now don't let pregnancy get you down
Plenty of fags - go out on the town
Have a binge with the girls, that's the least you can do
I won't expect you home until well after two
Remember, if we want to coin in the wealth
We don't want the little terror brimming with health
A baby who's sickly, with grievings and gripes,
Will appeal to the purse strings of do-gooding types.
The little terror was born, he burst on the scene
A healthier baby there never had been
Bright eyes, curly hair, and four dimpled cheeks,
Nan is all taken back, in a whisper she squeaks
"My gawd, it's enough to make you lose faith
We've got a prize fighter when we wanted a waif
The little terror's too healthy, too tubby, too pink

Oh, what to do now? Hang on, let me think.
We need a brat what's dysfunctional, ratty and mean
Who brings child experts and shrinks onto the scene
A celebrity one-parent family, trouble,
That draws us attention, our income will double.
We'll be on 'Supernanny' and 'Bringing up Tots"
'The troubled Teenager' : on TV there's lots
Of programmes that deal with recalcitrant youth
We'll get on the circuit, and then, it's the truth,
With brat camps appearing in shows like 'Trisha'
We'll get all the luxuries you heart could wish for,
With limousine transport, stay in hotels 4-star
Expenses and pampering, we will go far.
So stock up with junk food o'er brimming with E's
Telly and computer games, as much as you please.
Breathe smoke in his face, douse his Frosties in gin,
See what the little terror soon will bring in."
But the more his well being they would compromise
The more the little terror doubled in size.
Brighter eyes, glossier curls and to nan's great surprise
At school straight A's and the best pupil prize.
For his Mum and her Mum it was despair and woe
Only kid on the estate without an ASBO
15 GCSE's all at A or above
5 A-level's the same, after that a move
On to college at Cambridge, a first class degree
Then he starts his own firm, the forefront of I.T.
The milestones of his life, it became custom at each
That the family would gather and he'd make a speech
His first factory, first million, first helicopter was heard
His careful pronouncements, each well chosen word.
When he'd thank his dear nana for all she had done
To point a clear path for her favourite grand-son
For she knew he would say, there is only one truth
When you're directing footsteps through the perils of youth.
You have to accept that, whatever you say,
Youth's sure to go exactly the opposite way."
In her luxury annexe to his 8 million pound pad,
His nana would lounge - couldn't help but feel glad
In Armani and Lagerfeld, 9 inch heel Jimmy Choos

Puffing on gold tipped fags, with ten baths full of booze,
Nan would smile and herself be the first to say,
"Who'd have thought the little terror would have turned out this way?"
Whilst in her council flat, poor dim befuddled Shaz
Tended her other nine kids - she had gone back to Gaz.

THE ONE HUNDRED CLUB

In all the years that she had spent in her chosen profession, Maria Boswell felt she could never have been expected to anticipate the problem she was facing now in her last years before her own retirement. On leaving school, she had gone straight into nursing and she loved it. She decided to retreat from the bed pan and blanket bath when, after marrying Gerry, they decided to start a family. Then, when she felt the time was right, when the children could see themselves off to and back home from school, clean teeth, scatter cornflakes, microwave chips and toast burgers (except for Wayne, of course, who was now nineteen and in his total domestic ineptitude still completely reliant on his three sisters), she returned to the melee of the medical world.

She was at something of a disadvantage. Her lengthy sabbatical had put her somewhat off radar and she took what she could get. She entered the world of geriatric nursing, later termed care of the elderly. Again she found herself enjoying her job, and her reputation as a hard working and common sensical carer saw a steady advancement in her career. Now she stood as senior Nursing Officer in the Kay Court Residential Home in North West London.

But she had reckoned without Lilly Levy and her Hundred Club.

Kay Court was in an extraordinary situation. Next week Annie Fox would achieve her one hundredth birthday and would experience on her own behalf a ritual that was becoming all too familiar at Kay Court – the hundredth birthday tea-time celebration; a tea dance in the large lounge and conservatory (Bill Pugh, a mere 81 years provided the toe tapping waltzes and oom-pah-pah quicksteps on his gleaming marbled green and chrome accordion), a presentation by a local dignitary – someone self-important but well-meaning from the mayor's office - once it had been the mayor himself but then local elections were imminent – a presentation of a telegram from the Queen and a cellophane wrapped bouquet of seasonal flowers. The menu for tea would be a personal choice of the centenarian herself, "as long as it's not too over the top", frowned Bridgit O'Hara, the catering officer, thinking of the restraints of her budget. But Annie Fox had chosen fresh strawberry teas, "the scones must be home made and the cream clotted" – from Cornwall – where she had honeymooned with her Arthur all those years ago.

A loud and decisive crash from the direction of Lily Levy had bluntly curtained the possibility of any further dreaming and gentle reminiscence. And this sharp clearance of the throat brought Maria Boswell peremptorily back to her current concern.

Annie Fox's was the sixth hundredth birthday at Kay Court in three years. And all the ladies thus far feted – significantly no man had attained the honour – had survived to welcome Annie to their number. Lilly Levy was now 103, Sally Kershberg 102, Rose Rosenberg 101, Eva Moss 101 and Mildred Oster 100. They formed the 100 Club and were all too aware of their exclusivity and the proud tradition they brought to Kay Court at being statistically so renowned.

But whilst being aware of the acclaim that was heaped upon the apparent successes of Kay Court in nurturing and caring for such an unnatural proportion of residents in the healthy advances of old age, Maria recognised only too well the dark side of the situation.

The 100 Club had gelled into an unforgiving and formidable group, unassailable in its determination to have things its own way. They rallied to and closed ranks around the indomitable Lilly levy. Never saying a word, hunched sullenly in her soundlessly operating electric wheel chair, like an oversized, feather-worn, malignant mother hen, she brooded over her disapprovingly clucking flock of acolytes. Maria knew that little Annie Fox would not stand a chance. With her blue twinkling eyes, rosily powdered cheeks, sweetly pursed smile and bobbing white curls, she would be drawn into the muttering, tut-tutting coven – always closely gathered together in the corner of the large lounge furthest away from the possibility of any sunlight – and her demeanour would gradually and inevitably sour, her eyes' twinkle becoming a slanting glint, her heart shaped smile a distorting sneer, her cheeks hollow and pale and her hair yellowing and straight. They would sit aloof and silent, clustered intimately around the inanimate, heavily cardiganed blob that was Lilly levy, and five pairs of narrowed eyes would follow as one any movement that happened in the room. This intense scrutiny tended to unnerve the home's other inhabitanst who, on clement days, took to the conservatory or the garden – otherwise in small groups to their own rooms.

The main provocations of the malignancy of the 100 Club were the *youngsters* – they were the newer inmates not many years older than Maria herself.

Maria had grown used to the sequence of events. Inevitably it was during the quiet of a typical afternoon when she was in her office trying desperately to keep up with her paperwork - ever more determined efforts by government departments that every minute detail of life at Kay Court should be scrupulously recorded in triplicate - that there would be a commanding rap on the door. Lilly Levy's walking stick – but why she would require that in her confinement to a wheelchair defied credibility. The door would swing open, no word of permission needed from Maria. The group would appear, led by Lilly being propelled firmly by Mildred Oster, the most physically robust of the group. Close on Lilly's right stood Eva Moss. Tall, gaunt and unsmiling, she was Lilly's mouthpiece. Lilly never talked. Her lips remained fleshy, downturned and compressed. She hissed, the nostrils of her wide nose retracted and dilated and she coughed – but never spoke.

Eva Moss, her voice high pitched, reedy and sibilant, spoke Lilly Levy's sentiments.

"We have a complaint, Matron." The group shuffled into a tighter knot around the wheelchair. Lilly Levy's frown deepened. Like canoodling giant hairy caterpillars, her eyebrows moved closer together over her creased flat nose.

Maria knew that 'a complaint' would become a litany of grievances against the *youngsters* and very few of these, if any, she would be hearing for the first time.

Boisterous behaviour in the sun lounge; inappropriate programmes on the television; unwelcome drafts from the windows and patio doors left unnecessarily open, even though it is mid-July; pervasive unpleasant odours from take-away curries being surreptitiously delivered to the side door; late night noisy homecomings from visits to pop concerts at the local hall – and the noise of pop records being played with doors left open; that unseemly Valentine's Day dance where they took it in turns at the microphone to sing racy jazzy love songs at high volume – and so the list went on. Maria could feel herself tensing and she resented being forced to look upon this ancient sisterhood with anything less than veneration and respect.

Her gaze focused on Lilly Levy herself, whose blowsy features were compressed into a grotesque mask of distaste and disapproval. She remembered an incident in similar circumstances that she alone had witnessed some months previously. Lilly Levy had barked one of her chastening coughs and suddenly her eyes had bulged, her sallow complexion reddened and her tight lips inflated into a 'O'. Maria realised that the air forced up from her throat as a cough had dislodged her dentures and threatened to eject them into her lap. For a moment, the normally imperious crone seemed to panic, seemed vulnerable and ridiculous – beads of sweat broke out on her brow. But she swallowed hard and sat panting with a glassy stare. Maria could have laughed outright but she felt pity. However, now she had her remedy. Whenever she felt anger and awe at the behaviour of conniving old women, she pictured the teeth making their escape bid and pity cooled her temper.

After all, she had come to realise the irritation of the presence in the old girls' lives of the *youngsters* – having to share, on equal terms, all the intimacies of everyday life with strangers who were virtually the same age as their grandchildren. The umbrella terms of OAP, geriatric, the elderly blanked out the significance of forty years' difference – an alien culture forced onto an established and reactionary old age.

And – an even worse thought – but for the grace of God, Maria herself could well be a *youngster* in a couple of years' time. She was sure Lilly Levy and company (with added numbers) would well survive until then.

THE OTHER SIDE

"Mama – what is that noise?"

The small boy gazed up into the velvet dark, pitch dark heavens. Here and there pinpricks of stars twinkled brightly and sparsely. His eyes, if you could see them through the blackness, were mostly wide and dark. But something in the firm cool breeze was troubling them, bitter and smarting. Instinctively he scrunched up his eyelids and pushed his head further into his mother's side as they squatted together on the wet impacted sand of the beach. He tried to force his head (dark, richly black curls) between her slender arm and her warm body.

"What noise is that, Ali?"

"That noise. Roaring and swishing. Coming and going. Is it a monster? Will it come for us? Is it very big?" He felt her arm move to accommodate his comfort-seeking squirming. Her hand gently cupped the softness of his right thigh in a reassuring clasp.

"That is no monster, my son. That is the sea."

"What is *sea*?"

"It is water, my love. Water. Cold. Salty. Vast."

"But what is the roaring and hissing?"

"That is the sea moving, making waves in the stiff night breeze. Rushing it up towards us …" She felt him tensing in apprehension so she conceded, "But immediately away again. That is the swishing sound."

"But it will not hurt us?"

The mother understood too well her small son's constant fear of hurt and danger. The gun fights and bombing, long days on parched, dusty roads. The casual callousness of the authorities and fellow travellers. The irregularity of often foul tasting food. The sparseness of drinkable water. And now the wait on the inhospitable beach - never know was the cruellest of all. She released him slightly. "No, it will not hurt us. It will save us. It will carry us on its back from this side to the other side where everything is different. Life will be better for us – no bombs, no fighting, a new home. A new life for us all. But you must be brave. You have your life jacket and you have me and your father and your big brother. We will go together, stay together, be brave together."

"Yes, Mama." But the small voice in the dark emptiness sounded far from convinced.

The woman shed a tear. "It is only the salt on the breeze, she chided herself and shifted restlessly on the unyielding sand. She felt the tentative tug of a small hand scrunching the soft material of her veil.

"I will like the other side." The boy was reassuring himself.

Dawn was gradually building on the other side. The shifting waters were calmer, gentler. The wind had subsided. The light was still tinged with the gold and orange of a spectacular daybreak. The sky was edging from an exotic turquoise to a promising, optimistic blue.

But the beach was ugly – cluttered with the detritus of the clumsy and hurried activities of the nightly crossings. Huddles of dark, sodden bits and pieces – clothing, luggage, footwear, objects unidentifiable yet poignant. Together with the incongruous brightly orange splodges – eerily glowing in the amber light of dawn – of the many discarded life jackets.

But not all discarded.

Look carefully at that one, partly shrouded in the wafting floral pattern of a discarded shawl. The water moves it hypnotically forwards and backwards, to and fro.

Look closer still. A small brown fist clutching the silken, shifting folds. Dark curly hair now matted to the perfect roundness of a small skull. Dark eyes, wide, staring, unseeing.

The sea monster has been kind. Gently trying to nudge the small creature back to life. Backwards and forwards. To and fro. Then seemingly accepting that a calm soft rocking may be more apt. Sleep. Go to sleep. Backwards and forwards. To and fro. A sleep far deeper and longer lasting than the vast sea itself. Sleep. Now you are safe on the other side.

THE OTHER SIDE (2)

Now, prick up your ears and attend, I plead
To this chastening tale I am about to read
For you will hear in somewhat dubious rhyme
Of the perils to Maidenhood in bucolic Springtime
When modest sensibilities can be swept aside
And a pure girl so easily end up –
On the other side!

'Tis of your Charity Mickleblossom of whom I tell
A simple walk with her little dog in Dingly Dell
The sun it was shining, the first warmth of Spring
The sap it was rising, her heart yearned to sing.

Her young brain was giddy with thoughts of romance
Her feet fell to skipping, she wanted to dance
Her soft limbs responded to this sudden need
Inadvertently she let go of her little dog's lead

Sensing freedom he scampered away through the trees
Poor Charity panicked and fell to her knees
The guilt that she felt at her feelings so rash
From the near distance she heard a yelp and a splash

It was then she remembered a stream that was near
Oh, what had befallen her puppy so dear?
Fear lent her courage. In a trice she was up
And she ran to the aid of her much lovèd pup

The stream it flowed full, its waves overlapping
The poor pup struggled vainly, such splashing and yapping
But, fear not, gentle listener, Fate was kindly that day
Came a strong whirlpool eddy, swept puppy away
With a might surge of its rotating tide
Cast the little dog up on the stream's other side

On one bank stood Charity brim-full of tears
On the other her puppy soaking and shaking with fears
To save him was the problem that she must address
To wade over? But no, that might ruin her dress

In despair she called out, "Prettypaws, my dear
Stay still. Fear ye not. Your Mumsie is here."
When suddenly she sensed a presence nearby
A flicker of movement in the corner of her eye
With speed and as much elegance as a young maiden can
She spun round – emerging from the bushes she spotted – A MAN!

Her scream died in her throat, her attention drawn elsewhere
The shining curls of his locks of syrup golden hair
The sparkling of blue eyes that glinted beneath
Fine nose, aquiline nostrils, white pearly teeth

Firm chin with a dimple, strong oak tree-like neck
Shirt torn to the navel, tanned sweat-glistening pecs
Barrel chest that tapered to a narrow taut waist
Bulging thighs in torn breeches that were barely in place
His ankles were slender, his tanned feet quite bare
His whole demeanour was confident, he hadn't a care

All this she took in : her heart started to pound
And drunk with delirium she fell to the ground
Next she knew he was close to her, his breath was sweet
Strong arms as he lifted her, his burly back bent
She swooned as he carried her, felt total safety
As gently he settled her lolling against a tree

"My Prettypaws", she whispered through plush lips Cupid red
His periwinkle eyes widened. What was that she said?
"My little dog. The stream." She almost fainted 'tis true
But not quite. She waited to see what he would do

"Never fear, gentle maiden." Voice husky and deep
"I shall go." And she sat up. No fear now of sleep
He strode to the brimming waters. A manly swaying gait
Legs muscular and powerful. Figure upright and straight

He struck into the churning waves, gurgling and loud
To his knees, then his waist, then his shoulders he ploughed
His strong muscular arms held aloft o'er his bead
Like a proud Spanish dancer. She looked on with dread

Then he turned. He was holding with strength but with care
The little pup on his shoulder nestled into his hair
As he emerged towards her she couldn't help note
The silvery water drain from the sinews of his throat
As it torrented down over shoulders and chest
Powerful muscle extruded through his soaked clinging vest
Thighs working like pistons glimpsed through tattered torn drawers
Down over his dark calves, feet stomping like paws

'Tis odd that what's taken in in one brief glance
Is enough to put a girl into half an hour's trance

Enough to say, with one mighty arm he lifted her to her feet
And handed her her little dog in reunion sweet
"Come. I'll walk with you some of the way. That will be best."
His arm supported and enveloped her. Her cheek leaned against his chest

Once home she recounted to her sisters all seven
Her adventures that day, her experience of heaven
They clustered around her, all curls, ribbons and bows
They giggled and exclaimed with 'oohs', 'ahs' and 'ohs'.

Next day came Mrs Burden the Vicar's wearying spouse
She knew where to go when she wanted a grouse
Told Charity's mum that her girl had been seen
Canoodling with a man across the village green
A man, tall and burly, poorly dressed, tanned nut brown
Indubitably a brickmaker from the other side of town

Mother was astounded by her youngest daughter's capers
Fell back in her chair panting, an attack of the vapours
Called for smelling salts, with flapping hands her flushing face she fanned

Mrs Burden smirked with smugness – exactly what she'd planned

But her delight was short lived. Charity's sisters they knew more
And beaming with wide smiles they all crowded through the door
"Girls! Girls! Calms yourselves" cried Mother somewhat reviving with a flash
"I shall not hear a thing until all of you hush."

So all the girls lined up as they were wont to do
There was Hope, Piety and Innocence, Modesty and Charity too
Honest and Fidelity and … oh, one just isn't there
Let's get on with the story. We cannot wait for her

"Mum" cried the girls, in a chorus quite wild
"Be happy! And hurrah for your dearest youngest child
The young man whom she encountered and came unto her aid
Is indeed from the other side as the Vicar's wife said
But not from the low side, the brickmakers' shacks
The ramshackle hovels and the poor back to backs
But from the other side where our gentry reside
From Lord Edgemoor's mansion our humble town's pride

It was Tristram, his young son, whose presence was so timely
He was, in fact, in working garb, all tattered and grimy
He was out setting traps and heard dear Charity calling
And rushed to her aid in her dilemma so appalling

But now, dearest Muma, to your feet raise with pride
For he is here with his finest coach and waiting outside
We are sure he is here to find himself a bride
And transport dearest Charity to the other side!

THE SCROLL

The small girl sat at her desk – one of many in serried ranks within the large silent classroom – her head dutifully bowed over the script laid flat on her desk top. It was the period of quiet study before the end of the working day. To any observer, she was dedicated to intensive scrutiny of that day's reading, but she herself knew better. Today was a special day. Today, when she arrived home, there would be a special visitor. She could not subdue the anticipatory flutter in her chest, her feet were clenched together to prevent them impatient shaking, her fingers squeezed into tight fists and her eyes unable to focus on the theme of what she was supposed to be absorbing. Phrases she read scampered away. The afternoon seemed interminable.

Today would see the arrival of her great grandfather's sister – truly a venerable and honoured guest. Her mother had informed her of this oncoming visit.

Her great grandfather and his sister were geographically very distant relations and, being very elderly, were unable to travel far, if at all. So remote were they to her, her vivid imagination fleshed out the few actual details that had filtered through to her.

Above all was the artistry of her great grandfather's sister. This she had seen represented in some precious scrollwork that her mother had suddenly produced one day. She had returned from the bedroom with a shining ebony lacquered box, fixed with a catch of ivory and black ribbon. She placed the box on the floor near where the girl sat cross-legged and gently opened it. She sifted through various scrolls until she found the one she wanted. "This is your scroll", she said to her daughter. "It is fragile. I will unroll it. You may hold it but very, very carefully."

Mother did so and placed the extended vellum in her daughter's outstretched hands. The girl's eyes met an illustration of exquisite exoticism, vibrant colour and amazing detail. From the delicate curls of blue and silver foaming waves at the foot of the picture rose the elegant, curving figure of what must be a god, long robes gold and green swirling up from the waters to a masked face that combined fierceness and gentleness, awe, respect and caring, a configuration of black and red features on an ivory base – the brows glowing and forbidding, the eyes, silver and grey, demanding yet soothing, the lips blood red, half smiling, the cheeks hollowed and gaunt. Protruding from the folds of the voluminous sleeves of the robe were elegant pale hands with long slender fingers, extended by curling gold-tipped nails. These hands supported a swathe of white material cocooning an infant, of which could be seen only the head, one gently curled chubby hand and a dangling plump foot with podgy toes. In the background of all this, a distant landscape of bent and twisted dark limbs of trees, clumps of exotic blossom and craggy snow-capped mountains. The sky was azure blue with stylised curling white and silver clouds between the peaks.

The child's sloe eyes widened. Had there ever been anything so beautiful?

"This is your scroll, my daughter. Your great grandfather's sister has always seen it as her duty and pleasure to commemorate any significant family event with a scroll such as this. This is yours. You will see at the bottom the date of your birth – there, in red."

The girl looked carefully at the depiction and paused.

"Mother …" she began tentatively.

"Go on", her mother invited, a small knowing smile teasingly curving her red lips."

"The baby", began her daughter. She did not wish to be disrespectful by criticising the artwork but something troubled her. "The baby … its face."

"It is the face of a baby boy", explained her mother. "In it your great great aunt has put all the qualities a boy child requires – determination, stubbornness, defiance, moral strength. A girl child would be more serene and gentle."

The little girl was obviously still puzzled and not best pleased.

"Do not forget", continued her mother. "This picture was produced when the artist was a woman far advanced in years, though you would not know that from the perfection of the draughtsmanship. But she was rather deaf and difficult in her denial of this. The event of your birth was reported to her and she misheard your name. She prepared the scroll for the birth of a boy. You must forgive the frailties of old age. It comes to us all."

The girl sat still – a long pause – then a deep sigh. Her brow cleared.

"It is a beautiful picture", she said, "and very special to me."

Indeed, the girl's not inconsiderable artistic ability was often attributed to her great grandparents' generation, her great grandfather being a renowned screen-printer, and first in the functional dissemination of information, the wall newspaper of his day, and put in artistic reproduction, many of his sister's works.

Now the great great aunt would be arriving and the girl could share with her pictures that she herself had completed. She specialised in dogs, breeds she herself had imagined, often combinations of known breeds, lions, dragons and golden carp – but she also did somewhat otherworldly landscapes and perhaps too well observed caricatures of neighbours and friends – a particularly skeletal version of the old fruit seller at the entrance to the market who always frightened children with his sinister toothsome leer.

The school day ended and she rushed out into the street and walked hurriedly towards home – running was forbidden.

She had been warned by her mother of the great great aunt's situation. After 'the event' as it was euphemistically termed – after the earth had stopped convulsing and erupting – after the massive waves had thundered inland and equally destructively withdrawn – days after, the old woman had been found, shrouded in heavy, saturated blankets, aimlessly stumbling amongst the rubble of what had been a major road. To her great consternation, she had been affronted by a mighty, godlike figure, all gleaming acid yellow and black, face hidden by a white mouth mask and amber tinted goggles, a domed metallic helmet on its head. This rescue worker had scooped her gently into his powerful arms and taken her to his truck, in which, on a stretcher improvised from a garish poster-red door from the local cinema, she had been taken to a treatment centre. It took weeks to establish her identity, so intensive was her medical treatment, but eventually a grandson was identified in a city on the other side of the country – he and his wife and small artistic daughter.

Now, when that daughter arrived home, the family's guest would be there.

The little girl was shown into her own small bedroom which she had willingly vacated for the revered incomer. The old woman sat huddled defensively on the plush ink bedspread, pressing hard against her granddaughter-in-law. The small girl bowed solemnly. She unbent to meet the relentless yet vacant gaze of the grey watery eyes. Was there the faintest evidence of a smile on the pale, thin lips? The old woman suddenly turned her head and whispered hoarsely into the girl's mother's left ear.

"She says she is pleased to see you", interpreted the mother. A pause. More hushed tones. "She says you are very pretty." Again whispers. "She says you are too skinny and should eat more." Mother winked meaningfully as she reported this. "Remember, she is a confused old woman", the wink said.

The old aunt leaned away, releasing the mother. "That is all for now. Your great great aunt needs to rest. She has had a long journey. Go now, change from your school uniform and we will prepare our evening meal."

That was a very inauspicious start to the visit and matters improved very little. The little girl stood for scrutiny by the huddled grey crouching figure – even her kimono was a colourless, faded blue – there were whispered comments, frequently repetitive When the girl had presented some of her precious paintings, the old woman had hesitantly taken them in clawed, bony hands and almost instantly dropped them with nothing approaching even a careful perusal. "She probably could not recognise the breed", said mother. "Perhaps next time a country scene." But it made no difference. The girl was bitterly disappointed but tried not to show it.

Then things started disappearing. First two rice bowls from the kitchen shelves. Then father's shaving mug from the bathroom. A glazed earthenware figurine of a geisha from atop the bookcase. And finally a pad of the girl's drawing paper and some of her coloured paint sticks. Mother had learned to look for all those items behind the old woman's bed and she retrieved them without reaction or protest. But the art materials she had left. "We will buy you some more", she said. Until one day, having gently knocked on the sliding door, she entered the small bedroom to find the old woman at the small desk hurriedly applying the paints to the paper. Instantly the cover of the pad was slammed down. The old woman was summoned to the family meal. Mother was pleased, the instincts justified, the great great aunt was responding.

The little girl now visited the bedroom after school with greater regularity. She longed to see the splendid pictures her ancient relative was completing. Still, the great great aunt communicated through intimate whispers to the mother's lowered left ear. One day Mother said, "She says you are to look at this." The girl hoped it was to be a recently completed illustration, but it was a quite large sepia tinted photograph of a man in an old fashioned tight black suit, a butterfly collar to his white shirt and a narrow tightly-knotted black tie plunging into his dark waistcoat, He looked a stern man. He wore low over his narrow eyes a bowler hat. He had round rimmed glasses and a thin moustache that spread across his upper lip and down at each end making his expression severe and disapproving. His face was lean, his cheek bones prominent. More whispering. "She says this is your great grandfather. It is all she has left of him since 'the event'".

Not long after this, when the girl arrived home, the old lady was again on the bed alongside mother. Mother had the closed drawing pad on her knee. "She wants to show you her paintings. They are all of the old cherry tree that was in her yard at home. They show the tree in different seasons. Black and bare. Boughs of pink blossom. In full green leaf." A pause. More whispering. "You are to know that they are all drawn from memory. Now, come over here where you can see them when I turn the pages." The little girl settled close to her mother's right hip.

The dark card cover lipped open.

"Mother", the girl whispered.

Mother's elbow nudged her. "Now the next one", she said. The page flipped over.

The girl gasped. "Mother." She couldn't help herself. "They're just scribbling."

Yet the turn of another page. Mother's voice was firm and in its tone forbade any further hissed interjection from her child.

After four pages, the rest were blank. There was a long pause. Mother nudged the girl to her feet. "Go and change from your school uniform."

It took a huge effort for the little girl to walk towards the bedroom door, turn, bow very formally to her great great aunt and say, "Thank you, aunt, for showing me your paintings. They are very beautiful." She turned and left the room, sliding the door closed behind her. And she wept soundlessly, full tears plunging down her cheeks and chin.

Years later she was preparing to leave home to go to university to study Fine Ats. Clearing her room she came across the art pad that her great grandfather's sister had used all those years ago – the first four pictures of the seasons of the cherry tree and subsequent ones that the old lady had described in whispers – the family home, the countryside nearby, the mountains, the beach, the fishing village, local festivals. And they were all the same, not just scribbles but literally all the same, identical in the layout of the scribbling. A dark blue lightning streak that fizzed its way diagonally from bottom left corner to top right. The lower part of each sheet, swooping curls and coils of pinks and silvers and the palest of greens. Above there to the top of the pages scrawled patches of turquoise and blue, with golden angles and box shapes. And over all, a distorted spider's web of fine black, shattering the rest into uneven fragments of the whole – disintegrating the entire image. Each page identical, time and time again. She had once taken a measuring rule to them. There were less than millimetres of difference between the completed pages.

These she would store away, tougher with the fading photograph of her great grandfather – who, others had assured her – was not of her great grandfather at all. Goodness knows who it was or where it had come from. But the little girl had insisted that the photograph be carefully rolled into a scroll, tied with black ribbon, and placed in the shiny ebony box alongside her great great aunt's proper paintings – pictures she had come to love.

THEATRE SUPERSTITIONS

It is a fact well known that members of the acting profession – those theatrical luvvies who trod the boards - are given most determinedly to superstitious belief.

There are many, amongst them the most renowned one (a) mentioning the title of William Shakespeare's Scottish play neither on the stage or in any area approximate to it unless in rehearsal for or performance of the play itself, (b) never whistle on stage, (c) never, in rehearsal, utter the final lines of the play.

The 'Macbeth' superstition – (a) is because it is believed that the bard employs actual occult incantations, the speaking of which can manifest evil itself. The second (b) comes from the tendency in the 17th / 18th centuries to extravagant and ambitious spectacles in theatre presentations – storms at sea, earthquakes, the transformation scene, buildings on fire etc. etc. These necessitated the sudden and precise movement of vast items of scenery, hauled aloft on thick nautical ropes. Very often ex-sailors were called in to do this and their traditional means of communication at sea – which sheet to try on, which billowing sail to raise – was a vocalising of piercing whistles, heard through the worst of storms. They adapted this practice to the stage, the whistle being less evident but equally meaningful. Any extraneous whistle from an actor or bystander – a jolly turn, a signal of approval – could be totally misinterpreted and result in the crashing down of a tonnage of wooden framework and painted canvas exactly on the spot where the leading man was about to deliver his most important and dramatic soliloquy. The third – (c) – never conclude a play until in performance is less easily explained. It could be the idea of completing a magic circle, from beginning to end, somewhat tempting Fate, defying the Gods.

There is a (again 17th / 18th Century) lesser known superstition, again from the era when a substantial curtain divided the theatre, the actors from the audience, the colourful and magical era of escape from the mundane grey space of everyday life, An inadvertent merger of the two opposing worlds must be avoided. It was forbidden to peep out at the auditorium, why there was good reason to do so. Where the audience settled; indeed, were they all in? How many were there? Lord help us, were there any at all?

Ingrid Bergman, the famous actress more renowned for acting on screen than in the theatre, was known to be very apprehensive about appearing on stage before anything less than a full house. They could not keep her - or more likely her personal staff, dresser, hair stylist, makeup artist, secretary – away from the chink in the curtain and if empty seats were spotted she may well refuse to go on. The theatre management took to trawling the students from the local drama schools (this being London, of course there were plenty) to occupy any unsold seats free of charge – especially the front row which are never the most popular to the general public for a serious play. All that craning of necks to look up and see too much detail (tell-tale nervous ticks, unattractive sweat on the brow, bodily odours and a give-away aura of alcoholic imbibing.)

Of course, these days front of house and backstage are intimately linked with all manner of technological gizmos. Any such apprehensions of yore are definitely old hat.

The chink in the curtain – if there is a curtain at all – may be no more.

The practice developed of cutting a chink in the curtains and disguising it with painted gauze – this was solely and officially for the use of stage management – how else to keep in immediate touch with the front of house? Irresistible to avoid by passing cast members – and deemed bad luck. Perhaps they did spy misfortune – too many empty seats, rows of dozing old folk, swaying inebriated coach parties or – worse – a whole range of already restless school pupils, only there because it was preferable to an afternoon of double maths. Such gloomy tidings might well permeate the entire cast : spirits would sink, performances become below par or hurried so that they could get through the whole thing as quickly as possible. Have an influential critic in for one of those half-cocked displays to a play may scupper you even in London, never mind succeeding in the West End.

So it was Bad Luck!

But 'Do not peep at any cost' still applies. Beware the malevolent spirits!

THREE BALLOONS

The three balloons above his head
Bob, yellow, blue and gaudy red
As John his weary way plods home
On glistening paves, past walls of stone
His world is newly washed with rain
The pavement's damped a darker stain
Except where puddles gold and bright
Reflect the garish neon light.
The night is cold, raw to his face
Stark contrast to the cheery place
Where John has spent a festive eve
Finally begging to be allowed to leave
This celebration, bright and cheer
To acknowledge he's reached his eightieth year.

They'd sung 'For he's a jolly good fellow'
And hung balloons, red, blue and yellow
And put out sandwiches, crisps and pies
And as John rubbed his rheumy eyes
The landlord called 'Now, raise your beers
To John who's reached his eighty years.
It must be a compliment to our beer
For thirty years he's been coming here
In this public bar, a familiar face,
He certainly has earned his place
No-one sits on Old John's stool
Nor touches his tankard – that's the rule.'
Then 'Happy Birthday to you' they sang
And after that loud greetings rang
Of 'Happy Birthday, John! Many returns!'
With rounds of drinks they took their turns
Surrounded him with smiles and laughter
Warm goodwill ricocheted from the rafter
Danced down to join with cackling jest
The roaring fire in the chimney breast

Wine glasses sparking, horse brasses gleamed
The universe then to Old John seemed
A world of brilliant, magical light
Distant memories of a child's Christmas night.

Now the balloons bob, yellow, red and blue
The cold wind chills him through and through
He fumbles the key at his dark front door
Stumbles into the hall on the worn lino floor
Through the unheated hall to the dingy back room
Where the fire has died into unrelieved gloom
Sits huddled in his coat to retain the last heat
As the quarry tile coldness seeps up through his feet
The mantle clock ticks in the bulb's sallow glow
He squints at the sideboard, the dull metal framed row
Of grey-fading-to-khaki faces of those
Who long ago took up the dicky-bird pose
Whose memory within him fails to linger
As does the warmth in each stiffening finger
To go to his cold bed he knows it is time
But each night the stairs become more of a climb
So he'll sit here a while with his memories of light
That seem so far away though it's still the same night
Whilst, mocking his grey world just over his head
Bob three bright coloured planets –
blue, yellow and red.

TIM HOLT

Isolated within the stark yellow circle of light thrown down by his reading lamp in the vast cavernous winter evening gloom of the towering vaulted arch of the monastery library sat Tim Holt struggling with the intricacies of his now well overdue essay on the significance of the use of irony in the tragedies of William Shakespeare. His mind finished with the quotation he sought - inventions, or such like, 'that return to plague the inventor'. That wasn't it, but he was close. He closed his eyes, leant his head forward and rested it on his splayed hands. He felt the cold of his finger tips on his weighted forehead. And it was to his surprise, but not totally unexpected that into the spotlight of his mind's eye stepped – tall, mournful and copiously moustachioed- ed - the familiar stooping form of Mr Albert Shrubsore. Inventions returning to plague the inventor. How appropriate seemed Macbeth's ironic observation.

Albert Shrubsore had been, and probably still was, the Stage Manager of the modest Theatre Royal in Tim's home town, the seaside resort of Sandhaven Bay in Kent. Twice Tim had worked for him. It was his mother's idea. Tim's father was a bread delivery man; his mother had taken over the years a selection of clerical jobs. Tim had begun the first year of his sixth form A-level course and money was tight. In the summer his mother had moved to the local theatre to take over the manning of the box office so had been one of the first to become aware of the need to employ a temporary part time Assistant Stage Hand for the three week duration of that year's pantomime. No experience necessary. Must work evenings and weekends. Heavy lifting required. She quickly introduced Tim, a strapping second XV rugby player to the Theatre Manager and the job was his.

That was Tim's first pantomime, 'Peter Pan'. His second was to be 'The Snow Queen'.

Albert Shrubsore ruled the world of back-stage with undisputed authority, a world of garish billowing backdrops, swaying timber and canvas flats, the smells of glue, paint, hot electrics and ancient dust, the sweaty lights, the whispered, urgent instructions and sarcastic exchanges, suppressed laughter and giggles, but above all precise and unswerving discipline. An item of scenery placed one centimetre out of kilter could ruin an entire show. A prop handed out one second too late or an item of costume not available in the wings the minute it was called for, could very well bring the very roof of the building crashing down with calamitous implications for the whole history of 21st century English theatre. A grim determination pervaded the tinselled frivolities of an Albert Shrubsore pantomime,

But, above all, Albert Shrubsore prided himself on his inventions. In staging Peter Pan, he was in his element. Peter Pan and the Darling children had to be seen to fly. The tackle and harness necessary for this illusion could be hired from professionall suppliers but Albert Shrubsore saw little point in such needless expense. He had acquaintances who worked locally in in providing seafarers' chandlery - ropes, twines, spars and pulleys aplenty, and he had the whole of the autumn to draw up his plans, construct his contraption, develop his prototype and test run the final rigging.

Sharon Duckett, who was stage struck and available to the theatre as the lowest of the low on a Youth Employment Scheme, spent many precarious and uncomfortable afternoons swinging above the stage in a multitude of highly indecorous postures, either groaning in pain or sobbing with fear, that is when her breath was not entirely forced out of her lungs. But Albert Shrubsore was satisfied and all was in place when Tim joined his stage crew for the final dress rehearsal of the show.

It was on the fourth night that 'the inventor returned to plague'. There were four actors flying, six riggers operating the ropes and all would perhaps have been well had not the Director been determined to add to this already complicated scenario, a swift scene change from the Darling family bedroom to the land of stars and clouds so that the children of the local Eleanore Frosbit School of Dance and Drama could perform their starlight and snowflake ballet to the rather echoing recording of Aled Jones singing 'Walking on the Air. It was an overhasty shift of the twelve foot high Darling family chimney breast that knocked the not unportly actress playing Jane Darling in a copious winceyette nightgown and overlarge top hat out of her prescribed orbit into an indelicate collision with Peter Pan. The pair going into a spin which enveloped the other Darling boy, Wendy having reached the far side of the stage disappearing safely into the darkness of the wings. The three sturdy actresses, all until now playing with some conviction the parts of young boys, spun helplessly in a tight bundle some 14 feet above the stage, Peter Pan totally upside down, screaming curses that should never be heard in Never Never Land, in a mass of flailing green clad limbs, her companions desperately trying but failing to cover with their striped nightshirts their modesty, namely the generous curves that revealed together with sizeable brassieres and generous sized knickers that they were anything but prepubescent Edwardian boys.

The starlights and snowflakes exited in floods of hysterical tears, Aled Jones choked into silence and, incongruously, Captain Hook entered the fray, minced demurely down to the front of the stage, nodded to the gentlemen of the orchestra (all three of them) and together they launched into an uncertain rendition of 'If I ruled the World' which shouldn't really have happened until well after the interval as the curtain descended - all to the uproarious delight of the expectedly sparse Thursday night audience, most of whom took it to be part of the show anyway.

That was Peter Pan. The Snow Queen was to be Albert Shrubsore's opportunity to invent and experiment with trolleys.

It all stemmed from the fact that the script demanded a grand entrance from the Snow Queen herself gliding over the ice in a majestic, glistening and diamond encrusted sleigh. Albert Shrubsore would achieve this with a trolley, a low platform on smooth running well oiled castors. Not only this but his imagination transferred itself to the scenery. He would also mount the flats on trolleys. These, painted to represent the snow laden fir trees of an Icelandic forest, could then be moved about the stage in varying formations to depict different parts of the forest - so many short scenes happening in 'a different part of the forest'.

The choice of The Snow Queen as that year's pantomime was determined by the availability of a star name. Gloria Delmarco was a woman of a certain age who, after more years than she cared to count surviving as a choir girl and cabaret artist in, at best, third rate variety tours had landed the part in one of Britain's premier TV soap operas as a third rate chorus girl and cabaret artist of indeterminate age who had inherited the ownership of a rather seedy hotel, a prime location in the long running soap.

After many years her character and she had left the soap, the former perishing in a hotel fire, and she became available for 'star' appearances and charity functions. Her reputation for uncharitability preceded her, not a little due to a predilection for neat gin and frequent spliffs. But her public adored and missed her, she was sure. Also her ancient mother occupied a bungalow just outside the town which meant a decided economy when finding theatrical digs.

Into the first rehearsal that both Miss Delmarco and Tim Holt attended swept the star. Her contract stated that she was available for rehearsal only during the hours between 11 am and 2pm. She was tall, a proud bouffant of brass blonde hair (not her own), an aquiline nose, full scarlet lips, prominent even white teeth (not her own), and a pillowing pair of spectacular breasts (all her own). She posed theatrically, head thrown back, chest heaving, legs in knee high crocodile boots (four inch heels) aggressively splayed.

"Ah. Miss Delmarco has arrived," announced the director somewhat unnecessarily. 'Miss Delmarco' is how she insisted on being addressed, though the knowing boys in the chorus were only too well aware that her real name was Gladys May Budgen and, in all their catty asides, while exposed to her inaccurate and swooping soprano in her Act Two featured musical number, they referred to her as the MGB - Mad Gay Budgie.

Miss Delmarco was introduced to the trolley that would become her sleigh. Any sensible actress would have fled at the sight of such unlikely propulsion but Gladys, underneath it all, was a trouper and a sucker for a grand entrance. She sat with rictus grin and glazed eyes, one hand aloft in the deckchair placed precariously on the perambulating platform and slowly crossed the stage. All held their breath. She safely reached the far wings. A round of applause. She reappeared walking unsteadily towards centre stage, acknowledged the applause as if it was for her rather than a trundling low slung platform of old wood and hard-board, announced that was excitement enough for the day and left the building.

Tim Holt's lack of experience had in the past excluded him from all tasks backstage but the most menial. But now Albert Shrubsore's hand was forced. If he were to have a moving sleigh at the same time as all the fir tree flats gliding to form a different part of forest to allow for Miss Frosbit's protege gaggle to perform their ballet of starlights and snowflakes, this year to Bing Crosby's scratchy crooning of 'I'm Dreaming of a White Christmas', then he would need all the stage hands on deck.

Tim's job was quite simple. To operate a restraining piece of twine that would, with as little jerk as possible, impede the progress to the sleigh halfway across the stage so that Miss Delmarco could imperiously dismount and encounter the quivering children, Kay and

Gerda, for the first time in the evening. (Kay and Gerda were played by the same plump young actresses who had portrayed the Darling boys in the year previous and in the same striped winceyette nightshirts but without the top hat.)

It couldn't be simpler, if only Tim had not felt so humiliated and offended by the way Mad Gay Budgie treated the entire cast, crew and himself - primarily him himself. He came to her attention early on in the proceedings and the die was cast.

She sneered at him, "You, boy", referred to him as 'that child', and once, "Come over here. Good boy. Sit!" and shrieked with mirth.

Once, she had been taken unawares by the gliding movement of the painted fir trees. She had panicked momentarily, convinced that the scenery was toppling on top of her. She had lunged with a yelp into the wings, stumbled over a crouching Tim, recovered to realise fully what a fool she had made of herself , turned and struck out at the first object to hand - Tim's head. She accompanied the hefty thwack with, "You cretinous youth! Get out of my way!"

Not long later, at an evening performance, Tim sat huddled in the dark when she appeared to make an entrance in Act Two. She tottered alarmingly on her four inch heels, that she insisted she wore - "It's in my contract, darling", and he could smell the drink. She'd been imbibing steadily since before the start of that day's matinee. As she staggered stagewards, he could see that, in her present trajectory position, a collision with a fir tree flat was inevitable. He leapt forward, seized her firmly by the hips, directed her to her left and gently pushed her forward. She shuffled forward and turned angrily .

"Someone bloody goosed me", she hissed. Tim crouched at her feet. "It's that bloody spotty little runt. I'll sue you", she spat, turned and completed her entrance stage left with dignity.

Tim almost lost his job but it was very near the end of the run, hardly worth training up a replacement and Miss Delmarco was placated by the management with a crate of good champagne and a luxury hamper from Harrods.

Tim left his revenge until the last night. It was the Snow Queen's final traverse across the stage in her Ice and Diamond sleigh. The sleigh just didn't stop centre stage. It proceeded in a stately manner stage right taking two triffid snowy fir trees with it. There was a loud crash and a louder scream in the wings. A pause. Miss Delmarco appeared, limping grotesquely - she'd lost a shoe, her headdress of ice antlers and dangling crystals clung at a tipsy angle to her head, her fur cloak had slewed around so that she appeared to be struggling in a sack, her face was contorted into a mask of blazing anger and hate.

"Where is that bloody boy?" she screeched. " I'll murder him. Let me get at him. I'll tear his bloody head off his bloody shoulders." She limped blindly and wildly around the stage . The curtains slowly fell as the actress playing Gerda stepped nimbly in front of it, signalled to the orchestra (all four of them, this year) and went into a querulous reprise of 'He Ain't Heavy, he's my Brother'. This should only have been heard once, much earlier on in Act One.

The audience clapped enthusiastically . They thought it all part of the story. The Snow Queen's shouted threats fitted the plot perfectly.

Tim had shot off home. He wouldn't be looking for employment there next year. After all he'd be at university in the library catching up on an overdue essay on irony in the tragedies of William Shakespeare.

TO CREATE AN ANIMAL

If I could create an animal, it would be Eirys

He (that's He with a capital aitch)
Took a broad deep breath and sighed
Surely he had not got it wrong
By God! (he joked) he'd tried
He made the Earth, his sovereign globe
The emerald lands, the azure sea
The balmy breeze, the wintery wind
Gave rain and sun alternately
This precious jewel entrusted had
To his chosen one, to humankind
And what is happening now, he knows
Is certainly not what he'd had in mind!

"I will create an animal"
In omniscience he did decree
"With the better parts of all that live
On earth, in sky, on land, in sea.
And I will give in charge the earth
To this creature that will have true worth."

With majestic and celestial signs
He forthright summoned until Him
To aid him choose these 'better parts'
Angels, cherubim and seraphim
Wings fluttering like no sound ere heard
His heavenly host all clustered round
Bright halos fused to blinding glare
Then stillness – to make the choice profound.

First courage of marauding lion
Or lioness who protects her young
Then impishness of chimpanzee
Who is chatter, never holds her tongue

The thoughtfulness of elephant cow
Who protects the weakest of the herd
And lively merriment when on wing
Of every chirruping mockingbird
The steady seriousness and gait
Of sloth, who scarce that name deserves
The tigress's strength and flashing eye
Her fiery mask and steely nerve
The gentleness of cooing doves
Far sighted eagles soaring high
The cunning self-preserving fox
A little of dormouse, timid, shy
The majesty of peacock fanned
The grandeur of gorilla strong
The giraffes' ungainly comedy
The lark so soulful in its song
Awake all, innate innocence
A simple purpose, honest aim
To strive and live, survive and give
No pointless wish to hurt and maim.

And He was pleased. Now sprinkle dust
Perhaps more apposite to fairies
What shall we name this splendid being?
Cried the Holy Chorus –
'Call her Eirys!'

TROUBLE

"We should have given him 'Trouble' as his middle name",
Said Dad, as a letter from the school once again
Arrived in the post. It was always the same. No work done, bunking
off, on the roof, breaking lights,
Answering back, disrupting class, teasing girls, starting fights.
Now he sat, grinning shyly, nervous, picking at his tea.
Blond hair shining. "Sorry, Dad. It's school does for me."
Then the letters stopped abruptly and what neither parent knew
Was that unofficially he'd stopped going, found something else to do.
He'd just finished with the school, which had finished with him too.

So he spent the day
On a farmer's land
Real back-breaking work
But with cash in hand
He had found out that he loved it there
Free from classroom fug, out in God's fresh air
But he couldn't help give the game away
He scrimped and saved his hard-earned pay
Bought his unsuspecting family
The gift of a new colour TV.

Then the cops came knocking the front door instead.
"TROUBLE in town. He's the ringleader", they said.
Lads – TROUBLE – in the streets, beer cans, shouting and the rest.
Take this as a final warning; any more and it's arrest
"You're just TROUBLE, nowt but TROUBLE, I'm not having any
more."
Dad was angry and he shouted as his son slammed out the door
They heard later from a neighbour he was sleeping on the floor
Of a workmate's seedy bedsit. They did not hear any more
But for one typical tale that the neighbour relished telling
He'd been thrown out for setting the whole building smelling
As he improvised a curry on an illicit Baby Belling.
"His middle name is TROUBLE" Dad refrained that very night

"If there's TROUBLE to be found, he'll find it out all right!"

Then nothing for a long time, till a letter fluttered in
From the Army. They were formally notified 'Next of Kin'.
Cards from Aldershot and Germany, from Yorkshire and the
Cameroon
Saying "I'm all right. Hope you are. Perhaps I'll see you soon."

No return address to help them. Mum wanted to do more
Then one day there came another knocking upon the front door.
It was Sharon, how she loved him, then she just sat down and cried.
"I've got nowhere else to go", she said. "And the baby, he's outside.
I'm in TROUBLE. I am 4 months gone, the second's on its way
I have left him. I am desperate."
"Come in, lass. You'd better stay."

Dad said, "TROUBLE. Here's more TROUBLE" as Mum stirred the
baby feed
"Just more TROUBLE. I don't know how much TROUBLE do you
need?"

The rattle of the postman and lying on the floor
From the MOD, "To Afghanistan". He's on a six-month tour.
"He's a Corporal now", his Dad read out. "They don't tell us no
more."

Then the letters started, awkward, clumsy, spelling all to pot.
"How's Sharon and the kiddies? I am all right, except here it's stinking
hot.
Must go. The alarm's gone. I'm needed at the double.
I miss you. Lots of love to all." And then he signed it, "TROUBLE".

Another knock comes at the door. A Major, tall and grey
He didn't need to tell them, they knew what he'd come to say.

"Mentioned in dispatches" was their son
They'd been ordered to retreat
His squad was badly battered
They had to accept defeat.
Some lay dead and some were wounded

In the fire, smoke and rubble
He disobeyed and turned back
To help his mates in TROUBLE.

Dad goes quietly to the graveyard
Snow or sunshine, wind or rain
Sees black lettering on the gravestone
But there is no middle name.

TRUST

"Hey, you was in Brumley, wasn't you?"

I was stretched out on my bed half asleep when John's voice burst in on me. That's John Rollison, I mean. We was sharing a room at the time. I don't like to do that – I likes me own space. But if you have to share – and there's not always the option – then I suppose John's your man. He's clean, good clean habits and respectful of you. He doesn't even snore – well, in a heavy breathing kind of a way – and when he's out for the night, he's out dead, flat out. Not like some – grumbling and shouting, calling out, even swearing in their sleep. No, John and me gets on. Well, I know his surname – that's an indication. And he knows mine – Brightman. He laughed once and said, "We know our names – we're almost friends". But we both know the truth. You don't make friends in these hostels. Often you don't see other blokes often enough – certainly not enough to trust them. That's the word, the core of it – TRUST. They say you can only begin to trust a bloke if you can share with him and you still have your shoe laces in the morning. Yeah – me and John 'gets on' – put it no more strongly than that.

"Yeah", I said. "I was in Brumley."

"Well, it says here …" He was sitting on his bed with a daily paper – not necessarily today's – but he picked it up somewhere and it was passing the time. But then he can read. I think he knows I'm not good at that so he'll read me bits I might be interested in. "It says here that a Committee who inspect Her Majesty's Prison facilities has commented unfavourably on the conditions to be found in Category D Wing, Low Risk Inmates, of H M Brumley Prison."

I remember the memories came flooding in. Brumley. D Wing. That was my favourite place to banged up in. You left the hub of the prison – that's the centre part and all the wings lead off of it, like spokes in a wheel. D Wing had two floors and my favourite place was a cell I had right at the end of the second floor. Being at the end, there was no 'through traffic' as you might say. Being it was Low Risk offenders, there was no loud and aggressive behaviour, the screws themselves were more relaxed and at ease. My cell was at the end of the left.

The newspaper was right, it was an old and scruffy building. Thick brick walls covered with layers of peeling gloss paint – the last covering was a kind of deep cream but through the cracks and peelings showed green and brown and yellow – it was almost like the army's camouflage uniforms. The door was heavy grey metal with a small window. It wasn't a big room. There was a bed, a chair, a small set of drawers and a fold down table with an old rusted chair. There was a low box in the corner, varnished in dark brown but badly scratched, and underneath the lift-up lid – pardon me, if there are ladies hearing this – was a chamber pot crammed in and some bundles of thick perforated tissue paper.

That was all the ablutions there was. You still had to 'slop out' twice a day and go to the showers in the hub of the wing. Your towel you kept over the back of the chair. Not what you'd call 'luxury' then, but it was quiet and closed in. Away from it all. And being the end cell, it had an extra window on the end wall. Like the other, it was small and high up with thick reinforced glass but, if you stood on the chair, you could see out, over the yard, over the perimeter fencing, over to the outside world, hedges, trees, hills, the sky and in the middle distance a busy road with fast moving traffic both ways. And that was where I loved to be. Perched up there – a kind of birds' eye view – watching the world go by. Dozy and daydreaming. Once – and how stupid is this! – I got so carried away I fell off the chair. Crashed to the floor – bad bruises and a sprained wrist. Explain that away – they thought I was having fainting fits or even the start of epilepsy, one idiot medic suggested. But it was my cell, for three years. And try as I could, I could never get back in there gain. After one conviction I even requested it. "We are not a hotel service", was the officer's reply. "You go where you are sent. You have no family nor dependents so we can send you anywhere". And they did, over the years.

I always liked the small, cut-off solitary cells – but none of them were like Brumley D Wing Second Floor, left at the end.

It was one of my Social Workers – a young, rather overwrought, red-faced woman – Jean, her name – thick black hair, dark eyes, always seemed to have a cold – she was the one who gave me an explanation for me liking these small cramped places – the privacy and feeling of safety. And once she made the connection I felt stupid for not seeing it, it was so obvious.

It was when I was a kid. We had a small two up, two down terrace not far from the docks. Mum looked after us kids the best she could. I remember her as a small, thin, uncertain woman. No confidence.

Always scurrying around looking for the next thing to worry about – and she didn't have to look far because there was our Dad.

He worked all day in the docks – unskilled, whatever he could get his hands on. We were all right during the day – even when we wasn't at school. But in the evening, often after dark when the pubs shut or when he was thrown out, he would come home and suddenly the house was not big enough. His meal would be dried up in the oven, though there was a pan of gravy to slop over it. So *that* was not right and nor was anything else. On a good night he would slump his surly bulk into his old worn out armchair and grumble and snore the night away. We always hid in our back bedroom where we all shared a sagging double bed.

On a bad night we were all at risk. Fists and boots would fly at the smallest excuse. Plates, cups and vases would always be smashed, chairs would follow and then us. Mum would herd us upstairs in a squealing pack and she would stand defiant half way up the stairs facing his advancing wrath. We would burrow beneath the bed with stained and worn blankets and pillows pressed to our ears, but we couldn't block out her screams and his roaring rage and the thumps and crunches and crashes and thudding blows. Then finally silence. Then, muttering and stumbling and the other bedroom door slamming shut, their bed creaking and straining under his dead weight. And in the far distance, so it seemed, from downstairs, a desperate muffled sobbing.

This was the pattern of life.

Until one night, my oldest brother Eric could take no more. He was feeling his manhood, I suppose. He was taller than the rest of us, long gangling limbs, his feet and hands suddenly unnaturally large, his voice beginning to crack. He burst out of our bedroom door and down the stairs to confront Dad in all his rage. The din was awful – his hoarse desperate shouting added to the usual hideous high-pitched screams and the deep angry animal roars.

Eventually, a kind of silence and Dad staggering up to his bed. But this time the noise of the front door opening and Mum's footsteps and cries in the street outside. The busy voices of neighbours, bustle and confusion in the hallway. Mum's sobs, the neighbours cooing consolation like so many oversized pigeons and eventually the approaching sound of the ambulance's bell.

Eric was stretchered off to hospital.

Crouched in the bedroom, our fear was replaced by the intense curiosity to see what was going on and to experience first-hand the excitement of the visit of an ambulance. But the snoring, heavy presence in the front bedroom deterred us.

Today, Social Services and the police would be round to sort out the mess. But not in those days. Scuffles and violence were a recognised and tolerated condition of domestic life – certainly where we lived.

But Mother was alarmed and desperate. She devised a ploy to safeguard us – particularly the growing boys – when the evening became so advanced to indicate that when Dad eventually did arrive home he would be 'the worse for wear'.

If you went out through our downstairs back room to the small cobbled yard outside, there were three brick outhouses. One was the outside lavatory – no plumbing but with a door behind the bucket for the night soil men. Next was the coal hole. Then what was termed the wash house – a concrete shelf and underneath a washtub. She hauled out the tub. Her brother came over during the day and screwed in place a hefty metal latch which could be fixed and locked by a large solid padlock. It was in this damp, brick lined cubby hole that we were locked, shaking, whimpering and quivering until the worst was over. Sometimes there was the booming echoes and deafening crashes of an angry assault on the door. The padlock and latch would be ferociously rattled. We would cling together, pressed against the wall, as many of us under the concrete shelf as we could squeeze. Eventually the noise would subside and we would wait patiently for the easier scraping sounds of Mum unlocking our temporary …

Yes, prison cell.

At the end, on the left, 2nd floor, D wing, HMP Brumley.

It all makes sense. Doesn't it?

TRUST II

I call them her 'Joan of Arc' moments, when her natural instinct to do the right thing coincides with a steely, determined impetuosity that will brook no gainsayers. At these times she is armoured and unassailable. And this was one such occasion.

We'd been out to a nearby Italian restaurant for a casual supper with friends. It was a cold – very cold – January night and we, just the two of us, faced a short walk home. The darkness was still and biting bitterly. We were muffled up in heavy overcoats, wreathed with scarves, gloved hands and warm hats. Our eyes smarted, cheeks pinched, lips were dry and ears stinging. We hurried along the shop lined street that led to the turning into our residential avenue, tall Edwardian houses only slightly set back from the road, broad pavements, iron railings.

We came abreast of the local newsagent when a pile of rubbish – cardboard and rags – in the doorway suddenly heaved and the silence of the brittle air was shattered by a rasping, phlegmy cough.

Instinctively, as one, we paused, the loud tapping of my wife's heels on the paving stones suddenly stopping, emphasising the intense quietness of the icy night air.

We looked apprehensively at each other.

Again the grating, growly breathless lungs. The scruffy bundle on the floor lurched upwards and then appeared in the amber glow of the streetlight a pale domed head, tufts of grey hair and, in the shadows of full bristly eyebrows, a pair of dark glinting eyes.

My wife looked steadily at me. Her left arm, linked in my right, stiffened. I read her thoughts. She forced herself from me and walked over to the doorway.

"Are you alright?" Her voice was steady and concerned.

Again, the rasping cough.

"You shouldn't be out in this", she added. She returned to my side.

The figure in the doorway rose clumsily to his feet. The dark blanket shrouding his shoulders fell away to reveal another with all the incongruity of a Walt Disney character displayed in garish primary colours.

She glanced determinedly up at me. "We can't leave him like this."

Another wild gulping cough.

Her mind was made up. She squeezed my arm – in other circumstances this might have indicated affection but now it was decisiveness – and walked over to him.

"Let us offer you a bed for the night."

Pause. No response.

"We're only a short walk from here."

The man raised his hand and adjusted a dark woollen hat that had slipped too far back on his head. It was now pulled into an almost comical diagonal dark line just above his bushy brows. He looked from her to me. Maybe he thought in cases such as these he must look for a sign of approval from the male of the pair. He hadn't met St Joan!

I stepped forward. "Not far from here", I confirmed.

My wife stooped and collected his dark blanket from the floor. She handed it to me and stepped backwards. She nodded meaningfully towards the man. I moved to him, draped the dark folds over his stooping shoulders. He bent down and lifted two bags off the doorway tiles.

"Ta! Er ... thank you. That would be most welcome."

"Good. We'll lead the way." She relinked her arm in mine and we set off at a slower pace, conscious of a shuffling, dragging step behind us, heavy breathing and thick snuffling.

We reached our home, a strange procession. I went straight up the steps to open the door and my wife hung back to allow our visitor to slowly ascend to where I was standing. I went into the bright warmth of the hall and called, not too loud, "Naomi, it's us."

My wife addressed the man. "Follow me through to the kitchen. I'll put the kettle on. You'll need a hot drink." As they disappeared down the long hall to the rear of the house, I went straight into the sitting room. The door creaked horribly.

"I must oil those ruddy hinges", I thought, a promise I had made to myself too often of late.

"Hi, Naomi. Everything o.k?"

"Yes, fine, Geoff." She – our babysitter – was already closing her textbook and getting together her folders, scattered as they were on the maroon, corduroy settee. "Amy was her usual angelic self."

"And Danny?" I asked.

"In bed more or less on time." She stuffed Biros into her worn, denim pencil case.

"More ... or less?" I asked.

"In the end I had to go up and unplug his computer." She grinned.

"It's a pity you can't beat them <u>any more</u>. Another of the pleasures of fatherhood denied to me."

"Yeah – very likely." She was ready to go.

"Anyway, many thanks", I added. I reached for my wallet in my inside pocket. "How much do we owe you?"

"No, that's alright. Jenny paid me double last time – to get those concert tickets. Remember?"

"Yes. Cliff Richard, wasn't it?"

"Very likely. If I told you, you'd never have heard of them."

"Probably not."

She grinned. "Definitely not."

She moved out of the room quickly put on her coat and scarf, retrieved her books and bag from the hall table and went through the front door, down the steps into the street.

"Night. See you", she called over her shoulder.

"Goodnight. And thanks again."

I waited at the top of the steps and watched her cross the road. She lived only a few houses away so I saw her indoors.

In the kitchen I found my wife leaning against the sink, our visitor sitting at the table, a steaming mug in his still gloved hands, a box of biscuits in front of him.

"Would you like a tea?" she asked. "Geoff – this is Vince. Vince, my husband Geoff."

Neither of us moved to shake hands.

"Vince Brougham", the man confirmed. His voice was husky and assured.

"Great", I replied pointlessly. I looked at my wife enquiringly "Everything OK?", it read. Her ready smile signaled back, "It's o.k. Stop worrying."

But I was worried. I knew what had to be said. It may sound lame, probably pompous, but it had to be said.

"Er, Vince…." I began.

He put down his mug and looked squarely at me. His cheeks were flushed, the heat of the kitchen, I surmised. His eyes were dark brown, red rimmed and watery, his lips full, his face rounded greying stubble on his chin. There was an expectant panic.

"Vince …er … I … that is we, both of us, are glad to help you out. We are." I *was* sounding lame. I didn't want to sound lame. "It's a matter of … it's trust, Vince. We're trusting you. It's our home, and our two children asleep upstairs. We're happy to give you a bed for the night – but it is TRUST that we put in you."

He looked straight and unfalteringly into my eyes.

"And breakfast", chimed in Jenny, neatly slicing through another awkward pause.

Vince spoke. "Ta! I do appreciate what you're saying. I really do."

Jenny breezed across the kitchen and stooped to pick up the old blanket for a second time that evening.

"Right. Enough said", she stated decisively. "You bring your tea, Vince. Geoff, can you help with the bags? Let's get you to bed."

Eventually, Vince had retreated to the spare room. We were in our room, sitting side by side in bed. The room was in darkness, the door to the landing unusually left ajar and a small lamp on a side table in the wide landing left illuminated, a measure we hadn't taken since the children were small.

Jenny snuggled down in bed – I stayed sitting upright, bolstered up with many pillows. "You'll get cold", chirped Jenny.

"I'll be alright", I retorted. "I might lightly doze", I added nobly.

"I will deeply sleep." She was teasing me.

"I don't know how you'll be able."

She nudged her shoulder against me. "Because I know you're there. It's called TRUST." And she giggled softly. "Don't stay up too long."

I am prepared to swear on the Bible that I did not sleep a wink that night. Occasionally I tended to doze but the awkward lolling of my unsupported head prompted me awake. And I can assure you the house remained quiet and undisturbed. And as soon as I could, in the cold grey of morning – not wishing to be seen to be astir too early – I made my way to the bathroom.

The spare room door was slightly ajar. I used the bathroom, flushed the loo noisily and returned to the landing. All was still. I paused at the partly open door. I couldn't resist. I edged inside. I could always offer a cup of tea. But the room was empty. The bedcovers were somewhat ruffled, but the bed not slept in. No bags. No alien blankets. I went quietly back to our bedroom. Jenny was blearily awake.

"Jen … he's gone."

She sat upright.

"Check the kids", I said. "I'll go and look." I turned on the hall lights, checked the front door which was securely latched and went to the kitchen. All was as we had left it.

Jenny was half way down the stairs. 'The kids are o.k. Still asleep."

"There's no sign of him", I said. "He must have crept out in the night. There's nothing disturbed."

"You're right", she offered. "His bed's not been slept in."

There was a noise at the top of the stairs and Amy's voice, "Is everything all right, Mum? Dad?"

Jenny's voice was reassuring. "Yes, darling. Everything's o.k. Go back to bed whilst we use the bathroom."

"It's very early." There was a whine in Amy's voice.

"Yes, it is. Blame your Dad."

"Oh, Dad!" And Amy withdrew to her room.

Then started the usual early morning rush. Queues for the bathroom. Hunting for clothes and books and bags, sports kits and homework and mobile phones and pocket money and dance kit for Amy (it was Thursday). The breakfast and arguments and teasing and awful jokes and reminders that they'll be late and coats and scarves and gloves and a rush for the door and take cares and love yous and see you tonights and don't dawdles … and suddenly the house was quiet.

Jenny and I sat uneasily over a final mug of tea.

We froze. The sitting room door crashed noisily open. Shuffling footsteps down the hall and an all too familiar figure appeared hunched in the doorway.

"G'morning."

Jenny rose. "Vince. We thought you'd gone. You weren't in your room."

"No. I hope it's alright. The bed … the bed. I couldn't rightly use the bed. It was all clean. I thought there must be a settee for my blankets. So, I come downstairs. You were snoring – dead to the world. So, I took the liberty. Hope that's o.k. Given you a bit of a shock, have I? I'd never go without a thank you and goodbye. Trust me, you can."

Again, Jenny rallied. "Well, let's get you sorted. How about a warm bath? And the breakfast. What will it be? Eggs? Bacon?"

"You know what I would like? Really like? Bacon sandwich. Bacon sandwich with red sauce. And a cup of tea. Milky. No sugar."

"How about some Cornflakes first?"

"No … no, ta. Don't like Cornflakes without sugar and the doc says I can't have sugar coz of my diabetes. But bacon sandwich. Lovely."

Jenny led him upstairs to the bathroom and I stood halfway up listening. As soon as he was securely ensconced in the bathroom, I started a frantic, undignified hunt around the house – every room - for any sign of anything disturbed or, worse, missing. But there was nothing. All was as you would expect to find it.

Jenny was grilling bacon when I re-entered the kitchen. "Everything o.k?" She arched her eyebrows pointedly.

"Perfect. Not a thing out of place."

She indicated the biscuit tin on the table. "Not even a biscuit gone."

"So, you checked too?"

"Of course", she confirmed. "Even the cutlery drawer."

"So much for trust", I said ruefully. "Who is trusting who?"

"Shouldn't that be 'whom'?", she returned irritatingly.

"Whom is trusting whom?"

"Clever Clogs."

"But there is one thing troubling me", she said, flicking over a couple of rashers of bacon.

"What."

"Something did go missing when we got Vince home."

I bridled. I hadn't noticed anything.

"The cough. That juicy, phlegmy, rasping, grating cough – suddenly disappeared. Very theatrical."

"You mean ...?"

"Yes. I think we were conned. Just a bit. Now, where's the red sauce?"

TWO POEMS

or maybe one and a half!

1.
Whatever happened to the British summer
To our welcome cool seasonal grey
Kindly showers sometimes of hailstones
That serve to dampen down our day?

No! Now we've sun, we are down beaten
Its hot rays on us are glaring
And whilst we men observe our dress code
Our shameless sisters too much are baring!

Fearing lower limb discomfort
I phone our Chairperson, her voice was curt
Sorry to be disapproving, but
I cannot condone you wear a skirt.

But she softened to my sobbing
Oh, bring a skirt along with you
If the mercury hits the 30's
You can change in the ladies' loo.

Joyful, I phoned Fred and Chris. Fred contacted Betty
But to lend two skirts she was averse
Fred said, "It's just because she's jealous
We've got nicer legs than hers!"

The flickering flame of revolution
In the sun became a flare
We skirted lads are now revolting
And will occupy Daniel Owen Square.

To the Devil with propriety
We shall just do as we please
Wayward Writers gird up your loins

And get ready for our knees.

2.
There are those days full of incident
Shocks and blows, as Fate devises,
That you long next morn, at the crack of dawn,
For a day of no surprises.

There are other days that are dull and drear
That seem long with nought to do
So you wish on the morrow the day will bring
At least one surprise – or two.

'Twas such a day I set out early
On a drive, the clouds were grey
The road was monotonous, straight and bleak
Oh, for surprise to come my way!

Then there before me on the road
I couldn't believe my eyes,
An unnerving trepidatious sight
Well, I had asked for a surprise!

I applied my brakes, mounted the verge
Killed the engine, turned the key
Rose from my seat, advanced with dread
Oh, why had Fate chosen me?

As I advanced, heart beating loud
In anticipation's thrall
I saw what I thought I was going to see
Turned out not to be there at all!

Surprise upon surprise, I gasped
Felt dizzy and began to sway
Staggered to the car and with shaking hands
Turned the key and drove away.

UNCLE ABERNATHY'S ARTEFACT

Forgive me if I'm hesitant
I must proceed with care and tact
If I'm to tell the history
Of Uncle Abernathy's Artefact

It all began many years ago
In Primary School where he was sent
His teacher, Mrs Feather, was new
And of a strong artistic bent

In flowing floral frock and shawl
Green hair and fingernails too
She made the first of her decrees
An exhibition of Art by Classes 1 and 2

She brought mounds of clay and plasticine
Sugar paper and powder paints gay and bright
All parents were invited to attend
In four weeks' time on Friday night

Abernathy's family all went along
Such a cultural event was very rare
The children's work was all lined up
But by Abernathy there was nothing there

Grandpa sought out flustered Mrs F
Presaging some sort of disaster
Mrs Feather flushed and groaned and said
"I think, perhaps, see the Headmaster."

Headmaster in his study loomed
A towering figure in every way
He grimly said that in his school
He'd never put such a thing on display

Grandpa said "But ..." The Head raised his hand
And pointed to the open door
"Sir, take your child and leave my school
And darken my portal never more!

The Artefact your son has made
An offence to decent persons' eyes
Under wraps I gave it to the Caretaker
And ordered him to pulverise"

Thy never found out what it was
Turned the Headmaster white and Mrs Feather red
Put Abernathy in a different school
And not another word was said

UNTIL ...

The years passed by as years will do
All memories erased from the scene
T'was Abernathy's little sister's birthday
Sweet Augusta she would be sixteen

Mum – like all Mums – was in a tizz
Just not enough hours in the day
"I'll decorate the cake", Abernathy said
And Mum (in a tizz, as I said) let him have his way

With icing sugar, fondant and marzipan
Abernathy took the cake to Father's shed
By the family he was totally overlooked
When they took themselves off to bed

He worked all night with manic flair
In dawn's light his creation glowed quite pink
He called to his sister across the lawn
To come and see what she did think

There was a long pause, very long
The family froze, they felt unsure
A wailing scream grew louder, louder
Augusta burst in through the door

Her eyes were wide, she could not speak
She gasped, she sobbed, her wild arms flailed
Gradually she found her breath
"I'll not have that foul, foul thing!" she wailed

I grabbed Dad's spade and smashed it up
And threw it all around the shed
The dog was there. He gobbled it up
If it's as rotten as it looks, he'll soon be dead!

A calm Abernathy appeared with dog in tow
"You didn't like it then?" One of his quiet smiles
Mum said, "Watch the dog – he looks all right"
As he threw up all over the kitchen tiles.

As in Sleeping Beauty the deadly spindles
Were forbidden in every part of the land
So Abernathy's kin decided
That all future Artefactory would be banned

But Abernathy had a compulsive urge
A compelling obsession to be exact
To seize on any clandestine chance
To sculpt another Artefact

Like the time his cousin's sister Martha
Was set to marry her new beau
And Mum received a telephone call
Asking all the family to go

On the morn of the wedding another saying
"What a surprise! Really, how nice!
How quite unexpected for Abernathy to provide
A decorative sculpture carved out of ice."

Mum dropped the receiver, ran into the hall
And called upstairs to her husband, Bert
"Come on, Father. Stir yourself!
Another Abernathy Artefact Alert!"

Father rushed down, shirt tails flying
"Where is it this time?" With fear he shivered
"It's in the marquee at cousin's sister Martha's wedding
It's a six-foot ice sculpture being delivered."

Dad pressed the Red Button. Artefact Warning Alarm
And he and his other sons rushed out to the van
Quick call at the flame thrower shop for one each
Then on to the wedding as fast as they can

But too late! All around a state of confusion
All the people assembled first stood there appalled
In the centre of everything, gigantic and glacial
Abernathy's Arctic Artefact had been installed

The bridesmaids had fainted, St Johns in attendance
The bride keeling over as pale as a wraith
The groom's gulping whisky, his mother is hysterical
The vicar's defrocked himself and renounced his faith

And as for the best man he's lost all his faculties
In terror he's rooted to the floor
His voice gone completely. Will it ever return?
Have to deliver his speech by semaphore

The family rush in flame throwers ablazing
Great hissings of steam as they all take aim
The floor is awash with the melting obscenity
As the pink and white marquee goes up in flames

We will pass by discretely what Abernathy did
When they found him a safe job with Woodland Conservation
Where he uses his chain saw on a vast old oak tree stump
To carve out another artefactual aberration

They closed down the forest, drove out the public
By instinct all the birds and wildlife had fled
Plants withered and all the trees were denuded
The silence was that of the land of the dead

One final chapter in this grimmest of sagas
Abernathy had passed on. Reading his will
When they came to the clause of the final bequest
They listened with awe to the last codicil

For his life's work had been to create one more Artefact
More powerful than all the others before
And cursed be the bones of he who uncovered it
Bringing famine and pestilence, death and war!

WAYWARD WRITERS

Looking back on life, recently or remotely, it is the events we remember. The peaks and troughs. Not the stretches of ordinariness, the flatlands, the Cambridgeshire fens of existence that lie between. T.S. Eliot wrote that these are the periods of life that we 'measure out with coffee spoons'.

It was one of these lulls that I had drifted into. Occasions that were momentous for me had occurred, peaks and troughs in rapid succession, and I had emerged ruffled but not too badly damaged on a low plain – marooned, becalmed, 'a painted ship upon a painted ocean' – the paint being exclusively of grey, black and off-white hues. The only ripple on the surface, the only breeze in the sullen sky, the only slight movement of the lank sails was my growing concern at the situation in which I found myself – in a library not able to generate even the slightest interest in selecting a book.

But then a notice pinned up on an immaculately ordered board, neatly between 'Advice on Sexual Matters for Young Adults' and 'Beginners' Classes in Welsh' caught my eye. Wayward Writers. Occasional Thursday, 10 a.m., in Mynydd Isa.

Wayward Writers. I felt a vague stirring in my chest, a flicker of too long dormant flames in my belly, an itching dilation of my nostrils. That is what I needed. A dose of *Wayward*. Difference. Awkwardness. Challenge. Controversy. Unconventionality. Anti-status quo. Even a dash of outrageousness and perversity. Thursday morning in Mynydd Isa. A blast of waywardness. A splash of scarlet across my dull monotone seascape.

I looked more closely. Two women to be contacted by phone. I didn't even realise I had taken my biro and note pad from my jacket pocket. Phone Ruth or Helen. Now, which?

Ruth. An impressive Biblical name, powerful its mono-syllability. A woman of loyalty and courage who defied convention, the rules of her family and her race, who pursued her own agenda to the exclusion of all else – and won. A woman of threatening individuality.

Or Helen. A historical figure of extraordinary steadfastness and great beauty. 'The face that launched a thousand ships'. Who outfaced the King, her father and her nation's interests to elope with her Trojan lover, to cling to her forbidden passion even at the expense of a bitterly fierce ten-year war exploding around her.

Which of these?

I chose Ruth.

The voice that answered the phone was calm and to the point, wary but polite. No nonsense. In the background wild shrieks and screams, Bacchanalian and savage. The voice remained controlled and informative – but could I sense a tension, a tremor, the civilised veneer beginning to crack under the pressure of characteristics more primitive and, yes, wayward than she was prepared to give out to a total stranger?

The die was cast and the first Thursday approached. Anticipation trans-morphed into apprehension, that into a state approaching anxiety.

What was I letting myself in for?

All I had to go on was that the group would be female-dominated and would probably be restricted in number. After all, I could not see Mynydd Isa as being a breeding ground for the Wayward. There would be a certain exclusiveness just because of the sheer strangeness of their calling.

There would be a leader – not necessarily either of the two who flaunted their telephone details to the North Wales reading public. No, this leader, undoubtedly a woman, would have influence and ideas that reached far back towards the beginning of time. On anniversaries of the centuries of her creation, the group would be forced, however willingly on the surface, to celebrate the occasion with arcane rituals involving feasting, jollity and many candles. The leader would speak darkly of her past, employing subtle codes to carry her true import – references to nursing would indicate her magical facility to heal mortal ailments and sicknesses; veiled allusions to the RAF would reveal the ability of unassisted flight, with or without a broom.

Then there would be a strong Welsh influence – some kind of Druidical, primaeval association with ancient scientific knowledge, an expert in flora and fauna, and vegetable substances used in long practised arts of body and mind control. She – for it would be another 'she' – would masquerade as a skilled baker and cook. But her name. Ah, that would be special – magical and potent. For it would be one that had at least one hundred different variations in its spelling, that reveals the shiftiness and elusiveness of a true antediluvian spiritual presence that can never be conquered for it can never be contained and identified.

And what of the mystic East? A woman who shares the name of the loyalist handmaiden of the mighty Queen Cleopatra herself. A woman of endless experiences with an untiring capacity to be able to recount them to her spellbound acolytes. A far ranging and distant traveller and explorer, of great intuition and perspicuity. Her namesake may have majestically floated down the Nile on her Queen's burnished gold and silken sailed barge, whilst she herself only chugged up the Mersey in one of hardwood and rusting metal, but nevertheless she is to be crossed at peril, the glint of the eye, a final remnant of the cat gods of old Nile, being a dire warning of that.

There will be Elizabeths, of course, and diminutives of – Lizs, Bettys etc., with all the wile and regality of two noble Queens of this land; at least one representation of the little known Hawarden munchkins – a mini-race who, it is now acknowledged, inspired the invention of Dorothy's first friends in the Land of Oz (no-one any longer refers to the little fat one that Toto leapt on and ate in an early rehearsal). A tiny people, sweet and white haired who name all their female children after units for measuring liquids; the Germanic mystic who appears effortlessly to accomplish verses of exquisite delicacy which she delivers in a low, sincere and earnest semi-chant, reminiscent of the casting of magic spells.

And what else? Time and paucity of imagination defeat me.

There will be men, of course. Poor creatures, forced to sit submissively at the feet of three glorious viragos. I know it is my fate to join these cowed creatures – but first – a bit of 'Wayward'. I need some Wayward.

The morning dawns. I load my car boot with all I think and hope I might need to show I am a willing accomplice in the wildnesses and extravagances of the Wayward rites. Various contraptions and pieces of equipment, bottles and vials of rare liquids, hessian bags and sandalwood caskets of certain substances, cloaks, masks, wands and my favourite head-dress. Crystals and rare metals, exotic furs and feathers, lamps and lenses – ancient tomes and parchment scrolls that predate time itself.

I sigh deeply, gaze up to the turbulent heavens and go to pull down the lid of the boot. I pause. I have two more items to add.

A notebook and pen, in case, after all, that is all there is.

WHEN THE TWINS WERE BORN ...

When the twins were born, the family knew
A problematic situation would ensue
They'd read it all in Spock and Freud
A domestic dilemma to avoid
In an older child Dr Siegfried said
Green envy would rear its ugly head
About this there could be no doubt
Of joint he'd have his noise put out
To keep such jealousy at bay
The child should have his part to play
A responsible role as older son
In all that would be going on
So granny, grandpa, Auntie Sue
Great grandma, Dad, the neighbours too
All advised Billy what to do
To aid his mother in all things
And help look after his siblings.
Aged five, Billy took all this to heart
And solemnly vowed to play his part
Ready to take on every task
His mum wouldn't even have to ask
So trying to predict his mother's wishes
He thought that he should wash the dishes
Up on a stool leaning over the brink
He squeezed a bottle of Fairy into the sink
Then plug in both taps on full spate
He wandered off to find a dirty plate
But got distracted by his toys
(Such is typical of little boys)
Mum cried aloud in some distress
When she found the kitchen in such a mess
Her face was pale her eyes were wild
"When I get my hands upon that child!"

But Dad was calm – "Not worth a mention.
Bill was only acting with good intention."
With a smug, wry smile and a gentle laugh
He withdrew behind his Telegraph.

Next day Mother far from happy
Added yet another dirty nappy
To buckets full and smellily swashing
In the kitchen waiting for a washing
So Billy making sure he wasn't seen
Squished the nappies into the white machine
Pressed the button "Hot" the cycle long
And all too soon a revolting pong
Spread out and up the stairs it rose
And found its way up mother's nose
She rushed down as if to a fire
And found her expensive new spin-drier
Efficiently spinning and rotating
The foul brown mess throbbing and pulsating
She wailed "What now? I can't go on!
You must do something about your son!"
Dad cocked an eyebrow again so calm
"Poor Billy didn't mean any harm
No need to make a fuss and wail."
And he vanished behind his Daily Mail.

Next day you can imagine the scene
Billy polished the furniture with Windolene
Dad lay back "It's only a little mess"
Calmly turning the pages of this Daily Express.

Bill plugged in the iron but what's more
Burned a dark smoking hole in the kitchen floor
Dad yawned. "He's helping out. Can't you see?"
And went back to the lady on page three.

But trying to help Mummy and wanting to please her
To plug in the iron Bill disconnected the freezer,
Three days later poor Mother it just was not nice
To find rotting food floating in what used to be ice

Daddy calmly said "No need to rant and rage"
As he turned to the Mirror's sporting page.

Mum just had to act : take Billy to one side
"You are such a helpful little boy" she lied
"But in future if you want a job or two
Ask me first. I'll show you want to do."
"That's a good idea" Dad's calm voice came from afar
As he settled down with the Daily Star.

Next day, Billy said to help he'd be glad
Mum's smile was manic. "You can help your Dad.
Go outside and give his car a clean
Make it the cleanest it's ever been
When you've finished you show Dad what you've done
He'll be in his chair calmly reading The Sun
Billy's cheeks were ablaze with a proudful flush
As she gave him soapy water –
And a strong wire brush.

WHERE ARE YOU NOW?

21st July 2005

A bright summer morning on my way to work
Sitting at the rear
Of the top deck of a red London bus
Rolling with the gentle sway of the bus
Rocking with the stop and start of the bus
Relaxing in the familiar fog of the bus
The bus is my daily buffer
Between the rushing, roaring, gusting tunnels of the Tube.

And the efficient impersonality of my busy office
Not my office, *the* office which occupies my days.
The bus, a last chance to relax, to daydream
Today of my four free days stretching ahead
An effortless start at crack of dawn tomorrow
In the car, before the rush, a long weekend
North up the motorway. To a family wedding
My shoulders slope. My head inclines.
The sun is kind in its early morning warmth
And has yet to build to its cruel midday heat.
The bus is full. Passengers are puppets sharing strings
They loll to the left, loll to the right
In perfect unison with the sway of the bus
A big man, dark suit, thick neck
Slick black Brylcreem-ed hair accentuating
The perfect circle symmetry of a white sweating bald patch
Head down.
The pen in his fat finger pecks at the crossword
Ahead of him is a woman, green blouse,
Holding up knitting needles and meshed white wool
Whilst she peers intently down to the knitting pattern on her lap
Her dark hair falls forward and shades her face.
Next to her, smart grey suit, white collar
Tight curls of ginger hair
Eyes down through thick black-rimmed glasses

To the unfolded pages of a paperback book
And on my right, fidgety, fussing,
Delving into the dark mouth of his brown nylon rucksack
The long, elegant coffee fingers, a gold ring
Head forward, black beard
A hooded padded anorak (in this weather!)
A fly buzzes gently into view – totally ignored.
It rests on the dusty window to my left
I clench my rolled newspaper, prepared to strike
I will count up to ten and if it is still there
I'll strike.
It waits, oblivious of the seconds ticking away
Before the strike.
Six. Seven. Eight. It drones to the roof and away.
No death on the bus today,
The Lord of the Flies looking after his own.
The newspaper curled in my hot hand.
Part of the Olympics headline
And the date – Wednesday 6th July, 2005.
I look forward to tomorrow.

Where are you now?
A bright summer morning
I'm on my way to work
Sitting at the rear
Of the top deck on a red London bus.
The sun slants down, glares, unforgivingly searing.
The air is dry, hot, intensely still
Every breath an unrewarding effort
The windows, grimy, gritty, scratched,
Pressing closely in are not solid glass
But a hard compression of shards, splinters

Ready on impact to burst out in a hail of lethal shrapnel
That will pierce the wide eye of the startled passenger
Puncture the unprotected pink marshmallow flesh
Slash the lips of the shocked open mouth
Penetrate with vicious barbs the tongue
Shatter the teeth and bone cavity
Stifling the scream of terror that is heard before the blast

The yellow handrails that coil up to the roof
In the white heat of the moment
Will contort and curl
Hammer of burning metal and bubbling acid plastic
Snaking down to blister and brand
And the seats
Convulsing into a writhing mesh of molten black
Trap the limbs, pinion the legs, arms, torsos.
The silver blue and grey mosaic cushions
Rise incongruously into the blinding white tornado
And gently descend
Finally a cascade of funeral black snowflakes
Ironically settling, cool and mournful,
On the twitching carnage

My head throbs. My heart pounds
Sweat pours down face, back, chest
Panic knots tight in my gut and pressures upward
To my dry unswallowing throat.
I rise, stumbling forward, staggering, tottering
Walking suddenly an alien and unfamiliar activity
I lunge down the stairs
And am disgorged from the bus
An unwanted morsel, spat out onto the pavement
The taste of fear and shame repulsed
I stand bewildered and shaken on the solid stone
My fallen newspaper flutters to the ground
And reveals stark solid letters.
LONDON CAN TAKE IT. Monday 11th July 2005.
Where are you now?
I am slowly and shakily forcing my steps to work
One on one, getting progressively steadier
LONDON IS NOT AFRAID. Where are you now?
Already I am dreading my end of day journey home.

WHITE HOT

The End of Endeavour

From his lofty dais in the Congregational hangar of the Primus Intergalactic Starship Endeavour, the Supreme Commander and First Admiral gazed down at the thousands of upturned faces of his crew, their families and his passengers. Thus he addressed them.

"The momentous day has arrived when, after many generations, we shall begin leaving this our old home, P.I.S. Endeavour, and set out to explore and settle in our new home. I was a child when, from the dark far reaches of space, we first spotted this planet on which we have now landed – a gleaming green and blue jewel rotating slowly at a great distance. Throughout my lifetime we have drawn gradually closer and closer to this world. All the way our scientists have gathered information about this planet and their discoveries have grown more and more encouraging. Conditions of existence here are totally appropriate for us, not least the benign atmosphere and the presence of water and fertile soils.

After all this time, our decision to set out from our doomed planet – an entire population, in a ship that few thought could be successfully constructed on such a vast scale – has been totally justified. As a race we can be proud of such a great achievement. Generations before us, from the silent safety of outer space, witnessed the complete destruction of our home planet, engulfed in a blinding, blistering burst of fierce white-hot flame. Now we have landed, we hope (no – we are assured) in a gentler place.

Even as I speak, exit bays are opening to allow you to set out for all corners of this new land. Most of us will never meet again as, in your thousands, you begin the trek to your new lives. Our one anxiety is the brightness of the light outside. We have landed on a vast flat white plain which unremorselessly reflects the light of several suns. Whilst adjusting to this, you must wear your eyes at retract. The young, the very old and those in the process of producing young must lid their eyes totally. The cloudy, semi-darkness of our home planet is now but a note in the annals of history. It is with a heavy heart but with excitement at the challenge before us that I bid you this formal farewell. This is the greatest, most momentous day of the history of our race."

Almost imperceptibly, at the edges of the vast arena, the crowds began to disperse. It would be a long time before the hangar would resemble anything like emptiness.

It was at this very moment that Mrs Eda Havering-Lumpstock was surveying the bountiful spread of the extravagant buffet laid out in the grand hall of her small mansion set in the Gloucestershire countryside. She, of all the local WI membership, had been selected to host the first monthly meeting that their new royal member would attend. How could they have selected better? How dare they have selected otherwise? Her gimlet, eagle eye expertly surveyed the fine array of food elegantly set out on the brilliantly white damask table linens. This would be another jewel in the crown of her many successful social and cultural achievements.

Ah, a black speck. Of soot, no doubt, from the roaring fire in the grate. With brisk efficiency the finely manicured plum-red nail of her right forefinger flicked the black speck into the perfumed and creamily scented cushion of the cupping of her left hand and with a couple of brisk passes and a deft flick, she consigned the speck into the conflagration from whence she supposed it had come. It was engulfed in a blinding, blistering burst of fierce white-hot flame.

WHY DO I?

Why do I?
That is indeed the question
Why do I?
That is what I hear you ask
And I wish I could reward you with an answer
But that would seem too difficult a task

I've done it ever since I can remember
Suspect I did it as an infant in my cot
Certainly I did as I grew up and older
Had to do it, like scratching an itchy spot

Consequently it had never seemed an effort
Ideas flowed from brain to hand and on to pen
Flooded the grid of paper's feintist lining
With flowing words, again and then again

A curse I was to any English teacher
'For homework write a story' ordered the sage
But he hadn't reckoned with this pupil's efforts
As he had to read through to the fifteenth page

In turn, I'm plagued with poetic imagination
Nothing is simple, all will lead to something else
Sure there is no shortage of inspiration
Endless reading and the quirks of life itself

E'en so, the muse of lit. can be found wanting
Downcast eye and, woe, how still her quill
White blank page of A4, so uninviting
Requires the strictest application of sheer will

That was then and this is now, I cross my fingers
But my heart was chilled at something I was told
That with advancing age fails one's imagination
The purveyor of his wisdom herself is old

Still, with my pen I will go on and plough my furrow
Hope the sowing of ink's seed will come to creep
As the Bard wrote, there's "tomorrow and tomorrow"
I'll push my pen, there is no choice to stop

But still I haven't broached the question
Why I do it – that's for loftier brains than mine
Man must eat and drink and breathe to go on living
Maybe 'words' is a compunction that is mine

What draws fools to climb the highest mountain
Penetrate space, plunge the deepest of deep seas
Daub paint, rob banks, lie, cheat, take the fight to cancer
Be painted clowns, dare life on high trapeze?

Shakespeare again wrote that there is no difference
Between the present or the past to one who's mad
All have feet of clay, yet sublime inspiration
So I think I'll sign off now and be just a little glad.

~END~